Praise for
Heart Like Mine

"The voices are so down-to-earth and familiar and the events so much like real life that readers will feel like they know the characters . . . An uplifting and heartwarming experience."

—*Kirkus Reviews*

"Explores myriad themes sure to appeal to fans of women's fiction: love and loss, parenthood, grief, friendship, and complex family dynamics. Hatvany's compassion for each female character is evident throughout, and readers will find their hearts, at times, breaking in three."   —*Booklist*

"Beautiful and deeply moving . . . Amy Hatvany writes about the tangled web of family in a way that makes you laugh, cry, cheer, and ache. This book has so much heart."

—Sarah Jio, *New York Times* bestselling author of *Blackberry Winter*

"By turns gripping and revelatory, *Heart Like Mine* is a sympathetic exploration of blended family dynamics. Hatvany pulls no punches; her characters grapple with life's big moments— marriage, parenthood, death—but she renders each of them with compassion and understanding. An honest, hopeful story that resonates in all the best ways."

—Jillian Medoff, bestselling author of *I Couldn't Love You More*

"A heartfelt, moving story about the lasting effects of grief amidst family bonds and breakups, and the healing powers of love, honesty, and acceptance."

—Seré Prince Halverson, author of *The Underside of Joy*

"Hatvany brings sympathy and compassion to the page."

—Randy Susan Meyers, bestselling author of *The Comfort of Lies*

Praise for
Outside the Lines

"Will delight readers . . . vivid and written with a depth of feeling."
—*Library Journal*

"There are no storybook perfect endings here, but this compelling novel raises the possibility of a hopeful way forward."
—*The Seattle Times*

"A palpable love story, emotional search for and acceptance of a lost parent, and a bittersweet ending make for an enveloping, heartfelt read."
—*Publishers Weekly*

"Like a gorgeous dark jewel, Hatvany's exquisitely rendered novel explores the tragedy of a mind gone awry, a tangled bond of father and daughter, and the way hope and love sustain us. It does what the best fiction does: it makes us see and experience the world differently."
—Caroline Leavitt, *New York Times* bestselling author of *Pictures of You*

"This extraordinary novel about a woman's search for her lost father—and herself—touched me deeply. With her trademark insight and compassion for her characters, Amy Hatvany has written a beautiful and moving book. Were there Oscars for novels, *Outside the Lines* would sweep the categories."
—Melissa Senate, author of *The Love Goddess' Cooking School*

"*Outside the Lines* offers a fascinating look at the interior of a mental illness—the exuberance and self-loathing, creativity and destruction that then reverberate against the lives of family and loved ones. Hatvany's storyline is compelling, weaving back and forth between father and daughter, patiently explaining as it asks all the important questions."
—Juliette Fay, author of *Shelter Me*

"*Outside the Lines* is a tender and lovely novel that explores the boundaries of love and how we break those boundaries in its name. It's sad and funny, heartbreaking and heartwarming. You'll want to read this book slowly. When you're finished, you'll want to read it again."
—Rebecca Rasmussen, author of *The Bird Sisters*

Praise for
Best Kept Secret

"I was transfixed by Cadence and her heart-wrenching dilemma. The writing is visceral, the problems are real, and there are no clear solutions. You won't want to put it down."

—Emily Giffin, *New York Times* bestselling author of
Something Borrowed

"I'm telling everyone about *Best Kept Secret*. It's the realistic and ultimately hopeful story of Cadence, whose glass of wine at the end of the day becomes two . . . then . . . three . . . then a bottle. I love that Cadence feels so familiar, she could be my neighbor, my friend, or even my sister."

—Jennifer Weiner, #1 *New York Times* bestselling author

"One of the most compelling books I've read in years. This heartfelt, heartbreaking, and ultimately uplifting novel will start an important dialogue about the secrets we keep . . . and it could even save lives." —Sarah Pekkanen, author of *Skipping a Beat*

"This gripping novel probes the darker sides of motherhood and family secrets, and proves that redemption is never out of our reach. A captivatingly honest book that you won't soon forget."

—Lisa Tucker, bestselling author of *Once Upon a Day*

"Amy Hatvany's powerful language, delicious imagery, and tender treatment of motherhood is a love letter to women everywhere, who try and sometimes fail, but who always get back up again. She is a gifted writer." —Rachael Brownell, author of
Mommy Doesn't Drink Here Anymore

"Haunting, hopeful, and beautifully written, *Best Kept Secret* takes a brave and honest look at the slippery slope of addiction and the strength it takes to recover. I couldn't put this book down, and I can't stop thinking about it."

—Allie Larkin, bestselling author of *Stay*

ALSO BY AMY HATVANY

Best Kept Secret

Outside the Lines

The Language of Sisters

Heart Like Mine

safe with me

A NOVEL

AMY HATVANY

WASHINGTON SQUARE PRESS

New York London Toronto Sydney New Delhi

WASHINGTON SQUARE PRESS
A Division of Simon & Schuster, Inc.
1230 Avenue of the Americas
New York, NY 10020

First Washington Square Press trade paperback edition March 2014

WASHINGTON SQUARE PRESS and colophon are registered trademarks of Simon & Schuster, Inc.

For information about special discounts for bulk purchases, please contact Simon & Schuster Special Sales at 1-866-506-1949 or business@simonandschuster.com.

The Simon & Schuster Speakers Bureau can bring authors to your live event. For more information or to book an event contact the Simon & Schuster Speakers Bureau at 1-866-248-3049 or visit our website at www.simonspeakers.com.

Manufactured in the United States of America

10 9 8 7 6 5 4 3 2 1

Library of Congress Cataloging-in-Publication Data

Hatvany, Amy, date.
  Safe with me : a novel / Amy Hatvany.—First Washington Square Press trade paperback edition.
      page cm
1. Bereavement—Psychological aspects. 2. Children—Death—Psychological aspects—Fiction. 3. Transplantation of organs, tissues, etc. in children—Fiction. 4. Liver—Transplantation—Patients—Fiction. 5. Transplantation of organs, tissues, etc. in children. 6. Friendship—Fiction. 7. Domestic fiction. I. Title.

  PS3608.A8658S34 2013

  813'.6—dc23   2013017478

ISBN 978-1-4767-0441-8
ISBN 978-1-4767-0442-5 (ebook)

For Tina, my dearest friend and first reader.
I know all of my secrets are safe with you.

An invisible red thread connects those destined to meet, despite the time, the place, and despite the circumstances. The thread can be tightened or tangle, but will never be broken.

—*Chinese proverb*

Hannah

The first thing Hannah hears is Emily's soul-piercing scream. Next, the grinding screech of brakes and the sharp crunch as metals collide. The sounds twirl toward her in slow motion— still-frame, auditory blips. But then, in an instant, they stitch together into an image. Into a truth that steals her breath.

Oh, holy god.

She shoves back from her desk and races down the stairway, stumbling out the door and into the yard. With a wild-eyed gaze she sees it: the car she heard—a red convertible Mustang, top down, the engine still running. In front of it lies her daughter's purple, glittering ten-speed. The handlebars are twisted and broken, the black tires torn right off the wheels. Someone screams and it takes a moment for Hannah to realize that it is her. The sound slices up through her throat like a spinning blade as she runs over to Emily, whose small body was flung from the crash. Her twelve-year-old daughter is splayed upon the blacktop, arms and legs turned at strange angles from her torso. Blood trickles down her forehead from an injury on her scalp. Her mouth is open, her eyes closed.

She wasn't wearing her helmet. Oh god oh god oh god.

"Call 911!" Hannah shrieks. "Somebody, please, *call them*!" She is vaguely aware that her neighbors have rushed from their houses, too.

"I didn't *see* her!" a woman cries. She is standing next to the car, hands clutching the sides of her blond head. "She shot out from the driveway! I didn't have time to stop!" The woman is hysterical . . . sobbing, but Hannah doesn't care. She drops down next to Emily, scraping her knuckles raw as she lifts her daughter from the rough pavement, gathering her child to her chest the way she did when Emily was still a baby, their hearts pressed together in sweet, synchronized beats.

"Mama's here," Hannah says, her mouth against her daughter's dark, damp hair. "Don't you worry. Mama's right here." Emily is limp, unmoving.

A small gathering of people creates a protective circle around them both. It is a hot, sunny Saturday in late July. A day for barbecues and picnics, for Popsicles and campfires and s'mores. *This can't be happening. It can't be. She's all I have. Nothing else matters. Just her.*

Their next-door neighbor, Mr. Blake, sinks to his knees beside Hannah and slips an arm around her. "The ambulance is coming," he says. "Maybe you shouldn't move her."

Hannah ignores him. "She's going to be okay," she murmurs. "She *has* to be." She clutches Emily tighter.

After a few minutes that feel more like hours, like decades, a siren whines in the distance, growing louder as it draws close.

It isn't fast enough. Mr. Blake places two of his gnarled fingers on Emily's throat, and Hannah's first instinct is to yank her away, to protect her daughter from any more possible harm, but then she realizes what he's trying to do.

"She has a pulse," he says. "It's weak, but it's there."

Hannah nods, her lips pressed together so hard she can't feel them. She can't feel anything. The inside of her skull is a beehive someone just kicked. She can't form a thought. There is only the buzzing . . . the one word in her head, one incantation, one prayer.

She closes her eyes and whispers the word *please*.

Hannah waits. She sits in the emergency room, gripping the edge of her chair, her arms stiff and straight, her body rocking forward and back in small, measured movements. The space bustles with a state of urgency: nurses in brightly patterned smocks and sensible white shoes jog down the hallways; an aide rushes past with an empty gurney. The air, thick with antiseptic and sweat, tickles the back of Hannah's throat; she's afraid she might vomit. Patients cry out, phones ring, doctors are paged stat to the OR—sound effects like fishhooks in her skin.

She throws a quick glance at the people in the seats around her—a man with deeply lined skin and a thatch of white hair sits alone, holding a straw hat in his lap, tearing at its brim with shaking fingers. One of his legs bounces in a staccato rhythm; his plaid shorts expose thickly veined, knobby knees. For some reason this feels obscene to Hannah, almost as bad as if he had flashed her. Across the room, a couple hold each other's hands. Tears run down the woman's pale cheeks and she gives Hannah a look filled with palpable, aching empathy. Hannah bobs her head once, holding the woman's gaze for a moment, but then drops her eyes to the cold, glossy floor. It's too much for her, this kind of agony laid bare. Too raw and bloody. Too real.

The doctors are attempting to save Emily's life. They hurried her into surgery just moments after the medics rushed her inside the hospital. In a hazy fog, she signed all the forms the nurses put in front of her, giving the doctors permission to do their work.

"Please," Hannah said to the doctor hovering over Emily before they wheeled her away. "Help her." Emily's hair stood out like a swath of dark ink against the white sheet beneath her. Her skin was pasty except for the blackening blood on her face. She still hadn't moved.

"We'll do everything we can," the doctor said, giving her arm a quick squeeze before whisking her only child through gray double doors.

Now, two hours later, a nurse approaches Hannah in the waiting room. "Can I get you anything?" she asks. "Do you need to call anyone?"

Hannah shakes her head. Not yet. She'll phone her parents once she knows more about Emily's condition. When she can tell them their granddaughter will be okay. Mr. Blake had offered to come with her as she climbed into the back of the ambulance, but she told him no.

Thirteen years ago, at thirty-one, Hannah signed up for motherhood knowing full well she'd be on her own. She wanted a child so much that she was no longer willing to wait for the right man to come along, given the odds of finding someone who, unlike Devin, her fiancé for two years in her late twenties, *didn't* screw around behind her back.

Instead, she opted for a sure thing: sperm donor number 4873, a twenty-three-year-old premed student with dark hair and a family history vacant of serious illness. "Look at me," she joked to her best friend and business partner, Sophie. "I'm a cougar." Nine months after the procedure, Hannah held a red-faced, squalling baby Emily in her arms.

As she waits, Hannah's thoughts wander to all of those early nights she and Emily spent together—nights when Emily wouldn't sleep, when the only thing that brought her baby comfort was pacing the house for hours at a time.

"You are the reason I'm here," Hannah whispered into Emily's tiny, seashell-shaped ear. "You're my angel . . . my sweet, perfect girl." Emily gazed back at her with round-as-poker-chips blue eyes, and Hannah couldn't help but believe that, even as an infant, her daughter understood her, that the love she felt for Emily was a language only the two of them could speak.

She had support, of course. Sophie took over the bulk of the salon's administrative work for a couple of years right after Emily was born, and Hannah worked solely as a stylist. Jill, the nanny she hired when Emily was four months old, cared for her daughter while Hannah expertly cut and colored her clients' hair. While her parents were in Boise, too far away to be of much immediate help, they flew into Seattle at least once a year, and Hannah took Emily to their farm for almost every major holiday. There was nothing sweeter than seeing Emily at two years old chasing after the chickens that had free range of her parents' front yard, nothing that filled Hannah's heart more than her almost-teenage daughter still climbing up into Grandpa's lap for a cuddle.

They'd visited the farm just a few weeks ago, over the Fourth of July weekend, enjoying an enormous meal of her mother's crispy fried chicken and creamy dill potato salad, in which the celery *absolutely* counted as a serving of vegetables, her father insisted as he scraped the bowl clean. Emily was basking in her grandparents' attention, relishing her role as their only grandchild, but also missing her uncle Isaac. "Why didn't he come?" she asked as she stood on the edge of the wraparound porch, tilting her dark head and placing a splayed hand on her jutted-out hip. "He's supposed to light the fireworks."

"He really wanted to, honey, but he couldn't get out of a business trip," Hannah said. Almost twenty-five years ago, her brother had moved to Seattle because he'd received a full-ride structural engineering scholarship to the University of Washington. A year and a half later, Hannah followed him to the city in order to attend cosmetology school; her parents agreed to her moving away from Boise, too, only because her big brother would be close by. Hannah resented this a little at the time— what eighteen-year-old girl wants her big brother watching her every move? But later, especially after Emily was born, Hannah was grateful to have him around. Isaac was a doting uncle, devoted to Emily at least as much as her grandparents. He was certainly a positive male influence in her life—he taught her to ride her bike and fixed the broken toys Hannah would have thrown out. He played tag and roughhoused with Emily in the silly way that men like to do. His job demanded that he travel far too much to find a relationship that lasted longer than a few months, let alone become serious enough to consider having children, so he channeled all his paternal emotions into his niece. He took good care of them both.

A scowl took over Emily's face as she took a moment to consider Hannah's explanation for her uncle's absence. "That stinks," she finally remarked, then trotted off to pet one of the horses over the fence. She adored Isaac as much as he adored her.

"She's so much like you," Hannah's mother said, after watching this brief exchange.

With her long black hair and narrow face, Emily certainly *looked* like Hannah, but Hannah didn't think her mother was referring to their appearance. "Like me how?" she asked.

"She's a thinker." Her mother reached over and gave Hannah a knowing look. "But not afraid to speak her mind."

Hannah couldn't help but believe that her mother was right. Emily had been such a good baby, calm and serious, always seeming to absorb the world around her like a thirsty sponge, observing people's behavior, every detail. Cataloging them somehow. Deciding who was worthy of her attention and who was not. When Emily was a toddler, her belly laugh was infrequent enough that Hannah felt a true sense of accomplishment whenever she managed to evoke it. Emily wasn't withdrawn. Just . . . contemplative. She knew her own mind from an early age, stubbornly insisting on picking out her own outfits and meals, asserting her individuality wherever she could. Power struggles arose from time to time, with Emily's helmet being one of them. Hannah insisted that she wear it anytime she straddled her bicycle; Emily reasoned that if she was only riding on the sidewalk in front of their house, she shouldn't have to. "The cement on the sidewalk will crack your skull just as easily as in the street," Hannah told her more than once.

Hannah shudders now, thinking back to the many times she spoke those seemingly prophetic words. *Why* did Emily ride into the street when she knew Hannah strictly forbade it? Was she angry that Hannah said she had to come to the salon that afternoon because Jill was sick and couldn't come to the house? Was this simply a quiet act of rebellion that ended in disaster? What if Hannah had canceled her appointments for the day and instead spent the time with Emily? What if Emily had chosen to watch TV instead of slipping out the side door to the garage and climbing onto her bike? What if she hadn't zipped out of the driveway into the car's path? *What if, what if?*

Hannah closes her eyes and bites her bottom lip, trying to shut out the rampant noises around her. Nausea roils in her stomach and sour bile rises in the back of her mouth. She focuses on her daughter, imploring a God she isn't sure is there. *Please.*

Her phone vibrates in her purse, and she grabs for it. "Hannah?" Sophie's familiar voice, lilting with the soft trill of her French accent. After her parents' divorce when she was fourteen, Sophie and her mother immigrated to the United States to live with relatives, and while both spoke impeccable English, Sophie's words still sound as though they were made of music. "You missed your three o'clock color with Mrs. Clark. She was furious, *chérie*. Where are you?"

Hannah's chin trembles and her breath rattles inside her chest. "I'm at Swedish hospital. Emily's in surgery."

"*What?* Oh my *god*. What *happened?*"

Hannah tells Sophie about the red convertible, about Emily's mangled bike. "She wasn't wearing a helmet. I've told her a million times to put that damn thing on no matter what. No matter how hot it is or how itchy. Why didn't she *listen* to me?" Hannah's sobs tear at her throat as she speaks. "Oh *god,* Sophie. I'm so scared."

"I'll be right there."

"You don't have to—" Hannah starts, but Sophie has already hung up. Much of their salon's success was due her partner's unwillingness to take no for an answer. It was the reason Hannah owned half the business in the first place.

Almost twenty years ago, she and Sophie worked together at a large commercial salon where it was less about the quality of their work and more about how many clients they could shuffle in and out of their chairs each day. Finally, after a few years of dealing with a toxic atmosphere of gossipy and backstabbing stylists, Sophie talked Hannah into applying for a small business loan to start their own salon. They were so successful, in fact, that they had recently purchased a charming Craftsman house in a business district of Bellevue and planned to transform it into a second Ciseaux location.

"Ms. Scott?" A doctor in blue scrubs approaches, snapping Hannah out of her thoughts. He is older, a fact she finds strangely comforting, as though his years of wisdom and experience can somehow erase the perilous nature of this moment. His silver hair is damp around his forehead, and he clutches a surgical cap in one hand. "I'm Dr. Wilder. I was working on your daughter."

Was? Hannah stands, pulse racing, still clutching her cell phone. "Is she okay? Can I see her?"

"Soon." Dr. Wilder takes another step toward her and

gestures for her to sit. She complies, slipping her phone back into her purse, which she has only because another neighbor dashed into her house and grabbed it for her before the ambulance shut its doors. The doctor sits as well, taking her hand in his. His fingers are soft and warm. They feel capable. Hannah latches on to this thought as evidence that Emily is safe.

"Your daughter sustained life-threatening injuries," he says. His voice is low and calm; his gray eyes reveal nothing. "When her head hit the pavement, her brain began to bleed." Hannah nods, her jaw rattling so violently she has to clench her teeth to stop it. Dr. Wilder knits his thick, white brows together before continuing. "We were able to stop the hemorrhage, but I'm afraid the damage was extensive."

"What does that *mean*?" Hannah asks. Her heart thuds against her rib cage in a violent rhythm, hard enough to convince her it will bruise.

"It means she is alive, but only because we've put her on a ventilator." He waits a beat. "She's had no spontaneous brain function. None at all since she came in."

The buzzing in Hannah's head takes over her thoughts and the room starts to spin. She closes her eyes. "Is it a coma?" she finally manages to whisper. "Will she wake up?"

Dr. Wilder squeezes her hand. "I'm afraid not," he says. "There's no activity in her brain stem. If we discontinued life support, she wouldn't survive. I'm so sorry to have to tell you this, but there's simply no chance she'll recover."

Her eyes snap open. "Oh god . . . no!" She moans, a low, throbbing sound. Letting go of his hand, she bends at the waist, crossing her arms over her chest. Tears rush down her cheeks as she once again rocks in place. "Are you sure? Are you *sure?*" she repeats. She feels the eyes of the couple across the room upon her. The old man gets up and walks away, as though distancing himself from her could help him avoid a similar fate.

"Yes," the doctor says. "I'm very sorry." He doesn't speak again, waiting for Hannah to right herself.

When she does, she faces him with swollen eyes and red cheeks. "She should have worn that damn helmet," she says through quivering lips.

"Wouldn't have made a difference," he says. "The impact was too severe."

Hearing this, Hannah allows herself to feel a small flash of relief. "Isn't there something else you can do? Another surgery?" she asks, but Dr. Wilder frowns and shakes his head. Hannah feels her throat close up. She can't swallow, and for a moment, she can't speak. The walls seem to curve, compressing the air around her. She reminds herself to breathe. "I need to see her," she finally says in a hoarse voice, one she doesn't recognize as her own. Her body feels fragile, like thinly blown glass.

Dr. Wilder nods. "Of course," he says, then hesitates a moment before continuing. "And please, forgive me, but I need to ask . . . is your daughter an organ donor?"

"What?" Hannah says, blinking. She can't focus on his meaning. She knows she should understand it, but everything is muffled, as though they were having this conversation underwater.

"If she's a donor, it's possible she can save other lives when she passes."

When she passes? Hannah can't wrap her mind around the

thought. *I'll do anything,* anything *to make this not true. I'll sell the business, move back to Idaho with my parents like they've always wanted. I'll give Emily a quiet life in the country, let her frolic with goats and milk the cows, like I did growing up. I've been so selfish, having her live in the city. I'll give everything up. I'll change it all if she'll just stay with me.*

Hannah shakes her head. "I just . . . I don't . . . I can't think about that right now," she says.

"I understand how difficult this is," the doctor says. "I only ask because her organs will deteriorate as her condition worsens. The sooner we know if she might be a donor, the more lives she could save. That's all." He stands and motions for her to do the same.

Hannah stares at him a moment, wondering if she refuses to go, if she cements herself to the chair, would anything change? If she could somehow reverse the day, go back to the beginning and start over, do everything differently, none of this would have happened.

But the look Dr. Wilder gives her lifts her from her seat. With a deep breath, she follows him down the hall, suddenly facing the kind of decision that no mother should ever have to make.

Olivia

"We might have a liver," Dr. Steele says as he enters Maddie's hospital suite. He is a tall man, six foot five, with long, tapered fingers, seemingly more suited to a basketball court than to a hospital. As Maddie's hepatologist for the last eight years, he has gained Olivia's implicit trust.

"It's the right type?" she asks, clutching the novel she'd been pretending to read for the past three hours. She pushes herself up from the reclining chair in the corner of the room, her heart suddenly in her throat. Maddie's declining lab results place her as a Status 1 on the UNOS scoring system, which means as soon as a match comes up, it's hers.

Dr. Steele bobs his head. "A twelve-year-old girl was hit by a car. Her mother still needs to sign the paperwork, but the organ procurement team has been notified and is evaluating the match. It's looking good."

"How soon will we know?" Olivia asks as she sets the book on the chair behind her. Relief rushes through her, thinking that her daughter might survive. In exactly the same moment, she is struck by the plight of the other mother, the one whose child's life—all that potential and beauty—has been so swiftly and suddenly erased. She can't imagine the depth of this woman's pain, the unfairness of it all. It makes her ill to realize how fervently she's been praying for another child to die.

"Within the hour, I hope." He smiles, the gesture lighting up his dark brown eyes in a way Olivia hasn't seen before. Normally, he is the deliverer of bad news for Maddie.

"Thank you so much," she says to Dr. Steele, who nods and lets his gaze linger on Olivia's face a moment longer than she expects. She's accustomed to looks like this from men, filled with admiration and maybe even a little longing. It embarrasses her, really. Especially now, when she's certain her usually sleek blond bob is a frizzy mess and the makeup she applied yesterday afternoon is likely smeared around her eyes.

"You have tiger eyes," James told her the day they first met in the lobby of the attorney's office where she used to work as a paralegal. "Does that mean you're dangerous?"

Then-twenty-two-year-old Olivia shook her head and blushed in response, a little amazed that this polished, professional businessman with black hair and vivid green eyes was paying attention to her. He had to be at least a decade older than she was, though he carried himself with the slightly chest-puffed air of a much younger man. "I don't know," she said, raising a single eyebrow. "Are *you*?" This bold flirtation surprised her; it usually wasn't in her nature. But something about James pulled her toward him. She felt like a cat, wanting to arch her back, press her body against his, and purr.

James tilted his head back and laughed, a deep, resonant tone that made Olivia's skin tingle. Then, he reached over her desk and gently kissed the back of her hand. "Let me take you out for dinner tonight and you can find out," he said. She accepted his invitation to one of the most expensive French restaurants in Tampa, which he was only visiting for business.

"Please," he said, holding up the menu after they were seated. "Will you allow me? I want to introduce you to my favorite dishes." She let him order her meal; she let him instruct her on how to swirl the Merlot in her glass before breathing in its heady bouquet. He told her which fork to use and encouraged her to at least sample the escargot. She managed to choke a bite down so he wouldn't be offended, but whoever had decided that snails were a delicacy had clearly escaped a mental institution.

"You're so beautiful with those gorgeous brown locks," James said, leaning toward her across the table. He reached out and touched her hair. "But I bet you'd put every other woman in Florida to shame if you went blond."

Olivia felt a small twist in her stomach hearing his words, unsure if they were a compliment or an insult. Even so, she wanted to please him, so two months later, after several more comments like that, she let him set up an appointment for her to transform her into a blonde. Eight months after that, James proposed, wanting her to relocate to Seattle. "What about my job?" she asked. "And my mom?"

"I'll take care of her," James promised. "I'll get her a full-time nurse so she can move into her own place." He knew Olivia was especially close to her mother, who suffered from such debilitating arthritis that she was forced to live off disability. Olivia shared a small apartment with her, and there was no way her mother could pay the bills on her own.

"You would? Really?"

James nodded. "Of course. She'd be my family, too." Stunned by his generosity, Olivia accepted the flawless, three-carat diamond ring he presented to her. James kept his word, purchasing and moving her mother into an elegant two-bedroom condo near the beach. He helped Olivia hire a wonderful, live-in Jamaican nurse named Tanesa to care for her. A month later, they were married and left Florida, returning only when Maddie was born, and then again, three years after that, when Olivia's mother passed away after a heart attack.

Now, eighteen years later, Olivia runs her hands down her simple gray cardigan, smoothing out the wrinkles, wondering what James would think if he walked in and observed this moment with Dr. Steele. What he'd assume they had been doing. The thought lights a spark of panic in her chest and she swallows hard to extinguish it.

"I'll keep you posted," Dr. Steele says. "The social worker will be along soon. I've found a younger, less gullible member of the team. I think Maddie might like her."

Despite the weight of the moment, Olivia can't help but smile, remembering how a week ago, a meek, older woman with mousy hair and orthopedic shoes attempted to get Maddie to talk about any fears or concerns she might be having about becoming an organ recipient. Maddie peered at her, then cocked her head to the side. "Yeah," she said, deadpan. "I'm afraid of becoming possessed by the other person's soul."

"Maddie," Olivia said, knowing her daughter was testing the worker. Maddie couldn't rebel like a typical teenager—

she couldn't miss curfew or make out with a boy beneath the bleachers—so she tended to channel her hormonal angst into harassing hospital workers.

"What, Mom?" Maddie said, blinking. "I mean it."

Despite Olivia's best efforts to intervene, the poor woman went on for at least twenty minutes, trying to convince Maddie that those tales of possession were false, until Maddie could no longer keep a straight face. "I can't believe you *fell* for that one," she snickered, and the woman blushed, whipped around, and fled the room.

Now, Olivia nods and thanks the doctor again, watching as he strides out of the suite and down the hall. Then her gaze moves over to Maddie. Her daughter, petite for fifteen but unnaturally swollen, lies hooked up to machines pumping her full of the medications that are the only things keeping her alive. Her head is turned to the side, her sandy brown hair is straggly and limp, and her eyelids—covering beautiful hazel irises—are fluttery but closed.

As always, Olivia's gut clenches at seeing her daughter so distorted, so ill. Since she was seven, she has been plagued by a rare case of type 2 autoimmune hepatitis. When the immunosuppressant meds that controlled Maddie's disease stopped working a few months ago, her skin and eyes yellowed, and her belly plumped up as it began to retain more fluid and toxins than her bedraggled liver could process. The scarring on her organ has progressed to the point of her needing a transplant; if she doesn't get one, it is likely she will die in a few weeks. The thought makes Olivia feel as though she has been gutted. The past eight years have been tenuous, with Maddie in the hospital more often than she was out of it. Her health has been so fragile that she couldn't go to school or play with other children, for fear of picking up an infection that might kill her. All Olivia wants for her daughter is a normal life; a transplant is her only hope to have one.

Reaching over, Olivia pushes a stray lock of hair back from Maddie's face. "It's going to be okay, baby," she whispers, knowing she is reassuring herself as much as her daughter. *I can't lose her. I can't.* "We're going to get you well."

Maddie stirs, turns her head back and forth across the pillow. "Mommy?" she murmurs, and Olivia's chest aches. Maddie tends to call her Mom or Mother—sometimes Olivia, or even Mrs. Bell when she is feeling sassy. Mommy is an endearment left over from toddlerhood, a term that reappeared only after Maddie was diagnosed.

"I'm right here, sweetie," Olivia says, touching Maddie's thin arm with the tips of her fingers, careful to avoid the IV taped to the back of her daughter's hand. Maddie's veins are so exhausted from being prodded, they have shrunk away from the surface of her skin. When she was first admitted, it took the nurse an hour to find one that didn't collapse.

"Where's Dad?" Maddie asks as she finally opens her eyes. When Maddie first looked in the mirror and saw the whites of her eyes glowing yellow, she cried—a sound so haunting it tied Olivia's heart into messy knots. She tried to tell Maddie that she didn't see the yellow. All she saw was her daughter, her brilliant and beautiful child. That's all she sees now.

"At the office," Olivia says. "Do you want to talk to him?"

Maddie shakes her head. "Can I have my laptop?" Her voice is thick, groggy from the meds and lack of moisture.

Frowning, Olivia grabs the pitcher of water from the table next to Maddie's bed and pours her a glass. James bought Maddie the computer several years ago to help keep her entertained, and it seems to Olivia that her daughter spends too much time online, but she can't justify limiting something that Maddie loves—she is able to enjoy so little. Still, she hesitates. "Are you sure you feel up to it?" she asks. "Maybe you should get some more rest."

"All I *do* is rest," Maddie says, an irritated edge to her tone. She takes a sip of water, then sets the cup on the tray in front of her. "Please, Mom?"

Sighing, Olivia reaches into the drawer of the nightstand and places the laptop on the tray, careful not to knock over the water. "I'm going to call your dad, okay?" she says as Maddie turns on the computer. She needs to tell James about the possibility of the transplant, but she doesn't want Maddie to know until they are certain it will happen. No use getting her daughter's hopes up if the other girl's mother decides not to donate. Again, Olivia's stomach turns, imagining what this woman is facing. Could *she* make that kind of decision? Could she end her own child's life knowing another depended on it? She isn't sure that she could. *There's a very real possibility that this woman might say no.*

Maddie nods and waves Olivia away, keeping her fingers poised over the keyboard and her eyes on the computer screen, waiting for it to boot up. When Maddie was admitted to the hospital, three weeks ago, Olivia quietly suggested to her husband that their daughter might like to have a roommate to talk with during her stay, that Maddie had already spent too much of the last eight years in solitary confinement because of her illness. Tutors and homeschooling; weeks at a time in lonely hospital rooms with nothing to do other than watch movies or surf for silly videos on YouTube. But Olivia's husband insisted on privacy for Maddie, the fancy suite with the wide, comfortable bed and flat-screen TV, usually reserved for children of politicians or celebrities. As the owner and CEO of one of the largest investment firms on the West Coast, James had no concern about money. The ominous flash in his green eyes made it clear to Olivia that it wasn't worth trying to argue the point.

Once Olivia is in the hallway, she calls James's cell. Her breath becomes shallow as the phone rings, four . . . five . . . six times. At eight, she will have the electronic protection of voicemail and avoid having to speak with him directly. She won't have to worry about the words she chooses or the tone of her voice. James can take an unexpected pause in a conversation and turn it into a heavy silence he'd punish her with for weeks.

"What" is his greeting—not a question, but a challenge, because she's interrupting his day. Olivia swallows to keep from crying as she tells him about the little girl on life support. He listens, his impatience traveling on the line between them with invisible sparks. "So, it's possible, but the mother hasn't even signed off yet?" he asks.

"Right." Olivia knows she has to keep her voice steady. "I just thought you'd want to know . . . I thought you might come." *Your daughter needs you, you jerk.* Words she often thought over the past eight years, but would never, ever speak. James leaves the bulk of caring for Maddie to Olivia—he pays the bills, he visited the hospital when Maddie was admitted—but it is Olivia who spends every night with their daughter.

"I'm neck deep in closing a deal, Liv. I told you that this morning. Didn't I? Were you not paying attention?" His words are hard, pummeling her like barbed little fists. Olivia pictures him standing behind his huge burled walnut desk, looking younger than his fifty years. His six-foot-four, broad-shouldered build is imposing to anyone and anything that stands in his way. His suits are custom made to fit him perfectly, the hues of all his shirts carefully selected to set off his tan skin and salt-and-pepper hair. Everyone says they make a beautiful couple. On the surface, Olivia supposes they do.

"Yes." She bites the inside of her cheek to keep from saying more.

"I'll be there the minute we know for sure. Otherwise, I need to work. Call me when the papers are signed." He pauses, his voice momentarily softening. "Give Maddie a kiss for me." He hangs up without saying good-bye, and Olivia keeps the phone to her ear for a minute, thinking about their daughter, the one reason she didn't walk out on James eight years ago.

She had a plan—she'd squirreled away enough money from the allowance James gave her to take care of herself and Maddie for at least a year. Her strategy was to find a job with hours she could work when Maddie was in school. She would have changed their names if she had to. Dyed their hair and worn colored contacts. Started their lives all over again. And then, just before she began third grade, Maddie got sick, and Olivia knew she couldn't afford the kind of treatment her daughter's illness would demand. She couldn't work *and* get

Maddie to endless doctors' appointments. She'd never actually threatened to leave him—she was too afraid of what he might do to her if she spoke those words—but Olivia was certain if she did leave, that James would attempt to prove her an unfit mother, that she didn't have the resources to properly care for her sick child. And since there was no way in hell Olivia would let him take sole custody of her daughter, she resigned herself to the fact that as long as Maddie was ill, they had to stay with James.

But now, there is a liver. Olivia believes that if she has managed to survive a life with James this long, she can hold out a little longer. Maddie will miraculously be healed, and Olivia can start working out the details of her *new* plan. And then— finally—she will muster up the courage to make her escape.

Maddie

I wait until Mom leaves the room before I log in to my email account—the one linked to the Facebook profile my parents know nothing about. The one I created so I could pretend to actually have a life.

About six months ago, when I was just dinking around on the Internet, I stumbled across the Facebook profile of a gorgeous twenty-one-year-old girl in Austin, Texas, who was stupid enough to not use any kind of security on her page. (Not a single, solitary one. I mean, really. Who *does* that?) Despite her ignorance of privacy settings, as I looked through her picture albums, I thought, *I want to be her. She's everything I'm not—tall and thin with breasts like cantaloupes and a sparkly belly button ring. She has long, black, wavy hair, shimmery, tanned olive skin, and legs that are, like, twice as long as her torso. She dates hot guys with Abercrombie & Fitch–like style and gets to travel for her job as a car show model.* And then I thought, *Why* can't *I be her?* It's not like I'd be hurting anyone—I wouldn't be stealing her Social Security number or the password to her bank accounts. I wouldn't be using her airline miles or racking up charges at Victoria's Secret on her credit card. Using her pictures on my online profiles would simply give me a chance for a little vacation from pills and blood draws and IV fluids. It would let me be something other than sick.

I quickly discovered that while I *could* copy some of her pictures, there was no *way* I'd copy her status updates, since they tended to be filled with multiple exclamation points: "TGIF!!! Bring on the boys and beer!!! LOL!!!" (I might only be fifteen, but I'm not an idiot.) Instead, I amped up "Sierra's" (aka my) profile by liking what I hoped was a cool assortment of different pages. I kept it as close to the truth about me as possible, listing my music interests as hers (Coldplay, Fiona Apple, and Nirvana); giving her the books I adore (the Hunger Games series, Tolstoy's *Anna Karenina,* and *The Nanny Diaries*); and liking a few trendy pages: "Bacon" and "George Takei." I changed the girl's name (from Tiffani Myers to Sierra Stone), college (from none to WSU), and career (from model to aspiring graphic artist), then copied Tiffani's profile picture and other snapshots from her albums, making backup files on my hard drive so I could use the images as my avatar in the chat rooms I liked to visit and the games I liked to play online. (I had to restrain myself from sending Tiffani what I thought would be a helpful, anonymous message: "You *do* realize the Internet is forever, right? That pic of you lying across the BMW in a red bikini, men lined up take body shots off you? Your grandchildren are going to see that.") I accepted friend requests from anyone who wasn't already friends with Tiffani, amazed by the number of random strangers who "Sierra" was suddenly "friends" with simply because of the way she looked.

Now, as I lie in my hospital bed with zero emails in Sierra's inbox, I toy briefly with the idea of creating a profile as my *actual* self: a fifteen-year-old girl with a diseased liver, an emotionally distant father, and a sweet but overprotective mother. A girl who doesn't *have* any friends. Who has never gone to a school dance or had a boy try to kiss her. A girl who, if she doesn't get a transplant, is going to die.

I dig my fingernails into my palms and gulp hard, fighting back the tears. Most of the time, I'm able to keep the reality of my situation shoved into a corner of my mind. I can see it, I know the truth, but I can dance past it when I want, pretending to be Sierra instead of Maddie, hovering above what feels like an impending doom. Being in the hospital makes it impossible to ignore. I sleep most of the time, I can't eat, and the looks on Dr. Steele's and my mother's faces tell me that things aren't getting any better—they're getting worse.

When I first got sick, I didn't really understand what it meant. I knew I didn't feel good—I was tired all of the time and I didn't want to eat. I was six when I was diagnosed with celiac disease, which meant I couldn't ingest anything with any sort of gluten in it. When I did, I'd ache all over and get incredibly nauseous. A year later, it became worse. After a couple of weeks of thinking my symptoms were due to my secret stash of my dad's beloved multigrain bread, Mom took me to the pediatrician, who, while pushing gently on my abdominal area, discovered my liver was enlarged. Several blood tests and specialist visits later, my problem had a name: type 2 hepatitis, which, apparently, adolescent girls who already have some kind of autoimmune disorder like celiac are more likely to contract. It's rare, but it happens. Lucky me.

"It's treatable," Dr. Steele told us. He prescribed an initially high dose of prednisone, then gradually tapered the amount down to try and keep my immune system in check. The meds worked, at first. I was able to stay in school, though I couldn't run as hard or fast as the other kids in my class. And then one morning, in third grade, I woke up writhing and sweating in my bed. "I can't get up, Mama," I cried. "Help me!" I remember the fear, the agonizing ache in my bones. I remember vomiting so hard I saw streams of blood in the toilet. I remember my throat swelling and feeling like I couldn't breathe. I was in the hospital that night, and didn't leave for several weeks.

"Esophageal inflammation," Dr. Steele explained to my parents when he met us in the emergency room. "When the circulation in Maddie's body gets blocked because of scar tissue on her liver, blood can back up into other vessels. Mostly in her stomach and esophagus, which I think is what's happening now."

"And how do you propose to fix it?" Dad asked, holding on to the metal rail of my bed until his thick knuckles went white. I'd always hated my father's hands: they gripped too tightly, slammed too many doors.

"We'll try adding another course of anti-inflammatories and upping the prednisone. If that doesn't work, we may have to consider surgically inserting a shunt, to drain the fluid from her liver," Dr. Steele said, then looked over to me. "You'll have to stay here awhile, Maddie, so we can get you better. I promise, we'll take excellent care of you."

"I want her moved to a private suite as soon as possible," Dad said.

"Please," my mom quietly added to his demand, and Dad grabbed her hand hard enough that she flinched. He shot Dr.

Steele a charming smile. "I apologize. It's just . . . Maddie is my little girl. I only want the best for her. You understand."

Dr. Steele nodded slowly, then tweaked my nose. "I'll see you after your ultrasound, missy. Can I bring you a Popsicle from the cafeteria?" I bobbed my head yes, because at eight years old, I still thought Popsicles made everything better.

Seven years and countless hospital stays later, I *detest* Popsicles. I've also managed to build up a tolerance to the drugs that are supposed to suppress what Dr. Steele calls my "hyperimmune response," so they aren't working anymore. They make me fat and bloated and *still* my stupid immune system thinks my liver is its enemy and keeps trying to kill it. And the unfortunate side effect of that is killing *me*. Unless I get a transplant. Unless some other person with the right blood type dies and saves my life.

I try to distract myself from these depressing thoughts with a quick review of Tiffani's profile, scanning for material I might be able to snag for Sierra. I note that she's taking a trip to England for a car show next week, so I know there'll be new pictures to use. I cringe, imagining Tiffani's Facebook posts as she travels: "OMG!! Big Ben!!" and "I ordered chips and got French fries. LMAO, y'all!!"

My mom reenters the room just as I close the browser and lock the screen. She doesn't know much about computers past being able to email and surf the Web, but I password-protect mine, just to be safe. "Your dad sends his love," she says.

"*Awe*some. Why *be* here when he can just 'send his love'?"

Mom frowns at my sarcasm. "Maddie—"

"What?" I snap, closing my laptop. I get so tired of her pretending that Dad is such a great guy. I know she's trying to protect me. I know she hopes I don't notice what goes on in our house, but I'd have to be a moron not to. I'd have to be Tiffani.

Suddenly, the weight of overwhelming fatigue clamps down on my body. My heartbeat thuds inside my skull, chipping away at my consciousness, and I have to close my eyes. It hits me like this sometimes. I'll be feeling almost normal (well, normal for me, at least, which Dr. Steele says is probably how most people feel when they have a seriously bad case of food poisoning), and out of nowhere, I think, *Okay, this is it. These are my last breaths.* I try to have meaningful thoughts, to wish for world peace and the end to childhood famine and Miss America-y things like that, but usually, like now, I think about how I wish I could have a bowlful of chocolate gelato just one more time. I wish I could lie on the beach and get a sunburn, listening to the waves crash against the shore. I wish I wasn't going to die a virgin.

Mom rushes over to my bed. "Are you okay?" she asks, placing a cool hand against my forehead. I know I have a fever—my skin crackles beneath her touch. In the last year, there has only been a total of about a week that I *haven't* had a fever.

"I'm in a hospital, Mom," I say with a weak smile. "So, no. Not so much okay." I force my eyes open. "Thanks for asking, though."

"Sassy." Mom shakes her head, but smiles, too.

I pat the top of her hand. "These stupid pain meds are making me dizzy. I feel like shit." Mom is quiet, worried lines etched in deep parentheses around her mouth. I jiggle her arm gently. "What, no 'watch your language'? I must *really* be going to die this time."

Seeing the look of horror that takes over her face, I want to reel the words back the second they tumble out of my mouth. "Madelyn *Bell,*" Mom says. Tears gloss her pretty hazel eyes. "Don't you *talk* like that."

"Sorry," I say, with a guilty shrug. She hates it when I joke about death, but for me, it's the easiest way to deal. Plus, the way I figure it, if I'm happy and laughing, I *can't* die. God would have to be a total asshole to strike me down in the middle of a giggle.

Mom looks like she's going to say something, but then Dr. Steele rushes into the room, practically tripping over his long legs. I consider briefly that he and Tiffani, with their superextended, alienlike limbs, might make an excellent couple.

"We got it!" he says, and my mother starts to cry. I must look confused, because then he says, "She hasn't told you?"

I throw my gaze back and forth between them. "Told me what?"

He smiles, a wide motion that shows his gums, top and bottom, and his big Chiclet teeth. "We need to get you prepped for surgery," he says. "This is it, kiddo. Your whole world is about to change."

One Year Later . . .

Hannah

There is a moment—only a moment, right when she wakes up—when sunlight streams in through the streaked windows of her new apartment and the world is still too fuzzy to tell dream from sleep, that Hannah doesn't remember. She doesn't see the shell of Emily's body as it lay hooked up to machines in the ICU; she doesn't hear the steady *beep . . . beep . . . beep* of the EKG monitor. Dr. Wilder told her that this was the machine's heartbeat, not Emily's. Emily—*Hannah's* Emily, whom she fed strawberry waffles that morning—was already gone.

Emily is gone. The weight of this truth lands like a boulder on Hannah's chest, and suddenly, everything falls clear. She remembers it all, a scene stuck on replay in her head, no matter how hard she tries to stop it. She sees Sophie standing next to her, crying softly as Hannah leans over to kiss Emily's forehead.

Her daughter's skin was taut and cool; her head had been shaved for the surgery that didn't save her. Her eyes were closed, and there was a black-stitched, horseshoe-shaped incision on her scalp.

"Baby girl," Hannah whispered. "Oh, *sweetie*. I love you so much." Her jaw trembled, her entire body jittered. She looked at Dr. Wilder. "Please . . . are you *sure* there's nothing you can do?" The words caught in her throat like jagged bits of metal.

Dr. Wilder pressed his lips together and shook his head before speaking. "I'm so sorry. I wish there was."

Hearing this, Sophie released a shuddering breath and crumpled into a chair by the window, shoulders curled forward and her hands over her face. Hannah glanced at her, then back to Emily. She felt strangely hollow, as though her insides had somehow slipped out of her onto the floor. She searched her daughter's face for some hint of the girl she knew—the girl who scaled the pear tree in their backyard like a monkey, who sketched intricate drawings of dragons and queens, who danced in her room to rhythms that played only in her head.

"Can we wait for her grandparents?" Hannah asked. Sophie had called them when she arrived at the hospital and they were already headed to the Boise airport. Isaac was on assignment somewhere in Hong Kong and hadn't answered his cell, but Sophie left him a message to call as soon as he could.

"Of course," Dr. Wilder said. "But I need to know . . . have you decided if she'll be a donor?"

"She'd want that . . . don't you think?" Hannah asked Sophie. Her words quaked.

"Of course," Sophie said, dropping her hands to her lap. "She is such a kind girl . . ." Sophie's voice broke and tears streamed down her cheeks. Even crying, she was beautiful. Her red hair lay in a smooth sheet well past her shoulders, and her model-like cheekbones forced you to appreciate her clear green eyes and arched brows. She was the kind of woman other women accused of plastic surgery but was guilty only of exceptional genetics.

"She is, isn't she?" Hannah said, running her hand over Emily's smooth cheek.

"Yes," Sophie said softly. "Kind and generous." She let loose a heavy breath. "It's the right thing to do, *chérie*."

Hannah knew this was true. There had to be something good that came out of this horror. Some drop of joy amid an ocean of sorrow. "What do I need to do?" she asked Dr. Wilder.

"I'll contact the transplant coordinator," he said. "Zoe Parker. She'll take care of everything."

An hour later, a petite woman with short black hair and a clipboard entered the room and went over the entire process. Confidentiality was guaranteed—all the recipients would know was Emily's age and city, and that was all Hannah could know about the recipients. "I can tell you right now that there's a girl here in Seattle who desperately needs a liver," Zoe said. "She's been ill for years." She paused. "Your daughter will save her life . . . and many more."

Hannah nodded—she opted to donate every viable part of Emily: her heart, her lungs, her liver . . . even her skin to help burn victims—but inside she was screaming, *What about my daughter's life? Why can't someone save* her? Still, she signed where she needed to sign and wished with everything in her that she could cry. Since her initial tears in the ER waiting room, her breaths had become tight and dry, scorched and cracked as the desert. Nurses swirled around Emily's bed, injecting medicines into her IV that Dr. Wilder said would prep her organs for successful transplants. Hannah tried not to think about the surgery, about scalpels slicing into her daughter's skin. But over the next several hours, as she sat by Emily's side waiting for her parents to arrive, she couldn't stop the images from flashing through her mind.

Hannah heard her mother before she saw her. "Oh, no!" her mother cried out as she entered the ICU and saw Emily in her bed. Hannah turned around, noting that her parents hadn't bothered to change out of their work clothes before leaving for the airport. Her mother wore a white T-shirt and jeans smudged with dirt from her garden; her father, baggy Carhartt overalls with small holes in the knees. Her mother's gray-streaked black hair, usually worn in a tight bun at the base of her neck, hung loose about her face; her eyes were red, her jaw trembled.

Hannah stood, and her father strode across the room, taking her in his arms. He kissed the top of her head as she clung to him, her face pressed against his chest, breathing in the smell of hay, damp earth, and sweat. "It'll be okay, baby," he whispered.

"No, it won't," she moaned, and then Sophie entered the room after a trip to the cafeteria for a cup of coffee. Seeing Hannah melting into her father's arms, she quickly explained what had transpired since she'd called them earlier.

"No," Hannah's mother insisted. "I refuse to believe there's nothing they can do. There has to be *something*. Some procedure they haven't tried. An operation. We can't give up on her."

"It's too late, Mom," Hannah whispered. She felt like she was reciting lines from a play, acting out the part of the mother whose child was about to die. "They tried everything. But she's going to save other lives . . ." It seemed like the right thing to say, the only way to make sense of what was happening to Emily. "She's going to donate her organs . . ." Hannah's voice trailed off, and she finally pulled herself away from her father. Both he and her mother took a step over to Emily's bed, gazing at her with tears running down their cheeks.

This was how they all spent the next few hours, talking in hushed voices, murmuring words meant to comfort, trying to find a way to say good-bye to Emily. Hannah wondered if, after her daughter was gone, she could still call herself a mother. It struck her that when a spouse died, a person became a widow or widower, and when a child's parents died, he or she became an orphan, but there was no word to describe a parent who lost a child. Perhaps the pain of the experience was too vast to be captured, too gruesome to be wrapped up in one tidy little term.

Dr. Wilder returned around three in the morning, and seeing him enter, seeing the look on his face, Hannah knew it was time. Zoe had said the procurement process—dozens of tests run on Emily's body to ensure the organs were in the best shape possible for harvesting, as well as coordinating with the transplant center for delivery to all the various recipients—could take up to seventy-two hours, but the girl with the failing liver needed the transplant sooner than that, so Hannah had agreed to taking Emily off life support as soon as it was feasible to operate. She thought about the girl's parents, who were likely glued to their child's bedside, too, and for a moment, Hannah hated them. She hated them for anxiously awaiting Emily's death; she hated them for having a daughter who would live. The feeling passed as quickly as it had flashed through her, and she forced herself to focus on how grateful those parents must be, knowing a life had to be sacrificed for their daughter's to continue.

Hannah glanced around the room. Her father dozed in the chair, her mother on the small couch. Only Sophie was awake, sitting on the other side of Emily's bed looking weary and sad, one arm clutching her stomach, one hand curled into a fist over her mouth.

"Emily, honey," Hannah said, clasping her daughter's limp hand between both of hers. "It's okay, baby. You are the best thing that ever happened to me . . . did you know that?" She took in a shaking, shallow breath, then released it. "I'm going to miss you so much. I love you." The tears finally came, then, flooding her parched body. Her lungs convulsed, and her shoulders shook with violent despair.

Sophie rushed to Hannah's side, throwing her arms around her so she wouldn't crumple to the ground. Hannah pressed her face into her friend's neck, remembering the feel of her daughter doing this, too. Crying over a broken toy or fight with a friend. Looking to Hannah for comfort. Who would offer her child comfort now? At the sound of her cries, her parents awoke and joined her by Emily's bed, wrapping their arms around both Hannah and Sophie.

"I'm sorry," Dr. Wilder said, "but we really need to get her up to surgery."

"My god, give her a minute!" Sophie snapped, clutching Hannah more tightly. "She is saying good-bye to her *child*!"

"I understand," Dr. Wilder said gently. "But it's a time-sensitive process—"

"*Take* her, then," Hannah whimpered, cutting him off. "Oh god, please. Just take her. I can't . . . I don't know how to let her go . . ." She pulled away from Sophie and drew Emily to her chest one last time. She breathed her daughter in, sobbing, grief clawing at her lungs. "It's okay, baby girl. I'm here. Everything's going to be okay." She wept as she spoke these words, words she knew were pointless, words that Emily couldn't hear.

"No," Hannah's mother moaned; her father grabbed his wife to steady her.

Dr. Wilder came up behind Hannah and placed his hands on her shoulders. Gently, she released Emily from her arms. "I'll take good care of her, I promise," he said, and then she watched, helpless, as he took her daughter away.

A year later, Hannah can still feel the torturous pain of that moment in her chest. She has learned that the only way to escape it is movement, so this morning, after the scene plays out in her head, she forces herself out of bed. She slips on her shorts and tank top, pulls her hair into a ponytail, and tightly laces her running shoes. She doesn't look in the mirror, already knowing what she'll see: lined, sagging skin around her mouth and purple half-moons beneath vacant blue eyes. She's always been thin, but now her muscles are ropy, her rib cage exposed. She quickly brushes her teeth in the small bathroom, then trots down the steep stairs that lead from her apartment to the soon-to-open new salon below. It's only six thirty, so Hannah is startled to see one of the workmen already sitting in a heavily padded black leather salon chair, sipping a cup of coffee and staring out the large bay window.

"Good morning," he says as she enters what had been the living room of the house she and Sophie were almost done renovating. "Beautiful sunrise out there."

Hannah bobs her head. "You're here early." She recognizes him as one of the lead carpenters their general contractor hired, but doesn't remember his name. He is dark-haired and wears worn jeans with a long-sleeved, plaid flannel button-down and black, steel-toed boots. He has a faded but thick inch-long scar next to his left eye; it pushes down enough of the lid to make it appear that he is winking.

"You're here early, *Mike,*" he says with a slow smile, clearly understanding her struggle to recall who he is. "I like to get a jump on my day." He holds up his mug. "Coffee? There's plenty."

"No, thanks," she says. "I'm going for a run."

"I'll save you a cup, then," he says.

She doesn't bother telling him that she doesn't drink coffee, that her doctor said her anxiety is already so high that adding caffeine to the mix might shoot her blood pressure up to a dangerous range. She does give him a brief wave as she heads out the front door, happy to see that the landscaping she's been working on for the last two months is finally starting to take shape.

She didn't know much about gardening when she started back in June, but she threw herself into the project anyway, taking recommendations from the local nursery's staff, digging in the damp earth with her fingers to make room for the roots of a lilac bush and the whip-thin, yellow-popcorned branches of forsythia. There is a fountain built out of river stones, rose-bushes heavy with fragrant blooms. In the shadier sections, white-edged, pale green gatherings of bishop's-weed brighten the darkness. For Emily, she planted an enormous forget-me-not sea.

She starts down the street at an easy pace, relieved as her deepening breaths cause the claws in her lungs to retract. The sun is shining in a clear blue sky—a day so similar to the one of Emily's accident, Hannah stumbles as she makes the connection. She spent the anniversary of her daughter's death in the dark of her apartment, beneath the covers of her bed, feeling as though her every breath might be her last. Now, she focuses on the air moving in and out of her body, her feet pounding on the pavement, heel to toe, blood rushing through her veins and into her heart. She wasn't a runner before Emily died. She'd loathed exercise actually, never comprehending the masses who poured in and out of the gym. "I'll run if someone is chasing me with a knife," she used to joke with her clients who espoused the glory of released endorphins. "My endorphins aren't imprisoned," she said. "They're peaceful protesters."

Now, though, running is her medicine. The only way to calm her nerves, to keep her focused on something other than what she's lost. One foot in front of the other, one breath at a time.

When Hannah returns to the house an hour later, the rest of the work crew has arrived. Hammers slam against wood; nail guns spit out metal into the walls. The bamboo floorboards went in yesterday, and the bright white trim around the doors and windows should be finished today. Then, the four vanities with matching mirrors that Hannah found at an antique shop up in Anacortes can be taken out of storage and set up as workstations for her and her other stylists. She loves the contrast of the warm cherrywood set against freshly painted periwinkle walls. The flyers she sent out in a mass mailing last week announced the grand opening for August fifteenth. That gave them six days to get the rest of the work done, and with the way things looked now, they might be cutting it close.

Carl, the general contractor, stands in what will be the

clients' restroom, looking over the blueprints with Mike. He looks up when she comes through the door. "Just the woman I need to see," he says.

She nods. "Let me grab some water first." Sweat drips down her forehead; once in the small kitchen, she wipes it away with a paper towel, then pours herself a big glass of water from the pitcher in the fridge, gulping it down in one long swallow.

"Okay," she says as she approaches Carl and Mike again. "I'm all yours."

"Promises, promises," Carl says with a silly wiggle of his thick blond eyebrows. Hannah manages a small smile. He holds out the blueprints for her perusal. "Okay. So, Mike is installing the vanity for the sink today. I just need to know if you're good with where the plumbing comes in."

Instead of looking at the schematics, which she doesn't know how to read, Hannah eyes the pipes that are already through the wall. "Looks fine to me. It's such a small space; I want to be sure the door isn't going to hit anything when a client opens it."

"It won't," Mike assures her, reaching over to pat her arm. Hannah jerks away from his touch. Since Emily died, she feels as though her skin is on inside out, all her nerves exposed. Physical contact, except from those she already loves and trusts, is excruciating. Mike raises a single eyebrow at her, but she averts her eyes from his, instead focusing on Carl.

"I'll be upstairs if you need me again," she says, her voice wobbly and thin. *Don't cry,* she thinks. *Don't, don't, don't.* She spins around, feeling their gaze upon her as she ascends the stairs. The small bit of peace she felt during her run has evaporated.

The phone rings as she is running the water for her shower. She hesitates only a moment before turning the water back off and grabbing it. After Emily's funeral, she went through a phase of not answering her calls, which only led to the callers coming to her house to make sure she was okay. Verbal check-ins were still easier than face-to-face visits, so she has learned to always answer the damn phone.

"Good morning, Sophie," she says and drops to sit on the closed toilet seat.

"Good morning, love," Sophie says. "How are you?"

"I'm good," she answers. "Just got back from my run."

"Are we on schedule for opening?" Sophie asks.

"Looks like it," Hannah says. Initially, she and Sophie had planned to manage the renovation of the new salon together, but a few months after Emily's accident, Hannah latched on to the tasks of finding the right architect and contractor, of obtaining permits and designs, as a way to keep her mind busy. Spinning on thoughts of construction was the only thing that kept the grief at bay. Hannah decided the best way to stay on top of the project was to actually *stay* on top of it. Unable to live in the house she had shared with her daughter, she moved into the upstairs apartment of the new location. Hannah couldn't stand the emptiness of that house without Emily in it; she couldn't look at the street where Emily was hit without spiraling into hysterics or being overcome by rage toward the woman who'd killed her. It was an accident, Hannah knew. The police determined that the woman wasn't intoxicated and that she hadn't been speeding—witnesses confirmed that Emily really did shoot out from the driveway—so there were no criminal charges filed. And yet there were moments when Hannah couldn't help but blame the woman. On her worst days, she hated her. It didn't matter that the woman's insurance company was paying out substantial death benefits to Hannah. All that mattered was that Emily was gone.

After Emily's small funeral, Hannah had the majority of their things moved into storage and rented the home to an older couple who had no children. Seeing Emily's friends around the neighborhood after the memorial was too much for Hannah. They wanted to talk with her about Emily, to have Hannah offer them some kind of comfort in their grief, but she couldn't give that to them. She couldn't even give it to herself. Their visits reminded her too much of all she'd lost. When she moved, she felt relieved, like the cramped apartment somehow contained her sorrow. Kept it from overrunning her life. She welcomed the constant noise below her, the Skilsaws and sanders. She liked the idea of starting over, refinishing the old to make room for the new.

Sophie seemed to understand Hannah's inability to continue to work at the downtown Ciseaux, where Emily had grown up, where she had taken her first steps and played dress-up in front of the mirrors. For now, her savings and the death benefit payments are more than enough to cover the cost of renovation and give Hannah some to live on. Sophie agreed to be a silent partner at this location, with Hannah running the day-to-day operations.

"Your clients keep asking for you," Sophie says now. "They miss you."

"They can come see me here," Hannah responds with a sigh. The truth is, she hates the idea of seeing her clients again—the pity on their faces at Emily's funeral had been enough. She wants to exist in a new world with new clients, women who don't know that Emily is dead. Women whose mouths won't screw up into dark frowns and who won't ask how she is *doing*. What does that mean, exactly? How do they *think* she is doing? Her daughter is *dead*. A hard knot forms in her throat, and Hannah swallows around its sharp edges.

"Hey, Soph," she says, attempting to sound cheery. "I was just about to jump in the shower. Can I call you back?"

"I'll just see you later this afternoon, darling. The meeting with the caterer for the opening?"

"Oh . . . right. Of course." Like Mike's name, Hannah had forgotten this. With the launch of the new salon next week, they are planning a catered open house to welcome clientele to the location, but Hannah has yet to decide on a menu. Party planning is more Sophie's thing, so she asked her partner to join her. "I'll see you at three, then."

"Two, actually," Sophie says gently, and Hannah smiles.

"What would I do without you, Soph?"

"Good thing you don't have to find out."

They hang up, and Hannah strips off her clothes. As steam fills the bathroom, she moves her fingers across her belly, brushing over the stretched, soft skin and silvery lines that carrying Emily created. She wishes she had more scars than these. She wishes the evidence of her pain were somewhere other than inside her body, believing that if other people could actually *see* how deeply she is wounded, they'd know to just leave her alone.

Climbing into the tiled shower, she stands under the hot water, letting it scald her skin. For some reason, she thinks about the cars she saw on the road during her run this morning.

She watched the drivers talk on their cell phones and sip from their Starbucks coffee cups—how they took everything for granted. She wanted to warn them, to tell them how quickly everything can change, but she knew it was useless. There's simply no telling whose life will be touched by tragedy. There is only a before and an after, with no way to predict the moment when one is over and the other begins.

Olivia

During the months that James traveled to Tampa to see Olivia on the weekends, he talked a lot about what it was like to live in Seattle. "It gets a bad rap because of all the rain," he told her, "but it's actually really beautiful. More shades of green than I can name."

"I'd love to see it sometime," Olivia said, hoping she wasn't being too presumptuous. The truth was she wanted to visit the city so she could have a better picture of what he was doing when he wasn't with her. She could pull up vague mental images of him surrounded by people wearing galoshes and holding umbrellas as he strolled around the base of the Space Needle or stood on the deck of a ferry, but that was pretty much the limit of her visual knowledge about the Pacific Northwest.

"You will," he assured her. "But your mother needs you here, doesn't she? It's easier for me to come to you."

Reluctantly, she agreed with him. She couldn't afford a private nurse for her mother, and since they were only dating at the time, there was no way she would let James foot that kind of bill, even if he'd offered. So it wasn't until they were newlyweds that Olivia saw James's house. She gasped as their driver pressed the button for the automatic gate to open, allowing her a view of the imposing structure at the end of the road. The house was hers, too, she supposed, now that they were married. *Married,* she thought. *I'm twenty-three years old and married to an amazing, accomplished man. A man who adores me and has promised to take care of my every need.*

It was a new experience for her, being cared for. Since her parents divorced when she was five and her father decided he'd rather not bother spending time with his daughter, it had always been just Olivia and her mother. "We're better off without him," Olivia's mother said. They'd struggled over the years, trying to make ends meet, but her mother insisted that she'd never marry again—that overall, men weren't worth the bother of having them around. "They take what they want from you and then spit you back out," she told Olivia more than once. "They use you up and then throw you away."

Her mother's bitterness lingered in the air of their tiny apartment like secondhand smoke. Olivia did her best to not breathe it in, to believe that someday, she might find a man who would fall in love with her. She promised herself that when she got married, it would be forever. She remembered her mother constantly picking at her dad, screaming at him over silly things like him not taking out the garbage, and a small part of Olivia blamed her mother for her father's abandonment of them both. She swore that someday, she'd be a sweet, gentle wife who never yelled, so her husband would never leave. She pictured herself living with him—cooking for him and climbing into his bed at night, giving birth to their children, growing old in the house they picked out together. Years of watching *L.A. Law* with her mother primed Olivia for the idea of becoming a lawyer—she fantasized that she and her husband might work at the same firm, defending clients together. She tried to believe that she didn't have to share her mother's fate.

Later, after high school, the few men she dated before James were just boys, wanting to split the check and wait for Olivia to call them instead of picking up the phone themselves. They wanted to "hook up" and "hang out," vague relationship descriptors that left Olivia wondering if her mother was right—if any man was capable of true commitment. But James was different. James opened doors for her and pulled out her chair; he sent her long-stemmed red roses and helped her with her coat. He made her feel valuable and special. She glowed beneath the pleasure of his attentions.

"You're lucky he's rich," her mother observed, after meeting James for the first time. "He can take care of you."

"I don't care about his money," Olivia said, feeling her face grow hot. It was clear her mother didn't believe her, but Olivia spoke the truth. The fact that James had money seemed beside the point. What mattered to Olivia was that he wanted a happy, loving marriage as much as she did. "I'm ready to settle down," he told her after just a few weeks of dating. "I want to have the family my parents never gave me."

It surprised her, at first, that James pursued her so fervently, since it was obvious with his money and level of success, he could have any woman he wanted. "I'm not sure what you see in me," she said, feeling a little shy. She knew she was pretty, but she was far from the polished women with whom she knew James worked and socialized.

"I see your determination," he answered. "I see how kind you are and what an amazing mother you'll make. I see that you might teach me to be a better person."

His words pleased Olivia; she loved that for all his sophistication, he felt as though she had something to teach him, too. Just a few months later, she agreed to marry him in a quick civil ceremony at the Tampa courthouse. "Who needs all the fuss of a big wedding?" James asked, and while a part of Olivia would have loved that kind of fuss—it was, after all, the only wedding she ever planned to have—it seemed that after everything he'd already done for her, asking for him to pay for an event like that would seem greedy. He took her to Paris for their honeymoon, and they took moonlit walks along the Seine, sipped wine and ate buttery croissants in their enormous hotel bed, made love two or three times a day. Afterward, James would rest his head on Olivia's chest and she would run her fingers through his thick hair until his breaths slowed and deepened and he fell asleep. Olivia had never felt so content.

One evening, after just such a moment, Olivia tried to slip out from under the weight of him in order to use the bathroom, but James held on to her tightly. "No," he said. "I won't let you go."

She softened her body and gave him a little squeeze. "Just for a minute, love. I'll be right back." In her experience, most men were afraid of their emotions; she loved how vulnerable he was with her, how willing he was to express how he felt.

He looked up at her with so much love in his eyes, she was

almost startled by its intensity. "I need you, Liv. I need you so much."

"I need you, too," she said, feeling as though she was the luckiest girl in the world.

A week later, they arrived in Seattle, and James smiled at her in the back of the limousine as the heavy gate closed behind them. "What do you think?" he asked as they traveled up the driveway to the house.

Olivia couldn't respond, still staring at the red-brick palace before them. It was three stories high with several turrets, a circular driveway, and a detached five-car garage. Towering maples flanked each side of the building, and a large marble fountain served as centerpiece to the extensive grounds. A tall, black iron fence enclosed the entire property—wired to shock the hell out of anyone who tried to scale it, James told her. She knew James was well-off, but he hadn't made clear the exact level of his fortune. Olivia felt like it would have been in poor taste to ask for specifics.

The driver parked the car, then came around to open Olivia's door. Both she and James climbed out of the vehicle and stood beside it. "Welcome home, baby," he said, and then he kissed her, pushing his body hard against hers, making her feel drunk with arousal. When he finally pulled away, Olivia gave him a wicked smile.

"Let's make love in every room," she said, and immediately, James's body went stiff. He gripped her forearm until tears flooded her eyes.

"Don't talk like that in front of the staff," he growled. "I don't want them thinking my new wife's a slut." He released her arm, then smiled again, a wide easy motion, leaning down to kiss her cheek. "Come on, beauty. Let's get you cleaned up and I'll tell the cook to get dinner started. I asked her to stock all of your favorites. Chicken Caesar salad sounds good, doesn't it?"

Stunned, Olivia swallowed back her tears and nodded. *Did my husband just call me a* slut? The moment had happened so quickly, she wondered if she had imagined it. She glanced down at her arm then, and there it was: the bright red imprint of his fingers. She rubbed it, as though trying to erase the evidence. *He's just tired,* she told herself. *He didn't mean anything by it.* She promised herself to do as he asked, to be cautious of how she spoke in front of the people who worked for him. A man at his level of success had an image to maintain, and it was her job as his wife to support that. This was why he'd taken her on a shopping spree in Paris, helping her pick out an entirely new wardrobe: simple straight skirts, tailored slacks, and a rainbow of gloriously soft cashmere sweater sets. He bought her diamond stud earrings and a pearl necklace. "You know I already love how you look," he told her. "I only want you to have the best of everything." When she protested that she didn't need him to buy her so much, he shushed her. "It makes me happy to be able to give it to you," he said, and Olivia decided that she would do whatever it took to make *him* happy, too.

After he showed her their room—a master suite with an enormous walk-in closet and private bathroom all her own—she showered, dressing simply in a pale yellow sundress, then found her way back down the curved staircase into the dining room. A tall, slightly homely woman in a black chef's coat was placing a large salad on the table, but Olivia didn't greet her, afraid James might walk in and hear her saying the wrong thing. The woman pressed her lips together and nodded at Olivia, then exited the room.

She took a moment to absorb the simple, luxurious beauty of the space: creamy white walls were accented by crimson drapes. An enormous, brushed-nickel-framed mirror hung opposite the French doors that led out onto an extensive patio. This room alone was bigger than the tiny apartment she'd shared with her mother; its opulence outweighed any other home she'd ever entered. Walking over to the doors, Olivia stared out across the property on the backside of the house, which held a kidney-shaped, sparkling blue pool and what looked to be a modest but lovely guest cottage. She wondered briefly why James had never suggested bringing her mother with them, since he obviously had an appropriate separate living space, but then she brushed away the thought, knowing she should be grateful for everything he *had* done, both for her and for her mother.

"What do you think?" James asked, and Olivia put a splayed hand over her chest, whipping around to face him.

"Oh god, don't sneak up on me like that!" she exclaimed. "You *scared* me!"

"Sorry, darling. Bare feet on marble floors don't make much sound."

She dropped her arm back to her side. "*Bear* feet? I thought you had *people* feet."

James smiled indulgently at her silly play on words. "Let's eat, shall we?" He gestured toward the table and Olivia stepped over to it, sitting down in the chair he held out for her. She felt small in this high-ceilinged room, out of place in a house that was supposed to be her new home. *I'll get used to it,* she reassured herself, then forced a smile at James, who was filling her plate, then his, with greens and thin slices of chicken breast. She watched him pour the dressing over his salad, then asked him to please pass it to her. He tilted his head the slightest bit to the side. "Are you sure you should have any? You had that scone for breakfast."

His tone was gentle, but still, Olivia sucked in a tiny breath, suddenly self-conscious. *Am I getting fat?* They'd eaten out at so many fantastic restaurants in Tampa, indulging over candle-light dinners in buttery pastas and rich desserts. Perhaps it *was* time for her to scale back her diet. She smiled and nodded at him. "That's right. I probably shouldn't."

He smiled, reached over and squeezed her hand, then passed her a bowl filled with quartered lemons. "Here," he said. "With these and a little pepper, you won't even miss the dressing."

Now, thinking back to her arrival into James's world, Olivia is dumbfounded by how easily she overlooked those red-flag moments. She sits at the same dining room table almost two decades later, and wonders how different her life would have been if she had walked out right then, that first day in this house. If she had stood up when he refused her the salad dressing and told him to go fuck himself. If she had understood that that was only the beginning of what she would face.

But then she looks at their daughter, born just a year after they married, sitting across from her now with bright eyes, rosy cheeks, and a properly functioning liver—so much stronger and healthier a year after the transplant—and she knows that every sacrifice she has made has been worth it. Staying was the right thing to do. If she tries to leave now, there's no doubt that James will file for full custody of Maddie, so Olivia knows that she can't walk out the door until her daughter turns eighteen. She almost lost Maddie once—she won't risk it again.

"But I don't *want* to go to an actual *school*," Maddie says to her father, who is sitting, as always, at the head of the table, the two of them flanking him. "What's the *point*?"

"The point *is,* you are healthy enough to start living a normal life," James says, aiming a thick finger at his daughter. "The point *is,* I'm your father, and I say it's time for you to start living in the real world with real people instead of being on that damn computer all the time."

"She only has two years left until she graduates," Olivia says quietly. "Maybe she'll be fine with the tutor." She and James agreed that for the first year after Maddie's transplant, she would continue to be schooled at home so she could heal more effectively and be at less risk for infection. But now that her health is so much better, he is insistent that she attend Eastside Prep, the same elite, private high school he attended over thirty-five years ago.

"Maybe *you* shouldn't butt into a conversation I'm having with my daughter," James snaps, and Maddie's eyes grow wide. Olivia cringes, hating it when her daughter witnesses James's temper; she'd sheltered Maddie as much as possible from his darker side.

"Mom's right," Maddie says, dropping her fork to her plate with a clatter. "I've done fine with Mrs. Beck. I aced my SATs, right? I even took them early. That's because of her."

James shakes his head. "That's because you're brilliant, like your father." He winks at Maddie, who only frowns. Olivia breathes a silent sigh of relief that the pendulum of his mood seems to have swung back in a positive direction. To make sure it stays there, she decides the best thing she can do in that moment is to back up her husband.

"I think maybe your dad has a point, honey," Olivia says, tucking her hair behind one ear. "You are brilliant, but you missed out on so much while you were sick. I don't think you even realize how much." She glances at James, who gives her a brief, approving nod. The knot in her stomach that formed when he snapped at her relaxes.

Maddie rolls her eyes. "Yes, I do, Mom. I get it. I spent the last eight years doing nothing but think about everything I was missing. But that's totally my point. I already *missed* it." She waves a dismissive hand in the air in front of her. "Going to some stuck-up prep school where all the kids have known each other since they were like, in *diapers* would only make it worse. I'd be the weird, puffy girl who's carrying around a dead girl's *liver* inside her. I'd be a freak."

"That's not true," Olivia says. "And the only way people would know about the transplant is if you told them."

Maddie sighs. "As I'm taking eight hundred pills a day to ward off rejection. Sure, no one will notice *that*."

Olivia tries again, ignoring her daughter's exaggeration. "Well, some of the kids you'll know from elementary school. Maybe you can reconnect with old friends."

"Yeah, right," Maddie says. "Like the bonding we did over Play-Doh and hopscotch will just carry right on over to being BFFs now."

"Enough!" James bellows, startling both Olivia and Maddie. His eyes go dark as he glares at them; his brows furrow together into a deep V. Olivia can see the muscles along his jaw working in a tight motion, and she knows this means he is trying to restrain himself. She braces herself for what might come next.

After a moment, he shoves his chair back from the table and stands, pulls on his jacket, then walks over to Maddie. As he puts his hand on the back of her neck, Maddie freezes. Olivia holds her breath. "You're already registered," he continues, a cool edge in his voice. "I let Mrs. Beck go with a generous severance package. When school starts next month, you *will* be there. End of discussion." He squeezes his fingers on her neck once, and Maddie flinches, closing her eyes. A single tear slips down her cheek, and Olivia's heart aches at the sight. They are both silent, hands in their laps, as James grabs his briefcase and strides out the door.

After he leaves, Maddie opens her eyes and looks at Olivia. "I *hate* him," she whispers.

"No, you don't," Olivia says. "You're angry with him. You're disappointed. You're scared." Feelings Olivia is all too familiar with when it comes to her husband.

"What a fantastic way to feel about my own father," Maddie says with a sniffle. "*Please,* Mom. Don't make me go."

"You'll be fine, I promise."

"No, I *won't,*" Maddie groans. "I won't be able to *stand* it!"

Olivia twists her face into what she hopes is an encouraging smile. "Yes, you will," she says. "Believe me, honey. When it's for the right reason, you can handle more than you know."

Maddie

My mother is wrong, I think as I stomp up the stairs to my bedroom. *I do hate my father. If* she *had any backbone at all, she'd hate him, too.* Slamming the door behind me, I grab my laptop and plop down on my bed, quickly logging in to Sierra's Facebook profile to write a status update. "Parents are soooo LAME," I type. "Why do they think they can control my life⸮!"

After a few people "like" the post, I decide it sounds too immature and I delete it. I've listed Sierra's age as twenty-one, and I'm pretty sure by that point, most girls aren't constantly bitching about their parents. At least I hope not. Now that I'm fairly healthy, my plan is to get the hell out of this house the minute I turn eighteen. Two more years of dealing with my father will be enough; now, I have to deal with five hundred other kids at a school I don't want to go to⸮ Kids who won't know me or want to know me, because even though I feel better than I did a year ago, my hair is still stringy and my body has a weird shape. I'm not an hourglass; I'm a barrel.

This thought is too depressing to deal with, so I decide to log in to my favorite gaming site instead. I discovered Zombie Wars about six months ago, when I was still stuck in bed a good part of the day and about to go out of my mind with boredom. It's an online, alternate reality game set after the apocalypse, where you can create an avatar to join forces with other players to fight brain-eating zombies. I thought it was a little dorky at first, but once I got past the first couple of levels, I really started to get into the challenge of playing. Like pretending to be Sierra on Facebook and Twitter, I could pretend to be a butt-kicking zombie assassin who might just save the world. Maybe it *was* dorky, but it was definitely better than numbing my brain with daytime TV.

I click on my profile's inbox to see if any other avatars have interacted with mine, and suddenly, an instant message pops up on my screen: "Hey Sierra. I'm Dirk. Saw you take down that giant zombie yesterday with one shot between the eyes. Nice work. Want to build an alliance?"

My fingers poise over the keyboard, hesitant. I tend to only message with other girls in the game, forming virtual friendships with people I will likely never meet, but this is the first time my avatar has been contacted by a boy. How could I *not* respond? His avatar is handsome, a blond-haired, black-leather-clad boy with bright blue eyes and a strong jaw. It's almost eerie, how human he looks. In Zombie Wars, you can design how prominent you want your cheekbones, the shape and color of your eyes. Computer graphics are getting *crazy* realistic, and it's totally what I want to major in when I get to college.

I check out his avatar again and wonder if he's this attractive in person or if, like me, he has a reason to hide behind the screen. "Thanks," I type, and for some reason, my heartbeat speeds up. "I like yours, too. Been playing long?"

"Just a couple of months," he responds. "A friend turned me on to it, since he knows how obsessed I am with *Zombieland*."

"That's one of my favorite movies!"

"Best movie ever made. Well, beside *The Matrix*. And *Star Wars*." There is a pause, and then he sends me another message. "So, what do you think? Want to partner up?" He ends the question with a winking smiley face, and I blush.

"Sure," I reply, and before I can read his response, there is a loud knock on my bedroom door.

"Maddie, honey? Can I come in?" This is a new thing for my mom, having to ask to enter my room. When I was sick, she just came and went as she pleased, oftentimes even sleeping on the bed next to me instead of with my dad. But once I had the transplant and started feeling better, I asked her to knock, and—probably more difficult for her—to stay in her own bed.

"I'm kind of busy," I call out to her, trying to mask my sigh.

Dirk sends me another message: "R U still there?"

"One sec," I type. "BRB."

"Doing what?" She opens the door enough to stick her head inside. When she sees me with the laptop, it's her turn to sigh. "It's a beautiful day. Let's put that away and go for a walk."

"Later, okay? I'm journaling." One of the counselors I had to talk with after the transplant encouraged me to keep a diary about how I was feeling through the whole process. She told my mom about it, too, so now, whenever she catches me on the computer and gives me a guilt trip, I tell her I've been writing about my *feelings,* which usually makes her back off. "Can you close the door behind you, please?"

She stares at me with the hazel bordering on light-green eyes she passed down to me, blinks a couple of times, then quietly exits. My gut clenches, hating that I might have hurt her, but wishing she had something other than *me* to keep her busy during the day. What will she do when I go back to school? Dad won't let her work, I know that much for sure. The one time after my transplant that she suggested she was thinking about getting recertified as a paralegal, or how she might want to go back to school and become a lawyer, he totally lost it, throwing a chair across the room. A few inches to the left and he would have clocked her with it, which I'm pretty sure was exactly what he was trying to do. Not that she'd ever admit that about him. She'd make some excuse about what a tough childhood he had . . . how his father used to beat him and how he never really worked through his anger about that. "That's bull," I told her once. "Why don't you just leave him?"

"Because I can't," she said quietly, staring at me in a way that made me think that there was a damn good reason she hadn't left, and the only one I could come up with was me.

The message box on the screen blinks at me, and I look down to see that Dirk has asked me another question. "So, how old are you IRL? You're not really some gross forty-year-old guy wearing underwear in his mom's basement, eating Cheetos, are you?"

"LOL! No, definitely not," I answer, then pause before addressing the issue of my age. "How old are you?"

"Twenty-four."

"That's cool," I type. "I'm nineteen." I land on this age because it's closer to my own than the twenty-one I'd listed as

Sierra's, and it also gives him a chance to pass on hanging out with me in Zombie Wars since five years younger might be too much for his tastes. "Almost twenty," I quickly add, and then I wait for him to respond.

"Maybe I can take you out for your birthday," his message reads, and I smile wider, thinking how desperately I want to live in this world rather than my own.

Hannah

The morning of the salon's grand opening, Hannah drives to Sea-Tac airport to pick up her parents. They insisted on flying over from Boise for the event, but Hannah knows it's really just an excuse for them to check up on her.

After Emily's funeral, she went back to the farm for a few weeks, curling up in her childhood bed for most of the days she spent there. Her mother tried to tempt her with her favorite foods—fresh strawberry ice cream, bacon-wrapped meat loaf, and chicken potpie—as though calories could serve as some kind of magical antidote to grief. She managed to nibble on these offerings, but only to placate her mother. She couldn't taste a thing.

In the evenings, Hannah sat on the wraparound porch with her father, numbly staring out at the blossoming vegetable garden. In the old wooden swing, its joints creaking with each push forward and fall back, he would hold her hand and talk about Emily. "Remember her face when she learned how to open a pea pod?" her father asked. "'Look, Pop-Pop,' she said. '*Pea* seeds!'" His hands shook and a tear rolled down his creviced, sun-weathered cheek. "What was she . . . four, then?"

"Three, I think," Hannah whispered. Of course she remembered. Her mind was flooded with memories—made sodden by them. The first time Emily rolled over and then, six months later, when she pulled herself up to stand next to the couch. Hannah remembered her daughter's regularly skinned knees and her red apple phobia after seeing *Snow White*. She remembered the way Emily had let go of her hand the first day of kindergarten, her Hello Kitty backpack over one shoulder as she walked bravely down the hallway to her classroom, one white kneesock sagging around her ankle. "I can do it my*self,* Mama," Emily said, and Hannah glowed with pride that this pink-cheeked, bright-eyed child was hers, sure of herself in a way that many girls seem to lose track of as they journey toward adolescence. At twelve, Emily was already beginning to lose her girlish shine, jaded by the prepubescent hormones raiding her blood. She posted a Do Not Enter sign on her bedroom door; Hannah had to ask permission before tucking her in for the night. Long, deep snuggles were replaced by short, cheek-brushing kisses. Emily no longer talked freely about her days; Hannah had to grill her for even the smallest details. One night, a few days before the accident, Emily slammed her bedroom door, furious that Hannah wouldn't let her go to the mall alone with her friends. "I *hate* you!" Emily screamed. "I wish you weren't my *mom!*"

Hannah was already missing her daughter when she died, mourning the years that had so quickly passed them by. She was grieving whatever it was that allowed Emily to pull away so soon, so easily. That, of course, was before Hannah knew how deep real grief could go.

"She was an amazing girl," Hannah's father said, roughly wiping at his tears with the back of his free hand. "God just gained another angel."

God is a selfish bastard, Hannah thought. In the end, she left the farm after Labor Day, unable to manage her parents' sorrow on top of her own. She also couldn't handle their not-so-subtle suggestions that she should make her stay at the farm a permanent move. Though she emailed and talked with them on the phone at least once a week, today would be the first time she'd seen them in over six months. She'd gone back to the farm for Christmas, but only because they had pleaded with her. The truth was, without Emily, she would be all too happy to pretend that holidays no longer existed.

Pulling up in front of the airline's pickup lane, Hannah sees her parents already standing by the curb with their bags. They will stay at Isaac's house on Mercer Island, since she no longer has the space to host them. Her brother said he would come to the opening, too, but he wasn't sure what time, since he was flying in from a business meeting in Los Angeles and would be on standby.

"Hello, sweetie," her mother says, pulling Hannah into a tight embrace. She has a clean, soap and water smell that conjures up memories of Hannah's childhood: nights spent shucking corn with her mother in the kitchen, stirring enormous pots of what would become endless jars of blackberry jam. Pulling away, her mother cups Hannah's face with both hands. "You look good."

"Thanks," Hannah says, though her voice strangles on the

word. She knows "You look good" is her mother's code for "You look too tired and too thin and I can't believe you haven't come home in over six months." Just like when her mother said, "I support you no matter what you decide to do," after Hannah informed her she planned to skip the whole husband and marriage gig and go it alone as a parent. What she really meant was, "No man will ever marry you if you already have a baby. You're making the biggest mistake of your life." But then her mother held Emily for the first time, and Hannah knew it didn't matter *how* she became a grandmother—it only mattered that she was one.

The truth is that Hannah did date after Emily was born, thinking someday she might be able to get over Devin cheating on her, but she didn't introduce her daughter to any of the men with whom she spent time. She kept her parenting and dating lives separate, wary of bringing a man into Emily's life who might disappear on them both. She clung to what the experts said about the perils of dating as a single parent, how they cautioned against inserting someone into your child's life without some kind of assurance of long-term commitment. None of her boyfriends, even those she dated for more than a few months, made her feel safe enough to truly open up her heart and risk getting hurt again. She wonders sometimes if Devin's infidelities damaged her ability to trust to the extent that she *can't* fall in love. Once bitten, forever shy.

Her father hugs her next, and after getting their bags into the trunk, Hannah starts to drive them toward Isaac's house. "I thought you might want to get freshened up before the party," she says, after telling them where they're headed. "I'll come back to get you in a while."

"We're just fine, honey," her father says from the backseat. "It's only an hour flight."

Hannah glances at him in the rearview mirror. "Are you sure? I'm going to be pretty busy. You might get bored."

"We'll help," her mother says, reaching over from the passenger seat to pat Hannah's arm. She notices the back of her mother's hand, the skin creped and veined, a sharp, painful reminder that her parents won't be around forever, either.

Hannah tries to keep from sighing, knowing that they mean well, but that their "help" might add an extra fifteen minutes to each task. "Okay," she says, attempting to sound cheerful. "Great." She directs the car to I-405, heading north to Bellevue. Her father hums a nameless tune, a habit Hannah grew accustomed to years before. Wherever her father is, whatever he is doing, he is likely humming. That, along with the rooster's crow each day and the buzz of crickets at dusk, made up the sound track of her youth. She misses it sometimes, the simplicity of that life, but she also loves the quicker pace of living in a bigger city—the restaurants, the theater, the museums. She also loves having the mountains on one side of her and the ocean on the other; if she wanted to, she could ski and go swimming on the same day. She's not sure she could give that all up.

"Have you thought any more about moving back to the farm?" her mother asks as they pass through the Renton S-curves. Last year, her mother had campaigned the hardest for her to make the move. "You can open a small salon here," she suggested. "The women of Boise could use a little glamour."

Now, Hannah grits her teeth before speaking. "No, Mom." *Really? She's here less than twenty minutes and already pushing the subject?* Hannah realizes it's getting harder for her parents to handle the heavy labor on their property. Her father hired a foreman to manage the dairy business, and several laborers to take care of the two hundred acres of potatoes and corn. They have always wished for one of their children to someday take over the farm, but neither Hannah nor Isaac has any inclination to live in the country. Still, they are her parents, and Hannah feels guilty knowing that if she or Isaac doesn't move home, as her parents age, they'll likely have to sell the farm off, parcel by parcel, in order to survive. At the very least, they will have to fully turn its operations over to someone else, relinquishing to a stranger what they poured their hearts and souls into through the years. Hannah knows that, because he built the success of the property out of ten small acres he began with over forty years before, this prospect breaks her father's heart.

"A change of scene might be good for you," her mother says, wringing her hands together in her lap.

"Marcy . . ." her father says, a hint of warning in his tone.

"It's okay, Dad," Hannah says, gripping the steering wheel more tightly. She glances over to her mother. "I *have* a change of scene. I already moved—remember?"

"I'm just worried you did that to avoid your grief," her mother says. "Packing away all of Emily's things like that, pretending she never existed—"

"That's *not* what I'm doing," Hannah snaps. Her voice is raw. She clears her throat so she won't cry. How can she explain how she feels to them? How can she tell them that she's worried if she is surrounded by Emily's things, the weight of the memories might crush her? If she goes through Emily's clothes, her toys, her books, that she simply won't be able to survive? Having put her daughter's belongings into storage is keeping Hannah alive; having them around her might end her.

"Are you sure?" her mother continues. "I was watching Dr. Phil the other day—"

"Oh my god. Dr. Phil . . . really?" Hannah says. Besides baking and working in the garden, her mother's favorite pastime is armchair psychiatry, trained only by afternoon talk-show hosts.

"But, honey—"

"Enough, Mom, okay? Can we please just enjoy the day? It's important to me."

"Marcy," her father says again. He reaches over the seat, squeezes his wife's shoulder, and she finally falls silent.

Fifteen minutes later, as Hannah parks in front of the salon, her mother leans forward to peer out the windshield. "Is that it?"

"Yep," Hannah replies as they extricate themselves from the car and approach the garden gate. She finished the landscaping just yesterday, shoveling wheelbarrows full of smooth river stones into the empty spots of the flower beds, thinking about how Emily, at seven or eight, used to sit in their driveway and put together small, ragged towers out of rocks: Yard Henge, Hannah jokingly called them. "Structural engineer in the making," Isaac said proudly, when Hannah emailed him pictures of his niece's handiwork.

It's a mallet to her stomach, every time, realizing that Emily is no longer *anything* in the making. All of her daughter's dreams have vanished. She won't be a large animal vet or a Broadway star. She won't be an artist or a lawyer or a hip-hop dancer. She'll never have her first kiss. Hannah won't help Emily get ready for the prom, she won't take her shopping for a wedding dress, or one day cuddle a grandbaby. What was a future filled with infinite possibility seems hopeless to Hannah now. There are moments when taking her next breath feels like a pointless endeavor.

As Hannah and her parents make their way to the front steps, she notices that while she was gone, the caterers set up two round tables on the flagstone patio and the florist arranged the centerpieces. Small gatherings of chairs were placed in what will be shaded spots in the yard, so people can chat while they help themselves to the appetizers. "It's beautiful, honey," her mother says. "I can't believe how much work you've done since the last set of pictures you emailed us." She is trying, at least, to make up for her comments in the car.

"Thanks," Hannah says. "The contractor Isaac recommended did a really amazing job. Let me show you inside." She opens the front door only to find Sophie in the middle of berating one of the employees Hannah hired to work at this location.

"You will *not* wear that disgusting nose ring during this party," Sophie says to Veronica, a younger stylist with Crayola-red-hued short hair and pale, porcelain skin. Hannah interviewed her a few weeks ago, and Veronica's portfolio of the color work she'd done was stunning enough for Hannah to hire her on the spot. Today, Veronica wears black leggings and a fitted white blouse. She also has a small gold hoop hanging from the center of her nose, above her upper lip. Sophie, as usual, is dressed in her signature snug black T-shirt and jeans.

Veronica opens her mouth, but Sophie holds up her hand to stop her. "Uh-uh-uh, *chérie*. I don't want to hear it. I don't care what you did at your *other* salon—here you will look clean and professional. You will not wear jewelry that makes you look like a *bull*. This is Bellevue, not the *University District* or the *circus*. We do not cater to the steam-punk, liberty-spiked crowd here. Am I making myself understood?"

Veronica nods, as does Peter, the other stylist Hannah hired, looking a little afraid of Sophie, and then they head toward the back room to finish filling the small gift bags with salted caramels, various hair products and accessories, and coupons for services at both salons. Each party attendee will get one, and at last count before Hannah left for the airport, only twenty were finished. They expect at least two hundred people throughout the day.

Hannah clears her throat to get her friend's attention. She and Sophie had agreed Hannah would have complete charge of the second location, but clearly, Sophie still feels entitled to take the lead when necessary. Hannah finds this more amusing than annoying, wondering not for the first time if her friend's bossy nature is the real reason she opts for having lovers instead of boyfriends. "I have lovers because I'm *French,* darling," Sophie told her, when Hannah first brought the subject up.

"And the French don't get married?" Hannah asked, unable to disguise her amusement.

"But of course. And *then* they take lovers." Sophie grinned. "I'm simply skipping a step." Hannah knows that like her own, Sophie's cautious nature when it comes to relationships has more to do with a badly broken heart, but she never points that out to her friend. Hannah understands that sometimes, the stories we tell ourselves about the choices we make are the only things that keep us from being crushed by the truth.

Seeing Hannah's parents now, Sophie throws her hands up into the air. "Steven and Marcy!" she says, and steps across the small entryway to give them both kisses on the cheek. "Welcome to *Ciseaux,* part *deux*!" She sweeps her arm out from her body, gesturing to the rest of the room. "What do you think?"

Hannah takes in the space the way her parents might, seeing it for the first time. The pale-blond bamboo floors set against the periwinkle walls; warm cherry vanities with their matching mirrors adding an elegant Victorian feel to the otherwise modern-edged room. There are two low black couches in the reception area, and bright splashes of fresh yellow roses in tall silver vases on the reception desk. It's a different look than their downtown Seattle location, which is more chrome and black leather with red accents, softened by white linen paint on the walls.

"It's absolutely lovely," Hannah's mother says, and her father nods in agreement. They wander over to the back wall, where Hannah's father crouches down to inspect the hair-washing stations, verifying, Hannah assumes, that the plumbing was correctly installed.

Happy to see them momentarily occupied, Hannah leans over to whisper in Sophie's ear. "You were a little harsh with Veronica, don't you think?"

Sophie rolls her eyes dramatically. "You didn't hire her with that *thing* in her nose, did you?"

Hannah smiles. "No. She wasn't wearing it during the interview. I was planning to give the dress code talk later, but now that you've scared the shit out of them, I won't have to."

"You're welcome." Sophie kisses her cheek. "Now, I must make sure the caterer has the hors d'oeuvres scheduled to come out in the right order." She flits down the hall to the kitchen.

"What can we do to help?" Hannah's mother asks, having wandered back to stand next to Hannah. Just as Hannah is about to respond, she sees Isaac pull up behind her car by the curb. *Perfect,* she thinks. *He can keep them busy for me.*

"Isaac!" she calls out as her brother enters through the gate. He looks up, his face brightening as he sees her waving. Irish Twins, her parents always called them, born less than fourteen months apart. Isaac was older, but they were close enough in age as children to be either inseparable or at each other's throats. Both she and Isaac share their father's slim build and height, but while Hannah inherited her mother's black hair and blue eyes, Isaac has their father's stiff, blond buzz cut and brown irises. "Poop Eyes!" Hannah used to taunt him when he irritated her. "Scarecrow!" was always Isaac's retort. Hannah smiles now, remembering how they alternately teased and played with each other. She'd often considered giving Emily a sibling so her daughter wouldn't miss out on what Hannah cherished in her relationship with Isaac, but she'd never quite worked up the energy to get pregnant again. Now that Emily is gone, Hannah wishes she had made a different choice.

Her brother lifts her up in a huge bear hug, spinning her around before dropping her back to the ground. "Hey, Sis," he says. "How goes it?"

"Good," she says, tucking her flyaway hair behind her ears. "Better, now that you're here. I thought for sure you wouldn't make it until this afternoon."

Isaac grins, eyes sparkling. "What, and leave my little sister to fend for herself with the parental units? No way." Her brother understands her need for solitude more than her parents do. More than Sophie, even. He's the only one who didn't tell her that moving out of the house where Emily grew up was a bad idea. "You do what you have to to get by," he told her. "Everyone else can screw off, okay?"

Even though Emily's death hit him hard, too, he was there for Hannah. She knew that he couldn't have loved Emily more if she had been his own daughter. Isaac packed her room so Hannah wouldn't have to, and carefully moved her daughter's possessions into storage with the rest of their things, save the bare minimum of necessities she took with her to her new apartment. When Hannah expressed enthusiasm about the salon renovation, he made sure to connect her with the best architect and contractors he knew. He gave her room to grieve without telling her how she should do it. He treated her like he normally would, instead of like something he might break.

"Thank god. Mom already hit me with the whole 'I think you should move back to the farm' campaign."

"Oh no," Isaac groans. "Really?"

"Really. *And* an attempt to preach grief management according to Dr. Phil."

Isaac laughs. "Guess I got here just in time." He pauses, his expression suddenly serious. "You hanging in there, Hannah-banana?" Hannah's throat closes once again, and all she can manage is a brief nod. Isaac stares at her a moment, unsure if he should believe her, but then glances around the yard. "Everything looks awesome."

"Thanks."

Isaac smiles again when he sees their parents standing on the front porch. They wave excitedly, and Isaac waves back.

"Go," he tells Hannah. "Take care of whatever you need to. I'll keep them entertained."

Hannah gives him a quick, grateful hug, then heads inside the house to check on the stylists' progress on the gift bags. She's happy to see that they're all filled, but her blood suddenly runs cold with a memory of shopping with Emily to pick out what to put in her birthday party grab bags.

"I want sparkly *purple* pens, not pink!" six-year-old Emily insisted. "And Dora the Explorer is dumb—I want Hello Kitty erasers. And then I want chocolate Kisses and jelly beans, too!"

"You can pick *one* candy," Hannah said gently, and Emily proceeded to throw a tantrum right there in the Target toy aisle, knocking a few things off the shelves as she flailed. Minutes later, Hannah carried her out of the store, kicking and screaming, both of them in enormous need of a nap.

Why didn't I just give her want she wanted? Hannah thinks now. *Why did I fight with her on every little thing? If I'd known how little time I'd have with her, I would have said yes more. I would have played Barbies instead of telling her I needed to clean the house. I would have let her have ice cream for dinner, I would have read her that extra story after the six we'd already read.*

"Hannah?" Veronica's voice snaps Hannah out of her thoughts. "Are you okay?"

"Of course," Hannah says, blinking rapidly. "Just a lot on my mind today. What were you saying?"

"These were left over." Veronica holds up a few packages of caramels. "Do you have any kids? They might like them."

Her words slice into Hannah's chest. The question *Do you have any kids?* is the one she dreads most. How is she supposed to answer it? Saying no is too painful, but saying yes, but my daughter *died* is unbearable, akin to stripping naked beneath bright lights in a roomful of strangers. Just the thought of her daughter wrings her dry—she still can't fathom speaking casually to other people about her loss.

"You keep them," Hannah says. Her voice cracks on the words, and she wonders how many hidden land mines she'll face today, how many times her mother will tell her what she needs to do to process her grief and get on with her life. She doesn't *want* to join a bereavement group. She doesn't *want* to talk with a therapist or move back to the farm. The only thing she wants is the one thing she can't have. She wants her daughter back.

Olivia

The morning of Maddie's first day at Eastside Prep, Olivia lies in bed, watching her husband get ready for work. At four a.m., it's not light out yet, though she can hear a few early-rising birds chirping in the cherry trees outside their bedroom window. James stands in front of the mirror that hangs over the long, low mahogany dresser, carefully looping his tie into a Windsor knot.

"You look handsome," she says sleepily. Whatever their problems, the attraction she feels for her husband rarely falters.

"Well, thank you," James answers, turning to look at her with one corner of his mouth curled upward. "Want me to come back to bed?"

She smiles. "I think that's a fabulous idea." She pauses to stretch and adjust her pillow. "As long as you do all the work."

James laughs as he finishes with his tie, then takes a couple of steps over to sit down on the edge of their bed. The weight of him rolls her toward him. He places his hand on her hip and runs it down her thigh. "Another time, okay? I need to get to the office."

"Isn't there any way you can work from home for a little while so you can drop Maddie off with me?" Olivia asks, keeping her voice low and neutral. It makes sense to her that the least he could do is drive her to school, since he was the one insisting that Maddie attend his alma mater.

His hand freezes on her leg and a shadowy tension falls in a curtain across his face. He doesn't even have to speak. She knows his answer. She knows that tension is only a precursor to what could come next—a pebble next to the boulder of one of his rages—so she shuts her mouth and pulls the covers up to her chin. He finishes dressing and she pretends to be asleep when he kisses her good-bye.

Olivia *tries* to get back to sleep, but her thoughts spin too quickly, remembering the first time she really understood where that shadow on her husband's face could lead. She was seven months pregnant, it was a Tuesday night, and he'd come home late from a long day at the office, an occurrence that was more common than not. Olivia could almost see the stress rising off his body in wavy little lines, like steam from warm, wet pavement, and she wondered if a deal had gone wrong or if one of his VPs was giving him a hard time. She greeted him as she always did, at the front door with a martini and a kiss, but after the first sip he took of his drink, he stared at her like she'd done something wrong and the shadow appeared.

"What? Doesn't it taste okay?" she asked him.

"It tastes like shit." His green eyes were glassy, as though he might have already been drinking. James didn't drink often, but when he did, something about him shifted.

"What?" Olivia said, scrunching her eyebrows together over the bridge of her nose. She'd reapplied her makeup two times since six o'clock, waiting for him. "You're gorgeous no matter what," he'd said the few times she'd happened to go bare-faced, "but it makes me feel like you love me more when you make a little extra effort to look good."

Her initial, but silent, reaction was that he should love her no matter *how* she looked. In the end, however, she decided he was right. The only things she had to do during the day were clean the house, shop, and occasionally have lunch with her few girlfriends. Just because they were married didn't mean she could let herself go. She needed to stay the same woman he fell in love with in Florida, when she would spend at least an hour getting ready for one of their dates. Marriages ended because one or both of the people stopped doing the things that attracted their spouses to them in the first place, so makeup was the least she could do for the man who gave her so much.

Now, James dropped his briefcase to the marble floor with a loud *thunk* and loosened his tie. "I *said,* it tastes like shit." He took another sip, then promptly spat it back into the glass.

Olivia flushed and took it from him. "I'm sorry. Let me make you another one. Maybe I used too much vermouth." She started to turn away, but James grabbed her arm, causing most of the vodka to splash onto the floor.

"I don't want another drink." He looked at her with half-closed eyes and ran the tip of his tongue over his bottom lip.

"James!" she said, managing to set the glass on the entry-way table. She tried to wriggle away from his grasp. "Please. You're hurting me."

He pulled her in close and she could smell the alcohol on his breath. He kissed her then, hard, slipping his tongue into her mouth. "God, you're so beautiful," he murmured against her lips. He reached down and caressed her swollen belly. "How's our baby girl tonight?" James had been thrilled when they found out she was pregnant, making sure the cook stocked the house with food that would benefit the baby, then pulling some serious strings to get Olivia in to see the best gynecologist in the city, who at the time had a waiting list of a year. The only thing he didn't like about her pregnancy was her weight gain, though she exercised every day and denied every ice cream craving she could to ensure she didn't put on too much.

Olivia laid her hands flat against his chest and pushed him away. "She's good," she said, trying to keep her breath even. She'd grown accustomed to his flares of temper, which tended to blow in quickly and then evaporate, but when he drank, his tongue grew sharp and more dangerous. She knew the best thing to do was feed him and get him to bed. Everything would be better in the morning. "Dinner's on the table," she said, taking him by the hand and leading him toward the dining room. "Roast chicken and broccoli." A few months after their wedding, Olivia had convinced him to let go of their chef, reasoning that since he didn't want her to get a job, she was more than capable of learning to cook for her husband. It had actually turned into a task she enjoyed.

They sat down together, though she had already eaten. James hunched his shoulders over his plate, forearms resting on the edge of the table as he ate.

"I had lunch with Sara Beth and Waverly today," Olivia said, knowing that he liked to have a full inventory of how she spent her time. "We walked a few miles on the Burke-Gilman Trail and then had a salad at the Bellevue Club." James grunted in approval; Sara Beth and Waverly were the wives of two of James's friends. He'd introduced Olivia to them the first week she lived in Seattle, when the three couples went out to dinner to celebrate their new marriage at Seastar, one of John Howie's premier restaurants.

"Now *those* two are the kind of wives a man can be proud of," he said when they got home that night. From then on, Olivia took note of the women's sleek blond hair, toned bodies, and tanned skin; she watched the way they allowed their husbands to lead the conversations, throwing in the occasional witty, but always appropriate, comment. She saw how they made looking good for their husbands a full-time job. They gave her the name of the stylist who gave them their matching highlights, took her shopping, and helped her pick out more items for her wardrobe that accented her figure but didn't flaunt it. They were younger than their husbands, too, something that made Olivia feel like she could open up to them the way she did with the couple of girlfriends she'd left behind in Tampa.

"Don't you *want* to work?" Olivia asked them one afternoon over a late lunch. Though she enjoyed the fact that she no longer had to worry about pinching together enough pennies to support herself or her mother, Olivia did miss the complexities of her legal cases. She missed plunging into research, smothered by facts in the library, taking notes, writing reports for the lawyers in her firm. If she'd had the money when she was single, she might have gone to law school herself, but needing to take care of her mother had erased that particular dream. After high school, she cocktailed nights to put herself through the paralegal program at a community college, then found a job as quickly as she could. And then, she met James.

"It's a full-time job to look this good for our husbands, sugar," Waverly responded, laughing. Sara Beth agreed, and Olivia smiled and went along with what they said when really, she didn't believe it. In fact, it was a bit appalling to her that these women thought so little of themselves. Olivia knew James loved her for *her,* not just for the way she looked. She knew this because he had cried on her chest one night in Florida, after they made love for the first time. He told her that his own mother had never loved him, that his father constantly told James he was a worthless son. "He beat us," James revealed. "Me, mostly. I'd get between him and my mother and just . . . take it."

"Oh, honey," Olivia said. Her heart ached hearing how James had been treated, and she understood more than ever why a stable, happy relationship was so important to him. "I'm so sorry."

"I never thought someone like you would love me," he said, shuddering as he pressed his face into her neck. "I never thought I deserved anything this good."

So when James lost his temper or threw out a painful verbal jab, she remembered that moment. She remembered his tears, how his face was like a little boy's, scared of what she'd think once she knew the most vulnerable parts of him. She remembered that moment after he told her the drink she'd made him tasted like shit. And she forgave him one more time.

"We were talking about the baby shower," she said, thinking that the meal had improved his mood. He seemed much calmer than when he'd first walked in the door, so she figured it was safe to bring this subject up. "And they were wondering if my mother is going to come." She gave him her most charming smile. "I wasn't sure what to tell them."

James looked up from his plate, chewing a mouthful of chicken. "You tell them you need to ask your husband if he'll pay for your mother's flight."

Olivia bowed her head a bit, averting her face from his gaze. There was a strange light in his eyes—she wasn't sure what it meant. "Of course. If it's too much trouble—"

"You think I'd let you tell your friends that I wouldn't pay for your own mother to come to your baby shower? What kind of man do you think I am?"

Olivia took what she hoped was an inaudible, measured breath. She knew what he needed to hear. "I think you're wonderful. The most generous man a woman could ask for." She looked up, then reached over and grabbed his hand. "I love you so much, James. I know how hard you work for us . . . how hard you work for our baby girl. I am the luckiest woman in the world."

His expression softened, and minutes later they were upstairs in their bedroom. He disrobed her carefully, running the tips of his fingers over her skin, making her feel like every nerve was a lit sparkler. He moved her to the bed, took off his own clothes, and then joined her, taking care of her before he moved behind her—the only position that was comfortable for her this late in the pregnancy. Olivia moaned the way she knew he liked her to, the way that helped him finish, and she waited and waited for the end to come. After twenty minutes, when it still hadn't, she wondered if he really *had* had too much to drink at the office.

"It's okay, baby," she whispered, "if you can't." She thought she was giving him an out. She thought she was being generous.

But then James stopped moving, grabbed her by the waist, and wrenched her over onto her back. A sharp, twisting pain shot through her belly. She cried out, but before she could speak, he slapped her once, hard, across the face. Olivia closed her eyes and saw bright splotches of stars. She tried to keep from crying.

James dropped to her side and put his mouth up against her ear. "*You* don't tell me what I can and cannot do." He bit her earlobe until she yelped again. "Do you understand me?"

Olivia nodded, her chin trembling as she fought the tears in the back of her throat. *James just* hit *me. He hit me, he hit me.* She repeated the words over and over in her mind, until eventually, they held no meaning. She rolled away from him and pulled the covers up over her naked body. She felt his eyes boring into her back, but she couldn't look at him. She was too afraid of what she'd see.

The next morning, after he'd slept in the guest bedroom, he brought her breakfast in bed. "Good morning, beautiful," he said, placing the tray carefully over her lap. He'd made her scrambled egg whites with feta cheese and tomatoes—her favorite. "I squeezed you some orange juice, too," he continued, holding up the small glass before reaching out to caress her belly. "Can't give this sweet girl too many vitamins, right?" He smiled at her, the same wide, charismatic grin he'd given her the first day they met.

Olivia stared back, searching his face for some evidence of remorse for what he'd done. Some proof that she hadn't just imagined that moment in the dark. "Can you bring me a mirror, please?" she asked him.

He frowned. "What for?"

"I must look a mess," she said, reaching up to flatten her hair. "I just need to put on a little makeup." She smiled, and he brought her the lovely antique silver hand mirror he'd bought for her birthday. She took a deep breath, readying herself for a bruise on her face, some mark that would confirm that she hadn't been dreaming, but there was nothing. Her cheeks were rosy from sleep, and though her eyes were a little puffy from crying, no one, not even she, would have believed that James had slapped her.

He left for work soon after, and later that day, two dozen long-stemmed yellow roses arrived at the house, followed by an email confirming that a flight had been booked for her mother to come for the shower. In the end, though, her mother was too ill to travel, afraid her aching hip joints wouldn't be able to withstand a six-hour flight. "We'll take the baby to see her once it's born," James promised Olivia that night. "She needs to see her grandchild." *He was drunk,* Olivia told herself. *He didn't realize what he was doing.* Just this once, she could let it go.

This morning, after he left her alone to take their daughter to her first day of school, Olivia knew she had to let it go again. It had become an art on some level, navigating her husband's moods, reading his expressions and bodily tics. Much like a poker player, Olivia memorized James's "tells," the twitch beneath his left eye, the strange light in his eyes, the shadow across his face—minute signs that gave his impending reactions away. She knows that to some extent, Maddie has learned to read her father, too, but she can push him farther than Olivia can. Though he sometimes raises his voice at his daughter, though his eyes flash and his fists curl up in frustration, he never hits her. At least, he hasn't yet. Olivia believes that if James ever *does* hurt Maddie—even if he *threatens* to hurt her—that will be the catalyst for her to finally leave. Until then, she knows if she does, James will take Maddie away from her. It's not what he's said that makes her know this—it's who he *is*. He wouldn't let Olivia leave him without taking something from her, too.

Olivia knows little about family law, but she doesn't doubt that James has the power, money, and connections to take custody of their daughter away, so she stays. She stays and stays and stays, enduring whatever she has to so she can take care of Maddie. So her daughter will be okay.

Her alarm goes off at six a.m. and Olivia silences it, then rises from the bed. She knows Maddie doesn't understand why she doesn't leave James. Maddie has never seen her father hit her mother—James is too smart to let that happen—but Olivia is certain that Maddie suspects. She is also fairly sure that Maddie thinks she's a coward. But what her daughter can't comprehend is how much strength it takes to survive a life like this. It's a chess game—Olivia has to see ahead four, five, even ten moves to protect them both. It's exhausting, really, to live like this, to second-guess her every breath.

But this morning, James isn't home, so for the moment she can relax. She can fix Maddie breakfast, she can help her pick out what outfit she's going to wear. She can focus on what's important—she can take her daughter to her first day at a new school.

Maddie

"I don't *want* you to come inside," I tell my mom, who has been hovering around me all morning like I'm two years old and might be in need of a diaper change. "I can find my classes, okay? I'll be fine."

It's a slightly overcast September day, and we are sitting in the parking lot of Eastside Prep, watching the other kids mill around the entrance to the school, talking and laughing and generally looking more at ease than I've probably ever felt in my life. The girls all seem impossibly pretty to me, with long torsos and hip-hugging jeans, and the boys swagger with their backpacks slung over one shoulder, most of them with wannabe-surfer haircuts, their bangs too long over their eyes. I glance down at the black leggings and tan baggy sweater I decided to wear and suddenly wish I'd made a different choice. I've lived in pajamas and sweatpants for the last eight years, so I pretty much have the fashion sense of a third grader. And even though I'm telling my mother I'll be just fine,

I'm positive I'll never fit in with these people. Life is not a John Hughes movie, where the nerdy, weird girl ends up dating the captain of the football team. Life is me, sitting alone at a table in the lunchroom, wishing I could disappear.

Mom shifts her body to face me. "Are you sure? You remember the school nurse's name?"

"Mrs. Taylor," I say with a sigh. "And I will check in with her first thing so we can go over my med schedule." Mom had visited the school last week, bringing the nurse a stockpile of all my prescriptions and strict instructions to call her if I show even a hint of a fever.

"You remembered your hand sanitizer, right? You need to use it before and after every class and after you've been in the bathroom. Even after you wash your hands."

"*God,* Mom. *Yes,* I remembered it. You reminded me to put it in my bag, like, fifty-three times this morning." Even though I am doing really well with my new liver, I'm still at a higher risk for infection from simple things like a head cold or the flu. If my mom had her way, I'd probably be walking around in a full-on hazmat suit. I glance over at her—she's dressed casually in a swishy, knee-length, pale green skirt and snug white T-shirt—and I wonder if I'll ever have her looks. Her hair is always the perfect buttery blond shade with lighter stripes around her face; her skin is clear, her body is lean, spray-tanned, and strong. She looks a little like Jennifer Aniston, which I know my father likes to brag about to his friends, but sometimes it makes me wonder if I was adopted.

Grabbing my backpack from the floor, I lean over and give her a quick kiss on the cheek. "I'll be fine. I promise. I'll text you at lunch and let you know how it's going, okay?"

"Okay," she says with a nervous smile. "I love you, honey. You're going to do great."

"Thanks," I say and have to fight off the tickle of imminent tears in my throat. I climb out of the car and make my way down the sidewalk that leads to the front steps of the school. I look up at the imposing building, which my father said used to be a monastery. The face of it looks like a church, with Gothic arches and intricate stained-glass windows. Last night, I looked up the floor plan online, so I would know how to get to the office and my classrooms. I signed up for AP English and trigonometry, world history, psychology, Spanish, and an advanced computer sciences class. Luckily, I get a free pass from PE, since there's too much danger of being hit in the gut by a stray basketball or jabbed by an elbow.

A wave of other students practically carries me down the long hallway to the office, where I know the nurse is waiting for me. The walls are covered with posters: IF YOU BELIEVE IT, YOU CAN BE IT! and THE ONLY WAY PAST IS THROUGH! The words are set against impressive nature scenes, waterfalls and deep canyons, and are meant to be inspirational, but because they remind me of the lab at the hospital, they end up irritating me instead. There are a few other kids standing at the desk, so I get in line behind a girl with thick, cascading red curls and a purple checkered book bag slung over her shoulder. She turns around when my backpack accidentally brushes against her.

"Oh, sorry," I say. Her face is peppered with tiny freckles, and I think she'd be pretty in a girl-next-door kind of way if she weren't wearing so much makeup. Her eyes are thickly lined in black and her lips are sticky with bright pink gloss. She has on jeans and a long, tight green T-shirt with the word *Aéropostale* scrawled in sparkling white letters across her chest.

"No worries." She looks me over. "You new?" I nod, and she snaps her watermelon gum—I can smell it—before speaking again. "Cool. I'm Hailey."

"I'm Maddie." *She seems friendly enough. Maybe this won't be as hard as I thought.*

"Where'd you transfer from?"

"Um, I've sort of been homeschooled by a tutor for a while. Since fourth grade, actually."

"Really? Are your parents like, way religious or something?"

I feel my face flame and I clear my throat. "No. Not at all. I just . . . well, I've been sick a lot, like in the hospital so much that it was just easier to have a tutor so I wouldn't fall behind. That's all. But I'm better now, so I'm . . . here."

Hailey raises an eyebrow and leans away from me the tiniest bit, but enough for me to notice. "Sick with *what*?" From the look on her face, it's clear she's worried I'm contagious, that simply standing next to me puts her at some kind of risk.

"I had a bad liver," I say. "But I got a new one last year." I'm not prepared for her questions; the truth tumbles out of me before I can stop it.

"O . . . M . . . G." She spells the letters out with a notable pause after each, then widens her eyes, as though I just told her I had a third leg or an extra breast. "*That's* kind of creepy . . . isn't it?"

"Not really." I shrug, and attempt to appear confident, when I actually sort of agree with her. It *is* creepy, if I let myself think about it too long, the fact that I'm carrying around another person's organ inside my body. That a twelve-year-old girl had to die to save my life. I wonder about her sometimes, what she was like, if I would have wanted to be her friend. I wonder how her parents are doing, if part of them hates me for living when their child is dead. The transplant coordinator told me I could write them a thank-you letter—anonymous, of course—but when I asked my mom if I could, she told me my dad said no.

"Why not?" I asked, and she shook her head.

"Your dad just wants to protect us, honey," Mom explained. "He's worried if the donor family found out who we are, they might ask for money."

"They wouldn't do that," I said, not actually knowing if this was true, but I didn't think that the kind of people who would take their daughter off life support in order to save other lives would also be the kind of people to turn around and blackmail us after the fact.

"You never know," Mom said with a small shrug. "I know it's hard. I want to reach out to the mother of the donor, especially. Tell her how grateful I am for what she did for us. But we have to respect your dad's wishes, okay?"

I could tell that she thought it was crappy of Dad to not let us write to the family, too, but the truth is, I haven't been able to figure out what I'd say even if I could. Anything I come up with in my head sounds cheesy or I'm sure would make them feel worse than they probably already do. I feel pretty guilty, actually, knowing that I got to live when their daughter died, and I wonder if they'd even *like* me, if they'd wish someone else had been saved. It's a weird sort of pressure, feeling like I have to live up to a memory of a person I didn't even know. It's hard to feel worthy of this kind of gift. I mean, really, how do you find words to thank someone for saving your life?

Hailey's voice pops me out of my thoughts. "Is that why your *hair* looks like that?" She wrinkles up her pert little nose. My face floods red and I run my hand over my head, wishing I could melt right into the floor. One of the side effects of my meds is thinning hair; it's still long, but while I'd used a thickening shampoo and tried to tease it enough to make it look normal, apparently, I'd failed. Before I can come up with a proper retort, a woman sticks her head out of another office and calls my name. The nurse, I assume, who is expecting me.

"See you later," I mumble. *What a bitch.* If I'd been smart, I would have come up with a lie about moving or transferring from another high school and not said a word about the transplant. I wonder how long it will take for the whole school to hear all about the weird new stranger in their midst.

I make it through my meeting with Mrs. Taylor, working out a schedule for me to come to her office two times a day—once after third period and once after lunch—so I can take my pills. I sit through homeroom/AP English, somewhat slumped down in my seat, grateful that for the most part, everyone seems to be ignoring me. A few kids give me curious looks, a few others say hello, but that's it. The English teacher, Mr. Preston, assigns us *To Kill a Mockingbird,* which I've already read three times, so I tune out for the rest of the class. I wonder what Dirk (which he told me was his *actual* first name, chosen by his parents as a hybrid of the name of their favorite actor, Kirk Douglas) is doing right now. We chatted back and forth quite a bit over the last month, both inside the game with our avatars and on email and instant messaging. He sent me a picture of what he looks like in real life—kind of short, but muscular with a thick, wrestler's build and blond hair. He wears glasses, but they're the cool, funky kind, and he is definitely cute enough to date a girl way prettier than me. I sent him a head shot of "Sierra," the same profile picture I use on Facebook, holding my breath as I waited for his response.

"Wow," he wrote in his email. "You're hot *and* you like video games? How is that possible?"

"It's not, actually," I probably should have said, and sent him a picture of what I really look like. But then he'd know I'm only sixteen and he wouldn't want to hang out with me. I didn't think it was *that* much of a big deal, lying to him. We're playing in a fantasy world . . . and he is my fantasy.

The bell rings and I'm forced to stop thinking about Dirk. I maneuver my way through the crowded hallway and try to find my locker. I'm standing off to the side, attempting to peek around a group of kids standing in front of what I think is probably number 387, when a boy next to me looks over my shoulder at the piece of paper I'm holding.

"You want the next row down," he says, and I whip around to face him. He's taller than me, with brown hair that hangs a little too long over his blue eyes, and wears a black-and-white plaid shirt with his jeans.

"Oh," I say. "Okay. Thanks."

"You new?"

I nod, and he smiles, revealing shiny silver braces. "Cool. I'm Noah."

"Maddie." I wait to see if he asks me about where I've transferred from, but he only gives me a short wave.

"See you around," he says, and then I'm left to push my way through the crowd to my locker. Voices echo off the stone walls, making me cringe. I'm used to the quiet of the hospital ward or my house; the excessive noise makes me want to cover my ears.

I manage to make it through the rest of my classes without really talking to anyone else. I write down my assignments and organize my binder, really only excited about computer science, where the teacher, Mrs. Decker, promises we'll be scripting our own programs before the end of next week. I text a quick, nondescript message to my mom at lunch—"I'm fine"—and take my meds at the office as I promised. At the end of the day, I stop by my locker to grab the few books I'll need for my homework, and as I'm shoving them into my backpack, trying to ignore the buzz of people around me, I feel a hand on my shoulder. I turn around and see Noah.

"Hey," I say, trying to sound casual. I wonder why he sought me out again, but find myself sort of happy to see him. "What's up?"

He cocks his head to one side, and jerks his too-long bangs out of his face. "Is it true that you had some kind of *organ* transplant?"

He must know Hailey. Either that, or she's flapped her jaw to enough of the right people that the whole *school* knows about my operation. Sucking in a quick breath, I nod, not wanting to say anything more, but he keeps talking. "Which one?"

"Liver," I whisper. *I don't want to do this. I don't want to be here. I don't want to be different.*

"Do you have like, a *gnarly* scar?" Again, I nod, pressing my lips together. My scar looks like an upside-down T, starting in between my poor excuses for breasts and ending in a line that spans my entire abdomen, just above my belly button. Even after a year, it's thick and red and still a little bit painful if I twist too far in the wrong direction. I try not to look at it in the mirror.

"*Awesome,*" he says, and I let out a startled laugh. He jams one hand into his front pocket and swishes his hair out of his eyes again. "What's so funny?"

I shrug, then shut my locker. "I guess I don't really think of my scar as 'awesome.' "

"Dude, why *not*?" he says. "You're like, a Franken-babe."

I stare at him, wondering if he has any idea just how shitty it is to call a girl anything related to a monster. My eyes fill and I drop my gaze to the floor before pushing past him and speed-walking down the hall. I will *not* let him see me cry.

"Hey!" Noah calls out. "I meant that as a *compliment*!"

I pretend not to hear him as I shove through the mass of students gathered at the front doors. I see my mother's midnight blue Mercedes in the parking lot, and I rush down the stairs. Once inside the car, I drop my backpack to the floor between my legs and let the tears come. I curl my shoulders forward and put my hands over my face.

"Maddie, sweetie . . . what's wrong?" Mom asks, reaching over to rub my back. "*Tell* me."

I shake my head, as tears and snot run down. I feel like I've been holding my breath the entire day, waiting for that moment when someone would make me cry. I knew going to this school was going to suck. I knew there was no way I'd fit in.

"Oh, baby," Mom says. "What can I do? Can I help?"

"He called me a *monster,*" I sob, dropping my hands to my lap and leaning over the console to rest my head on her shoulder. "He asked about my scar." I don't know how to explain just how exposed Noah's words made me feel. I can imagine the nickname catching on, how I'll have to endure it being launched at me as I walk down the hall, listening to the laughter and whispers behind my back.

"Who did?" Mom wraps her arm around my shoulders and squeezes me to her.

"Nobody. A boy. A stupid asshole *boy*." She doesn't scold me for my language, so I continue. "And a girl said my *hair* looks bad. She seemed all nice at first and then she totally insulted me!" I pause to take a shuddering breath as my tears begin to subside. "I'm so *ugly*, Mom! I hate it! Can't I just stay home and have a tutor again? *Please?* Can't you talk to Dad and make him *understand?*"

"You are *not* ugly," Mom murmurs against my head, apparently choosing to ignore what I said about Dad. "Your hair is a little thin, that's all. It just needs the right cut and maybe some color." She pulls away and reaches into the console to grab a stack of junk mail that has been sitting in there for god only knows how long. My mom is organized about many things, but for some reason, her car is always a mess.

"What're you doing?" I ask with a sniffle.

"Looking for something." She rifles through the various envelopes and flyers until she comes up with a pale yellow card with an image of a pair of black scissors at the top. It looks vaguely familiar to me. "We got this a few weeks ago, remember?" she says. "Announcing a new salon opening? You liked the name . . . Ciseaux." She pauses. "We'll go there right now and get you all fixed up, okay?" She hands me the card, and I take it, noticing that she has tears in her eyes, too.

I know she is latching on to the only thing she can think of to help me feel better, so I nod, even though I know that having shiny hair isn't going to magically change anything. I'll still be the girl who hates how she looks.

I'll still be the girl with the scar.

Hannah

The front door of the salon opens just as Hannah is finishing up with Julie Stein, a woman who attended the Ciseaux grand opening party and has been coming twice a week for a blow-out ever since.

Veronica, sitting at the reception desk waiting for her five o'clock, greets the woman and teenage girl who enter. "Welcome to Ciseaux," Veronica says with a big smile, as Hannah trained her to do. They have moved past the nose ring incident with Sophie, and so far, Hannah is happy with Veronica's performance and her attire. "Whom are you here to see?"

The woman wraps her arm around the girl's shoulders. "We don't actually have an appointment." She gives Veronica a cautious smile. "Do you take walk-ins? My daughter needs a cut and color."

"Let me check the schedule," Veronica says, quickly pulling up the program that manages the stylists' calendars on the computer. She peers at the screen, then spins her seat around to face the stations. "Peter? It looks like you're open."

Peter frowns as he pauses from sweeping up around his chair. "Sorry, doll. I would, but Paul and I are having dinner with my mother at six."

"You definitely don't want to miss *that,*" the woman says and chuckles, but the sound is hollow, similar to the way Hannah has learned to force herself to laugh over the past year. When you laugh, people assume you're okay. You're smiling, so everything's fine . . . right? They don't notice the twitch at the corner of your mouth or the quiver of your chin. They don't see that the smile doesn't quite reach your eyes. It's easy to miss the small details that show how a person is really feeling, to gloss right over them and move on with your day. It's a phenomenon Hannah counts on, actually, so she can avoid too much discussion about her grief.

"I have time," she volunteers, hanging her dryer on the hook on the wall next to her station. Julie was her last appointment, but Hannah prefers to work as late as possible, so this unexpected walk-in is a good thing. Upstairs in her apartment, nights spent alone are the hardest—the silence confronts her with weapons she doesn't know how to handle. Most of the time, after her last client, she'll go for her second run of the day, the first being in the morning before the salon opens. After she returns, she'll check in with Sophie to see how sales are going downtown and how her latest lover is. She'll clean the apartment, do laundry, warm up a frozen dinner, then eventually fall asleep with the TV on. When she can't sleep, she takes one of the Xanax her doctor prescribed.

Now, though, she smiles at the woman and her daughter, trying to ignore the biting grip in her stomach as she is reminded, once again, of the things she will never do with Emily. "I'll be right with you. Please, have a seat."

A look of immense gratitude washes over the woman's face, and Hannah wonders what could be so important about a cut and color for her daughter. She gives Julie the hand mirror and spins her around so she can check out the back of her now-smooth, shiny jet-black locks. "Good?" Hannah asks.

"Beautiful," Julie says, peering at her reflection. "You do the *best* work. I'm sending all my girlfriends here. Have they called?"

"A few, yes. I appreciate it so much."

"Word of mouth is the best advertisement, right?" Julie says as Hannah releases the cape from Julie's neck and asks Veronica to ring her up.

"Make sure you give her ten percent off for the referrals," Hannah says, then turns her attention to the woman and her daughter, beckoning them toward her with a wave of her hand and a smile. "Come on back."

They rise from the couch in concert, walk around the reception desk, and make their way to Hannah's station. "Have a seat," Hannah says to the daughter, who looks to be about fourteen. She has a slight build like her mother, but her torso is thicker—not fat, exactly, just more rounded. Her light brown hair is long and stringy, riddled with split ends, and desperate for some kind of color to bring it to life. The girl's eyes are reddened around the edges and slightly puffy, as though she's recently been crying. She looks so sad, so anxious, Hannah's mothering instinct kicks in and immediately longs to soothe her. "I'm Hannah," she says.

"Maddie," the girl mumbles, slumping into the chair. She avoids looking in the mirror, which as a stylist, Hannah has learned to recognize as something women who have self-esteem issues tend to do. If they don't *see* their perceived flaws, then they don't have to feel inadequate. Hannah's heart squeezes, wondering what could have made this girl feel so bad about her looks.

She suddenly recalls a conversation she had with Emily a few months before her accident, when Hannah found her daughter standing in front of the mirror in her bedroom, wearing only her white cotton training bra and panties. As Hannah stepped inside her room, Emily clutched the flesh around her belly between tight fingers and made a strange, growling noise.

"Honey, what are you doing?" Hannah asked with a frown.

"I'm so *fat!*" Emily wailed, letting go of her stomach and dropping her hands to her sides.

"No, you're not," Hannah said calmly, putting her arm around her daughter's shoulders and looking at their reflection. At twelve, Emily was dark haired and pretty, but short for her age, so her middle was a little thick in comparison to the rest of her body. Hannah was five foot seven with a naturally thin build, which was definitely a product of heredity more than of diet and exercise. The sperm donor Hannah had chosen was six foot four, with no history of obesity in his family, so she was hopeful Emily wouldn't struggle with her weight. Hannah had seen too many clients zip into the bathroom to vomit after sampling from the platter of buttery, sweet pastries Sophie insisted on setting out every day—it terrified her that Emily might someday fall victim to similar behaviors. "You just haven't had your growth spurt yet, sweetheart. I didn't get mine until I was fourteen."

Emily leaned her head against Hannah's chest, regarding her mother's reflection. "Are you *sure*?" she asked with a sniffle. "Katie Shaw is my age and is like, an *Amazon* woman or something. She's totally skinny and her boobs are *huge*!"

"Trust me, you don't want huge boobs." Hannah gave her daughter a quick jiggle, hoping she could make Emily laugh.

"How do *you* know what I want?"

Hannah sighed, then turned to face her daughter, pulling Emily's attention away from the mirror. She set her hands on her daughter's shoulders and met her eyes with a determined gaze. "I know that you're beautiful exactly as you are right *now*. And I know it's tough to see your body get a little heavier before you get taller and even it all out. It was like that for me, too, Em. You just wait. In six months, you'll look in the mirror and see something entirely different."

Emily's blue eyes lit up when Hannah said this, filled with hope. Only her daughter never got to see her body change. Now, Hannah's mind flashes to the image of Emily on the day of her accident, her limbs twisted on the pavement, her daughter lying motionless in the hospital bed. She shakes her head, trying to dislodge the memory. She focuses on throwing the black protective cape over Maddie, fastening it around her neck. "Too tight?" she asks, and Maddie shakes her head, too. "Okay, then. What are we going to do for you today?"

Maddie barely lifts one of her shoulders, still keeping her eyes on the floor. Hannah looks to the girl's mother, eyebrows raised.

"She had a rough day at school," the woman says, apologetically. "I was hoping a new look might lift her spirits. We got your flyer, so we thought we'd come give you a try."

Hannah returns her gaze to Maddie's reflection. "Eastside Prep?" It was the high school closest to the salon, attended by the children of only the most elite families in Seattle.

"Yeah," Maddie says, like she's tasted something sour.

"You're a freshman?"

Maddie shakes her head. "Junior. I'm sixteen."

Hannah must look confused because the woman jumps in to explain. "Maddie's had some health issues, so she's a little petite. She's been tutored at home since she was nine. School is . . . an adjustment."

"I'm sure nobody wants to hear the boring details of my life, *Olivia,*" Maddie says, but there is a small spark of levity in her voice, and Hannah suspects that she must be close to her mother in order to tease her like that. Emily had called Hannah by her first name instead of Mom a few times, mostly in the months before the accident, and only when she was frustrated. Hannah read somewhere that this is a normal thing for teenage girls to do, a way they test out being separate beings from their mothers. A first snip at the proverbial apron strings.

Peter returns from the back room, where he'd grabbed his coat. Always the impeccably dressed hipster, today he wears black skinny jeans and turtleneck sweater paired with funky, red-rimmed oval glasses. His blond hair is spiked up, and his cowboy boots click-clack on the hardwood floors. "Good night, ladies!" he says, then blows us all a kiss. "Stay fabulous!"

"I like his glasses," Maddie says, after he closes the front door behind him.

Hannah smiles. "He's an original, for sure." She looks over to Veronica, who is just hanging up the phone, looking irritated. "What's up?" Hannah asks.

"My five o'clock just canceled." Business has been good since opening, but for stylists, time is money, so each time a client cancels at the last minute it's like having your paycheck docked for an offense you didn't commit. She sighs. "Is it okay if I go? I already cleaned my station."

Hannah nods. "Of course. I'll see you tomorrow." She turns back to Olivia and Maddie. "Sorry for the interruption."

"You're the boss?" Maddie says, perking up again.

"I am," Hannah says, smiling. "My best friend, Sophie, is my business partner, but she runs our downtown salon." She gently lifts up Maddie's hair, examining the strands. "So, I think we need to get rid of these split ends first, don't you? It will really give you more body on top if we lose about four inches."

"Okay," Maddie says. "It's like, totally stringy, right?"

Hannah's heart clenches hearing Maddie insert the word *like* in her sentence, a verbal tic Emily had picked up from her friends at school. She manages a smile. "I wouldn't say 'stringy.' I would say 'volume challenged.'" Maddie giggles, and so encouraged, Hannah continues. "Let's cut it to just above your shoulders, okay? Once we get some of the weight to stop pulling at the roots, it will automatically thicken up. And then we'll add some layering, and maybe deepen the color a bit, to bring out your eyes . . ." She looks to Olivia, who is watching their interaction from where she stands a few feet away. "If that's okay with Mom." Olivia nods, relief palpable in her expression. Hannah notes that she is quite beautiful, though with her dark eyebrows, Olivia isn't a natural blonde, she suspects.

"Can I go *red*?" Maddie asks, twisting her head back and

forth, finally reviewing her reflection. "Like, flaming, Jessica Rabbit red?"

Hannah laughs. "I think that might be a little extreme for your skin tone. Not to mention hard to maintain. The best way to bring out your natural beauty is to go just a few shades darker or lighter than your own color, which I assume this is? Or have you colored your hair before?"

Maddie shakes her head. "I've never even been in a salon."

"Well, then," Hannah says. "I feel privileged you're here." She hesitates a moment before putting her hand on Maddie's shoulder—other than the hugs from Emily's friends at the funeral, Hannah hasn't touched a child since she last held Emily in her hospital bed. She's a little worried she'll burst into tears when she does. But then her hand finally drops, and there's no electric sensation as Hannah had feared, no devastating jolt throwing her to the floor. "Come on," she says. "Let's get you shampooed."

Hannah takes her time washing Maddie's hair, giving her the full-on "relax" massage treatment. Pushing the tips of her fingers in steady circles on Maddie's scalp, Hannah remembers the many times she washed Emily's hair at the other salon; her daughter would sometimes fall asleep under Hannah's touch. Maddie's eyes close, and she even lets out a quiet, contented groan. Olivia sits down in the shampoo chair next to the one Maddie is in and watches them.

"Have you been busy since you opened?" Olivia asks as Hannah finishes rinsing the shampoo from Maddie's head and then applies a thickening conditioner.

"Yes, thank goodness," Hannah says with a smile. In fact, they've been busier than Hannah thought they'd be over the past month, though that has a little to do with the fact that Cerina, the other stylist she hired, quit her first week, deciding that she'd rather work for Gene Juarez. "Your highlights are beautiful. Where do you get them done?"

Olivia's shoulders twitch, like she's uncomfortable receiving the compliment. "Henry DeLong's, in Mercer Island. Do you know it?"

"I do." Henry is one of Ciseaux's chief competitors, in business for well over twenty years, with a focus on high-end services and excellent client care. "You're dark haired, naturally?" Olivia nods, and an odd look appears on her face, as though she is recalling an unpleasant memory. Hannah rinses the conditioner from Maddie's hair, pats it dry, then they all relocate to Hannah's station. "Can I get you something to drink, Olivia? Coffee or tea? Water?"

"I'd love some water." She looks at her daughter. "Baby, it's almost time for your afternoon meds, too, isn't it?"

"Mom!" Maddie exclaims. "I know! It's programmed into my *phone*. You don't have to *remind* me."

Olivia looks a little hurt, and Hannah starts to head toward the kitchen, but Olivia stops her with a hand on her arm. "Please, let me get it."

Hannah tells her where to find the chilled bottles of Perrier and Evian, then turns her attention to cutting Maddie's hair. She carefully runs a wide-toothed comb through the strands. "So . . . tough day at school, huh?" The words catch in her throat a bit; she thinks of the many times she asked Emily the same question.

Maddie nods. "Being the new kid sucks."

"I'll bet."

Maddie glances up at Hannah in the mirror, watching as she combs long strands upward and snips off four inches. She looks like she's deciding whether or not to say more, so Hannah keeps quiet, a skill she's learned over the years that works well with her clients. A good stylist is part artist, part therapist, part priest.

"I just want to be tutored at home again, but my dad says no way and my mom won't fight him on it." Maddie glances toward the kitchen, where her mother went, then looks back at Hannah, suddenly looking worried. "Don't tell her I told you that, though, okay?"

Hannah smiles and takes another snip at Maddie's fine hair. "Okay."

"Thanks," Maddie says, obviously relieved. She watches Hannah work, and Olivia returns with their waters. Without saying a word, she hands a bottle to Maddie, along with a few pills from her purse. Maddie sighs, but takes the medicine.

"Do you mind if I ask why you were out of school so long?" Hannah says, checking to make sure her cuts are even on both sides of Maddie's head.

Olivia looks at Maddie, waiting for her to be the one to decide if she'll answer the question. "I have immunosuppressant hepatitis," she says, then screws up her face. "*Had,* I guess. I got a liver transplant last year, so I'm better. But I still have to take a bunch of stupid medicine, and now the kids at school all know and they basically think I'm a freak."

No. Hannah's breath seizes in her lungs. Her fingers lose hold of her scissors, and they clatter to the floor. *It couldn't be.*

"Honey, I'm sure they don't think that." Olivia reaches out and squeezes her daughter's hand, and Hannah squats down to pick up her scissors, taking a moment for a couple of deep, controlled breaths. *Is it possible this is the girl Zoe mentioned? The timing is right—a year ago. Is Emily's liver the reason Maddie is sitting in front of me right now?*

She's often thought about the lives Emily saved—the person who can see because of her corneas; her daughter's heart beating in another child's chest. It was the only part of losing Emily that was bearable, knowing that other families were able to avoid the kind of debilitating grief Hannah now endured. Over the last year, through Zoe, the transplant coordinator, she's received notes from many of the parents of the recipients of Emily's organs, but Hannah hasn't been able to bring herself to read them. Like going through her daughter's things, she isn't sure she would survive it.

Now, her pulse thuds wildly inside her neck, flooding upward into her head, making it almost impossible to hear what Maddie says next.

"That boy called me *Frankenstein,* okay, Mom? I *told* you it would be like this. I just want to stay home." She lifts her chin and looks away from the mirror again. Her bottom lip trembles, and she bites it.

Olivia sighs, then looks at Hannah, who has managed to straighten herself behind the chair. "Do you have children? Do they give you a hard time, too?"

Hannah's throat closes and her mouth goes dry. *What can I say?* Should she avoid the question? Tell the truth? She coughs, fluffing Maddie's hair to stall a moment. Finally, she looks at Olivia. "My daughter died." She says the words quietly, but inside her head, they bounce around like an echo. And then, she can't help it. Her eyes grow blurry and a single tear slips down her cheek. It's the first time she has made the statement out loud to a stranger.

Olivia's hand flies to her mouth, and Maddie freezes in her seat. "Oh god," Olivia says, dropping her arm back to her side. "I'm so sorry. I didn't mean to upset you."

Hannah shrugs, a minute gesture, then wipes the tear away. "No need to be sorry. It's a natural question. I just don't talk about it much." Her voice shakes, and she grinds her molars together to keep from completely breaking down.

Olivia stands unexpectedly, and the next thing Hannah knows, she is being hugged. She immediately tenses, unused to spontaneous affection from strangers, but then slowly relaxes into the warmth of Olivia's embrace. "We came so close to losing Maddie," Olivia murmurs. "I can only imagine . . ." She pulls back and searches Hannah's face with clear, practically amber eyes. "How old was she?"

"Five," Hannah whispers. The lie pops out of her mouth, and she doesn't understand why. It isn't illegal for organ donors and recipients to know each other's identities, but there is a protocol they are supposed to follow in order to contact each other, and Hannah doesn't know if she'd be breaking some kind of official rule by voicing her suspicions. It's entirely possible that Maddie didn't get Emily's liver—that Hannah is imagining connections that aren't there. But then again, what are the odds? And maybe more important, how can she find out for sure?

Olivia

The instant Maddie was born, Olivia didn't think she would ever be unhappy again. How could she, with this beautiful baby girl in her arms? Maddie was a sweet, smiley infant with huge, round eyes and a cap of dark hair. In the hospital, the first time James held her, Olivia saw something in him soften. His shoulders visibly relaxed, his hard edges went blurry. "My angel," he cooed. "My little butternut squash."

"Butternut squash?" Olivia repeated with a tender smile. She shifted beneath the covers. The labor had been a long one; she felt like she'd been torn in two. "You're comparing our child to a gourd?"

James chuckled. "I have no idea where that came from," he said, unable to take his eyes off Maddie. "She's ruined me." He put the tip of his index finger in Maddie's tiny starfish hand and she stared up at him, blinking and seemingly enraptured. Finally looking up at Olivia, his eyes were shiny. "Thank you," he said, and his voice wavered. *The first year of marriage is the hardest,* she told herself. *Now that Maddie is here, we'll settle into becoming a family.*

Once they brought Maddie home, though, James seemed to harden again. He focused as he always had, completely on work, leaving the house at six a.m., returning at the very earliest twelve hours later. Olivia often suspected that if success were a drug, James would have chopped it up and snorted it. He'd worked so hard to build his company—taking on three jobs in college so he could pay his own way. In his senior year, just before graduating, he was accepted for an internship at an investment firm, where he was mentored by William Stern, chairman and CEO of Stern Global—one of the most respected money-management companies in the world. "William taught me everything I know," James once told her. "His first rule was be ruthless. He was in business to make money, not friends."

James took that philosophy to heart when at twenty-nine, he decided to launch his own firm, taking all of his clients from Stern Global with him. And later, even with a baby at home, he was obsessed with every deal, every stock bought or sold, doing whatever it took to keep the money pouring in. Olivia told herself that he needed to work this hard to prove his father had been wrong—that James wasn't worthless. She tried to understand why being at the office was more important than being home, but with a new baby, it was hard to not beg him to cut back. Before Maddie was born, Olivia had asked him to let go of the housekeeper like he had the chef, reasoning that since she wasn't working, she was more than capable of taking care of their home without hired help. And for a little while, she did. But now that Olivia was alone with Maddie most of the day, nursing, changing diapers, trying to sleep when her baby slept, she knew the house wasn't as clean as James liked it and the meals she prepared weren't up to her own standards. She considered asking him to hire a baby nurse, but it felt so overindulgent she couldn't bring herself to do it. *Other women do this on their own every day,* she told herself. *Not everyone has the luxury of being able to afford help.* And the truth was, Olivia didn't want *hired* help—she wanted her husband's.

"I'm so tired I can't see straight," Olivia told her mother during the phone call they shared each morning. Olivia could hear the noisy jangle of the television in the background; both her mother and her nurse, Tanesa, were big fans of *The Price Is Right.*

"That's how it is with a baby," her mother said. Her voice was weak; all the meds she had to take for her heart made her woozy. "I promise, it will pass."

"But James is never home to help me." Olivia knew she was pouting, but she was too exhausted to care. She also knew she wouldn't get much sympathy from her mother, who'd actually welcomed the solitude she experienced after Olivia's father had left. Olivia didn't want to give her mother a reason to say "I told you so" by complaining too much about James.

"They never are," her mother said simply, and a few minutes later, they hung up the phone. Olivia knew that despite her mother's misgivings about men in general, she didn't want the marriage to end because then James would stop paying for her condo and her nurse. Olivia had only hinted to her mother about the sometimes malicious edge to James; she never said a word to anyone about the time he slapped her. It would be on the tip of her tongue, but something would hold it back. Fear, maybe, that if she said it out loud, she'd be forced to act—to leave him or file a police report. As long as she was silent, it remained a secret, and nobody could judge her for not walking out the door.

Olivia wasn't exactly sure why she hadn't. Part of her felt like what he'd done was her fault, that maybe the tone of her voice that night had brought out the worst in her husband—that he felt like she was judging him. Another part of her was sure that no one would believe her. James never showed his darker side in public—he opened doors for her and kept his hand at the small of her back, a tender act of possession. Also, he hadn't raised a hand or his voice to her again since—he'd been kind and attentive, rubbing her sore feet and massaging her aching shoulders. He'd even attended the baby shower Waverly and Sara Beth threw for her, playing silly shower games and opening their presents. He agreed to name their daughter Madelyn, after Olivia's grandmother. He indulged her every whim to decorate for the nursery—he sent her flowers at least once a week. It was easy to convince herself the slap was just a one-time thing. She put that night into a box and buried it somewhere deep inside her, leaving no marker so she could easily ignore the spot.

As the months passed, Maddie began sleeping more and Olivia started to feel better. She found a routine that worked for them both, taking long walks each morning with Maddie in the stroller, strapping her daughter to her chest as she vacuumed and dusted the house. She often had lunch with Waverly and Sara Beth, smiling as they oohed and aahed over adorable seven-month-old Maddie. "She's just a little *peach*!" Waverly exclaimed. "I want to take a big *bite* out of her!"

Olivia laughed. "I know, right? There's something about her chunky little thighs that makes me want to nibble them." She looked over to the car seat next to her, where Maddie was contentedly chewing on a gel teething ring. Her daughter gave her a drool-soaked grin, showing just the tips of her two front teeth poking through her gums.

"You look like you've lost almost all the weight," Waverly observed, running her sharp gaze over Olivia's body.

Olivia shifted in her chair, suddenly hyperconscious of her own new shape next to her friends' leaner silhouettes. While it was true she had already lost the twenty-five pounds she'd gained with the pregnancy, her body had definitely shifted—her hips widened, her breasts swelled, and her stomach developed a small pooch that wouldn't disappear no matter how many crunches she did at the gym. Just last night, after Maddie had settled to sleep in her crib, James had stared at Olivia's naked body as she stood in front of the mirror next to the closet, brushing her hair.

"I'll pay for a tummy tuck, you know," he said out of no-where, as though Olivia had been complaining to him. Which she hadn't. In fact, while she knew her body had changed, Olivia actually felt *better* about it after giving birth than she ever had before. She was amazed by what it had pulled off, and figured a slightly rounded belly and a little jiggle on her thighs was a small price to pay for the miracle of their daughter's life.

"*Excuse* me?" Olivia said, setting her brush on the dresser, then spinning around to face him. She reached for her robe from its hook on the closet door and wrapped it tightly around her, tying it at the waist.

James waved a dismissive hand in her general direction. "Maddie's seven months old, Liv. If your shape hasn't bounced back on its own by now, it never will." Seeing the look of horror on her face, he laughed. "C'mon. Don't be upset. It's nothing to be ashamed of. You'd be in and out in an afternoon."

"I don't *need* a tummy tuck," Olivia said, feeling the heat creep up her chest and neck onto her face.

James's eyes narrowed. "You think it's attractive, all that *fat* bouncing around when I'm fucking you?" Olivia cringed. "I'll have my assistant make the appointment," he continued, as though his words hadn't just stabbed her in the heart.

Olivia knew better than to try to argue with him, and in the end, she was happy with the results of the procedure, if not the manner in which it came about. Now, as she drives Maddie home from Ciseaux Salon with her newly darkened and shaped pageboy, she worries about what kind of message she has just given her daughter—that as long as she looks beautiful on the outside, how she actually *feels* doesn't matter.

"Do you think Dad will like it?" Maddie asks as they enter their house, gesturing to her hair. Her daughter looks like a different person than the one Olivia picked up from school—her shoulders are pushed back, she walks as though there is an invisible string pulling her up at the top of her head. Hannah did a beautiful job on the color—deepening the natural brown just enough to warm up Maddie's pale skin. The layers she added create the illusion of fullness, and the longer, feathery bangs frame her daughter's hazel eyes perfectly, bringing your attention directly to them. She went into the salon looking like a little girl; she came out looking like the pretty young woman she actually is.

"I think he'll love it," Olivia says, hoping with everything in her this turns out to be true. James won't be thrilled she made this kind of decision without consulting him, but Maddie's happiness might outweigh his need to control how the change came about. She puts her purse on the entryway table and smiles at Maddie. "I'm starved. What sounds good for dinner?"

"Pepperoni pizza!" Maddie says with a playful, sparkly smile.

"Nice try. Too much grease. I think we can manage tomato, mozzarella, and basil, though. And a salad." She waits a beat, hesitant to bring up anything having to do with school, not wanting to ruin Maddie's markedly improved mood. "Do you have homework?"

Looking away, Maddie shrugs one shoulder, as though she were trying to shake something off her skin. "Not really. Just some reading. And a trig work sheet, so the teacher can figure out what we already know. Or don't know."

"Okay, so, why don't you work on it in the kitchen while I cook?" This is new for Olivia, being able to spend time with Maddie, doing something other than caring for her daughter's immediate physical needs. She tries not to worry about something going wrong, that Maddie's body will reject her new liver or be riddled by some dangerous infection, but there are times she can't help it. Like tonight, when Hannah told them about losing her daughter, fear overwhelmed Olivia again.

"I sort of was going to check my email," Maddie says.

"Later," Olivia says. "Homework first."

Maddie sighs, but follows her mother into their enormous kitchen. She sets her backpack on the counter and settles onto one of the barstools, watching as Olivia digs through the refrigerator for the ingredients she'll need. "That was really sad about Hannah's daughter," Maddie says, as she pulls out her notebook.

"It was," Olivia agrees. She feels horrible about accidentally bringing up such a painful subject for this woman they just met. Olivia hadn't asked for any details—whether or not Hannah was married or how her daughter had died. "I like her."

"Me, too," Maddie says. She holds her pencil over a piece of paper. "Maybe *you* should get your hair done by her, too. You could go back to your natural color. We could match!"

Olivia smiles as she sets the ball of gluten-free pizza dough on the marble-topped counter and unwraps it. "I could. But your dad wouldn't be happy. He likes me blond."

Maddie makes a face. "And you *always* do what makes Dad happy, right? Not what *you* want to do?"

Olivia cringes, not looking at her daughter as she rolls out the dough into a thin circle. She wants to tell Maddie her plan. She wants to show her the cash she has stashed away, little by little over the past ten years. Money she made from the small bits of jewelry she sold—pieces James would give her after a particularly bad fight or bruise left on her skin. But this isn't the kind of thing Olivia discusses with Maddie—she wants her daughter to have plausible deniability if James should ever confront her. She has to keep Maddie safe.

"How about I think about it?" Olivia says, as she runs a sharp knife through a Roma tomato. Maddie shrugs again, keeping her eyes on the work sheet in front of her. Olivia hates that she hasn't been a better role model. "I stay with him for you," she longs to say. "I keep myself small, I keep my mouth shut all because of you!"

But she knows Maddie is too young to understand these kinds of decisions. Her daughter still sees the world in stark divisions of right and wrong, black and white, when the truth is, life is so much more complicated than that, colored by infinite shades of gray.

Maddie

My dad comes home just as Mom and I are finishing dinner, around eight o'clock. He walks into the kitchen, loosening his tie as he enters. He stops short when he sees me sitting at the table, his eyes wide, and stares at my head.

I set down my fork and speak so Mom doesn't have to. "My hair was so trashed from all my meds, I asked Mom to take me and get it fixed." I feel Mom's eyes on me, hoping she'll understand that I'm trying to keep Dad from getting angry. "I really love it, Dad. All the girls at school are like, fashion models or something. I'm just trying to fit in. And I feel so much better now." I wait a beat, trying to gauge how he'll react from the look on his face. "Do you like it?"

He hesitates before responding, looking to my mom then back to me again, his expression softening. "You look beautiful." I can almost hear Mom's internal sigh of relief. "How was your first day?" Dad asks.

"Okay," I answer, not wanting to get into what had happened with Hailey and Noah. Knowing my dad, if he found out what they said, he'd be on the phone with their parents in a hot minute, which would only make everything worse. "I still need to do some reading, though, so I think I'm going to head upstairs."

"Clear your plate, please," Mom says, then stands up, walks over to Dad, and gives him a kiss. She could win an Academy Award for her acting. He wraps an arm around her waist, squeezes her tightly to him, and makes the kiss deeper, which totally grosses me out. That's how it is with my parents, though. They run hot and cold, and I'm never sure which side of them I'm going to get. It's different when it's just me, alone with my mom. She's way more relaxed. She smiles more and even acts a little goofy. But when she's around my dad, it's like she turns into a skittish cat. She gets all twitchy and guarded.

I grab my plate from the table, hurry over to the sink to rinse it off, then put it in the dishwasher. Small chores like this are a new thing for me, since for years, I ate most of my meals in my bed, but I try not to complain about having to do them. It could always be worse, I figure. I could always be dead.

I rush up the stairs to the safety of my bedroom, the one place in the house that is completely mine. When I was twelve and stuck in the hospital for a month after having a shunt inserted in my liver to drain the toxins my body couldn't process on its own, Mom distracted me by bringing in endless stacks of decorating magazines and catalogs. "You're almost a teenager, now," she said, as we flipped through the pages together. "We should redo your room."

She was right—I'd outgrown the décor she'd picked out for me when I was a toddler: cotton candy pink walls and white lace curtains. "I like this one," I said, pointing to a page in the Pottery Barn teen catalog.

"Neon green and turquoise, huh?" Mom asked, eyeing the polka dot bedspread and thin-striped curtains. "Are you sure? It's a little bright."

"I *like* bright," I said. I tapped the page with my index finger. "This is the one."

"Let me talk to your dad," she said. In the end, he agreed. The one bonus of being a sick kid, I guess—parents who are willing to overindulge you. He even hired a decorator to manage the project since Mom was busy at the hospital with me. When I finally came home, the walls of my room were white, and the rest of the room was accented by loud spots of turquoise and bright green on my bedspread and curtains—exactly what I'd wanted. The decorator gave me a queen-size, four-poster bed and an entire wall lined with white bookcases. She filled the corner with a huge turquoise beanbag chair and fuzzy neon green pillows. Now, everything about the room is comfortable and plush. It is by far my favorite place to be.

As my computer boots up, I stand in front of the mirror above my chest of drawers, regarding my new reflection. I wasn't lying to my dad that I loved my new hair—in two hours, Hannah somehow made me look like an entirely different person. I tuck one side behind my right ear, turning my head back and forth and making kissing lips at myself, wondering what Hailey might say about me now. I still need to put on a little makeup and go shopping for some new clothes, but maybe now she and Noah will at least leave me alone.

My laptop chimes, letting me know it's ready for me to log

on. But instead of immediately checking my email to see if I've heard from Dirk, I open Facebook and look up Hailey's profile. Even without her last name, it only takes a few minutes to find her under Eastside Prep's page. She's listed as one of the people "liking" the school, and with her mop of red hair, her profile picture isn't hard to pick out. Like Tiffani's, Hailey's account is set to public, so I don't need to send her a friend request in order to read all the posts on her wall or dig through her About.me page, either. She has over a thousand friends, she likes pages like *Cosmopolitan* and *Your Daily Horoscope,* and her most recent post was ten minutes ago: "Yo! Green beans = Yuck!" Eighty-seven of her friends "liked" this.

"Seriously?" I say aloud. "How old *are* all of you?" I scroll down through her other posts, most of them fairly similar in tone. She seems a little in love with herself, posting self-portraits clearly taken with her cell phone—her chin down, eyebrows suggestively raised, with coy, fishing-for-compliment statements like "Who says a girl needs makeup to feel good about herself?"

"You *might* need it to cover up Mount Vesuvius on your chin," I mutter, despite the fact that I realize making fun of anything to do with Hailey's appearance makes me just as ugly as she was to me. I consider using my Sierra account to post inappropriate YouTube videos on her wall or signing her email address up to receive endless amounts of spam, but decide that cyberbullying might be a bit more retaliation than she actually deserves. Teenage girls are supposed to be catty to each other—at least, that's what I gathered watching movies like *Heathers* and *Mean Girls,* along with countless episodes of *The Secret Life of the American*

Teenager when I was stuck in the hospital. Hailey's comment about my hair might have only been reflex, and not necessarily evidence that she is related to Satan.

Hoping it's not too late to chat with Dirk, I quickly log in to my email, smiling when I see his name in the inbox. Over the last two weeks, we'd all but abandoned the Zombie Wars game, choosing instead to chat over instant messaging and through emails. I learned that he works as a systems engineer for Google, helping to write the complicated scripting that makes things like Gmail and Google+ function on a day-to-day basis. He has two younger sisters—both still in high school, but they live in North Seattle with his parents, so at least I'm not in danger of running into them at Eastside Prep—not that they'd know it was me, since the only picture he has is the one I sent him of "Sierra." His apartment is downtown on Capitol Hill, a small studio inside a converted brick warehouse. "It definitely needs a woman's touch," he wrote. "I'm sort of a slacker when it comes to decorating. Unless you consider stacks of empty pizza boxes artistic expression."

"Hey Sierra," his note tonight reads. "I've been thinking, and I'm pretty sure it's time I get your digits. I mean, we've been talking online for a month now, right? I'd like to hear the voice attached to that pretty face. Call me tonight. I'll be up until midnight."

He included his number at the bottom of the screen, and I take a deep breath, considering whether or not talking with him on the phone is a good idea. I'm not sure if I *sound* like I'm almost twenty years old, or if I'll give myself away when I don't have the added protection of the computer screen. But my curiosity gets the better of me, and I grab my cell phone out of my backpack, dial his number, and immediately head inside my closet, shutting the door behind me so my parents won't hear me talking.

I can do this, I say to myself. *I can be Sierra.* The phone rings six times before he answers. "This is Dirk," he says. His voice is low and warm, and I suddenly feel like I can't breathe. "Hello?" he says after a moment of silence. "Sierra?"

"Yes. Um, I mean, no." I cover my eyes with one hand and shake my head. *Oh, god. I'm such an idiot.*

"No?" The way he says it makes me picture the word curling up at the end.

"Well, sort of." *I should just tell him the truth. I should just get it over with and get on with my life.*

"You're sort of Sierra? Sounds like a name for a bad sitcom. *Sort of Sierra,* starring Blake Lively as the girl wrestling with an identity crisis." He says it in a deep, mocking movie voice-over tone, which makes me laugh. *So he's not just charming on the computer.* "I'm happy you called," he continues.

"Me, too." I drop my hand from my face into my lap. "I mean, I'm happy you asked me to."

"So, what's this 'sort of Sierra' biz?"

I pause, feeling my pulse thud inside my ears. "Well . . . that's not actually my name."

"Oh." He is quiet, then clears his throat. "Like it's a moniker for the game?"

Tell him, I think. *Tell him who you are, NOW.* "Yeah," I say, the lie slipping out of me so much more easily than the truth. "I just like it better than my name, so that's what I go by online."

"What's your real name, then?" he asks, sounding clearly relieved.

"Madelyn. But I mostly go by Maddie."

"Maddie," he repeats. "Well, *I* think it's pretty, but coming from a guy named Dirk, I can totally understand wanting to use a different one."

"It could be worse," I offered. "You could be Cornelius."

"Ha! Totally true." He's quiet again, and I struggle to find something interesting to say. I don't really know how to talk with boys, and all I can think is I'm going to say something that's going to give me away. But then I don't have to speak, because he does. "It's nice to finally hear your voice, Maddie. I mean, it's cool and everything talking online, but this is better." He sounds so relaxed, so comfortable with himself, I feel terrible for deceiving him. "What are you up to tonight?" he asks.

"I got my hair cut and had dinner with my parents. Exciting, right?" I remember reading somewhere that the closer to the truth you keep a lie, the less likely you are to be found out. I'd already told him that "Sierra" still lived at home with her parents while she went to school to become a computer graphics artist. "What about you?"

"Well, I was helping my dad rebuild the engine on a '69 Corvette a little while ago, and now I'm back at my apartment, sitting on the couch, talking with a super-cute girl on the phone." My face warms, and for a moment, I feel like that girl—the girl in the picture I'd sent him. But then it hits me—*that's* the girl he's thinking of, not me. He's imagining Sierra's long, smooth torso, not my thick belly, marked by an ugly red scar. *He's not imagining the Franken-babe.* Even with my new haircut, I'm pretty sure if he saw me on the street, he'd look the other way.

"Maddie?" I hear my mom's muffled voice, coming from the hallway. "Can I get you anything, sweetie?"

I sigh and shift a little on the floor. "Hey, can you hold on a sec?" I say to Dirk.

"Sure," he says, so I set my phone down and quietly step out of my closet into my bedroom. I open the door to see my mom standing there, her face turned away from me, showing me only the right side.

"I'm fine," I say. "Thanks. Just going to read and go to sleep, okay?" She nods, and I notice her eye is watering. "Are you okay?" I ask, and she nods again. "Mom, look at me."

She turns her head a little bit, and gives me a half smile. "I just wanted to check to make sure you'll remember to take your meds."

And then I see it—the red mark on the other side of her face, next to her ear. "Oh my god. Did he *hit* you?" My stomach clenches. I've seen marks on my mother's body before—small, fingertip-size bruises on her biceps, a slight pink swelling around her eye—but she denies my dad had anything to do with them. She always has a good story.

"No," she says, but her voice breaks on the word. "I opened the pantry door too fast and smacked my cheek. That's all." She leans toward me and gives me a quick kiss. "I love you, sweetie. Get some rest, and I'll see you in the morning." She turns quickly and moves down the hallway toward my parents' room.

"Mom?" I call out, not knowing what I could possibly say to make her feel better. She pauses just in front of their door, then turns back, a questioning look on her face. Though her eyes are shiny with tears, she is so beautiful. My heart suddenly hurts. "I love my new hair," I finally say, faltering. "Thank you."

She holds my gaze a moment and then smiles. "You're welcome, sweet girl." And then she is gone.

I keep my hand on the doorknob a moment, wishing I had the courage to run down the stairs and scream at my father. I wish I knew how to stand up to him—I wish I knew the right words to say. But before I can think of any, I remember Dirk, waiting for me on the phone. I rush back inside the closet, making sure I've shut my bedroom door behind me. "God, I'm sorry," I say, breathlessly. "That took longer than I thought."

"It's okay," Dirk says. "I like it when a girl plays hard to get." Despite the weight I feel in my chest after seeing my mom, I smile. "Everything okay?" he asks.

"My parents had a fight," I say, before I can stop to wonder if telling him this is a good idea. "My dad's got a temper."

"Like how bad a temper?"

I swallow hard, trying to push down the lump in my throat. "Pretty bad," I whisper. I can't help it, a tear rolls down my cheek.

"Hey . . . are you okay?" Dirk asks, with real concern in his voice.

I take a deep breath. "I'll be fine," I say, hoping that somehow, I can find a way to make those words come true.

Hannah

That night, after Olivia and Maddie leave the salon, for the first time in months, Hannah doesn't go for a second run. Instead, she quickly cleans up her station and heads upstairs to her apartment, where she reaches into the top drawer of her dresser and pulls out the thank-you notes Zoe has forwarded to her. She counts them—eight in all—wondering if she can handle reading them without falling apart. But then her desire to know whether she has a letter from the parents of the child who received Emily's liver takes over and moments later she is sitting on her couch, sorting through the stack of envelopes. She puts them in order by the dates on the postmarks.

With a deep breath, she opens the first envelope and removes the card, which is white with the simple words *Thank You* in shiny silver letters on the front. Inside, are these hand-written words:

We wish there was a way to express just how deeply we are grateful for the gift of your daughter's heart. Our son, Marcus, had been on the UNOS list for almost six months and his doctors weren't exactly hopeful that we would find a donor in time to save his life. When they told us about your daughter, some of our first thoughts were of you, what an incredible person you must be to give such a gift to another person's child.

We know that there is nothing to lessen the sorrow of losing her, but we want you to know that she is our hero. We think of you both every day, of your selflessness and generosity. We thank God for the gift of our child's life and will always grieve the fact that it had to come at the loss of yours.

Thank you seems too inadequate a phrase to capture how we feel, but we hope you find some comfort in knowing that your daughter—and you—will never be forgotten.

Sincerely,
Pat and Sheila

Hannah's eyes blur as she reads, and when she is finished, she lets loose a rough sob from her chest. *Emily's heart saved a little boy.* She finds her spirits lifted knowing this, knowing his parents are truly grateful. She quickly begins to open the other cards, most of them similar to the first. There are notes from the parents of the children who received Emily's lungs, her corneas, her intestines, her kidneys and skin, but none for her pancreas or liver. Hannah knows that the fact that there isn't a note from the parents of the girl who Emily's liver saved doesn't mean Maddie is that girl.

Still curious to know more about Olivia and Maddie's family, Hannah grabs her laptop from the bedroom and sits back down on her couch. Once it boots up, she types, "Olivia Bell, Seattle," into a search engine, surprised by how many links immediately populate the screen. Olivia's name is in almost all of them, but never alone—always following her husband's. *JAMES AND OLIVIA BELL HOST A BENEFIT FOR SEATTLE CHILDREN'S HOSPITAL*, a recent headline reads, just above a picture of the two of them dressed in elegant attire—Olivia wears a simple silver sheath, cut perfectly to fit the lines of her lithe frame, and James, a tall man with salt-and-pepper hair and broad shoulders, is movie-star handsome in a classic black tuxedo. Hannah stares at his face a moment, wondering if she is just imagining the slightly glassy, reptilian look to his eyes. She reads the brief paragraph beneath the photograph:

James and Olivia Bell honored the doctors at Children's Hospital this weekend with a benefit that raised well over two million dollars for the facility. Bell Investments is one of the largest firms in the Northwest, and supports not only the hospital but several other charitable organizations in Seattle.

Okay, Hannah thinks. *So maybe he's not a reptile. Maybe the camera just caught him at a bad moment.* But she can't help but notice the body language between him and his wife—how his arm is wrapped tightly behind her back, gripping her waist— the fabric is wrinkled and cinched beneath his fingers. And yet, her torso is turned from his like she's trying to pull away, and her eyes look up and over the camera. Hannah thinks about the strain having a sick child can put on a marriage, and she wonders what their relationship is like after years of managing Maddie's illness.

Clicking through various other articles, Hannah learns more about James than Olivia. She reads about his phenomenal financial success, a man who rose from meager beginnings and built himself into an empire. In one magazine article, the journalist asked him about his family, citing an interview James's father had given, in which he took credit for instilling "Jimmy's" innate business sense. The journalist noted that James instantly went silent when his father was mentioned, then finally replied, "My father is dead. And my name's not *Jimmy*."

"And your mother?" the journalist pressed.

"I didn't have one," James said, then refused to discuss the subject further. Hannah wonders what could have created such a substantial rift between James and his parents. There are pictures of him shaking hands with the governor and the mayor, shots of him playing golf with Bill Gates. In every picture he is smiling, a wide, car salesman grin, but again, in every image, his eyes appear vacant to Hannah, as though at any moment that smile might vanish and you'd be fighting for your life.

After reading a few more articles about James Bell and his family, Hannah is no more certain if Maddie is the girl who received Emily's liver than when she started. Closing the browser, Hannah shuts her eyes, suddenly not wanting to read any more about the Bells. Her body aches, missing Emily, and she wants to go for that second run, but it's past eight o'clock and too dark for her to be out on her own. As a few tears slip down her cheeks, she hears the front door of the salon downstairs open, and she quickly wipes her face and sets her laptop on the small coffee table in front of her.

"Hannah?" Sophie's voice travels up the narrow stairway. "Are you here?"

Hannah sniffles and stands. "Come on up," she calls out. She wonders if she should tell Sophie about Olivia and Maddie right away, or wait until she finds out more about them. Her friend appears in the doorway before Hannah has a chance to decide. Sophie's red hair hangs over one shoulder, expertly folded into a tight fishtail braid, and she's wearing dark jeans with a navy blue silk tank top. "I'm here to take you out for drinks," she says. "I need a wingman. Wing woman?" She pauses, tilting her head to one side. "Whatever."

Hannah smiles and takes a step over to hug her friend. "I don't think you need my help meeting men."

"No, but you need mine." Sophie pulls back and kisses both of Hannah's cheeks. "I do believe it's time to dust the cobwebs off your vagina."

Hannah laughs, surprised by the sound. Genuine amusement has all but evaded her over the last year—she's a little amazed that her body still knows how to react to the feeling. "My vagina's just fine, thank you very much. Perfectly happy."

"With a *vibrator?*" Sophie snorts. "Hardly." The only reason Sophie knows Hannah has such a device is that she's the one who gave it to her. And besides, the truth is that Hannah could care less about sex at the moment—with herself or anyone else. She's fairly certain she's forgotten how to do it.

Sophie looks down the bridge of her nose and raises her arched brows. "You need to be careful with those things. I've heard they can desensitize you." Hannah shakes her head, but Sophie continues. "*Really,* darling. One day it's the vibrator, the next it's the paint shaker at the hardware store."

"Oh my god, Sophie, that's *disgusting*!" Hannah squeals, immediately visualizing herself naked, splayed upon Home Depot machinery, surrounded by an audience of slack-jawed carpenters and plumbers. But then she dissolves into laughter, the deep-seated, internal body-scrubbing variety that leaves her feeling lighter and slightly bruised.

Sophie grins, then grabs Hannah's arm and pulls her toward the bathroom. "Let's get you ready."

"I really don't feel up to it, Soph." Hannah dreads the idea of sitting in a club, bass music thudding in the air, surrounded by totally-inappropriate-for-dating twenty-five-year-olds. Clubbing is a young person's game, and now that they are in their midforties, Hannah feels as though she and Sophie don't qualify. And really, she has no interest in meeting a man. What would be the point, now? What would she have to offer anyone, other than sorrow?

"You can't let yourself waste away in this apartment," Sophie says, seemingly undeterred. "Do you think Emily would want that for you? Do you think it would make her happy to see her mother hiding from the world?" She pauses, then answers her own question. "Of course not. She wanted you to fall in love."

Hannah can't deny this is true. When she was a toddler, Emily often asked when she would get a daddy like all of her friends. "Where's *my* daddy?" she'd say, and Hannah would cuddle her close.

"I wanted to be your mama *so* much, I couldn't wait for a daddy to come along," she told her daughter, unsure of the appropriate time or manner in which to explain artificial insemination. It would have been easier if Emily had been adopted. Over the years, Emily brought the subject up every now and then, bemoaning the fact that she didn't have a father.

"You could get married to Mr. Tate," she said, suggesting that her first-grade science teacher would make Hannah a perfect match. "He has two dogs and pizza is his favorite food!"

"Mr. Tate is very nice," Hannah agreed, "but I think we're doing just fine on our own." She paused, worried by the disappointment scribbled across her daughter's face. "Aren't we?"

Emily shrugged, and Hannah couldn't help but feel her daughter's longing for a father was an indication that the life Hannah had built for them wasn't enough—that she was failing Emily in the most fundamental way. Emily was twelve before she finally understood the logistical circumstances surrounding her conception, and she was not happy about them.

"So my dad is just some random guy you picked out of a book?" she asked, disgusted.

"He wasn't random," Hannah explained. "I picked someone very healthy and smart."

"It's totally creepy," Emily said with a dramatic shudder. "Do you tell the guys you go on dates with how you had me?"

"Some of them, yes." It wasn't something that Hannah offered up front, but if a man asked, she told him the truth.

"Maybe you shouldn't," Emily concluded, and every time Hannah went on a date after that, her daughter would inquire if she thought he might be "the one." Hannah hated to disappoint her, but the truth was she didn't believe in soul mates, that there was one perfect person for her in the world. She thought of relationships as many possible paths she could walk down, but so far, she hadn't found one she wanted to travel.

She had thought she found it with Devin. The first day she saw him sitting alone at a table at the coffeehouse she used to frequent before work, she was struck by his rugged good looks.

He had short brown hair, eyes almost the exact shade of copper pennies, and wore jeans and a T-shirt amid a sea of men in well-cut suits. He caught her staring at him and his lips curved into a slow, languid smile. Not wanting to gawk, she averted her eyes as quickly as she could, but she couldn't deny the attraction she felt. After she paid for her drink, she was about to go talk with him, but he beat her to it; before she realized he had left his table, he was standing next to her. He was tall and thin, but muscular, too. As he rested an arm on the counter, she could see one of his exposed triceps working beneath his skin and she had to restrain herself from reaching out to caress its contour.

"Do you need any furniture?" he asked, and she laughed.

"Well, *that* has to be the strangest pickup line I've ever heard," she said, wrapping her hands around her travel mug.

He smiled and tilted his head at her. "Am I trying to pick you up?"

Hannah's chest flushed with heat, but still, she looked him straight in the eye. "I hope so," she said, grateful that he laughed, too.

They sat down together and drank their coffee, making small talk and stealing lust-laden glances at each other. Their attraction was immediate and visceral, something she felt like she couldn't deny. It turned out that Devin designed and built beautiful custom furniture for a living. He had just opened a small studio with a storefront a few blocks from the salon, so he invited her to come see it that night. Normally, she'd play a little bit hard to get, but something about Devin made her say yes right away.

When she arrived at his studio, it was illuminated by candlelight, and her first impression was that he was laying the romance on too thick for a first date. But then, as he began to show her the pieces he'd built, he explained how the candlelight brought out the truest beauty of the wood, the wisps of texture and changes of color in each. She ran her fingers along a burled walnut end table, marveling at the pattern of the grain.

"Mesmerizing, isn't it?" Devin said, standing so close to her she could feel the heat coming off his body.

"Completely," she said and turned to face him. He kissed her and led her to the bed he kept in the back room. Their lovemaking was beautiful and slow; Devin coaxed pleasure out of her body the same way she imagined he created art out of wood. His skin held an intoxicating scent of sandalwood and sap—she breathed him in like he was her new oxygen. Hours later, sated beyond anything she'd ever experienced, she felt sure she'd found her match.

Within a couple of months, they were engaged. Devin moved into her apartment, and for a while, everything was better than Hannah could have imagined. She introduced him to Sophie and Isaac, and then took him back to the farm to meet her parents. Everyone agreed he was the right fit for her. They talked about the babies they would have, the house they would build together just outside the city. They occasionally argued about money, but Hannah assumed this was a normal part of being in a long-term relationship.

After about a year together, though, Devin began staying nights at the studio again. "I work better at night," he told her. "I like the quiet and the dark."

She tried to be understanding, but she had a hard time with the distance he suddenly put between them. Then one evening, at an opening they hosted at the studio for his new line, Hannah saw him in the corner leaning a little too close to an obviously younger, twentysomething girl in a red dress. She giggled when he whispered in her ear, and Hannah felt sick.

"It was nothing!" he said later when she confronted him. "She's interested in marketing the line for me, so I was just being friendly."

"It looked way more than friendly," Hannah said, trying not to cry. She loved him so much she tried to overlook that one moment, what she hoped was a simple misjudgment of his behavior. But then as time went on, even when he was with her, he was constantly checking his phone, telling her over and over again it was business related. But the look on his face as he read whatever was on the screen was one of pure lust. She recognized instantly because it was the way he'd stopped looking at her.

Her suspicions ate away at her thoughts, so much so that one night when he was in the shower, she opened his laptop, which he'd left on the coffee table. His email was still up on the screen, and as she clicked on one message after another, reading the notes from a woman named Nadia about the recent nights she'd spent with Devin at his studio, she felt increasingly ill.

"What the hell do you think you're doing?" Devin demanded a few minutes later as he stood in the threshold between the hallway and the living room. He had a white towel wrapped around his thin waist and his hair was still wet.

She looked over to him, her eyes glassy with tears. She pointed at the screen, her entire body shaking. "How long have you been screwing around on me?"

"I'm not," he said, though his shoulders curled forward, as though a weight had suddenly been set upon them.

"Please don't lie to me." She swallowed back the bile that had risen in her throat. "Please. I asked you how long."

"I don't know," he said, clearly deflated. "A while. I think I have a problem, Hannah. I think I need help."

She stood up, clenching her fists at her sides. "I think you're right," she said. "And you're not going to get it from me. Get the hell out."

It took almost a year after Devin left for Hannah to work through the shock she felt over his betrayal. Only then did she start focusing on what it was she really wanted in her life, and it turned out what she wanted was Emily.

Now, fourteen years later, Hannah sighs, defeated by Sophie's logic. Emily would want Hannah to be happy. She would want her mother to move on, so Hannah allows her friend to drag her into the bathroom.

Sophie puts her finger under Hannah's chin and lifts it, examining her face. "Have you been exfoliating? Your skin is positively *gray*."

"It hasn't exactly been high on my list of priorities. I'm a little busy running the salon."

"Pfft!" Sophie dismisses Hannah's excuse with a wave of her hand. She grabs a bottle of astringent off the counter and douses a cotton ball before cleaning off Hannah's face. As she carefully swipes on a mineral base, Sophie chatters about business. "I can't believe how many new clients I have time for now," she says. Part of the reason she and Hannah decided to open a second location was how many potential clients they'd had to turn away because of lack of space on their stylists' schedules. Even during an economic downturn, they'd been lucky enough to prosper. "The only things that are certain are death and taxes," Hannah liked to joke. "And the need for twice-weekly blow-outs."

Sophie quickly applies Hannah's makeup, then takes her into the tiny bedroom and stares into the closet, clucking with disapproval. She finally pulls out a pair of decent boot-cut jeans and a fitted scarlet sweater. "Put these on. And don't smear your lipstick."

Hannah complies, and twenty minutes later, she and Sophie are seated in the bar of Daniel's Broiler, an upscale restaurant not far from the salon. The lighting is warm and low, and a grand piano tinkles quietly in the background. At least Sophie hasn't brought her to a club. Hannah figures she can have a drink or two to placate her friend and then go home.

Sophie orders them both a glass of Merlot and with a stealthy eye, surveys the room. "By the window," she murmurs. "Bachelors on the prowl."

Hannah gives them a perfunctory glance, pretending to take in the stunning view of the city lights. The two men look to be in their late forties and are attractive enough—one with thick, slightly wavy black hair and the other a cropped-cut blond. Both are wearing jeans with casual button-down shirts, along with expensive-looking silver watches. The black-haired one catches her eye and smiles, so she quickly looks away. She decides the only way to keep Sophie from inviting them over is distraction, so she tells her friend about Olivia and Maddie appearing at the salon. Not wanting to appear obsessed, she doesn't mention that she spent an hour reading about the family on the Internet.

"Do you really think it's them?" Sophie asks after she takes a sip of wine. "I mean, what are the odds?"

"There are only something like two hundred transplants a year in the Northwest," Hannah says, reciting what she learned from Zoe. "And only a handful of those are livers, since the parameters to qualify as a match are so hard to meet. I think the odds are pretty good, but I don't know for sure yet."

"Did you tell them that Emily was a donor?" Hannah shakes her head, and Sophie sighs before going on. "Why not?"

"I don't know. I just . . ." Hannah trails off, then takes a quick sip of wine. "I told them she died, I just didn't say when or how." Sophie gives her a pointed look, and Hannah groans. "I was blindsided, Soph. I was in the middle of cutting Maddie's hair. What was I going to say? 'Oh, by the way, I think you might have my daughter's *liver* inside you?'"

"Why not?" Sophie repeats the question, and before Hannah can answer, the men they were eyeing from across the room are standing next to them.

"Hi," the blond one says to Sophie, holding out his hand. "I'm Robert, and I'm pretty sure it's a crime that women as beautiful as the two of you are sitting alone."

Hannah tries not to roll her eyes as the man with black hair slides onto the stool next to her. "Hello," she says, primly. "Are you lost?"

He smiles. "If I am, you're certainly a lovely roadside attraction."

Hannah cocks her head. "Did you just compare me to an enormous ball of *twine*?" Up close, she sees that he is quite handsome, with dark eyes to match his hair, tan complexion, and a slow, easy smile. He looks like the kind of man who doesn't have a hard time getting women to fall in love with him—and once they have, he probably loses interest.

He laughs, then holds out his hand. "I'm Seth."

Hannah tells him her name, then briefly places her hand in his, noting his soft skin and manicured nails. *Metrosexual,* she thinks. *He's never done an ounce of hard labor in his life.* He stares at her face, as though attempting to figure something out.

"What?" she asks, taking another sip of wine. "Do I have a piece of spinach in my teeth?"

He smiles again, but squints a little, too. "I'm just trying to figure out how high this wall of yours is, and whether or not I have the strength to climb it."

There's no malice to his tone, but still, Hannah bristles. "Does that line get you laid a lot?"

He sits back and lets out a quick, low whistle. "Ouch."

"God, sorry," she says, immediately feeling guilty for being rude. She knows she's being a bitch, but she can't help it. How can she even consider dating, when Emily is dead? Dating someone would imply she is moving on, letting go of the life she had with her daughter. Emily was the foundation upon which Hannah structured her entire life. All her decisions, her goals, her day-to-day choices were based on how Emily would be affected. Her daughter was the center of her world, and now, Hannah has no way to gauge what to do next, no scale to weigh what might be right or wrong for her. All she has is her gut instincts, and right now, they're telling her she's not ready to be here.

She looks in the mirror behind the bar, noting that Sophie is leaning in toward Robert, whispering something in his ear. She's fairly certain her friend won't be going home alone tonight.

Suddenly, Hannah's empty stomach seizes and she feels as though she might vomit. The wine has made her queasy. She grabs Sophie's arm. "I think it's time for me to go," she says.

Sophie stops midsentence and turns toward her. "But we just got here, *chérie*. And Robert's asked us to join them for dinner. You should eat."

"Yeah," Robert says, placing a light hand on Sophie's lower back. "Don't leave poor Seth all alone."

"Poor Seth will be just fine," Seth says, quietly.

Hannah sets her glass on the bar, causing the wine to slosh and spill onto her hand. "I'm sorry, but I really don't feel well," she says, swallowing down the bitter swell of acid that rises in her throat. She shouldn't have come. She should have stayed home, where she was safe. She will climb into bed, take a Xanax, and drift off to sleep . . . into the only kind of true relief she can find.

Sophie frowns, and her brow furrows. "Do you want me to drive you home?"

"No," Hannah says with a quick shake of her head. "Don't worry. I'll grab a cab." She stands, picks up her purse from the bar, and gives Sophie a kiss on the cheek. "Thanks for trying," she whispers into her friend's ear. "I'm just not ready for all of this." Pulling back, Hannah smiles at Robert and Seth. "Be nice to Sophie," she says. "Have a good night."

Pushing her way through the small crowd of people gathered at the bar, she tries to keep her breaths even and measured so she doesn't cry. At the elevator, she pushes the down button over and over, as though the motion could hurry the machinery, and then, she hears her name being called.

"Hannah, wait," Seth says, half-jogging toward her. She

keeps her eyes on the numbers as they light up over the eleva-tor door. Seth stands next to her, not too close, his hands linked loosely behind his back. The elevator dings, and the door opens. It's empty, so the two of them step inside and Seth presses the button for the lobby. "I really am sorry for the wall comment," he says. "It's kind of an occupational hazard. I didn't mean to offend you."

This piques Hannah's interest, and she eyes him briefly. "What do you do?"

"I'm a psychologist. Reading people is part of my job, and sometimes I do it at the wrong time with the wrong person." They are quiet a moment, the only sound the buzz of the cables guiding the elevator to the ground, but then he speaks again. "What about you?"

"Bricklayer," Hannah says wryly. "Professional wall builder."

"Ha," he says with a chuckle, and because he laughs at him-self, Hannah decides she needs to apologize again.

"I'm sorry for being rude, too," she says. "I'm having a bad night." *A bad year, actually,* she thinks but doesn't say.

"It happens," Seth says gently. "Don't worry about it."

"Thank you," she says and then realizes she hadn't yet an-swered his question about what she does for a living. "And Sophie and I own Ciseaux Salon, one downtown and one here on the Eastside. We're stylists."

"Ah," he says. "No wonder you're both so beautiful." He glances at her with warm brown eyes, and suddenly, Hannah feels exposed, as though he can see right through her. "What-ever it is you're dealing with," he says, "I hope it gets better, soon."

"You're doing it again," Hannah says, though not unkindly.

It wasn't that he *made* these observations that bothered her—it was the fact that he was *right* about them. She thought she was a better actress than that. She thought she did such a good job of hiding her pain. Was she really so transparent? Maybe he was just really good at his job.

"I'm telling you," Seth says as the door opens and they step out into the lobby, "it's like having psychological Tourette's."

She laughs a little at his words, and once they're on the street, Seth hails her a cab. She shakes his hand and looks him straight in the eye. She notices when he smiles, the lines around his eyes crinkle into small fans.

"Good night, Hannah," he says. "Take care."

She nods. "You, too." She climbs into the back of the cab, and he closes the door behind her. She tries not to, but after she gives the driver her address and he pulls away from the curb, she looks back at Seth standing on the sidewalk. She wonders what it would be like to let a man like that into her world, and if Emily would have liked him. Before she knows it, she is crying, loud, gulping sobs that shake her core.

The cabbie glances at her in the rearview mirror. "Everything okay?" he asks, gruffly.

Hannah sucks in a quick breath and nods. "Just take me home," she says, knowing that without Emily, no matter how hard she tries, things will never be okay again.

Olivia

Olivia walks down the hallway of Lakeview College, clutching her purse between her fingers until her knuckles turn white. An hour ago, after dropping Maddie off for her second day at school, she withdrew enough from the bank to pay her tuition in cash, and she's terrified that some punk kid might decide to mug her and snatch away the handbag that holds her future.

The idea of working toward a degree in criminal justice came to her one night last year, not long after Maddie's transplant, when she and James got into an argument that ended with a three-inch round bruise on the back of Olivia's thigh, where her husband's heel landed when he kicked her. She doesn't remember what the argument was about, but she does recall lying on the floor of their bedroom afterward, thinking if she didn't find a way to leave James, someday he was going to kill her.

She already has an A.A. in criminal law—it was a prerequisite for her certification as a paralegal—but she knows if she is ever going to make it to law school, she'll need a four-year degree. Once Maddie turns eighteen and is safely ensconced at college, there will be no more threat of a custody fight and Olivia can leave James. She wants to be prepared. She wants to find a job, first, something that will pay her enough to support herself—something that will allow her to say "no, thanks," to alimony offers from James's legal team. After witnessing Waverly's husband divorce her five years ago, seeing the hateful way she went after every penny she could get, Olivia is hesitant to become one of those women who live off their ex-husbands' fortunes. She doesn't care that the law says she's entitled to 50 percent of James's money, or that after her living with his abuse for almost twenty years, he deserves to pay a steep price for all he has done to her. She only wants to be free from him, and needs to do whatever it takes to cut all ties.

Olivia enters the admissions office, glancing around the room to make sure there is no one there she knows. However unlikely it is, she is terrified someone will see her and tell James what she's up to. If someone *does* tell him she was at the college, her plan is to say she was only doing research on whether it might a good school for Maddie. She isn't sure if he'd believe this, but she isn't going to let anything stop her. For now, she will register for one course, Criminology 201, scheduled three mornings a week, while Maddie is at school and James is at work so her absence will go undetected.

As she stands in line to pay her tuition, unsure if she is doing the right thing, she feels her heart bang against her rib cage in an anxious rhythm. But all she can think about is last night, after James told Maddie her hair was beautiful and their daughter went upstairs to her room. When he was sure Maddie was out of earshot, he grabbed Olivia's arm and twisted it behind her back. With a sharp intake of breath, Olivia bit her bottom lip and tried not to make a sound—she didn't want Maddie to come back and see what her father was doing.

"You should have asked me first," he said, pressing his mouth against her ear. She winced as he squeezed her forearm tighter; her shoulder felt like it might pop out of joint.

"I know," she said, hoping to placate him. "But she had such a hard day. She was *crying,* James. She felt so different from the other girls and I just needed to do *something* to make her feel better." She closed her eyes and waited for him to release his grip on her.

After a moment he did, but when she tried to take a step away from him, he grabbed her hair at the nape of her neck and yanked it, hard. Her hand flew to the back of her head, and she cried out, her eyes filling with tears.

"It's not your *place* to make those kinds of decisions," he said, spitting the words out through gritted teeth. He gave her hair a tug in emphasis. "Next time, you call me first. Do you understand?" She nodded, head down, and he released her again. This time, though, she stood still, waiting for him to tell her what to do. Her eyes flitted to the sharp silver pizza cutter resting on the counter, and she suddenly flashed on grabbing it and slicing it across his face . . . his neck . . . his chest. She imagined the blood and what were sure to be his howling cries as he fell to his knees on the pristinely white kitchen floor. She'd watched *The Burning Bed.* She knew that women in situations like hers sometimes committed such heinous acts. But that wasn't what she wanted—to murder him. She wanted him to *see* her thrive without him. Someday, she wanted to rub her freedom in his face.

"I'm sorry," she said quietly, glancing up at him. His eyes squeezed into slits, and before she knew it was coming, he threw out his arm and backhanded her across her face. She cried out again, curling her shoulders forward and pressing a palm against where he'd hit her to try to reduce the sting.

"You should be," he said, then strode over to the table, where he sat down and took a bite of pizza. She cleaned the kitchen up in silence, feeling his eyes on her the entire time, and she wondered if he sensed what she was thinking, if he knew she had a plan.

Now, after paying her tuition and confirming that the college will only communicate with her through an email address James doesn't know about, Olivia makes her way back to her car, unsure how she should fill the rest of her day. For years, all she has done is take care of Maddie—her daughter is the foundation upon which she structures her time. She feels a little out of sorts until her cell phone rings, startling her. She grabs it from her purse, instantly worried something has happened to Maddie at school, ready to jump back into her caretaker role.

"Hi, Olivia," a woman's voice says. "This is Hannah, from Ciseaux Salon?"

"Oh, hi." Olivia clears her throat and straightens in her seat. "Is something wrong? Did my debit card not go through?" James sometimes would transfer money out of her account without her knowledge, just to show her he was the one who controlled it. Normally, she checked the balance before even buying groceries, but yesterday at the salon she'd been so worried about Maddie being upset, it hadn't even crossed her mind.

"Oh no, nothing like that," Hannah says. "This might be a little presumptuous, but I wanted to extend an offer for you to make an appointment with me for yourself. I know Henry's a master with highlights, but I'd love to be able to win you away."

Olivia laughs. "That's funny. Maddie liked you so much, she basically suggested the same thing." She pauses. "When should I come in?" She doesn't really need a touch-up, but she likes Hannah, too.

"I have some time free early next week. Thursday morning at ten thirty? Or we can meet after hours, if that's easier."

"Thursday morning is fine," Olivia says, wondering if she is imagining that Hannah sounds a little nervous. "But hey, maybe we could get together before that? For lunch, or a cup of coffee?" She doesn't know the words are there until they come out of her mouth. She's been so wrapped up with Maddie and her illness, Olivia hasn't made a new friend in years. The more time she spent in the hospital or at home taking care of her daughter, the more her interactions with Waverly and Sara Beth tapered off. They sent get well cards and flowers, stacks of books and magazines, but after Maddie's transplant, neither of them came to visit her. For the most part, Olivia spends all of her time with her daughter or alone.

There is a beat before Hannah responds. "Sure," she finally says. "I'd like that. There's a cute café right around the corner from me. Are you free today?"

"I am," Olivia says.

Three hours later, after a trip to the gym and a quick shower, Olivia parks her car in front of Café Veloce and makes her way to the entrance. It's a warm September day—the air is sweet and the sun bathes everything in a golden light. The beauty of this season is one of Seattle's best-kept secrets, the reason why many natives are able to survive the other brutal months of near-constant rain. She sees Hannah already sitting at an outside table, and Olivia skips speaking to the hostess and joins her.

"Hi," she says, slipping into the black wrought-iron chair. "Nice to see you so soon."

"You, too." Hannah smiles and takes a quick sip of her iced tea. "Did you have any trouble finding it?"

Olivia shakes her head. "Not at all. GPS is a godsend." She picks up the menu, perusing the options. "What's good here?"

"I'm a big fan of the black-and-blue salad—blackened flank steak with blue cheese dressing. Or the grilled shrimp."

Olivia sets the menu back down and smiles. "The salad sounds perfect." Their server approaches and they both put in their orders. "So," Olivia says, wondering if she sounds as awkward as she feels. She's never been very good at this part—the small, getting-to-know-you chitchat. "Busy morning?"

Hannah nods. "But I have about an hour and a half before my next client."

"Did you always want to be a stylist?" Olivia asks, folding her hands on the table in front of her, taking in Hannah's delicate features, her wavy black hair and round, blue eyes. There is something so fragile about her—practically hollow—and Olivia knows that losing her daughter must have affected her deeply, carving away something fundamental from her personality. All of Hannah's decisions—like Olivia's—were likely made from one vantage point: that of being a mother. The times when

Maddie was really ill, teetering on the brink of death, Olivia had often wondered how she would survive without Maddie there as the focus of all her actions, how she would learn to move through the world when her child was no longer there to guide her. She looks at Hannah and sees herself—the childless mother she might have been. It makes her feel as though she already knows Hannah, that in some way, perhaps they are meant to be friends.

"I did," Hannah says. "I used to braid the hair on the horses I grew up riding." She smiles. "I cut it once, too, much to my father's horror. Poor Blackie with his stubby tail."

Olivia laughs. "You grew up on a farm?"

"Yep. In Boise. But both my brother, Isaac, and I moved to Seattle after high school."

"And your husband?"

"I've never been married, actually," Hannah says, visibly flinching.

"Oh, wow," Olivia says, immediately backtracking. "I guess I just assumed . . . because of your daughter. I'm so sorry. I don't usually put my foot in my mouth so much, I swear." *I apologize to James, constantly, too,* Olivia realizes. It's her first line of defense with him—if she is properly penitent, she sometimes can keep his anger in check. This apologetic stance makes her feel ashamed of herself. It also makes her wonder once again what kinds of lessons she is teaching her daughter.

Hannah waves her hand in the air, as though to dismiss her concern. "You couldn't have known. I was engaged once, but it didn't work out and I didn't want to wait around for the 'right' relationship to become a mother. If I had, I never would have had Emily. I used a sperm donor."

Olivia takes a moment to digest this piece of information, thinking how much confidence it must have taken for Hannah to raise a child completely on her own.

The two of them take a few bites before speaking again. "This is wonderful," Olivia says, a little afraid to ask Hannah for details about what happened to her daughter, knowing from her own experience just how overwhelming it can be to discuss anything remotely painful having to do with your child.

"She was hit by a car," Hannah says, as though what Olivia is thinking were written across her face. "I miss her every day." Her bottom lip trembles and she blinks away a few tears. "And I don't talk about it very much because when I do, it feels like it's happening all over again. Most people don't understand that. But with what you went through with Maddie . . . maybe you can."

Olivia sets her fork down and reaches across the table. She squeezes Hannah's hand, her heart aching for the pain she knows Hannah must be in, but also grateful that Hannah feels connected with her, too. "A little bit. We were very lucky to find a donor. A few more days and it would have been too late." Even now, even though Maddie is better, Olivia's throat still thickens when she speaks these words.

Hannah drops her gaze from Olivia's and pulls away, using the tip of her fork to toy with her salad. "Do you know . . ." She trails off, then starts again. "Do they tell you who the donor is?"

"Only general information." Olivia takes a quick sip of water before continuing. "Maddie really struggles with her guilt about that . . . that she lived and the other person didn't.

She's too young to understand that life is rarely balanced or fair." Olivia wonders if she sounds as bitter as she sometimes feels about her life with James. And really, does she *have* a right to be bitter, considering *she's* the one who hasn't left him? She often imagines what other women would say, women who'd never been beaten by their husbands: *I would have walked out the door the minute he raised a hand to me,* they'd claim. *I'd* never *put up with a man who hit me.* Even if your child's life hung in the balance? Olivia would want to ask. Even if you would likely lose custody of your daughter if you tried to walk away? She looks at Hannah, unaccustomed to discussing such intimate details of her life with other women—Waverly and Sara Beth kept everything on the surface, and Olivia tends to do the same. But something about Hannah feels different, and for the first time in years, she feels like she might be able to open up.

"No, it's not fair," Hannah says. She waits a beat, taking a quick sip of her iced tea. "Can you contact them at all? The donor's family?" Olivia flinches this time, and Hannah quickly speaks again. "I'm sorry. You don't have to say."

"That's okay," Olivia says, forcing a small smile. "Yes, we can contact them. But James—my husband—is a very private person. He'd rather we remain anonymous." A familiar pang of guilt strikes Olivia's chest as she thinks about the mother of the girl who saved Maddie's life, how much Olivia wants to thank her for the sacrifice she made. Her eyes fill with tears and she blinks them away.

"Oh," Hannah says, clearly taken aback.

"He only wants to protect us," Olivia hurries to explain, hating that she always feels as though she needs to make excuses for James's behavior. "If I had my way, I'd want to thank the family, for sure, but it's not really worth trying to argue with him, you know? Once he's made up his mind there's not much I can do." Olivia wonders if Hannah can see the anxiety she feels even discussing the possibility of going against her husband's wishes. She thinks back to the night not quite a year ago when James forbade her to send a thank-you to the donor family.

"I won't risk them coming after us for money," he said. "I've worked too long and too hard."

"I don't know why they would," Olivia said, attempting to reason with him.

James rolled over in their bed and gave her a cold look. "Are you saying I'm being paranoid?" Olivia reassured him that of course that wasn't what she was saying, and fortunately, she was a good enough actress that he believed her.

Now, she waits for Hannah to ask her why Olivia wouldn't even attempt to change her husband's mind and wonders how in the world she might respond. But Hannah doesn't ask this; instead, she asks, "How long have you been married?"

"Seventeen years." Olivia says this as though it is a jail sentence. "I met James in my early twenties, before I really even knew myself, I guess. And then we had Maddie so quickly . . ." She trails off, letting Hannah draw her own conclusions about the quality of her marriage. "I actually just registered for college today. Only one class, but I'm planning to get my bachelor's degree in criminal justice." Olivia wants to reel her revelation back in almost immediately, unsure whether she can trust this woman she barely knows.

"Really?" Hannah lifts her thin brows and smiles. "That's wonderful."

"I haven't told James about it yet. We're . . . he's . . ." She takes another deep breath before continuing. "It's complicated. He wouldn't exactly approve. So please . . . if you don't mind keeping it to yourself . . ." Olivia can hear the rising panic in her voice, so she knows Hannah hears it, too. Hannah gives her a puzzled look, as though trying to sort out why Olivia would want to hide this information from her husband. And while it's not like Hannah even *knows* James, like she'd call him up to tattle, Olivia hopes it's clear to her new friend that her going back to school is not something she wants discussed with anyone else. But then Hannah speaks and puts Olivia's fears to rest.

"We all have our secrets," she says. "I promise, yours will be safe with me."

Maddie

On my second day of school, there is a piece of paper stuck to my locker. I grip the strap of my backpack tighter and slow my pace, wondering if someone crafted an image of what they thought a "Franken-babe" might look like and pasted it in the hallway for everyone's amusement. People mill around me, chatting and laughing, totally oblivious to the tears stinging the backs of my eyes. I knew a stupid haircut wouldn't make a difference. I got up an hour early this morning just so I'd have time to style it the way Hannah had shown me; I picked out what I thought was a pretty decent outfit of jeans and loose-fitting blue blouse—I even put on some of my mom's mascara and lip gloss, but none of it matters.

I keep my head down as I take the final few steps to stand in front of my locker. "Excuse me," I murmur to the couple of kids in my way, and finally, as they step aside, I put my shaking fingers on the combination lock and force myself to look up. It's a standard piece of white paper, eight and a half by eleven inches, and on it is a detailed cartoon sketch of a guy who appears to be Noah, kicking himself in the butt. In the corner, written in tiny, chicken-scratch letters is this: *I'll kick my own ass so you don't have to. Sorry for being a jerk. Peace, Noah.* Careful not to tear the paper, I take it off my locker, fold the small bits of tape over the edges, and read the words again.

"You like it?" Noah asks, and I whip my head to the right, realizing that he was hiding around the corner, watching me. Today he wears black skinny jeans and a black T-shirt with the words THINK OUTSIDE OF THE QUADRILATERAL PARALLELO-GRAM beneath the picture of a cube.

"Yeah," I say, nodding. "You're a good artist."

"Thanks." He swishes his bangs out of his eyes and squints at me. "You changed your hair."

I nod again, and he smiles, showing his silver braces. "Nice." He pauses and I'm quiet, too, unsure of what to say. He glances down at the piece of paper in my hands, then looks back to me. "I *am* sorry if I hurt your feelings, you know. I've just never met someone like you."

"Someone like me, how?" I feel my face start to flush, bracing myself for another insult.

"Like, you defied *death*. Which is totally awesome."

I shift my backpack on my shoulder and smile. "I guess I'm just not really used to thinking about it that way." I pause. "Or talking about it with people I don't know. So what you said . . . what you called me . . . it kind of took me by surprise."

"Well, now you know me. And you don't have to talk about it if you don't want to. I just didn't want you walking around thinking I'm a jerk."

"I don't," I say, a little surprised to realize that I mean this. A *real* jerk wouldn't admit he had been one—he would have pasted an *actual* picture of Frankenstein's monster on my locker instead of an apology.

"Cool." The muscles in his face visibly relax. "So, I'll see you in computer science?"

"Oh. Okay." I hadn't noticed him there yesterday, but that probably had to do with me avoiding eye contact with anyone in the room other than the teacher. I glance at the clock on the wall above my row of lockers. "I should probably get to class."

"Yeah, me, too." He stiffens his posture and raises a single hand in a mock salute. "Later," he says, then takes off down the hall. *People make mistakes,* I think, and decide to try and let it go. There have been plenty of times I've said things to my mom that I didn't mean—words pop out of my mouth that I don't even know I'm thinking. I wonder if my dad has ever apologized to Mom for all the times he's said she is stupid or fat; I also wonder if at this point, if he did, would she even be able to forgive him?

After I hung up with Dirk last night, I heard my parents continue to fight in their room. My dad's low, rumbling voice reverberated through the walls. "You coddle her too much," he said. I couldn't hear my mother's response, but I did hear her sharp, strangled cry a moment later. My stomach clenched, certain that he had hit her again.

I don't understand why she lets him treat her this way—why she lies to herself, to *me,* about what he does to her. Knowing he hits her is like carrying a sharp black stone around in my chest. I'm afraid that someday, I'll take too deep a breath and it will slice my already damaged insides to shreds. I'm often torn between wishing my father were dead and being terrified that if I speak up to anyone—if I tell a counselor or call the police—his anger might turn toward me. And then I feel guilty for keeping my mouth shut, like I'm not the kind of person who deserves anything good. I wonder what the parents of the girl who gave me her liver would do if they knew how selfish I am—what lengths I go to in order to protect myself instead of my mother.

Last night, instead of going to help her, I lay on my back in bed with my bottom lip trembling, pulling the covers up to my chin and trying to pretend I didn't hear my mother crying. I stared at the ceiling, remembering when I was eleven and went through a phase of being fascinated with the solar system—entranced by a night sky I was so rarely healthy enough to step outside and see. Mom came home one afternoon with ten packages of those glow-in-the-dark sticky planets and stars. "For your very own universe," she said, then spent the afternoon climbing up and down a ladder, carefully adhering each and every sticker to the ceiling. A woman like her deserves better than my dad.

As I sit through my morning classes, I try not to think too much about my parents. I try to listen to my teachers, but much of what they talk about I already learned from Mrs. Beck last year—I wonder if I can talk to the school counselor about graduating a year early.

I don't see Hailey until I'm in the lunchroom, after I've already stopped by the office and taken my meds. I'm waiting in line for the salad bar when I feel her standing next to me—or rather, I *smell* her—the sickeningly sweet scent of watermelon gum. She's flanked by two other girls, both as pretty as she is, one with wavy brown hair and the other, stick-straight blond.

"Hi, Maddie," Hailey says, popping a bubble inside her mouth with a loud snap. "This is Kyla"—she gestures to the blonde first—"and this is Jade." Both the girls nod at me, and I give a brief bob of my head, too. It seems safer than talking.

Hailey peers at me. "Your hair looks way better."

"Thanks," I say, gripping my tray tightly so it doesn't shake. I hate that smug look on her face, like she's well aware that the only reason I *changed* my hair was what she said to me about it yesterday. She is wearing a short black skirt and tight white sweater. Her legs look like pale stilts.

"I saw you talking to Noah Bedford this morning." She pauses to blow a pink bubble, sucking it back into her mouth before it pops. "You know him?"

"Not really," I say. "I just met him yesterday."

"He's such a *geek,*" Hailey says and then looks at me expectantly. I know I'm supposed to agree with her, but my phone buzzes in my pocket, saving me. I'd turned it to vibrate after I left the office a few minutes ago, in case my mom sent me a text during lunch. There hadn't been any marks on her face this morning, but she moved a little more slowly than usual and I wondered if she had injuries I couldn't see.

"Sorry," I say. "I should check this." Quickly setting my tray on the table next to me, I pull out my cell and see Dirk's name and picture on the screen. "Thinking about you today," his text says. "Hope everything is okay. I'll call you tonight."

Hailey peeks over my shoulder. "Is that your *boyfriend?* He's totally hot."

"Yeah," I say, the lie slipping out before I can stop it. "He's super-smart, too." This part isn't a lie—Dirk didn't go to college; instead, he taught himself everything he knows about computers by hanging out in online, geeked-out chat rooms. He was twenty when he landed his first job at Google, and over the last four years, he moved up from an entry-level position to being one of the top programmers in his department.

"What school does he go to?" Kyla asks, pulling a wisp of hair out of her overly mascaraed eyelashes.

I straighten and pick up my tray again. "He doesn't. He works at Google." I say this proudly, as though I had something to do with it.

"He does *not*," Jade says, rolling her blue eyes. "How old is he?"

"Twenty," I say, thinking this is more plausible than the twenty-four Dirk actually is. "We met online."

Hailey looks skeptical, too. "You're a junior, right? And he's cool with that?"

I shrug again. "It's only four years' difference. If he was twenty-four and I was twenty, no one would care. So it doesn't really matter to us. We just like each other." I'm a little terrified how easily this blatantly false explanation comes to me. Maybe pretending to be Sierra Stone has turned me into a professional liar. Maybe I should become an actress instead of a graphic artist.

"Do your *parents* know?" Kyla asks.

I shake my head. "No *way*. So you can't tell anyone, all right? It's a secret."

All three girls look at each other, as though gauging if they are willing to agree to my request, and then, as soon as Hailey nods, Jade and Kyla do, too, and I know that I may have managed to win them over. Even if I'm not one of them—if my hair isn't perfect and my body is far from lean—they think I have a hot, older boyfriend, and for now, that's all the power I need.

Hannah

On Friday night, Hannah's cell phone rings just as she's locking the front door to the salon. She fumbles for it, worried that it's Olivia, canceling their plans for the evening. After their lunch earlier in the week, Olivia invited Hannah to her house for dinner, and for the first time in months—even if it is for the wrong reasons—Hannah is actually looking forward to something other than going to sleep.

"Hi, honey!" her mother chirps. "Did I get you at a bad time?"

Hannah wedges the phone between her shoulder and ear as she makes her way to her car. "I'm just locking up," she says. "And I'm on my way to a friend's house for dinner." *Friend might not be the exact right term,* she thinks. But what else should she call Olivia? She wants to tell Olivia about her suspicions of who they are to each other—she knows she *has* to—but she doesn't know how. She's worried now, too, considering that Olivia said James doesn't want any contact with the donor family. The way Olivia talked about him, Hannah got the distinct impression that James's word was pretty much law in the Bell household, and she wonders what would happen if Olivia went against it. Hannah doesn't want to do anything that might put Olivia in a bad place with her husband, so until she's absolutely positive Emily was Maddie's liver donor, she's decided to keep her mouth shut.

"How nice!" her mother says, sounding as enthused as she might have if Hannah had just told her she won the lottery. "I won't keep you long. I just want to know if we'll see you for Thanksgiving this year."

Leave it to her mother to be planning a holiday meal almost three months ahead of time. "I'm not sure yet. I'll have to see how busy things get at the salon." Hannah climbs into her car and starts the engine, slipping her earpiece on so she can continue their conversation while she drives. "Is Isaac planning to come?" She feels like the only way she'll survive the holiday with her parents is having the protective layer of her brother there, too.

"Oh, you know your brother. It's always last minute with him." There is a melancholy edge to her mother's voice, and immediately, Hannah slips into an all too familiar sense of I'm-a-bad-daughter guilt for living so far away from her parents. She thinks about how much she misses Emily—how it feels as though there is a gaping, aching hole in her life—and she wonders if, even though she and Isaac are still alive, her mother feels the same way when they both can't wait to escape the confines of the farm. She has always seemed supportive of their decisions and proud of their accomplishments, but Hannah knows all too well that parents often wear a mask to protect their children from how they really feel.

"I'll try to make it work, okay, Mom? I promise." Hannah slowly backs out of her driveway, more of a cautious driver than she ever was before Emily's accident. It took her almost a month after the funeral to be able to get behind the wheel of a car, and now, she tends to ride her brakes and take corners in slow motion.

"Okay, honey. Thank you." Her mom pauses a moment to clear her throat. "So, your father had his yearly checkup the other day."

"Is everything okay?"

"Well, mostly. His blood pressure is a little elevated and his cholesterol levels could be better. Dr. Warren thinks he needs to slow down. That he shouldn't be doing this much heavy labor at his age." She pauses again, for effect. "I told him we've asked you to move home to help out, but it doesn't look like that's going to happen anytime soon."

"God, Mom." As though Hannah isn't already feeling guilty enough.

"What? I'm simply telling you about my conversation with your father's doctor."

"Uh-huh." Hannah leaves her response at this, knowing the more she engages her mother on this subject, the more her mother will push.

"Who are you having dinner with?" her mother asks brightly, apparently satisfied that she's accomplished whatever she meant to with the story about her father's checkup.

"Just a woman I met at the salon," Hannah says, thinking the fewer details she gives, the better. Even over the phone, her mom has a way of sniffing out when Hannah is hiding something. "We hit it off and she invited me over."

"Well, I think it's wonderful you're making new friends."
Hannah hears her father's voice in the background, and then
her mother speaks again. "Dad sends his love, honey. Call me
soon, okay?"

"Okay," Hannah says, grateful to hang up. As she drives
along, the guilt Hannah felt during the phone call nags at her.
She worries that she is being too selfish. If her parents did lose
their farm, would she be able to live with her decision to stay
in Seattle? She isn't sure that she could. Now that the second
salon is up and running, could she find a way to make living back
in Boise work? Maybe she could let herself be lulled into the
simplicity of planting a garden and watching it grow. She loved
helping her parents when she was a child—riding on the tractor
with her dad and pulling weeds with her mother—but as soon as
she turned fourteen, all she could think about was a life beyond
digging her hands in the dirt, a life without the constant scent
of manure in the air. For years she was happy—happy living in
Seattle with Emily, happy with her career and being a mother.
But now that Emily is gone and Isaac still traveling so much, is
there really anything keeping her here? Sophie could easily buy
out Hannah's interest in their business and run both salons, then
Hannah could put the profits from the sale into the farm. She
could lose herself in learning how to manage a new business, just
as she lost herself in the renovation. She could keep her parents
happy and her mind busy. She could keep her grief at bay.

Her GPS spouts off navigation instructions to Olivia's Me-
dina address, interrupting her thoughts. Hannah takes several
deep breaths, trying to prepare herself for the evening. She's
a little concerned she might say something to give herself
away—that she might mention Emily's real age or the fact that

her daughter was an organ donor. She promises herself that once she is certain, one way or the other, she'll tell them the truth.

"Your destination is on the right," Hannah's GPS informs her as she pulls up to a tall, black iron gate and presses a blue button on the wall, as Olivia instructed.

"You made it!" Olivia's voice comes through the speaker, and the gates slowly begin to swing open. Part of Hannah wants to turn her car around and make a run for it. She shouldn't be here. She shouldn't be doing this. But the other, more desperate part of her convinces her to stay.

"I did," Hannah says, placing her hands directly on ten and two on the steering wheel.

"I'll see you in a minute," Olivia says, and Hannah pulls through the gate and tries not to gasp at what she sees. The house rises atop perfectly manicured grounds—a red-brick mansion better suited for an English moor than the Eastside of Seattle. There is a huge fountain in the center of the circular driveway and a vast collection of giant rosebushes in front of the house. Hannah suddenly wishes she'd taken the time to wash her dingy blue Honda, and that she'd picked out a better outfit than jeans and a faded black sweater. She turns off the engine and stares at the front door, wondering if she shouldn't just sit Olivia down the minute she walks inside and tell her the truth, but then Olivia appears on the porch, wearing jeans and a poet-style white blouse. She looks happy to see Hannah.

"Hey, there," Hannah says, smiling as she climbs out of her car. "I think you might need a nicer house. This place is clearly bringing down property value in the neighborhood."

Olivia laughs. "I know, right? When James first brought me

here, I felt like I should have worn a ball gown. Or remembered to shave my legs, at least." She trots down the steps and walks over to Hannah's car, giving her a quick hug. "I'm so glad you're here."

"Me, too," Hannah says with what feels like a somewhat shaky smile.

Olivia loops her arm through Hannah's and they make their way inside. "By the way, James's business trip got cut short so he's here. He can't wait to meet you," she says, but the high-pitched trill of her voice makes Hannah think this might not be exactly true. She suddenly feels anxious about meeting him.

"Let me go get Maddie," Olivia says. "I can't seem to get that girl off the computer lately. Or the phone."

"That's like most teenagers . . . isn't it?" Hannah asks, knowing full well that Emily would have spent entire days online or texting if Hannah had allowed it.

"I suppose so," Olivia says, putting her hand on the end of the curved railing that edges the stairway. "I guess I was just hoping once she got out of the hospital she would want to spend time with real people instead of imaginary ones." She sighs. "Wishful thinking, I suppose . . . I'll be right back."

She runs up the stairs, and Hannah takes a moment to let her eyes wander over the subtle elegance of the entryway. She feels dwarfed by its vaulted ceilings and elaborate crystal chandelier, and she wonders if the gold-framed Van Gogh *The Starry Night* hanging on the wall is an original.

"You must be Hannah." A man's resonant voice jolts Hannah out of her thoughts, and she looks up to face James Bell standing about ten feet away from her. He is taller than she thought he'd be, well over six feet, broad shouldered, and unlike in most of the pictures she has seen of him online, his hair is definitely more salt than pepper. He wears Levi's, a wrinkle-free, short-sleeved blue linen shirt, and no shoes. His bare feet throw Hannah a bit—she imagined him as always fully dressed, topped off by coordinating belts and expensive Italian loafers.

"I am," she says, smiling. "It's nice to meet you."

"You, too." He takes a step toward her and holds out his hand, which she shakes. His skin is cool, and she shivers not because of that but because of the appraising look he gives her. She suddenly feels as though she's too tall, too plain, too flat chested.

"So . . . you're the magician who transformed my Maddie into a woman?"

Hannah hesitates before answering what seems more like an accusation than a question. Does James not like Maddie's new hair color and style? "I'd say at sixteen, she's still very much a *young* woman," Hannah finally says. "But yes, that's me."

James bobs his head once, as though satisfied with her response, and Hannah wonders if she's passed some kind of test. "I wasn't supposed to be home from San Francisco until much later tonight," he says, "but my dinner meeting was canceled so I caught an earlier flight. What a surprise to learn you were coming over." He pauses to give her another look loaded with some kind of meaning—what kind, Hannah isn't sure. She holds his gaze, though, feeling like they are in some weird game of chicken—whoever blinks first, loses. She doesn't blink.

"A bad surprise?" she asks evenly.

"Not at all." He pauses. "You've made quite the impression on my wife. Maddie, too."

"A good one, I hope." Hannah gets the feeling that James wants her to bow to him somehow, to thank him for honoring her with his presence. She guesses he's the kind of man who needs a lot of adulation, and all other matters aside, this is reason enough not to like him.

"It's a beautiful night," he says, not commenting on what kind of impression she's made on his wife and daughter. "Shall we go sit on the patio?"

"Sure," Hannah says, following him through an ornate dining room and already wide-open French doors. The backyard is as beautiful as the front, every shrub and clump of flowers expertly arranged, the lawn lush and closely clipped. James gestures for her to sit in one of the padded Adirondack chairs, and she complies. "Can I get you a drink?" he asks. "A cocktail or some wine?" He steps behind an outdoor bar, where there is already a half-gone martini resting on the counter. Maybe that explains the slightly glassy look in his eyes.

"No, thank you," Hannah says. Her nerves are jittery enough that she'd love a drink to take the edge off, but she knows she needs to keep her head clear so she doesn't end up saying something she'll regret. She needs to stay in control. "I'd love some iced tea, though, if it's not too much trouble."

"Not at all," he says and quickly brings her a glass with a wedge of lemon on the side, carrying his drink in the other hand. He sits down next to Hannah, uncomfortably close, but she doesn't want to offend him, so she doesn't scoot away. She wonders if this is part of his professional success, creating the subtle illusion of power over his business rivals by invading their personal space.

She experiences a brief moment of panic that perhaps James

is acting like this with her because he already knows who she is. Does someone with his kind of power have the connections to unseal confidential medical records?

He looks her over again, this time more slowly, and again, Hannah feels uncomfortable. "My wife says you live above your salon in an apartment?" He says this like it couldn't possibly be true.

"I do. It was easier to oversee the renovation that way. The whole place needed to be gutted, so my contractors did the apartment first, then tackled the downstairs." Hannah remembers how, at Isaac's request, Carl and his crew quickly transformed what had been a three-bedroom second story of the house into what is now a cozy, five-hundred-square-foot studio. She guesses from this line of questioning that James doesn't like his wife making friends with women not already in their social circle—that she has to somehow earn his approval. She also gets the impression that this is likely an impossible task.

"Ah, a businesswoman who likes control over her projects." He gives her a pointed look. "Am I right?"

Hannah cocks her head at him. "If you mean I like to make sure things are done correctly, then yes. But I also think it's important to trust the people I hire to do their job."

"You're a better boss than me, then," James says with a low chuckle and takes a sip of his drink. "Olivia also tells me you've never been married."

"That's right." Hannah holds her breath, waiting for him to bring up Emily next. But he doesn't.

"Are you not interested in the institution?" he asks, setting his glass on the table and staring at her with bright green eyes.

"Or are you just picky?" He smiles as though he is joking, but there is a hint of mockery in his voice. He strikes her as the kind of man who thinks that women who choose to be single are either man-haters or lesbians, and Hannah briefly toys with the idea of telling him she's both, just to mess with his head, even though she's neither.

"God, Dad," Maddie says, as she and Olivia join them on the patio. "Leave poor Hannah alone. So she's not married. Who *cares*?"

Hannah stiffens a bit, certain Maddie's challenging her father will lead to some sort of immediate parental backlash, but James only chuckles. "I was just making conversation with our new friend." He looks at Olivia, who remains silent, and then back at Hannah. "Right, Hannah?"

Before Hannah can respond, Maddie flops down in the chair next to her and slings one leg up and over the armrest. "Please. You were interrogating her." She looks at Hannah. "Ignore him, okay? He thinks that every woman needs a man to be happy."

"And you think I haven't heard you on the phone this week, giggling?" James asks his daughter, but there is a teasing edge in his voice. "You think I don't know you're talking to a *boy*?" Maddie blushes, and she drops her gaze to the ground. "Aha!" James continues, triumphantly. "I thought so. What's his name? Do we know his family?"

"James, honey," Olivia finally says, though her voice is muted, less bubbly than it is when she speaks to Hannah. She sounds like Hannah used to when she attempted to talk Emily down from an impending tantrum—placating and vaguely pleading. "We have a guest. Maybe we should talk about this later."

"Maybe we should talk about it *now*," James says to his wife, and though on the surface, his tone seems playful, Hannah can hear the condescension shadowing the words. Olivia cringes and looks at the ground. *No wonder she keeps secrets from him,* Hannah thinks. She can only imagine what might happen if Olivia said something James didn't want to hear.

"His name is Noah," Maddie says, quietly. "And he's just someone I met at school. We have a class together. That's all." She looks at her father with a strange light in her eyes. "You wanted me to make friends, didn't you? Isn't that why you made me go there?"

"Maddie," Olivia begins, but James holds up a hand to cut her off. "And what is Noah's last name?" he asks, ignoring his daughter's questions.

"Bedford," Maddie answers, and James smiles. "I know his father," he says. "Good man. Real estate investor."

"What's your favorite subject?" Hannah asks Maddie, hoping to rescue her from her father's focus. Maddie seems more willing to challenge her father than Olivia is, though there is still a hint of fear in her face when she speaks to him. Hannah wonders if she keeps secrets from her father, too. And maybe more important, what secrets *he* might be keeping from *them*.

"Math and computer science, definitely," Maddie says. "I think I might want to get into computer programming. Or digital graphic arts."

"Like CGI for movies, you mean?" Hannah asks, but James interrupts before Maddie can respond.

"Maddie has always had a fascination with technology."

"Dad . . ." Maddie begins, but James interrupts her.

"No, honey. It's true. Remember when you were five and snuck my cell phone out of my briefcase and tried to take it apart to see how it worked?"

Maddie grins and looks at Hannah. "I thought he was going to be mad at me, but instead he took it to work to brag to his friends about what I'd done. Of course, I couldn't put it back together."

James laughs, and Hannah smiles, happy to see that he has a softer side—at least, when it comes to Maddie.

"I'm sorry about the loss of your daughter, Hannah," James says quietly. "A car accident, I understand?"

Hannah snaps to attention, once again panicked. "That's right," she says, making sure to keep her voice steady.

"James, honey," Olivia says. "I'm sure Hannah doesn't want talk about that right now."

Talk about what, exactly? Hannah wonders. What in the hell had she been thinking, coming here like this? What was she expecting to happen? The truth is that she genuinely likes Olivia and Maddie and wants to spend more time with them. Yes, there is the possibility of them being linked through Emily, but even without that, Hannah would want to get to know them better. She decides to focus on that, and nothing else.

"I'm just expressing my condolences, Liv," James responds.

"Thank you, James," Hannah says. "Like I told Olivia, I'm not really comfortable talking about the details, but I do appreciate your kind thoughts."

"See that?" he says, turning to Olivia, who nods in submission. "How's dinner coming along?"

"Almost ready, I think," Olivia says, flashing him a toothy smile that matches his own. Their gestures appear false to

Hannah like *Here, look at us, gleefully smiling at each other.* Olivia glances at Hannah. "Will you excuse me a minute? I should check the temperature on the roast."

Hannah rises from her seat. "Let me help you," she says, leaving Maddie in the company of her father. She follows Olivia through the dining room into the elaborate kitchen, which is full of restaurant-size stainless-steel appliances and an eight-burner stove. And even though the garlicky aroma of roasted meat wafts through the air and several pots simmer on the stove, the space is immaculate, not a splatter of sauce or bread crumb to be found. "Your house is spotless," Hannah says.

"James likes things clean," Olivia says with a small shrug.

I'll bet he does, Hannah thinks as she slides onto one of the barstools at the marble-topped breakfast bar. *I'll bet he runs his fingers over the top shelves, looking for dust.*

Olivia reaches into a drawer and rifles around until she pulls out an electronic meat thermometer. "I'm sorry if he made you uncomfortable." She opens the oven and slips the metal prong into an enormous prime rib roast, then turns to look at Hannah. "He can be a little direct."

"That's okay," she says, thinking "direct" is a polite way to say "rude." She wants to ask what's really beneath James's smooth exterior, but instead she asks about Maddie. "So, if she's already talking to a boy, things must have gone better for Maddie the rest of the week at school?"

"I think it was the hair," Olivia says, seemingly relieved that Hannah has abandoned the topic of her husband. "Or at least, how she felt after getting it done. Thank you, again, for that."

"Just doing my job," Hannah says. "And it was my pleasure."

Despite the brief moment of apprehension she felt when Maddie first sat in her chair, Hannah realizes this is the truth. She sees a bit of her daughter in Maddie—not in a weird, Maddie-might-be-possessed-by-Emily's-soul kind of way, but rather, in the way Maddie projects a sense of fragility laced through with defiance—the lift of her chin when she challenged her father a few minutes ago, but also, the way it trembled.

Olivia removes the thermometer, grabs a pair of oven mitts, and pulls the roast from the oven, setting it on the counter to rest. "I imagine that being around her isn't the easiest thing for you." She takes a sheet of foil and tucks it around the meat, then turns her gaze to Hannah, her palms resting flat on the counter in front of her. She looks a little shaky, and Hannah wonders why.

"The years when Maddie was so sick," Olivia continues, "when she couldn't even get out of bed to go to the bathroom, seeing other children in the park or just walking down the street was sheer torture. I resented their health, the way their mothers just seemed to take for granted the fact that they could run and jump and play." She sighs. "And then when we came so close to losing her, I thought about how if we did, I'd never want to see another little girl again. How hard it would be."

Hannah grips the edge of her stool, just as she had gripped the edge of her chair in the waiting room of the ER last year, desperate for Emily to survive. "It's not always easy," she says in a ragged voice, then clears her throat. "Maddie is the first one I've spent any time with, really, but she's older than Emily was." She waits a beat, wondering just how much she should share about how she feels, but then the truth comes tumbling out. "But they're everywhere, you know? I can't avoid them.

I'll be jogging and see a little girl with black hair and skinny arms and think she's Emily. And then my heart will just stop. It literally skips a beat. For an instant, I'll think the doctors were wrong—that they made a mistake and it *wasn't* Emily who died." Her bottom lip quivers as she gives Olivia a wan smile. "Ridiculous, right?"

Olivia shakes her head. "Not at all." She walks around the island in the center of the kitchen, joins Hannah at the breakfast bar, and takes her hand. Hannah holds her breath, waiting for her to say something about the mother of the child who saved Maddie—she wants Olivia to be the one who brings the subject up—but then Maddie enters the room.

"I think Dad's head is going to *explode* if he doesn't have dinner soon," Maddie says, stopping short when she sees Hannah and Olivia holding hands. "Is everything okay?"

"Everything's fine," Hannah says, pulling her hand back to her own lap. "Your mom and I were just talking about how great your hair looks. And I *love* your outfit." Maddie is wearing black leggings, which flatter her thinner limbs, and a lace-edged, Kelly-green peasant blouse, which camouflages her thicker middle and brings out the color of her eyes. "It's very hippie-chic."

"Mom took me shopping this afternoon," Maddie says, rocking from her heels to her toes and back again, clearly pleased by the compliment. "The woman at Macy's was *way* helpful in picking things out. I basically got a whole new wardrobe."

"A new wardrobe for your new life," Olivia says, and Hannah can't help but feel a biting twinge of grief in her chest. *A life Emily might have made possible,* she thinks. After meeting James tonight, she's become even more determined not to share her suspicion about their families' possible connection unless she's absolutely positive she's right. Then it can be Olivia's decision to tell James or if, in the end, she'll just have one more secret to keep.

Olivia

On Monday morning, James brings Olivia breakfast in bed. "Wake up, beautiful," he says as he sets a tray on the bed next to her. "The breakfast fairy has been hard at work."

"What's all this for?" she asks as she braces her arms behind her and uses them to push herself up into a sitting position. A glance at the clock tells her it's six thirty—she slept through her alarm, and she can hear the water running in Maddie's bathroom.

James takes the napkin and sets it carefully across Olivia's lap. "Do I need a reason to spoil my wife?" He moves the tray over her legs and lifts up a cup of coffee for her to take from him. "Two Splendas, no milk. Right?"

Olivia smiles and gently retrieves the white mug from his hands. "Right." She takes a small sip and gives him another smile. "And of course you don't need a reason. Thank you, honey." She wishes she could just accept this loving gesture from her husband at face value, the way she used to, instead of wondering what his motives might be.

"You're welcome," he says as he picks up the fork and scoots a bite of scrambled egg whites onto its tines. "It's the least I can do for my amazing wife." He hands her the fork, watching as she chews. "Good?"

"Very," Olivia says, nodding.

"I was thinking we should all take a cooking class together. Maybe Thai food, since Maddie loves it so much."

Olivia sets her fork onto her plate and sips at her coffee. "Really? You could find the time?"

James nods. "It might not be until the first of the year, after the fourth quarter numbers come in, but it would be fun, don't you think?"

Olivia nods, and James leans over to give her a kiss. "I have to go," he whispers against her lips. "But I'll be back."

"I'll be front," Olivia jokes, and he laughs. A few minutes later, he heads to the office, and even though she knows better, even though she's been through this with him a hundred times before, Olivia can't help but wonder if she really needs to leave him after all.

A few minutes before ten o'clock, after dropping Maddie off at school, Olivia walks into her criminology class with her belly squirming. She wonders if this is how Maddie felt her first day at Eastside Prep, twitchy and insecure, wishing she could melt right into the floor. The room buzzes with the low hum of conversation, punctuated by the occasional squeals of girls closer to Maddie's age than to Olivia's. Eyeing the boys wearing jeans that ride low on their skinny hips, exposing the tops of their boxers, she has to squelch the motherly urge to tell them to pull up their pants.

What the hell am I doing *here?* Olivia thinks as her fellow students file through the wide double doors and into their seats in Whitaker Hall, practically carrying her along with them. *James was so sweet to me this morning. Do I really need to go through with this?* She clutches the strap of her purse, thinking she should probably just make a run for it. James might call her and she wouldn't answer, and then what would she do? *Tell him you were swimming at the athletic club,* she thinks, trying to calm herself down. *Tell him you were vacuuming or taking a shower. Tell him whatever you have to. This is your plan. You need an education. You won't be able to take care of yourself or Maddie without one. He may have been sweet to you this morning, but you know all too well how quickly that can change. You can't back out now.*

Her phone vibrates in her bag and she jumps at the sound, wondering if it's possible she's just manifested a checkup call from her husband. But then she looks at the screen and sees a text message from Hannah, wishing her good luck. "Thanks," Olivia quickly responds. "I'm scared as hell." A moment later Hannah answers: "Don't be. If you need a cover story, just say you were with me. I've got your back." Olivia smiles, then quickly deletes the messages, in case James decides to do a random check on her phone. She knows he wasn't crazy about Hannah, though once dinner was on the table Friday night, he'd been nothing but the most charming, animated version of himself. It wasn't until later, after Hannah had gone home and Maddie was ensconced in her room, that he told Olivia how he really felt.

"She's very guarded," James said as they got ready for bed. "And how successful can she really be if she's living in an apartment above her salon?" He leaned over the counter to peer closely in the mirror, then plucked a few stray eyebrow hairs with his fingers.

"She owns a house, too," Olivia explained, crossing her arms over her chest and resting her shoulder on the threshold of his bathroom, hating that her husband measured a person's worth by their level of wealth. "She just had a hard time living there after her daughter died, so she rents it out. Too many memories."

"That's another thing," James said, straightening, then staring hard at her in the mirror. "She barely mentioned her daughter the entire night. Don't you think that's strange?"

"No, I don't." Olivia took a measured breath, knowing she was walking a fine line with him by defending her new friend. "She's grieving, James. Talking about it—especially with someone she's just met—is probably like digging around in an open wound." And then, because she couldn't help but try to drive her point home, she continued. "You don't like to talk about how your father beat you . . . right? How your mother let him? When feeling our pain is too much to handle, we push it down. It's human nature."

He turned around slowly, and Olivia braced herself, thinking he might lunge at her, but he only stared, his green eyes wide and disbelieving that she had the nerve to challenge him. "And what are *you* pushing down, O-li-vi-a?" He spaced out her name into four distinct syllables, and his tone was shot through with contempt. He wanted her to say that she didn't *have* any pain, that her life with him was one beyond her happiest, wildest dreams. But Olivia only stared back at him, unwilling to give him what he wanted. She held her breath—it was dangerous to defy him like this, knowing how deeply her silence would offend him.

Finally, he blinked, and shook his head. "Just be careful," he said. "I don't trust her."

You don't trust anyone, Olivia thought, and now, as she slides into a seat in the last row of the auditorium, she wonders if Hannah picked up on how James felt about her, and if she senses the real reason why Olivia needs someone to have her back with her own husband. It's a little odd that Hannah is willing to lie for Olivia when they barely know each other, but it has been so long since Olivia felt like she had anyone on her side, she decides not to question Hannah's motives. It feels too good to have a friend.

"Hi!" a young woman chirps as she slides in next to Olivia. "This seat isn't taken, is it?" She is a tiny thing with almost white-blond hair and pale blue eyes—more like the negative image of a picture than an actual girl. She wears a light blue broomstick skirt and a snug matching T-shirt. When she lifts her arms over her head to take off the book bag that is slung crosswise over her chest, Olivia sees a quick flash of her flawless pale stomach, and she can't help but think of the thick, red scar across her own daughter's flesh.

"Nope," Olivia says. "It's all yours."

"Thanks!" The girl plops down next to her and drops her bag to the floor in between her legs, quickly pulling out a small laptop and placing it, along with her cell phone, on the half desk in front of her. She presses a button to boot up the laptop, and suddenly, Olivia is embarrassed by the three-ringed notebook she bought at the campus bookstore. She glances around the room to see that the majority of students are sporting shiny silver netbooks or iPads. Apparently, the method for taking notes has changed since Olivia last went to school. She suddenly feels very, very old.

"Do you know anything about this professor?" the girl asks, keeping her eyes on the screen of her phone, rapidly tapping out what Olivia assumes is a text message.

"I don't," Olivia answers. It amazes her, how many technological tasks teenagers are able to juggle simultaneously. Maddie doesn't watch television unless her laptop is in front of her, too, or she's playing Angry Birds on her phone. She's always plugged into *something*—usually two or three things at a time. There doesn't seem to be a nonstimulated moment, a chance for her brain to breathe. It worries Olivia sometimes, that Maddie spends so much time interacting with what *other* people's imaginations have dreamed up that she'll never learn to imagine things on her own.

"I've heard she used to be a cop and is kind of a badass." The girl glances away from her phone and looks at Olivia. Her eyelashes are so pale, they're almost invisible. "I'm Natalie."

Olivia introduces herself, too, and just as she speaks her name, a short, broadly built woman enters from the side door of the auditorium. She charges up the steps to the stage and makes her way over to the podium, moving with a decided swagger—a don't-mess-with-me swing of her shoulders and hips. She wears black slacks and a blue button-down shirt with thick-soled, no-nonsense black shoes. Her blond hair is pulled tightly into a bun at the base of her neck, and as far as Olivia can tell, she's not wearing a stitch of makeup. She *looks* like a cop—hard and unyielding. *Maybe Natalie's right.*

"Hello?" she says, then blows into the microphone. "Is this thing on?" The chatter in the auditorium continues, ignoring her question, and so she leans closer to the microphone and opens her mouth again. *"SIT!"* she bellows. This unexpected noise causes Olivia to jump and all the conversation and movement in the room to cease.

"Holy *shit*," Natalie says under her breath as the rest of the students silently find their seats.

Satisfied, the professor smiles—a beautiful movement that suddenly makes her appear warm and thoughtful instead of hard shelled and rough. "I'm Regina Lang," she continues in a pleasant, normal tone. "Please call me Professor Lang or Regina. Mrs. Lang is my mother." Everyone titters appropriately at her joke, and she goes on. "If you're not supposed to be in Criminology 201, you should leave now. Otherwise, let's get started." She flips open a laptop in front of her, and a large theater screen behind her lights up with an image of a man choking a woman. His fingers are wrapped tightly around her neck, and he is grimacing, the muscles in his arms straining beneath his skin in ropy cords. The woman's face is red and her eyes are bulging, her hands tear at the man's wrists, seemingly trying to get him to release her. And even though Olivia knows these people have to be actors—the picture can't be real—her muscles immediately go rigid. *Is that what I looked like ten years ago?* she wonders. *Before Maddie got sick . . . the night I first decided I needed to leave James?* She pushes those thoughts down, trying to breathe, wanting to hear what Regina says next.

"I want you to think about what you would do if you were this man's lawyer," Professor Lang begins. "If this scene is what the police walked in on after a neighbor called 911 and the woman in the picture decided to press charges against her husband for attempted murder." She pauses. "Is there any defense for this man? If there are pictures of his finger marks around his wife's neck? If she has years of hospital records listing numerous broken bones—spiral fractures of her forearms, a shattered cheekbone?"

"He's indefensible," a girl's prim voice pops up from somewhere in the auditorium. "And she's an idiot for not reporting it sooner."

Her words make Olivia feel ill. She leans forward, arms over her stomach, and Natalie puts a hand on her back. "Hey, are you okay?" she asks, and Olivia straightens. "I'm fine," she whispers. "I just didn't have breakfast."

Natalie reaches into her bag and pulls out a cereal bar—the kind Maddie can't eat because of her celiac disease. Olivia gives Natalie a brief smile and thanks her, taking the bar, even though she doesn't think she can eat it. She turns her attention back to what Professor Lang is saying to the girl who called the woman in the picture an idiot.

"And what do you base your judgment of this woman upon?" Professor Lang's expression is blank, and Olivia can't tell if she agrees with the girl's proclamation or not. "Do you know her? Do you understand there are a hundred possible reasons why she might not have reported her husband's abuse?" She pauses, runs her gaze over all the students. "Anyone want to hazard a guess at a reason?"

"Maybe he's threatened to take custody away from her," Olivia says loudly, unsure why, exactly, she speaks up, but that it likely has to do with the fact that Regina seems to understand something Olivia thought no one else could. "Maybe he's extremely powerful and respected in the community. She knows if she presses charges against him, he'll find a way to prove her unfit and she'll lose her children."

Professor Lang peers at the back row, making a visor out of her hand. "Can you say that again, please? It's a large room, and I don't think everyone caught it."

Olivia takes a deep breath before repeating herself, and is ridiculously pleased when the professor nods in agreement. "That's right. People tend to have this image of abused women as weak, low income, and uneducated, when in fact, the opposite is often true. Many women stay because their husbands are upstanding, successful men and they think no one will believe them if they tell the truth about what's going on behind closed doors. Abusers are expert manipulators—of their victims and everyone else in their lives." She pauses, moving her gaze over the room. "But here's my point—and the reason I opened class with this particular picture. If you feel like you can make a case to defend the husband, then you should think about focusing your studies on defense law. If your heart aches at the plight of the wife and you feel like you sort of want to tear the husband's eyes out, you might do better in prosecution. I use the picture to show you how polarizing legal issues can be, and how varied and muddy our individual reactions are, too. We're all shaded by our personal experiences and perceptions. That's the most difficult aspect of working in the legal system, whether you are a cop, lawyer, or judge. Staying neutral, relying on process and procedure to do its job, can seem impossible. And yet, if you remain in this program, you'll need to learn how."

The room is silent again, everyone seeming to allow her words to sink in, and for the rest of the class, during which Professor Lang goes over the syllabus and discusses the literal definitions of *probable cause,* Olivia is haunted by the image of that woman on the screen. She wonders if becoming a lawyer is really such a good idea, considering her life with James. Would she be better off prosecuting the men who abuse their partners, or defending the women who sometimes snap and kill them? Will she be too close to the issues involved to do her job? When she was younger and working as a paralegal, she'd always imagined herself as a defense lawyer, researching case law to vindicate her wrongly accused clients. But what would she do if her client were guilty—if he wrapped his fingers around his wife's throat and squeezed until she was almost dead? She isn't sure if she could defend a man like that now. She's afraid she might just shoot him instead.

These questions concern her deeply enough that after class ends, Olivia works up the courage to approach her professor on the stage. She waits as the other students talk with her then walk away—she doesn't want anyone else to overhear her. When the last of the other students is gone, Professor Lang looks up and smiles at Olivia. "Ah, a grown-up. What can I do for you . . . ?" She trails off, waiting to hear Olivia's name.

Olivia introduces herself, then shifts her weight from foot to foot, gripping the straps on her shoulder bag, as though this might keep her from running away. "Well," she begins, haltingly. "I was hoping I could ask you about a hypothetical situation."

"Of course," Professor Lang says, tilting her head toward one shoulder, slipping both hands into the pockets on her slacks, then rocking forward and back, toe to heel.

"Great-okay-thanks," Olivia says, hurriedly, squeezing the

words together so that they almost come out as one. "I'm wondering . . . what if you had a student who is interested in the law, but she's not sure if she would be a good candidate for becoming a lawyer."

"Why not?" Again, Olivia can't tell what her professor is really thinking from the expression on her face—it's careful and measured, something she must have learned from her years on the police force. She confirmed her previous career during her lecture, citing a back injury for her early retirement from the force and subsequent switch to teaching.

Olivia swallows to help wet the case of dry mouth she's suddenly developed. "Maybe she's had some trauma in her life," she says quietly, not making eye contact with her new teacher. "And she's worried she'd be too personally influenced by this to do a good job . . . as a defense lawyer *or* a prosecutor." She pauses, finally looking up. "Do you have any advice I could pass along?"

Professor Lang blows out a quick shot of air from between pursed lips before speaking. "Well, that depends. What kind of trauma are we talking about?"

Olivia hesitates, unsure how close she should keep her hypothetical situation to the truth. "Let's say she's been attacked. More than once."

"Like raped?"

Olivia's face burns and her stomach twists at the sound of this word. She's struck silent by images of James on top of her after he's hit her—after she's told him no over and over again—pushing himself into her anyway, like he is jabbing her body with a knife. *Is it rape when your husband tells you he's only doing it to show you he's sorry?*

She bobs her head, trying to keep her expression clear of the revulsion she feels. "Yes," she finally says. "And beaten." She thought she could do this without falling apart. She thought if she made it seem like it happens to an imaginary woman, she wouldn't give herself away. Professor Lang's expression—blond brows stitched together, the deep curve of a concerned frown—tells her different. She knows Olivia is talking about herself.

"I would tell her that she needs to get serious professional help before she makes any kind of commitment to this career path. Or any other, for that matter. Things come up when you're trying cases . . . triggers that spark all sorts of weird emotional baggage. Victims of abuse can sometimes turn their past suffering into motivation to help other people, but only if they've dealt with it on the deepest levels." She gives Olivia a good, long look. "Even then, it's a challenge for them to work within a system that betrays them more often than not."

All Olivia can manage to say is "Oh." She is reeling—not only from the images of James swirling in her head but from the realization that if she ever leaves her husband, if she ever works up the courage to confess how he treats her, she won't be seen as the woman who nobly endured years of abuse in order to protect her daughter—she'll be seen as a victim. The idiot woman who let her husband beat her. Who let him rape her and never said a word to anyone. Shame burns through Olivia's body, making her feel ashy and weak. She suddenly wants nothing more than to escape this room. What the hell was she thinking, talking to her professor about this?

"Does that help any?" Professor Lang asks.

"I think so," Olivia says, forcing a weak smile. Yes, it helps.

It helps Olivia realize that she's made a huge mistake, attending this class. And another mistake, talking to her teacher. "Thanks for your time. I appreciate it."

"That's why I'm here." Her professor closes up her laptop and slides it into a carrying case, then looks at Olivia again. "It was you, right?"

"Me?" The word barely squeaks out of Olivia. *Is she going to make me admit what James does to me? Oh god. I'm so stupid.*

Her professor nods. "Right. You spoke up in the back row, at the beginning of class?"

Relieved this is what Professor Lang wants to know, Olivia bobs her head, once, and turns, ready to walk away, but then her teacher stops her with a hand on her arm. "A person like that could talk with me anytime she wants . . . okay? I can help." She pauses and gives Olivia another look that leaves no doubt she sees right through her. "My hypothetical door's always open."

Olivia pulls away, feeling her professor's eyes on her back as she leaves the auditorium. She walks quickly to her car, knowing she needs to get home, and suddenly, no matter how hard she fights them, she's unable to stop the memories she pushed down earlier from tumbling through her mind—the image of that night ten years ago, the first time James put his hands around her neck and took her breath away.

Maddie

I was six the first time I saw marks on my mother's skin. I hadn't been diagnosed with my liver disorder yet, so I was like any little girl—I went to school and played with other kids at the park. I still spent a lot of time with my mom, though, because my dad was at the office more than he was home.

"He has to work hard to take care of us," Mom told me when I asked why Dad wasn't going to come to my dance recital like he'd promised he would. I was going to be a purple flower and I wanted my daddy to see it. I was going to do the *splits*.

"But I want him to *come*," I replied with a stomp of my foot. I wanted a daddy who spent time with me, who built forts in the living room and gave me airplane rides in our front yard, spinning me in circles until I was too dizzy to walk. What I had was a daddy who'd rather be at work, buying money, which is what he once told me was his job. "Buying and selling money, peanut," he said, giving me a quick tweak on my nose. "People give me money to make them *more* money. Everyone wants more money . . . don't you?"

He looked at me expectantly, so I nodded solemnly, knowing he wanted me to agree with him, and I, as always, wanting to make him happy. Part of me believed that if I was just good enough—if on the nights he came home before I went to bed, I remembered to fold my napkin in my lap at the dinner table and not slurp from my glass of milk—he would stop being gone so much. If I picked up my room and didn't leave Legos on the floor for him to accidentally step on with his bare feet in the middle of the night, he would be like the fathers I saw drop their daughters off at school, giving them kisses on the head and quick hugs by the front doors for everyone to see.

"I know you do, baby," my mother said, tucking my blanket up around my neck. "I'll talk with him, okay?"

Later that night, I woke to the sound of my parents fighting in their bedroom, my father's angry voice and my mother's quiet cries as familiar to me as my own. Pushing back my covers, I tiptoed out of my room and down the hall to theirs, standing as still as possible so they wouldn't know I was awake. I pressed my palms and one ear flat against the door and listened.

"Are you saying I'm a *bad father*?" I heard my dad say, the words sounding more like an animal's growl than a man speaking. "Are you saying I don't provide the both of you an amazing life? A beautiful house? Everything and anything you might need? Is *that* what you're saying to me, Liv?"

"She needs you, James," my mother responded. "She needs her father to be with her. She doesn't need more things or more money. She's only *six*. She loves you so much and you just walk away from her over and over again." There was a brief moment of silence and I strained to hear if they were whispering. But then my mother continued. "Please. Come to the recital. Be the father you never had."

My father's feet pounded across the floor—I felt the vibration from where I stood. "*I* am not my *father*!" he shouted. There was a loud crash, and my mother gave a short, high-pitched scream before the noise was cut off and everything went silent, except for my father grunting. My heart pounded against the inside of my chest and my eyes filled with tears. I was desperate to open the door, but too terrified of what I might see. My mother cried out again, a strangled noise, a word I couldn't fully understand. It could have been "help."

"Shut . . . up," Dad spat the words more than he spoke them, with a distinct pause in between. I could picture his face, the way I'd seen it a hundred times before when they fought—puffed up and red, green eyes pressed into angry slits, the corners of his mouth pushed down into sharp points. "I've had *enough* of this shit. I am a *good* father. I take *care* of my family. I give you both everything you could possibly need, and still, it's not good enough for you. I *saved* you, Olivia. I turned you into the woman you are and *this* is the thanks I get?" I heard him take a couple of heaving breaths . . . I heard my mother struggling to speak, her words sputtering and blocked. *What is he* doing *to her?* I put one hand on the doorknob, trying to work up the courage to fling the door open and get him to stop yelling at her, but I couldn't do it. My chin began to tremble and I thought about calling 911, but what would I say? My parents are fighting? Was that a *real* emergency, like a fire or a robber? I didn't know.

But then my mother's voice finally broke through, heavy sobs cutting her words into fragmented pieces. "Please," she begged. "No . . . more . . . I'm sorry." She took a couple of breaths, a ragged, hiccuping sound, then spoke again. "You're a good father, James. The best."

"Damn *right* I am," my father said, but his voice was shaky, too, and I wondered if he was crying. "Don't make me be like this, Olivia. You *know* I hate to be like this."

"I know," Mom whispered in a hoarse voice. "I'm sorry. Let's just go to bed, okay? Let's just sleep."

I waited for my father's response, but when one didn't come, I was suddenly afraid he'd open the door and find me there, so I dashed down the hallway as silently as I could. I had just crawled back in bed when I heard their door open, and the distinct sound of my father's footsteps padding down the thickly carpeted hallway. I closed my eyes and tried to steady my breathing enough that I'd appear asleep, in case he came into my room. He did that sometimes, when he got home late from the office. He'd pull a chair up next to my bed and watch me. Sometimes he'd run his hand over my face, or kiss my forehead, and sometimes, on my favorite nights, he even whispered that he loved me. But this time, when he came into my room, he climbed right into bed with me, cuddling me close, his thick, strong arms wrapped tight around me.

"Are you awake, Maddie?" he whispered. "Daddy needs to talk with you." He gave me a tiny shake, and I fluttered my eyelids open, pretending to just be waking up.

"Daddy?" I said, sleepily.

He kissed the top of my head and pulled me closer. "You love me . . . right, honey? You know I'd never do anything to hurt you." His voice was high and strange, not the strong, confident tone he usually used. He sounded like a child.

"I know," I said quietly, wondering if his not doing anything to hurt *me* made it somehow okay with him that he hurt Mom. Why else would she cry like that, if he wasn't hurting her? My stomach twisted, imagining what he might have done to steal her words.

"I try so *hard*," he said, pressing his mouth up against my ear. His breath was hot, and it smelled like stale coffee. "I don't want to be like him. I *don't*, I *don't*." I assumed he was talking about his father, and then he confirmed it. "My father was a horrible man, Maddie. He used to whip me with the metal end of a leather belt. He beat me . . . he kicked me until I bled. He broke my arm once, and when I tried to run away, he locked me in a closet for *two days*." He sighed, a shuddery, broken sound, like he was trying not to cry. "I would *never, ever* do that to you. You know that, right?"

I nodded, scared to tell him the truth, which was that I didn't know anything when it came to him—that no matter how much I wanted to be with him more, part of me was terrified of his anger, of the odd, bright light that appeared in his eyes whenever he was about to yell. I was too afraid to say that he might not do anything like that to me, but I wasn't so sure he hadn't done something like it to my mother. "I love you, Daddy," I said quietly, knowing this was what he needed to hear, hoping this reassurance was enough to make him leave my room.

He did, eventually, and in the morning, when I joined my mother at the breakfast table, he had already left for work. I hugged her like I normally did, and she cringed just the slightest bit as she squeezed me back, and I worried I might have hurt her. "Are you okay, Mama?" I asked, and she nodded. I pulled back to look at her, and she dropped her chin.

"What would you like for breakfast, sweet pea?" she asked with a false, light note. "Can I make you some rice flour pancakes? We have blueberries, I think, too." She turned her head toward the stove and that's when I saw them—the black and blue fingerprints on the sides of her neck . . . the red and swollen swath of skin across the front. She'd tried to cover them with pale, powdery makeup, but it didn't work. It reminded me of the time I accidentally spilled grape juice smack-dab in the middle of my white-carpeted bedroom floor and tried to hide it by moving a bright blue area rug over the mess—it was the first place my mother looked when she walked through the door.

"What happened, Mama?" I asked, tears stinging my eyes. At the time, I wasn't exactly sure what he had done to her, but I knew it was bad. I knew those bruises hadn't appeared out of nowhere.

"Nothing, baby," she said. Her hand flew to her throat. "I'm just clumsy." She gave me a wide, shaky smile. "Now, what can I get you to eat?"

I remember that night now, as I sit in my closet again, talking with Dirk on the phone about our parents. For the last week, I've waited until I was sure mine were asleep to call him, not wanting my dad to freak out on me. He totally embarrassed me when Hannah came over for dinner, and I'm a little bit worried that he might call Noah's father and find out that it *isn't* Noah whom I've been talking with every night. I hang out with him a bit at school, but only because our lockers are close together and we sit next to each other in computer science. Noah is nice, even a little bit cute in a nerdy sort of a way, but he hasn't even asked me for my number.

"Mine met when they were sixteen," Dirk tells me. "My

dad moved from San Diego to Seattle because my grandpa got a job at Boeing, and ended up buying a house right next door to my mom's family. They got married two weeks after they graduated from high school and have been together ever since."

"Sounds like a movie," I say, wishing my parents had such a sweet love story.

"Yeah, it does, doesn't it?" Dirk says. "They have their share of arguments, but they still sort of act like teenagers." He pauses. "What about your parents?"

I think about this a moment, unsure how to describe my parents' relationship. I used to think it was sort of romantic that my dad flew across the country every weekend for almost a year just to see my mom and then brought her to live in his beautiful house. But I realized how sad it was that in order to marry Dad, Mom had to leave behind everything and everyone else in her life, including her own mother. She lost contact with all her friends there and for the most part, was too busy taking care of me after I got sick to make new ones. That is part of why I like Hannah so much—she seems to genuinely like my mom. And maybe more important, she doesn't seem intimidated by Dad.

"If you met them, you'd think they're in love," I tell Dirk. "My mom is really beautiful and my dad is totally handsome and successful. They look great together, you know? In public, they're always smiling and laughing and holding hands. But that's not how it is at home."

"Your dad's always had a temper?" Dirk asks, hesitantly. It's the first time he has brought the subject up since our initial conversation.

"For as long as I can remember," I say, my voice almost a

whisper. "He just . . ." I trail off, trying to figure out how to describe my father's unpredictable behavior. There are moments with him that feel normal, when we talk and laugh about things the way a regular father and daughter do, and then, something will change. A tone in my voice might set him off, or more likely, a tone in my mother's voice. "He's moody," I conclude. "And we never really know which mood we're going to get."

"Well, that sucks," Dirk says. "I'm sorry you have to deal with it." He waits a beat. "But I suppose the good news is you can move out pretty soon, right? Get some distance from him? My relationship with my parents got way better when I got my own place. I really like hanging out with them now. Because when I've had enough I can leave."

He's so nice, I think, once again feeling horribly guilty for lying to Dirk about my age . . . my looks . . . about everything. I keep telling him I'm not ready to meet him in person yet because I recently had my heart broken and I'm a little afraid of it happening again. He told me not to worry about it—that he is okay with just getting to know each other until I am ready, becoming friends, which only made me feel worse. I'm not sure how I got to this place—pretending to be someone I'm not. In the hospital, when I first created "Sierra's" Facebook profile, I was just messing around—playing virtual dress-up with someone else's life. It was an escape, something to think about other than the fact I was probably going to die. But I'm better now, and actually have a chance for a life of my own. The longer I wait to tell Dirk the truth, the harder it's going to be.

"You still there?" he asks.

"Yeah," I say, then take a deep breath, trying to find the right words. *This is it.* It doesn't matter that, because of Dirk,

Hailey and her friends have decided I'm worthy of hanging out with them. It doesn't matter that I've been sitting with them at their table in the lunchroom, or that they invited me to come hang out with them at the mall this week. What I am doing is wrong, and I need to set things straight. "I have to tell you something," I say, haltingly.

"You're finally going to take me up on dinner?" he asks, his voice so hopeful, so sweet, I feel sick to my stomach.

"No . . ." I swallow hard, once, to soothe the dry ache in my throat. "I'm still not quite ready for that."

"Okay, then. You actually *are* a weird old man living in his mother's basement, eating Cheetos?"

I laugh. How can I hurt his feelings with the truth? And really, what harm is it doing, just talking on the phone? We're friends, that's all. As long as I keep refusing to meet him in person, I can make him believe I look like that picture of "Sierra"—and pretend I have a chance with him. It's not like I'm delusional. I know it won't ever actually happen. I'll eventually have to stop answering his calls—I'll have to block his email and instant messaging ID and tell Hailey that he and I broke up. But for now—just for now—I want to allow myself this one good thing.

"No, definitely not." I take another deep breath, and suddenly decide on a different truth I can tell him, something a little closer to who I actually am. "I just wanted to say . . . to tell you . . . well . . ." I clear my throat. "I used to be really sick. Like in-the-hospital-all-the-time sick."

"Really? What was wrong? Are you okay?" There is real concern in his voice again, and I can't help it—I flush with pleasure, thinking he already cares about me that much. And then

I remember once again, he doesn't care about *me* . . . he cares about the hot girl in the picture.

"I'm okay now. I had a pretty bad liver disease, though, and needed a transplant. Which I got a year ago last July."

"Holy shit, Maddie," he says. "You're sure you're okay?"

"Yeah, I'm good. I had a couple of small infections after the surgery that I had to go back to the hospital for, but they treated me with a couple rounds of IV antibiotics and then I was fine. Now, I just have to take a bunch of pills every day to make sure my body doesn't reject the new liver. The survival rate is pretty high compared to like a heart or something, so, so far, so good."

"*Wow.* Why didn't you tell me before?"

"I dunno. I guess I was scared to. It's kind of weird to talk about." I feel a strange sense of relief, telling him about the transplant, like maybe because of it, he might someday forgive me for lying to him about what I look like.

"Weird, like how?" Dirk asks, and because he sounds so sincerely interested, I tell him the truth.

"I'm walking around with a piece of a stranger inside me. It's just weird."

"Well, can you meet them? The donor's family, I mean? Then they wouldn't be strangers."

My throat clenches and my eyes fill, thinking of the girl who died last year, thinking about her parents who have to be wondering about the life their daughter saved, and I feel guilty for an entirely different reason than lying to Dirk. "No," I tell him. "My dad won't let us. He's worried about our privacy or something." I don't mention that my mom told me that he's also worried they might ask us for money because I haven't told Dirk that my dad is rich. If I did, that might lead to questions about what he does for a living and then I'd have to make up more lies.

"Shouldn't that be your decision?" he asks. "You're the one who had the surgery. If you want to write them and say thank you, you should."

He's right, I think. I'll only use my first name, so it's not like they'll know who the rest of my family is. I'll write the letter and send it to that nice coordinator at the transplant center who gave me her contact information in case I ever had any questions. My parents will never have to know. I've been over-analyzing what I should say, how I should present myself to this family, when all I really need to do is tell them how much I appreciate the gift they gave me and how sorry I am that their daughter died.

I wipe away the few tears that have escaped down my cheeks, staring up at all the new clothes my mom and I bought last weekend. I realize that it's moments like *that* that I'm grateful to have—strolling through the mall with my mother, or sitting here, right now, talking with a boy on the phone. Tiny, happy moments that make up an entire life—a life that, until a year ago, I never thought I'd actually get to live.

"You're right," I say. "You're totally right." We hang up a few minutes later, with him promising to text me in the morning. And even though it's past midnight when I slip out of my closet and into bed, I turn on my bedside lamp and open up my laptop, determined to write the letter I've waited far too long to send.

Hannah

When Zoe Parker first walked into Emily's hospital room, she was the last person Hannah wanted to see. It was her job, as the transplant coordinator, to go over the entire process with Hannah, to talk with her about where Emily's corneas and heart and lungs would go. Later, Zoe was the one who forwarded the thank-you notes from the organ recipients' families and tried to push Hannah into attending one of the donor family support groups, which Hannah repeatedly, but politely, refused to do. Hannah was not a joiner. Growing up, she didn't play on any teams or become part of any clubs. The idea of sitting in a room, staring at other parents who had lost their children, bemoaning their mutual misery, made Hannah feel like her skin was suddenly too tight for her body.

"Talking about your grief helps process it," Zoe gently suggested. "I know you're keeping busy, but I'm afraid that if you don't learn how to sit with your pain over losing Emily, it's going to come crashing down on you when you least expect it. I want you to be ready for that."

"I'll manage," Hannah responded, wondering how, exactly, Zoe thought a person could be "ready" for grief—as though it were an Olympic event one could train for with tear-duct-strengthening exercises and emotional sit-ups. The grief Hannah felt about Emily's death wasn't a momentary event; it was a constant, aching throb in her body, a sliver lodged deep in her heart. From the first moment she saw her child lying motionless in the street, no matter how hard she worked, how busy she kept, it had never left her. She couldn't imagine that it ever would.

After too many conversations like that one, she stopped answering Zoe's calls. So on Thursday morning, after she gets back from her morning run and sees Zoe's name on her caller ID, she hesitates before answering. But curiosity gets the better of her and she picks up before the call goes to voicemail.

"I just want you to know that I forwarded you a thank-you note from the liver recipient yesterday," Zoe says after Hannah says hello. "You should get it today."

Hannah's stomach spasms, and she wonders if it's too much of a coincidence that she will get this letter just over a week after meeting the Bell family. Have they guessed who she is? She wouldn't put it past James to run a background check on her. No matter what Olivia said, it was pretty clear from his behavior the night she went to their house for dinner that he didn't like her. At the very least, he was wary of her. The entire evening had felt like the two of them were boxers, carefully circling each other in the ring. "Is it the recipient or the parents?" she asks, thinking this is the best way to find out if James had anything to do with the timing of the letter.

"The recipient," Zoe says. It is her job to read through the thank-you notes before sending them on, vetting them for any identity-revealing or otherwise inappropriate information. "She sounds like a sweet, smart girl who's still trying to figure out who she is after the transplant. A lot of kids struggle with that issue. They've spent their lives totally defined by their illness, and suddenly, they're not sick and have no idea who they are without a diagnosis. Getting well mentally and emotionally is a whole different ball game from their physical recovery."

"I can only imagine," Hannah says. Olivia said that James basically forbade them from contacting the donor family. If this was true, the letter couldn't be from Maddie . . . could it? *Maybe I'm wrong about everything. Maybe I was just telling myself what I wanted to believe.* There will be no way to know until she holds the letter in her hands. She glances at the clock. It's eight fifteen and her first client is due downstairs at nine—she needs to get dressed. "Thanks for the heads-up, Zoe. I really appreciate it."

"Of course," Zoe says, but she hesitates a moment before ending the call. "How are *you* doing? Have you given any more thought to joining one of our groups?"

"Not really," Hannah says, trying to repress a sigh but failing. "I'm fine. Thank you. Really busy with the new salon, and I've made a great new friend." She says this to prove to Zoe that she's moving forward with her life—new friendships must serve as evidence of that. Her mother clearly thinks so, but that's only because she doesn't know who Hannah's new friend actually is. Sophie has a different opinion on the matter, and because of this, Hannah has deliberately avoided her since the awkward night her friend took her out for drinks; for now, she is communicating with Sophie through text messages and emails only.

"That's great, Hannah. I'm happy to hear it. We're here if you need us, okay? Any time at all."

Hannah thanks her again, then hurriedly hangs up so she'll be able to shower and get the salon open in time for her client. Veronica and Peter don't typically schedule their clients until after ten, which is fine with Hannah. She's glad she has a reason to make herself get out of bed.

A few minutes before nine, Hannah jogs down the stairs and unlocks the front door. Just as she is opening it to go check the mail—which usually doesn't come until the afternoon, but her excitement over the news of the letter makes her optimistic—she sees a man at the bottom of the steps, his hand on the railing. It takes a moment for it to register, but then it comes to her—he's the psychologist, Seth. "It's you," she says, keeping her hand on the doorknob. She feels the heat rise to her cheeks and a sudden twist in her stomach; she's unsure if these are symptoms of attraction or annoyance.

He looks up at the sound of her voice and smiles, his eyes crinkling in the exact way she remembers. "I think so. If I'm *not* me, then I put on the wrong man's underwear this morning."

She can't help it—she laughs. "What are you doing here?"

"I'm your nine o'clock appointment," he says, taking the steps two at a time, then stands in front of her.

"You are?" She gives a brief shake of her head. "I don't remember putting you on my schedule."

"A nice girl named Veronica set it up for me yesterday, when I called." He runs his fingers through his slightly overgrown dark hair, then drops his arm back to his side. "I usually just buzz it myself with the clippers at home, but I figured since you have *two* salons, I should come see what all the fuss is about." He grins and tilts his head just the slightest bit to the left, in a charming, I'm-accustomed-to-getting-what-I-want fashion. "Do I get to come inside, or do we do this on the porch?"

Hannah waits a moment before opening the door. Just showing up like this, unannounced, seems a little presumptuous on his part. Cocky, even. She really *isn't* ready to date anyone and wonders if she's sending him the wrong message by letting him in. Sensing her hesitation, Seth holds up his hands, palms facing her. "Just here for the haircut, I swear." He pauses. "Also? I'm an excellent tipper."

"Oh well, in *that* case," she says, smiling as she swings open the door. *It can't hurt to cut his hair,* she reasons. *I can keep it professional.* A minute later, he is seated at her station. She wraps the black protective cape around his neck, then takes a moment to push her fingers through his thick locks, checking the length. "Just a trim, then? Or are you wanting to do something different?"

"Is there more a man can *do* with his hair?" he asks, scrunching his dark eyebrows together. "I usually just set the clippers to three and go for it."

"I could give you a faux-hawk," she suggests.

"Um, no," he says. "My clients will think their shrink needs a shrink."

"Okay," Hannah says, feeling more comfortable talking with him than she thought she would. It's probably a therapist thing—a test they have to pass before getting their licenses, knowing how to set other people at ease. "Do you trust me?" she asks. He says that he does, and she proceeds to shampoo

him, which she has always secretly thought an oddly intimate
thing to do for a person she's just met.

As he leans back in the chair and lets her firmly massage his
scalp with the tips of her fingers, he closes his eyes and releases
a low, guttural groan. "I should prescribe this as a treatment for
my clients suffering from anxiety."

"What kind of counseling do you do?" Hannah asks, figur-
ing the least she can do is make small talk with the man. She
does this with all of her clients—even the ones she doesn't particularly like.

"Individual, mostly. Some marriage and family, but I tend
to avoid couples."

"Why's that?" She checks the temperature on the water with
the edge of her hand before rinsing off the shampoo, taking a
moment to examine Seth's face more closely. A few feet away,
it had convinced her it was perfect, but in fact, one eye is a little
higher than the other and his nose is a little big for the rest of
his features. He has full lips and he trims his nose hair, which is
more than Hannah can say about some of her male clients.

"Well, because by the time most couples wind up in counseling, it's too late."

"So you're telling me you're an optimist," Hannah says
wryly.

Seth chuckles. "With some things, yes. But couples experi-
encing a crisis in their marriage usually have such deeply rooted
resentments it's almost impossible to untangle the truth of their
issues. I sometimes have luck if they see me separately first,
then together, but I have the most success with people who are
motivated to work on themselves, not change the behaviors of
another person." He opens his eyes as Hannah finishes rinsing

him, and she wraps a towel around his head. "Have *you* ever been married?"

Furrowing her brow, she motions him back toward her station. "I thought you were just here for the haircut."

"I am," he says, walking over to the chair and sitting back down. He grins at her in the mirror. "Just making idle conversation. Isn't that what I'm supposed to do with my hairstylist? Or should we be gossiping about movie stars and reality TV?"

"Have *you* ever been married?" she asks, grabbing her comb and sharpest scissors from her drawer.

"Ah, answering a question with a question. Classic deflection technique." She finds herself mildly irritated by his observation, so she doesn't respond, only runs the comb through his hair and begins snipping. Seeming to register her annoyance with him, he continues. "Yes, I was married. I've been divorced almost ten years now, though. No children. I wanted them, she didn't."

"Didn't you talk about that before you got married?" Hannah asks, grudgingly interested in what he has to say.

"Yeah, but I was stupidly convinced that she must have had some trauma in her childhood that made her not want to have a baby. That if we could just figure out what it was, she could deal with it and then she'd change her mind." He pauses and lets loose an almost inaudible sigh. "I couldn't accept that some people just aren't wired to be parents. I pushed and pushed until she couldn't take it anymore. It ended."

Hannah pauses before taking the next cut, a little surprised—but oddly appreciative—that he is being so open with her. "Do you still want them?"

"Theoretically? Yes. I love kids. But I also don't want to be one of those guys who needs a walker to attend his children's high school graduations. So it's probably not going to happen." There is a tangible sadness behind these words, and Hannah decides to take it a little easier on him and share a bit about her past.

"I've never been married," she says, as she carefully trims the hairline over his ears. "At first, it was more of a rebellion against my parents, you know? They met when they were thirteen and have been happily together for over fifty years. It all seemed so boring, being with the same person day in and day out . . . *forever*."

"And you didn't want to be bored." Seth listens to her intently, his brown eyes never leaving the reflection of her face as she speaks. She imagines his clients feel that he hangs on their every word.

"Exactly," she says. She tells him how she moved away from the farm, went to beauty school, met Sophie, and eventually opened the salon. "I dated quite a bit throughout my twenties . . . you know, just having fun . . . and then I got engaged. It didn't end well."

"What happened?" He pauses. "If you don't mind my asking."

She shrugs, thinking if he could be so honest about the reasons behind his failed marriage, the least she can do is return the favor. "Well, when one of you wants to get married and the other wants to sleep with another woman, it's really not meant to be."

"What a fucker," Seth mutters.

"Yes," Hannah says, laughing. "As a matter of fact, he was.

Literally." She sighs, surprised at how easy it is to talk with him. "I thought I was going to be with him for the rest of my life, you know? Marriage, babies, the whole deal. And after what he did, I started *really* thinking about what I wanted for my life besides my career, and I realized it was having a baby. On my own."

"And did you?" he asks, an unmistakable lift of hope in his words. She suspects he is imagining dating her and meeting her children—maybe someday, if all worked out between them, becoming a stepfather. When Emily was alive, Hannah had played this fast-forward game with some of the men she dated, picturing what their life together might be like, what each one would look like standing next to her and Emily, but none of them ever seemed right to her. They didn't fit into her daughter's future, and now that Emily is gone, Hannah has stopped planning a future of her own. That is the real reason it wouldn't be fair to date Seth—because she knows at this point, no matter how sweet and smart and funny he might be, she doesn't have it in her to commit to anything more than a haircut.

"My daughter died last year," she says, a familiar tension gripping the muscles in her chest. She doesn't know why she has decided to tell him this, but then he reaches up and grabs her hand, stopping her from her work.

"Oh my god, Hannah. I'm so sorry." He says this simply and with so much sincerity, it makes her want to cry. She bobs her head once in acknowledgment. "Was she ill?" he asks.

"She was hit by a car." The moment of the accident flashes in front of Hannah and she has to close her eyes and swallow hard to contain the sharp sob she feels building in her throat.

She wonders if it will ever get easier to say these words—to tell someone the truth.

"What was her name?"

"Emily." Hannah whispers her daughter's name like a prayer and forces her eyes open to look down at Seth. They hold each other's gaze for a moment before Hannah finally drops hers to the floor, then resumes the final touches on his cut. When she's done, she adds a dab of styling paste to hold his hair in place. He is quiet while she does this, and it's not until the front door opens and Veronica and Peter walk through it together that Seth speaks again, examining his reflection in the mirror.

"I look like a new man," he says. "Thank you." She gave him a George Clooney style—close cropped, pushed forward, and slightly spiked and messy in the front. It suits him.

"You're welcome." Grateful that he seems to intuit that she can't talk any more about Emily and doesn't press her for details, Hannah carefully removes the cape, and Seth stands up, smiling at her.

"Good morning!" Peter says cheerfully as he takes off his coat and proceeds to his station. Veronica waves, too, as she walks past them toward the kitchen for her morning coffee. When she's sure Seth's back is to her, she points at him, widens her eyes, and mouths the word "cute!" at Hannah, who chooses to ignore her.

"Good morning," Seth says to Peter, then he and Hannah step over to the reception desk, where she runs his credit card and takes what she hopes are imperceptible deep breaths to calm her racing pulse. She's not sure if the anxiety she feels is over telling Seth about Emily or about the way he *looked* at her when she told him—like he understood something deep within her core. As he puts his wallet in his back pocket, Hannah struggles to find the right words to express how she feels. She finally lands on "I'm happy you came in."

"Me, too," he agrees, then runs a light hand over his newly shorn hair. "I'll never buzz it again." They briefly discuss when he should schedule his next appointment, and just as he is about to leave, Sophie breezes in through the front door.

"Good morning!" she says, then stops short when she sees Seth. "Well, now. Hello." She gives Hannah a pointed look, then takes a step over to kiss Seth's cheek. "Remember me?"

"How could I forget?" Seth says. "Robert hasn't stopped talking about you."

Sophie flushes and lowers her eyes, clearly pleased to hear Robert has been discussing her with his friend. From their limited communication over the past week, Hannah knows Sophie has seen Robert several times since the night they met, but her friend hasn't gone into much detail. Hannah was assuming that he was just another one of Sophie's casual flings, but from the look on her face, she wonders if the relationship might have the potential to be something serious.

"What's up, Soph?" Hannah asks lightly. "Don't you have clients this morning?"

"My partner's been avoiding me," Sophie answers in an equally cool tone. "So I cleared my schedule for a visit."

Seth's gaze ping-pongs between them before he grabs his coat from the rack by the door. "I need to get to the office, too," he says, then looks at Hannah. "Thanks, again."

She smiles at him as he leaves, then turns her eyes back to Sophie. "I have another client in half an hour," she says, purposely not telling her friend who that appointment is. She might not have looked at her schedule closely enough for it to register that Seth would be her nine o'clock this morning, but she *does* know Olivia will be there at ten thirty—she made that appointment herself the day she first called Olivia. Knowing Sophie disapproves of Hannah's interactions with Olivia, she can't imagine that the two of them meeting would go well. She needs to get Sophie out of here as quickly as possible.

"Plenty of time," Sophie says. "Let's go upstairs." Reluctantly, Hannah tells Peter where she'll be, and a moment later, she and Sophie are seated on the love seat in her small living room. "So . . . Seth?" Sophie says, raising a perfectly plucked eyebrow. "What else haven't you been telling me?"

Hannah shrugs. "I didn't know he was coming. Veronica made the appointment."

"Mmm-hmm," Sophie murmurs. "He's very handsome. Robert says he's a good guy."

"I'm sure he is."

"Did you sleep with him?"

"No!" Hannah says. She doesn't say anything more, waiting to hear whatever it is Sophie came to say. All she can think about is the letter Zoe said would arrive today, and she wonders how having Seth show up could have so easily distracted her. She needs to check the mail.

"Then what aren't you telling me?"

"Nothing." Hannah shifts her body, turning it slightly away from Sophie. Her friend knows her well enough to recognize when she's lying, so when she feels Sophie try to catch her gaze, she looks down, suddenly very interested in picking at a loose thread on the love seat.

"Your mom told me you went to someone's house for dinner the other night."

"When did you talk with her?" Hannah says, finally looking up.

"She called me Monday, just to check in. And Isaac emailed me." Sophie gives Hannah a pointed look. "He said you've been avoiding him, too."

Hannah tries to think if this is exactly true. Isaac had shot her a few texts over the last week, but she's been so distracted by meeting Maddie and Olivia, she can't remember whether or not she answered them. And she just spoke with her mother Friday night on the way over to Olivia's house. Why was she "checking in" with Sophie after that? The idea that they were talking about her behind her back infuriates Hannah, so she stays silent, giving Sophie what she knows is a defiant look.

Seeing this, her friend sighs. "We're just worried about you. That's all."

"Don't be," Hannah says. "I'm fine." *Am I really so dysfunctional? What's next? Some kind of intervention?*

"Fine spending time with the family you're stalking?"

"Jesus, Soph. I'm not stalking anyone. I just had dinner with them." She decides to keep quiet about the fact that she also had lunch with Olivia and that they've been texting back and forth every day since. "I *like* Olivia and Maddie," she continues. "*James* Bell is different story. He's kind of an ass." She waits for Sophie to ask for details—her friend is usually anxious to gossip about anyone and anything—but Sophie only frowns.

"Hannah, you know I love you, but if they're the family you think they are, then you definitely need to be honest with them. What you're doing isn't fair. To them *or* you." She reaches over and tries to grab Hannah's hand, but Hannah jerks out of her reach.

"I'm *fine*," she snaps again. "I wish everyone would *please* stop telling me what to do." She grips the edge of the cushion between her fingers. "I'm going to tell them, okay? When I know for sure, one way or the other." A few tears slip down her cheek and she angrily wipes them away. "I can't *do* this right now, Soph. I have a client, okay? Can we talk later? I'll come over, I promise. We'll have dinner and catch up. I know I've been distant . . . I just . . ." She trails off and her bottom lip trembles before she can go on. "I'm finding my way through this as best I can."

"I know," Sophie says. "But I wish you'd stop thinking you have to go through it alone."

Olivia

Olivia lowers herself onto one of the couches in Ciseaux's reception area just as Hannah comes down the stairs.

"*There* she is!" the female stylist who greeted Olivia when she came in says, as she runs a comb through her client's long black hair.

Seeing Olivia, Hannah looks shocked—or is it panicked? Olivia is more than a few minutes early—she decided to come right over after dropping Maddie at school. Maybe she'd forgotten about their appointment.

"Olivia . . ." Hannah begins, but just as Olivia stands to greet her, a stunning, willowy redhead steps out from behind Hannah and stares at Olivia with piercing green eyes.

"*The* Olivia?" the redhead inquires with a tilt of her head. Confused, Olivia looks to Hannah for clarification.

"Yes," Hannah says quietly. "Olivia Bell."

"Hello," Olivia says, slightly unnerved by the intensity of this woman's gaze.

"Sophie Renard," the woman says with a melodic trill as she strides across the room to shake Olivia's hand. "Hannah's business partner . . . and best friend."

"Oh!" Olivia says, glancing over to Hannah, whose expression has morphed from one of shock to one of apprehension. She looks back to Sophie and quickly grasps her hand. "Lovely to meet you."

"Yes," Sophie says. "I've heard so much about you. *And* your daughter."

Before Olivia can ask what, exactly, she has heard about them, Hannah comes around the reception desk, too, putting her arm around Sophie and giving her a tight squeeze. "Sophie was just on her way out," she says, then looks to Olivia. "I'll be right with you, okay?"

"Is Hannah doing your hair, too, now?" Sophie asks.

Olivia nods, raising her fingers self-consciously to tuck her hair behind one ear. "If this is a bad time, I can reschedule," she says, feeling as though she's just walked in on a conflict she would be better off avoiding.

"It's not a bad time," Hannah says, practically shoving Sophie toward the front door. "Veronica, can you please get Olivia some coffee or water? I'll be right back." She opens the door, keeping one arm wrapped around Sophie as they move across the threshold and onto the porch. Olivia watches their animated conversation through the large bay window.

"Can I get you something to drink?" Veronica asks dutifully.

"No thank you," Olivia says, keeping her eyes on Hannah, who looks as though she's about to cry as Sophie speaks to her. After a few minutes of this, Sophie hugs Hannah, a long, hard movement, during which Hannah's arms hang loose at her sides. Olivia strains to hear what Sophie says next and thinks she hears the words "If you don't tell her, I will." With that, Sophie finally trots down the stairs and out of the yard. *What would Hannah have to tell me?* Olivia wonders. *If, that is, Sophie was referring to me.*

Hannah stands extremely still, her shoulders curled and her head down, until her friend climbs inside her car and drives away. Olivia feels the urge to go console Hannah, but something holds her back—a sense that her presence wouldn't be appreciated. She watches as Hannah takes a deep breath and straightens her posture, then strides toward the front gate, where she checks the white mailbox, which turns out to be empty. Hannah looks up to see Olivia staring at her, and she manages to smile as she scales the front steps and reenters the salon.

"Sorry to keep you waiting," Hannah says, smoothing down a few flyaway strands of her black hair. The corners of her mouth twitch, as though her pleasant expression is taking more effort than usual.

"No worries," Olivia says. "I'm a little early." She pauses. "Is everything okay?"

"Of course!" Hannah says brightly, and Olivia hates that her new friend feels that she has to hide whatever's really going on. But then she thinks about the many times she's lied to the people in her own life and she knows she doesn't have the right to judge Hannah for any secrets she might feel the need to keep.

Another woman enters the salon, and Veronica rises to greet her. The two of them wander over to Veronica's station, and Hannah leads Olivia to hers. "Busy morning?" Olivia asks as she lowers herself into the chair and Hannah adjusts the protective cape around her neck. Olivia panics briefly, wondering if there are marks on her skin that Hannah might see, but then she comes to her senses, remembering that James hasn't choked her in over a decade. But the memory of the night he did has haunted her ever since her brief conversation with Professor Lang; just this morning, she woke up in a cold sweat after dreaming it had happened again.

"A little hectic," Hannah says, giving her another false smile, then goes on to tell Olivia that the man she met the other night came in for an unexpected appointment.

"Did he ask you out?" Olivia says, watching Hannah's face in the mirror to gauge her reaction to the possibility.

Hannah blushes and shakes her head. "Strictly business," she says, but her suddenly shy smile tells Olivia otherwise. "So," Hannah continues, "are we just touching up your highlights today?"

Olivia twists her head back and forth, staring at her hair—the shade one she has kept so long, it feels like her own. "I'm thinking of going dark again," she says. "Back to my natural color. Like Maddie's, maybe." She looks anxiously at Hannah. "What do you think?"

"I think you'd look amazing. Let me go grab my sample book and we can talk about shading." A few minutes later, they've decided on a warm chestnut with undertones of auburn and honey, which will only show when the sunlight hits them.

Nerves swirl in Olivia's belly as she watches Hannah squeeze various pastes into a plastic bowl and begin to mix the color. "James isn't going to be happy about this," she says in a voice she's afraid reveals more than she'd like.

Hannah stops what she's doing and puts the bowl down on the counter. She furrows her thin, dark brows. "It's your hair, though, right?"

"Of course," Olivia says. "It's just . . ." She falters, then begins again. "He prefers me blond."

"And what do *you* prefer?" Hannah asks. When Olivia doesn't respond but instead holds utterly still, Hannah leans down and speaks next to her ear, so that no one else can hear. "I might not know you well enough to say this, but it worries me how scared you are of him."

Hannah's words make Olivia feel as though something inside her has dropped down several levels. "I'm not scared," she murmurs, but she knows she's not convincing Hannah—or herself.

Hannah turns the chair around and takes off Olivia's black cape. "Come on," she says, ignoring the questioning looks from Peter and Veronica as she guides Olivia toward the stairs that lead to her apartment. Once they are in her living room, with the door closed behind them, Hannah lets go of Olivia's hand and turns to face her. "You can trust me," Hannah says.

Instead of answering, Olivia moves her gaze over the small space, taking in the spare furnishings, the few books on the shelves. There is a purple velour love seat, a short walnut-hued coffee table, and a flat-screen television hung above the mantel, but otherwise, the room is practically empty. Anyone could live here. Why doesn't Hannah have any pictures of her daughter? If Maddie had died, Olivia imagines pictures would be her only link to her child—she would want them everywhere. She wonders if seeing them is too much of a reminder for Hannah of all she'd lost. "What a pretty apartment," she remarks. Her voice sounds strange, not tethered to her body.

"Olivia," Hannah says, undeterred. "Please. Talk to me."

"About what?" Olivia responds, her tone as light as she can possibly make it. *This isn't why I came here today. I came to get my hair done.*

"James. Why you have to keep secrets from him. It's not normal, the way he talks to you."

"You only met him once. He was just . . . in a bad mood." Olivia turns away, feeling guilty about lying to Hannah. She looks out the bay window at the blue September sky, but Hannah doesn't give up. She steps over to Olivia and stands in front of her. Olivia tries to avert her gaze from Hannah's, but she can't seem to look away from her friend's pleading eyes. She notices they are lighter in the center, like the sky, but rimmed in dark navy—framed like a picture.

"Does he *hurt* you?" Hannah asks, her voice low and thick with compassion.

Olivia presses her lips together and shakes her head, still unable to take her eyes off Hannah's. Her gut churns, as she realizes that Hannah isn't going to give up. What gave the truth away? James didn't touch her in front of Hannah the night she came over; Olivia didn't have any telling bruises. Tears threaten in the back of her throat, and she swallows once, hard, to force them down. She can't say it. She can't. She can't tell a person she barely knows what her life has become, what she's endured, what she's allowed her daughter to live with . . . and why. She has to stick to her plan. Get a degree, get a job, get Maddie away at school, and *then* she can leave him. Only now she's not sure she can follow through. What seemed so plausible in theory seems impossible in practice; she didn't return to class after that first day, unable to face what that picture had brought up within her. The disgust she felt, relating to the woman it depicted, the black, aching sense of shame that flooded through her veins. *I'm not strong enough,* she thinks. *I'm not strong enough to save myself. This is my life—I created it. I allowed it to happen. There's no way out for me.*

"His father beat him horribly," she finally says. "He's just a product of his environment . . . you know?" She pauses, searching Hannah's face for the judgment she expects—the same disdain she heard in that young girl's voice during class when she said the woman in the picture was an idiot. But all she sees in her friend's eyes is concern—a soft, warm place to fall, someone willing to bear witness to her pain. "It doesn't happen very often," she whispers, suddenly unable to keep the tears from spilling down her cheeks.

"Oh, Olivia," Hannah says, reaching out to take her friend's hands. She pulls them to her chest, so their faces are only inches apart, their foreheads almost touching. "It shouldn't happen at all."

In the end, Olivia doesn't change a thing about her hair. Instead, she sits with Hannah for the next two hours—the length her appointment would have been—pouring out the dirty details of her life. The words come slowly at first, stuttering out of her in fits and bursts. And after she is done describing how it all started, trying—and failing—to pinpoint the exact moment when everything about her marriage changed, she can't believe the woman she's talking about is her. She can't comprehend the sheer number of times James has raised a hand to her, the humiliation and degradation she's lived with for almost two decades.

She takes in a few deep, shuddering breaths and waits for Hannah to speak, to ask her why she didn't call the police or walk out the door years ago. But Hannah is silent. Olivia shakes her head. "I don't know how he does it," she says helplessly.

"Does what?" Hannah asks.

Olivia's bottom lip trembles and she has to bite it before she can speak. "Makes me feel like *I'm* at fault. We go months and months when everything is fine and then, out of nowhere, he comes home and I do what I always do . . . say what I always say in the exact same way I always say it, and suddenly he's a different person. It happens so *fast*. And when it's over, it's like I stepped out of my body and watched it happen to another person. Like it wasn't real. So then I think I'm crazy, that I'm making it worse than it really is, because *he* pretends like it didn't happen, too, so I think, *Okay, maybe it didn't. Maybe I'm imagining things.*" Out of breath and realizing that she's babbling, she stops herself and looks at Hannah through watery eyes. "You think I'm stupid, don't you." A statement, not a question, because she is so certain it's true. "For staying with him."

"Of course not," Hannah says, gently enough that Olivia almost believes her. "But I guess I wonder . . . can you help me understand why?"

Olivia wipes away her tears with the tips of her fingers.

"I was ready to leave. I had money saved and a plan for us to start over without him . . ." She trails off, staring out the window again at the clear blue sky, trying to recall the sense of determination she felt in the weeks after James had choked her, when she first knew she needed to escape. "But then Maddie got so sick so quickly and I could never afford the kind of care she needed on my own. And I just knew if I tried to leave, he would threaten to prove I was unfit and take custody of her away from me." She swallows a sob, but still, her voice feels shredded as she speaks. "He could have, too. He has those kinds of connections. That kind of power. I couldn't lose Maddie. I *couldn't*. So I stayed."

"I get it," Hannah says, though her eyes cloud with an emotion Olivia doesn't know her well enough to recognize. "Does Maddie . . . ?" Hannah begins, blinks a few times, then starts again. "How much does she know?"

"She suspects," Olivia says, still tearful, "but he's never hit me in front of her." She knows how empty this statement sounds, though she still wishes it could absolve her of the choices she's made.

Hannah leans forward, intent. "Has he ever hit *her*?"

"Never," Olivia says vehemently. "He loves Maddie."

"Do you love him?" Hannah asks, visibly relieved to hear that James doesn't raise his fists to his daughter.

Olivia presses her lips together, hard, and bobs her head. This is maybe the hardest thing for her to admit—that despite everything he's done to her, the horrid way he's treated her over the years, a part of her is still enamored with James. She thinks of the moments they've shared—lying together in bed, his body curled up behind hers, the tears he's shed when he allows himself to talk about his past, the insecurities he's allowed only her to see. His fits of anger are always tempered by long stretches of passion and gentility. Her feelings about him are strung together in wild, complicated knots—fear braided tightly with adoration, tenderness shot through with shame. She has no idea how to unwind one from the other. "I can't leave him," she says to Hannah now. "I want to . . . but I just can't."

"With the right lawyer, you can fight him," Hannah says, with a determined edge in her voice. "You and Maddie can get away. You can call the police, you can get a restraining order . . . and he'd have to pay child support. He can't just stop Maddie's health insurance, either. He'd be legally required to take care of you both."

"You don't understand," Olivia whispers. "He'll *take* her so he won't have to." She goes on to explain her plan to get a degree and leave when Maddie went to college. "But it was a stupid idea, really. I'm not going to be a lawyer. I'm not going to be anything." She hears the defeat in her words and she hates it. She hates how weak she's become, how inadequate she feels to change her own life.

"You can be whatever you make up your mind to be," Hannah says and then releases a long, slow breath. "I won't try to tell you what you should do. Only you can decide that." She hesitates and opens her mouth, as though about to speak again, but quickly closes it.

"What?" Olivia asks. "What is it?"

"I just . . ." Hannah begins, then trails off, her lips pushed into a deep frown. She appears on the verge of saying something important, something Olivia might not want to hear. She looks nervous. *This is it,* Olivia thinks, her stomach twisting. *This is where she tells me she thinks I'm an idiot for being with James. This is where the truth comes out.*

"I just want you to know that I'm here for you," Hannah finally says. "Okay? However you might need me."

"Thank you," Olivia says shakily. She looks at Hannah, wondering how they got to this intimate place in their new friendship so quickly, and concludes that perhaps it's because they *don't* know each other very well that Olivia feels safe enough to open up. Sometimes it's easier to talk to someone who doesn't have preconceived notions of who you are, no expectations based on past behavior, no running commentary on the choices you've made in your life. Hannah seems to take Olivia exactly as she is in this moment, and it's because of this that—for the first time in as long as she can remember—Olivia feels like she's finally found someone she can trust.

Maddie

I feel better somehow, after writing the letter to the donor's family. Like a weight I'd been carrying around has lifted and I can breathe easier knowing I've done the right thing. It must show, because as I slide into my seat in computer science a few days later, Noah throws a playful punch from where he sits across from me, lightly brushing against my shoulder.

"What are *you* so happy about?" he asks. He stretches his long legs out in front of him and leans down to pull his binder from his book bag.

"Nothing much," I say with a shrug, uncertain if I really want to tell him the reason for my good mood. I'm sure Zoe, the transplant coordinator, has reviewed the letter by now and forwarded it to the family. I wonder if I'll ever hear back from them, though it doesn't matter, I suppose. All that matters is that I finally told them how much I appreciate their gift to me. And maybe more important, how sorry I am for everything they lost. "I just took care of something I've needed to do for a long time, you know? I feel relieved."

"I get you," he says, bobbing his head. He opens his binder and wiggles his mechanical pencil between his index and middle fingers before speaking again. "So, hey . . . I was thinking. Are you busy after school today? I thought we could maybe hang out in the computer lab. See if we can figure this scripting assignment out together." He glances at me sidelong, and I notice he's blushing. *He likes me,* I think, and the realization creates an unexpected, fluttery sensation in my chest. The pencil wiggling speeds up as he waits for my response.

"I can't," I say. "Sorry. I promised I'd go to Bellevue Square with Hailey and Jade." His face crumples, and I immediately feel awful for hurting his feelings. "Can we do it tomorrow?" I ask. "Or Monday?"

"Sure," he says, but he doesn't look at me. He sets his pencil on top of his desk. "Are they like, your *best friends* now or something?" He doesn't even attempt to hide his disdain. Hailey made it clear that she doesn't like Noah, and apparently, the feeling is mutual.

"No," I say. "I'm new here, okay? I'm just getting to know everyone. They asked me to go and I said sure. That's all." He rolls his shoulders as though trying to dislodge something from the middle of his back. I want to say more, to tell him that all of these weird who-is-supposed-to-be-friends-with-whom rules are something I've never dealt with before. I don't know where I fit in. And even though Hailey was seriously rude to me on my first day, I definitely understand that I don't want to be on her bad side. Right now, she thinks Dirk is my boyfriend, and even though it is a lie, it makes me feel like I'm just as good as she and her pretty friends.

Noah ducks his head so his hair falls over his face, ignoring my explanation. Sighing, I rip a small corner of paper from my notebook and quickly write down my phone number with a small note. *Text me later. Please?* I fold it up into a tight square and then chuck it across the aisle. It lands right in front of him, but he hesitates a moment before opening it. Though once he does, a smile spreads across his face and he surreptitiously reaches into his sweatshirt pocket, turning away from me. I feel my phone buzz inside my own jacket a second later, and I pull it out to read his text. "Is it later yet?"

I look at Noah and smile, and when he smiles back at me, I feel something in my stomach flip over, the same way it did when Dirk first spoke my name. *What is* that *about?* But before I can send a response, the teacher raps on her desk with a ruler as an indication that it's time for class to begin.

A few hours later, after I meet Hailey and Jade in the parking lot and we're on our way to the mall, I go back to that moment in class when Noah smiled at me. Specifically, I think about his mouth—the way his lips might feel against mine. Suddenly, the fluttering I'd felt earlier in my stomach moves into my pelvis and I have to suck in a quick breath.

"You okay?" Jade asks, twisting around from her place in the front passenger seat to look at me. Hailey is driving—the candy-apple-red BMW her dad bought her for her sixteenth birthday—and it was made clear that, as the new girl in their little circle, my place is in the back.

"Yeah," I say, embarrassed my breath had been loud enough for her to hear. It's a little weird to picture Noah kissing me—I'd pictured Dirk doing it a hundred times, but it was different with him, since I'd never actually had him standing in front of me. With Noah, I could imagine how he'd smell—like Axe cologne and bubble gum—how he'd have to brush his bangs out of his eyes. I know his touch would be gentle and suspect his braces might click against my teeth.

"What time does your boyfriend get off work?" Hailey asks as she turns in to the parking garage of the mall. "Maybe he can come meet us."

"He's traveling right now," I say, trying not to stammer. "Some kind of programmer conference in Texas." This is true, actually. Dirk texted me yesterday morning to say he would be out of contact for a few days, on a business trip to Dallas. Which doesn't make sense to me, exactly, since I'm pretty sure he'll have his phone with him when he's there, but maybe he'll just be too busy working to talk or text with me. At least, this is what I hope. I wonder if he isn't losing interest in me altogether. And then, surprisingly, I realize that might not be such a horrible thing.

"Too bad," Hailey says, giving Jade a quick, meaningful stare as she pulls into a parking spot and turns off the engine. "We wanted to see him for ourselves."

"I can show you his texts," I offer, thinking this would be enough to placate them, but they refuse and we make our way into the mall. Hailey and Jade walk together, their arms brushing against each other's, and I try to keep up with them.

"Where do you like to shop?" I ask, but they are already headed inside Forever 21, which I think is sort of an ironic name considering the three of us are only sixteen. Loud, bass-driven music pumps through hidden speakers, and an assortment of teenagers and grown women—whom I think should probably be old enough to know better than to wear the styles the store carries—mill through the various racks and displays.

"What about this?" Hailey asks, holding up a sparkling turquoise tank top with the word SLUT emblazoned across the chest in tall, dark letters.

"OMG, super *cute!*" Jade squeals. "Do they have it in pink?"

I wonder what I'm doing hanging out with girls who think the word *slut* is super-cute. With their text-speak and exclamation-mark-studded speech patterns, I'm pretty sure Jade and the long-limbed car model Tiffani would totally hit it off.

Hailey doesn't answer; instead, she pushes the top closer to me. "Do you like it? Maybe we all could get matching ones."

"I like the color," I say, trying to find something positive about the top. "But my dad would freak out if he saw me wearing it." I pause. "Wouldn't yours?"

Hailey flips her red curls over her shoulder and shoves the top back on the rack, where Jade is digging through for a different color. "He doesn't care *what* I do," she says. And even though she tries to sound proud, I can hear a gloomy shadow of disappointment behind her words.

"I'm sorry," I say, knowing how much it hurts to feel invisible to my dad. Maybe Hailey and I have more in common than I previously thought.

"What for?" she asks, and I just shake my head, thinking this isn't the best place to have a conversation about our fathers. We spend the next half an hour or so looking through the rest of the racks, pulling out various items we like—Hailey and Jade more than me, since most of the styles are cut for size-two-and-below body types, not for my slightly bloated, after-the-liver-transplant shape. I do manage to find a pair of sparkling black leggings I think I might be able to squeeze into, and when we head toward the dressing rooms, Hailey slips into one with me, leaving Jade on her own.

"Um . . . did I grab one of your outfits?" I say, immediately terrified by the thought of undressing in front of her. No one other than my parents and doctors has seen my scar, and Hailey is probably the last person I'd choose to add to that short list.

"Nope," she says. "I thought we could share." She lowers her voice to a conspiratorial whisper. "I think Jade likes to look at my boobs."

I give her a weak smile, knowing she's joking but still trying to figure out a way to get her to leave me alone. "I'll just let you go first," I say, moving like I'm going to push the curtain back, but she stops me.

"Oh come on. Let's try things on together. It'll be fun." She smiles, and a mischievous light pops up in her green eyes. As she is pulling her shirt off over her head, I try not to stare at her breasts, which are practically spilling out of a black push-up bra. But she catches me. "Perv," she says, laughing.

"What's so funny?" Jade's voice comes through the thin wall between our two dressing rooms. I hear the panic floating in her tone—she's worried, I'm sure, that we're talking behind her back. Which Hailey did, but I'd never tell Jade that. I don't want to be that kind of person.

"Maddie just said something *totally* hysterical about having sex with her boyfriend," Hailey says, giving me a quick wink. "She'll tell you later."

"Hailey," I say through gritted teeth. "Don't *lie* to her." *Now that's funny,* I think. *Perhaps I should take my own advice.*

"Whatever," Hailey says. She grabs a thin silk blouse with cap sleeves and puts it on, regarding her reflection in the mirror. "What do you think?"

"I like it," I say, grasping the leggings to my chest, wondering how I can avoid getting undressed. "I'm pretty sure these will fit me."

"The waist looks like it might be small for you. You better at least try them." Hailey pulls off the silk top and shimmies out of her Levi's. She's wearing a lacy black thong to match her bra, and I wonder why the hell anyone would purposely put her underwear up her butt like that. She grabs another pair of jeans from the pile on the bench and tries them on.

"I think I'm good," I say, watching as she examines her half-naked image, twisting around to see herself from the back. I can't believe how perfect her body is—smooth, pale skin and not an ounce of fat on her. She tilts her head as she looks at me over her shoulder.

"You think I care about your *scar* or something? It's no big deal."

Maybe not to you, I think, but what I say is "I know. I just don't think I'm going to buy anything, anyway. My mom took me shopping last weekend for a bunch of new clothes."

"Whatever," Hailey says again, then throws me the silk top. "Can you put that on under your shirt then, please?"

"Why?" I ask, staring at the top as she takes off the jeans and puts her own back on.

"Because I want the red one, too, and I can't wear *both* of them under my own shirt. It'll be too bulky." I must still appear confused, because she lets loose an irritated sigh. "I'm not going to *pay* for them, okay? " She keeps her voice low, almost too quiet for me to hear. "I'll buy the jeans, but we're wearing the tops on our way out."

"I don't know," I say slowly. "I don't think that's a good idea."

She laughs. "You don't think it's a 'good idea'? " She says this in a high-pitched, mocking tone that makes me cringe. "Seriously? We do it all the time. Stores write this shit off—they expect it to happen. It's not like we're hurting anyone."

"Still," I say, swallowing the anxiety that rises in my throat. I suddenly don't care about getting on her bad side because I realize something important. Hailey is, without a doubt, an idiot. I should have hung out with Noah in the computer lab. I hold out the top to her. "It won't fit me, anyway."

Frowning, she glances at the top, then back to me before snatching it from my hand. "You're not going to tell anyone, are you? "

"No," I say. "I just don't want to do it." I pause. "I'll wait for you outside, okay? " She doesn't answer, so I slip out of the dressing room and walk over to the jewelry display, wondering if my mom would like anything they carry here. I want to call her, to ask her to please come pick me up so I don't have to hang out with Hailey a minute longer—I even finger my cell phone in the pocket of my hoodie, ready to dial her number—but I can just imagine how *that* story would get twisted and told at school: *She had to have her* mommy *come get her at the mall.* Better I just hold my ground against shoplifting and make it through the rest of the afternoon as best I can.

"Those are pretty," Hailey says as she sidles up next to me, the jeans she tried on slung over her forearm. She must have seen me touch a pair of small sparkling silver hoops on the rack.

"Yeah, they are. I was thinking my mom might like them." I look over and see Jade by the cash register, paying for a couple of T-shirts. She looks up and waves at me with a knowing half smile on her face, and I wonder what she is wearing under her already bulky blue sweater—what items *she's* in the middle of stealing.

As I'm staring at Jade, Hailey takes another step and bumps into me. "Oh, sorry," she says. "I wasn't looking where I was going."

"That's okay," I say. "And *I'm* sorry, you know . . . if I was weird about that whole thing." I might not like her very much, but I still don't want to piss her off.

"What whole thing?" she asks, widening her eyes and raising her thin eyebrows, throwing a quick, meaningful look over to the salesclerk.

"Nothing," I respond, realizing she doesn't want to talk about it, especially not while we're still in the store. I wait with her in line while she buys the jeans, holding my breath to see if the clerk notices the slight bulge beneath her shirt, but nothing is said, and after Hailey produces a black American Express card to make her purchase, we are on our way out of the store.

"See?" she says to me as we walk into the crowded corridor. "No worries."

"Totally easy," Jade agrees.

"I guess," I say, checking my phone to see if Noah has sent me another text. I'm rewarded by the sight of his name, which I'd added to his phone number after the first message he sent me during class. When I click on the text, my stomach flip-flops again because he's written this: "I think UR 2 pretty 4 a geek like me." I stop walking and read the note again. I've never been told by *anyone* other than my parents that I'm pretty. Dirk doesn't count, because he's talking about a picture of a different girl. But Noah, he sees me . . . the *real* me. And I know it can't be easy for him to put himself out there like this, to ask me to hang out with him and send me this sweet text. Because he *is* kind of a nerd, but I realize that I like that about him. And then I realize why—because he's a bit of a misfit, like me.

I'm trying to figure out how to answer him when I look up to see that Hailey and Jade are about fifty feet ahead of me already, oblivious to the fact that I've fallen behind. No matter how I feel about them, I don't want to lose my ride home. I shove my phone back in my pocket and start to trot to catch up with them, just as I hear a man's deep voice call out behind me. "You! Stop, please," he says, and I whip around to see a large security guard making his way through the crowd, pointing a chubby finger right at me.

"Hailey!" I call out, speeding up my pace, bumping into a few people around me. She stops and turns around with a bored, seemingly annoyed look on her face, but then she sees the guard and her expression flips into one of panic as she grabs Jade by the arm. And they take off without me.

For some reason, I start to run after them, even though I haven't done anything wrong. I wonder if being with them makes me an accomplice to a crime, if not telling the clerk what they were up to makes me just as guilty. My heart begins to race as I think about what might happen if my dad finds out that I got caught hanging out with girls who shoplifted. It's not like I knew they were going to do it, but that won't matter to him. I can hear his loud, angry voice, my mother's quiet pleas behind a closed door for him to calm down. And then the moment will come when she cries out before going totally silent. I see me, outside their room, knowing exactly what my father's done to her. Knowing it's my fault.

"Miss!" the guard calls out, snapping me out of this horrifying thought. "Don't make me chase you!"

Craning my neck to see over the crowd of people in front of me, I catch a glimpse of Hailey and Jade disappearing around a corner. *Bitches.* I stop running, realizing that it only makes me look like I have something to hide. The guard catches up with me, and I hold both my hands up, palms facing him, breathing hard. "I'm sorry," I say, hoping I can talk my way out of this. "I didn't know you meant me."

"And that's why you ran, right?" he asks, a smirk on his red, round face. He's breathing hard, too. "Do you mind showing me the contents of your pockets, please?"

"My pockets?"

He gives me an exasperated look. "Yes." He motions me over to the bench by the wall, and I do what he asks because I don't know what else to do. I look up, straining to see if Hailey and Jade have come back, but of course, they haven't. They're probably halfway to Hailey's car by now.

"I'm not sure what you're looking for," I say, pulling out my phone and then reaching into my other pocket for my small wallet. My fingers brush up against something sharp, and it takes a minute for me to identify it. The earrings. The ones I'd been admiring when Hailey stood next to me in the store, when I looked away from her and she bumped into me. My next breath seizes in my throat. "I don't know how these got here," I stammer, taking them out and holding them in my open palm. "Seriously. My friend must have put them in there."

"Uh-huh," the guard says, snatching them out of my hand. "You need to come with me, miss."

"No," I say, "you don't understand. I didn't take anything. I told them I wouldn't." Tears fill my eyes and my jaw begins to tremble. "Please. You have to believe me. I didn't do anything *wrong.*" I consider telling him about my transplant, thinking it might win me some sympathy, but then he looks down at the earrings and back at me, clearly not believing a word. *Well, here it is. My lies are catching up with me.* And then, because there's nothing else I can say, I follow the guard down the long, narrow hall, terrified of what will come next.

Hannah

After Olivia leaves the salon, Hannah feels as though she sleep-walks through the rest of her appointments. She suspected there was something off about James Bell, but her mind reels after learning that he's an abuser. She can't get the picture of him hitting Olivia out of her mind, and the image infuriates her. Despite Olivia's assurance that he's never raised a hand to Maddie, Hannah worries that it's only a matter of time before he loses control.

The mail doesn't come until almost the end of the day. When her final client leaves at six o'clock, and Peter and Veronica are both cleaning up their stations, Hannah rushes out to the mailbox. Rifling through the various advertisements and bills, she finally pulls out an envelope from Life Choices Northwest, immediately recognizing Zoe's tight scrawl. Blood rushes past her eardrums, and she grips the letter tightly as she makes her way back into the salon. Peter looks up from sweeping and smiles. "Going for a run?"

"Not tonight," Hannah says. Her throat is dry—it cracks on the words. "It's been a long day. Do you mind locking up?"

"Of course not," he says, though he gives her a strange look; it's rare for her to leave the salon before either of her employees. She waves and then heads upstairs to the safety of her apartment, locking the door behind her.

Once she sits on her couch, though, the letter in hand, she hesitates before opening it. She wonders if it will make a difference in how she feels about Olivia and Maddie, knowing for certain if they share the connection to her that Hannah suspects. If it will, in fact, give her any sense of peace. But curiosity takes over soon enough and she carefully tears the letter open.

It is typed, which Hannah didn't expect. Most of the other notes she received were handwritten on store-bought thank-you cards—brief but heartfelt expressions of gratitude from the parents of the recipient—not the recipient himself or herself. This one is a little over a page long, double-spaced, and typed in an elegant font. Hannah takes a deep breath, forcing herself to read the entire letter before looking at whom it is from.

Hello,

I know this letter is late—I know I should have sent it a long time ago. I don't really have an excuse . . . I guess I wasn't sure there was anything I could say to express just how grateful I am for the gift your daughter gave me. The gift you gave me. I was afraid I'd make you sadder than you already were.

I'm really so sorry about your daughter. Every time I sat down to write, all I could think about was how nothing I could say would make it any better that she had to die so I could live. I still feel really guilty, to tell you the truth. It's not fair how this whole organ donor thing works, but my mom always tells me that life isn't fair most of the time so I should probably stop expecting it.

Well, anyway. I don't really know how to explain why I was afraid to write you this letter. It's hard to feel like I deserve something this amazing. I can only imagine what you've gone through. All I know about your daughter is that she was twelve and that she was hit by a car. I wish I knew more. I wish I knew if she liked computers or boys, what her favorite foods were and what TV shows she liked to watch. I lay in bed sometimes at night, imagining getting to know her somehow, thinking that if she was a girl like me when I was twelve, we might have some things in common and it might be easier for you to know that I'm the one who she saved.

The truth is, I'm still learning how to be anything but sick. I've been in hospitals almost my whole life and now I'm out in the world, back at school, and even though it's totally weird and totally great pretty much all at the same time, it's only because you made the incredibly hard decision to let your daughter save me. Thank you seems too small a thing to say for something so huge, but that's why I'm writing you today. To say thank you for letting your daughter go so I can stay. I promise to live the best kind of life I can. I won't waste this gift—I'll do something big and good for other people whenever I can.

You don't have to write me back if you don't want to—if it's too hard or whatever. I understand. I just needed you to know

*that I'm grateful. What you did for me . . . what your daughter
did for me . . . will never be forgotten.*

Sincerely,
Maddie

It's Maddie, Hannah thinks. *I was right—Emily saved her.* Hannah's whole body begins to shake, and she grips the paper in her hand so tightly, she has to set it down for fear of ripping it apart. Maddie—sweet, funny, smart Maddie—wrestling with guilt for being the one who lived, worried that she didn't deserve it. Olivia had mentioned this before, but it didn't sink in for Hannah until just now—until she read it in Maddie's own words.

She goes over the letter a few more times, hearing Maddie's voice in her head as she does. She wonders how she can possibly tell them who she is now, knowing what she knows about their family, what James might do to Olivia for allowing Hannah into their life. She struggles to think of what words she should use and if she can find a way to say them. She longs for Emily so much in this moment—to curl up on the couch under a blanket with her daughter, to eat popcorn and watch a stupid movie with her, letting any worries quietly slip away. Emily was like a balm to Hannah when life wounded her, and now, Hannah has no way to soothe the prickly ache of her pain.

With a shuddering breath, she carefully refolds the letter into thirds and puts it back in the envelope. After setting it on the table, Hannah rises from the couch and slowly walks over to the built-in bookcase next to the fireplace, standing in front of it a moment before finally reaching for the one photo album she brought with her from the house. Its cover is distressed brown leather, similar to a bomber jacket, with thick, off-white stitching along the edges. Her daughter is in its pages—shots of her as a baby, chubby, drooling, and sweet; as a toddler, hugging the teddy bear who, for no discernible reason, she named Steve. There are pictures of her with Hannah, Emily fast asleep in her mother's arms, pictures of Emily's first steps, her first dance lesson, her last birthday party. Hannah recalls the night of that party, when Emily asked her to please stay in her bedroom while she and her friends watched movies and ate pizza in the den.

"But what if you need something?" Hannah said, trying to hide her disappointment that her daughter didn't want her to be part of the celebration.

"We can get it ourselves," Emily responded with a sigh. "I'm not six anymore, Mom. I love you, but I just want to hang out with my friends." It had hurt Hannah, the ease with which Emily pushed her away, and now, she thinks that perhaps it was a mistake to create a life fulfilled only by work and time with her daughter. She wonders if after Devin cheated on her, she latched on too firmly to the promise of a child's unconditional love. She wonders if there even is such a thing.

Hannah opens the album to the pictures she took that night—a smiling Emily when her friends arrived at the front door, presents and overnight bags in hand; the four of them standing around the fudge brownie ice cream cake Hannah had made, the light from twelve candles bathing their young faces in a warm but slightly ghoulish glow. She runs her fingers over Emily's face in the pictures, trying to remember how it felt to touch her daughter's perfect skin, and is shocked to realize she can't. She closes her eyes and tries to hear Emily's voice—her lilting giggle and slightly gravelly, melodious tone. "Stevie Nicks, Jr.," Hannah had jokingly called her, baffled as to why her daughter sounded a little bit like she'd been smoking cigarettes since she was a toddler.

These are the kinds of things Maddie might want to know about Emily, Hannah thinks, and suddenly, she knows she can't put off telling Olivia the truth a moment longer. She sets the album back on the shelf and reaches into her purse for her cell phone. Olivia picks up on the second ring, her voice strung tight when she answers.

"Are you okay?" Hannah asks, hoping Olivia doesn't sound so stressed because she somehow discovered that Maddie wrote the letter. Would Zoe notify her parents? Would Zoe even know that James had forbidden them to contact the donor family? Maybe it was too late for Hannah to do the right thing.

"I don't know," Olivia says. She isn't crying, but her tone is definitely strained. "No," she continues. "I'm not. I'm at the police station."

"Oh no, what happened?" Hannah's mind races with ugly explanations for why Olivia might be there. "Did you call them? Are you hurt?"

"It's Maddie," Olivia says. "She went to the mall with some friends and got caught shoplifting. She swears it's a mistake, that she didn't take anything, but the guard found some earrings on her. I tried to talk them out of it, but the store is going to press charges and I'll have to tell James." She takes a heaving breath. "He's going to lose his mind, Hannah. I'm afraid of what he might do."

"Do you want me to be there when you tell him?" Hannah

offers, thinking James would be less likely to harm his wife and daughter with a witness present, but also knowing that there is nothing she can do to protect Maddie and Olivia once they are alone with him.

"I don't know," Olivia says, and that's when she starts to cry. "I just don't know how I got to this place . . . It's so stupid. *I'm* so stupid."

"You're not stupid," Hannah says gently. It makes her sick to know that James has convinced Olivia of this. She wonders if he also has something to do with what Maddie said in her letter—that she doesn't feel worthy of the transplant. The thought that he's made his daughter feel that she is somehow defective incenses Hannah. "Are you done with everything there? Can you take Maddie home?" Olivia says yes, and Hannah continues. "Okay, then. I'll meet you at your house. We'll figure it out when I get there."

"You don't have to come—" Olivia begins, still sniffling, but Hannah cuts her off.

"I know I don't have to," she says, her hand resting over the open pages of the photo album. She thinks about Emily, if she had been the one arrested for shoplifting, how Sophie would be right there for her. Olivia doesn't have anyone else. *It has to be me.* "I want to."

Olivia thanks her, and they hang up. Hannah takes a few deep breaths, knowing that the last thing Olivia needs right now is to find out that Hannah has been lying to her, but no matter how hard it might be, no matter the price she might pay, it's time for Hannah to tell her who she is.

Olivia

Maddie is quiet on the drive home from the police station. Olivia tries to get her to talk, to tell her the last names of the girls she was shopping with so maybe James will have somewhere else to direct his anger, but her daughter stays silent until they turn the corner to their street and Maddie sees Hannah's car waiting for them at the gate.

"What's she doing here?" Maddie asks, uncrossing her arms from her chest and looking over to her mother with eyes puffy and red from crying.

"I called her and she offered to come over," Olivia explains. Her heart aches seeing her daughter's distress. "I need to figure out how we're going to tell your dad what happened."

"And you need Hannah to help you with that?" her daughter asks tearfully. "So I can feel even more humiliated than I already do?"

"Maddie . . ." Olivia says as she presses the remote on the visor to open the gate. She knows her daughter gets a little snotty when she's actually just scared, but a teenage temper tantrum feels like the last thing Olivia can deal with right now. James will be home soon, and Olivia has no idea how to talk with him about Maddie's arrest without it escalating out of control. The last time Olivia really had to discipline Maddie was before she got sick—it wasn't like she misbehaved much when she was bedridden or stuck in the hospital. When she did—when she talked back or threw a hissy fit before yet another blood draw—Olivia mostly overlooked it because Maddie *was* sick—she was entitled to act out. Punishing a sixteen-year-old for getting caught shoplifting versus punishing a six-year-old for coloring on the living room wall is a huge mental leap for Olivia.

"Never mind, Mom. You don't get it."

"Don't get what? I thought you liked Hannah." In front of them, Hannah drives through the open gate and proceeds toward the house. Olivia feels a strange sense of calm, knowing her friend is here to support her.

"I do like her . . . it's just . . ." Maddie shakes her head and looks away from Olivia again. "Nothing. Don't worry about it." Her daughter's bottom lip trembles as Olivia puts the car in park.

"Sweetie, I *am* worried. I'm worried about you, about why you'd hang out with girls who would do something like this."

"It's not my *fault*!" Maddie says. "It's not like I *knew* they were going to steal. They asked me to go shopping with them, not shop*lifting*! I said yes because I'm the new girl and I want to make friends. That's all. End of story. *God*!" She throws open her door and climbs out of the car, racing past Hannah to the front porch, using her key to enter the house.

"Is she okay?" Hannah asks as she approaches Olivia, who has also exited her car. Hannah glances around, a little nervously, it seems, tucking her black hair behind her ears. Olivia wonders if she's looking for James.

"She's scared," Olivia says, looking at her friend with tears in her eyes. She can hardly believe that it was only this morning when they sat in Hannah's apartment discussing the truth of Olivia's life with James. Now, she blinks a few times and tries to smile. "Thanks for coming. I really appreciate it."

"Of course," Hannah says, then hesitates as she had earlier in the day, opening then closing her mouth like she is about to say something else then thinks better of it. Olivia realizes this is something Hannah has done more than once since they met. She waits to see if Hannah will say more, but her friend remains quiet and they both follow Maddie inside, putting their purses on the entryway table.

"Maddie?" Olivia calls out, and her voice echoes. "Honey, please. Come talk with us. I'm not mad. I believe you, okay? I know you wouldn't steal. But we need to talk about all this." She looks to Hannah, who nods encouragingly, then Maddie appears at the top of the stairs, her arms crossed over her chest again. Hannah gives Olivia's forearm a quick, reassuring squeeze.

"Talk about what?" Maddie says, still tearful. "How Dad's going to react? He's going to lose his shit. *That's* how he'll react."

"Please don't swear," Olivia says, feeling helpless, mostly because Maddie is right. James will freak out over this, whether or not Maddie actually took those earrings. It won't matter to him that the other girl may have put the earrings in his daughter's pocket—what will matter is that Maddie got caught. What will matter is that he'll be furious she's done something that could make *him* look bad. Olivia has the brief, wild thought that they could simply pack their bags right now. They could climb in their car and drive away from this life and not have to deal with any of this. But where would they go that James couldn't find them? How would they survive?

Maddie throws her hands up in the air. "Why not? What does it matter? Dad's going to *kill* me, Mom. You know he will. He's never . . . it's always you . . . but now . . ." Her words stutter out of her, and Olivia knows exactly what her daughter is afraid of—that James will hit her now, too. A hot wave of guilt rushes through her for letting herself be fooled even for a moment that she'd managed to protect Maddie from her father's abuse. No matter how much Olivia has tried to hide his behavior, Maddie is still its casualty—collateral damage from a war quietly raging between her parents.

"Oh, honey," Olivia says, starting up the stairs, wanting to do nothing more than comfort her daughter, but then Hannah speaks, stopping Olivia in her tracks.

"Sometimes you have to stand up to a bully to make him back down," she says, and Maddie looks quickly at Olivia, then over to Hannah again.

"You make it sound easy," she says, her words stilted and slow.

"It's not," Hannah says. "But if you're prepared, if you have a plan of attack, you can do it."

Maddie still looks doubtful. "You don't know what he's like—"

"Yes, she does," Olivia says quickly, cutting Maddie off. "I told Hannah everything this morning."

"Told her what?" Maddie lifts her chin, challenging Olivia to admit what she's never acknowledged. She's let her body speak the truth to her daughter—her bruises and her tears—but she's never had the courage to say it out loud. *It's time,* she thinks. *There's no use in pretending anymore.*

Olivia takes a deep breath, holding it as the words tumble out of her in a ragged whisper. "That your father hits me." She stares at Maddie, imploring her to forgive her for not telling the truth sooner. Her daughter's expression softens, and Olivia knows she's done the right thing.

"We can call the police," Hannah says. "We can tell them you're afraid for your safety and they'll come."

At the thought of bringing the police in on the situation, every ounce of courage Olivia might have been feeling evaporates. She shoots Hannah a panicked look. "I can't," she says. "Not yet."

"When, then?" Hannah asks, sounding desperate. "When he breaks your bones? Or when he finally hits Maddie? Will that be reason enough for you to leave him?" She takes in a sharp breath and then continues, her hands balled into tight fists at her sides. "I know I said this morning that I wouldn't tell you what to do, but I was wrong. I was wrong because you still have your daughter, Olivia. She's bright and beautiful and kind and she's right *here.*" She waits a beat, as though considering the wisdom of what she wants to say next. "Do you have any idea how much I'd give to have Emily with me again?" Olivia begins crying when Hannah mentions the death of her own daughter. Hannah continues. "Do you? I would do anything. *Anything* to have the chance to save her, to protect her . . ." Her voice breaks and she has to clear her throat before going on.

"To keep her alive. *This* is your chance. You can either take it or not. But if you don't and James hurts her more than he already has—if he beats her the same way he's beat you—you'll regret it for the rest of your life. You won't be able to stop blaming yourself, not even for a minute. You'll know if you'd just done one thing differently, she'd be okay. I live with that feeling every day . . . knowing if I'd made different choices the day Emily died, she might still be here."

Olivia's shoulders shake as Hannah finishes speaking. Maddie rushes down the stairs and throws her arms around her mother. "It's okay, Mama," she says. "We'll figure it out and we'll be okay." Maddie glares at Hannah over her mother's shoulder.

"I'm sorry," Hannah whispers, her shoulders slumped. "I shouldn't . . . it's not my place to talk like that to you . . . I just . . ." She trails off, and Maddie's gaze softens the slightest bit. She pulls back from her mother, and Olivia looks at Hannah through watery eyes.

"But you're right. We can't live like this anymore." She sniffs and takes Maddie's hand in hers, taking another calming breath before going on. "So I think it's best if we don't tell your dad about what happened at the mall today. He doesn't need to know." She turns toward Maddie and puts her hands on her daughter's shoulders. "Hannah is right. You are good and kind and smart and you deserve better than being afraid of your own father. I'm sorry I've let it go on so long . . . I just . . . I never thought . . . you were so sick and I didn't know how—" Olivia stumbles over her words, trying to find a good explanation for why she stayed with James. But maybe that's the problem. When it comes right down to it, there isn't one.

"I get it, Mom," Maddie says through her own tears. "It's okay." She glances over to Hannah, who is tearfully watching their exchange. Olivia reaches out a hand to her friend, but Hannah takes a step back from them, frowning with her blue eyes wide.

"What is it?" Olivia asks her, dropping her arm back to her side. She pauses. "I'm not angry with you, if that's what you're thinking. What you said about losing your daughter . . . how you'd do anything to save her and keep her safe . . ." She puts a splayed hand over her chest. "Oh my god, Hannah, that so hit home with me. I've been pretending like I have some kind of control over how James will react, like I can manage his behavior or turn it away from Maddie or whatever, but the truth is that even if I could, it doesn't matter. I shouldn't be with a man I'm afraid might beat my child." She drops her hand back to her side and takes a deep breath. "I shouldn't be with a man who beats me."

Hannah shakes her head, indicating that isn't what she's worried about. "I need to tell you something," she says. Her voice is thin and quiet. "Both of you."

Olivia freezes, suddenly apprehensive of what her friend might have to say.

"Tell us what?" Maddie asks, pulling away from Olivia and cocking her head to one side. "My dad's going to be home any minute. If we're going to leave . . ."

"I don't think we can leave *tonight,* honey," Olivia says, temporarily sidetracked from whatever it is Hannah needs to say. "I want to, but I think it would be better to plan a little bit . . . to figure out money and where we're going to live . . ."

"I need to *tell* you both something!" Hannah says again—

loudly this time—and both Olivia and Maddie startle at her insistence. Hannah is breathing hard; her chest heaves and her entire body jitters.

"Hannah," Olivia says nervously. "What is it?" She looks at her new friend, worried that James will walk through the door, see them all crying, and demand to know what happened. She needs to get Maddie showered and fed; she needs to calm herself down before dealing with her husband. But Hannah has been there for her today—more than anyone else ever has. No matter how emotionally exhausted she is, Olivia owes it to her to at least listen.

Hannah doesn't answer her; instead, she steps over to the table where her purse lies next to Olivia's and reaches inside it. She pulls out a white piece of paper folded into thirds. Silently, she hands it to Maddie.

"What's this?" Maddie asks as she carefully opens the paper. Her mouth drops slightly open as she looks at the writing on the page, and Olivia throws another questioning glance at Hannah. But before Hannah can speak, Maddie crumples the paper in her grasp and stares at Hannah. "Where did you get this?" she demands.

"Zoe Parker," Hannah says quietly. The name rings a bell for Olivia, but she can't quite put her finger on why.

"The transplant coordinator," Maddie says, gripping the paper so tightly it begins to tear.

"Please don't," Hannah says, panic lighting up her words. She holds out her hand, as though to take the paper back. "I want to keep it. It was such a beautiful letter, Maddie. It meant so much that you wrote it." Her chin quivers as she speaks; her blue eyes are still glassy with tears.

Olivia shakes her head, trying to comprehend what Hannah has just said. Why would Maddie write Hannah a letter? And the transplant coordinator? What the *hell* is going on?

"It's *you*?" Maddie says, her eyes wide with disbelief as she releases the paper and lets it flutter to the floor. "*Your* daughter . . . ?"

"Yes." Hannah squats down and grabs the letter, tucking it back inside her purse. Olivia watches this, and suddenly, it begins to dawn on her what might be happening. *No. There's no way. Hannah's daughter wasn't the right age to be Maddie's donor.*

"But you said she was *five*," Maddie says, as though she could hear Olivia's thoughts. She stares at Hannah accusingly, her eyes flashing in a way so similar to James's eyes when his fury takes him over, it makes Olivia's heart skip a beat.

"I know, but—" Hannah begins.

"Wait a minute," Olivia says, cutting Hannah off, not wanting to believe that what she suspects is going on between her friend and Maddie is the truth. She turns to her daughter, looking at her sternly. "You wrote Hannah a letter? Why?"

"I wrote a letter to the parents of the girl who donated her liver to me," Maddie says, then narrows her eyes at Hannah. "How did you find us?"

Olivia is stunned; a hundred thoughts tumble through her mind at once. Did Hannah seek them out? Did she somehow figure out a way to meet them? *No, she couldn't have,* Olivia decides. *We walked into her salon on a whim. Completely on our own. There's no way this could be true.*

"Maddie, wait a minute," Olivia says, putting her arm around her daughter's shoulders. "This can't be right. Tell her, Hannah. Tell her she's wrong."

Hannah turns to face Olivia and shakes her head. "I wish I could but . . . Emily *was* Maddie's donor. I didn't know for certain until I got Maddie's letter today." She takes in a deep breath and releases it before going on. "I didn't mean to lie about Emily's age . . . I was just completely blindsided when you came into the salon and it just sort of popped out when you asked me about her. And then you told me about James basically forbidding you to contact the donor family and I was afraid of what he'd do if he found out who I was. I didn't want to say anything that could get you in trouble with him until I knew for sure."

"Hold on," Olivia says, clutching Maddie's shoulders so tightly her daughter flinches. She relaxes her fingers and takes a couple of deep breaths. "You've been *lying* to me?" Olivia's mind whirls. *What if James finds out about this? What will he do to me?* She can almost feel his fingers around her throat. She has to get Hannah out of this house. James will be home any minute. He can't know who Hannah is.

"I was afraid if I told you about Emily, you'd stop talking with me," Hannah says hurriedly. "I've been so closed off since the accident and you and I connected so easily . . . I just . . . I didn't want to lose that. It was stupid. I'm sorry, Olivia. I'm so, so sorry."

For a moment Olivia's heart softens, understanding why Hannah was afraid to reveal her suspicions to them. Olivia puts her fingers to her forehead and grips them there, trying to sort out her conflicting feelings. She wants to understand why this happened, but she also knows if James finds out, he'll lose his mind.

Before she can respond to Hannah, the front door swings

open and James strides across the threshold. As he looks them over—assessing the tears, the smeared makeup, the angry expression on Maddie's face—they all freeze where they stand.

"What's going on?" James says, quickly dropping his brief-case to the floor.

"Nothing, honey," Olivia says, shooting Hannah a look that makes it clear she shouldn't speak. "Just a misunderstanding. Everything's fine."

"It doesn't look like nothing," James says, crossing his arms over his broad chest. Olivia knows that no matter what she and Maddie decide to do—how long they stay with James—she can never tell her husband Hannah's true identity. She'll simply tell him they had a falling-out and his appraisal of her had been right—Hannah couldn't be trusted. No matter how hurt Olivia might be that Hannah lied to them, suddenly, it isn't just herself and Maddie that Olivia needs to protect from James. It's Hannah, too.

"Believe me, it is," Olivia says, hoping she sounds convincingly lighthearted considering the weight that now sits on her chest. "And Hannah was just leaving."

Hannah holds her gaze for a moment, her blue eyes pleading and sorrowful, but then she presses her lips together and nods, slinging her purse over her shoulder. She pushes past James, who stands like a bouncer in front of the doorway, and then stops once she reaches the front porch. The light casts a warm, pale glow on her face, and Olivia stares at the woman who only moments ago she thought might become her closest friend, wondering how she never even suspected the truth. Wondering if she'll ever get to see Hannah again.

Maddie

After the door closes behind Hannah, my mother, father, and I stand in silence. I keep my eyes on the floor, knowing if I look up, I'll give something away. I'm worried he'll see that Mom and I want to leave him. I'm terrified of what he'll do.

My mother is the first to speak. "Why don't you go upstairs, Maddie?" Her voice is surprisingly calm, considering the panic I see skittering across her face. I glance up at her, and she gives me a quick, encouraging nod. "I'll call you down when dinner's ready. I think I have what I need to make those sesame rice noodles you like."

"You haven't eaten yet?" my dad asks. He looks twitchy, bubbling at the surface like a pot about to boil. "It's after eight."

"I'm not really hungry," I say, hoping to help my mother.

"It's been a busy afternoon," she says, stepping over to stand next to my dad. She runs a hand along his forearm with a gentle touch. "Maddie and I went shopping at Bellevue Square after school and lost track of time. We came home to find Hannah waiting for us, which I thought was a little strange since I hadn't invited her." She smiles at him, and I can't believe how easily she came up with this lie, how efficiently she hid how I know she's really feeling. Maybe I came by my *dis*honest tendencies more honestly than I thought.

"That's why you were arguing?" He sounds doubtful, looking back and forth between Mom and me. "There was definitely something going on here, Olivia. Don't try to tell me there wasn't." He sounds exactly like the bully Hannah described him as being only minutes ago. *Hannah. The mother of the girl who saved me.* I can barely wrap my mind around the idea that this is true.

"No, no. You're right, honey," Mom says. "We were arguing about that. I thought it was odd for her to just show up without calling first. Too pushy and overly familiar when we barely know her. She got defensive when I called her on it, and everything went downhill from there. Nothing serious . . . just uncomfortable, you know?"

I hold my breath, watching as she spins this fragile web of lies, wondering if he will fall for it.

"I told you there was something off about her," Dad says, the puff of his chest relaxing as he speaks. "Didn't I?"

Mom nods. "You did." She sidles up against him and puts her arms up around his neck, waiting for him to kiss her. He does, pressing his body hard against hers. I cringe, understanding for the first time, really, how much moments like this must cost her. I'm amazed seeing her manage him, and I understand that we might have to wait to leave—that we need to have a good plan and some money before we walk out the door. But right now, the fact that she told the truth about what he does to her—that she trusted me to be able to handle it—will have to be enough.

My phone suddenly buzzes in my pocket and I grab for it, not wanting to irritate my dad when Mom has just coaxed him back off a dangerous ledge. "I'll be upstairs," I say and head to my room without waiting for either of my parents to respond. Once the door is closed behind me, I flip on a light and check the screen to see whom the text is from, smiling when I see Noah's name and a short message: "Can u talk?"

I shoot a text back: "Yeah, but need to take care of something first. Call you in a bit." After I press send, I boot up my laptop, ready to do something I should have done a long time ago. If I expect my mom to be honest, I need to expect the same thing of myself.

It only takes a few minutes to log in to Facebook and Zombie Wars and completely erase any evidence of Sierra Stone. I delete her profile on Twitter, too, which I hadn't used much since the only followers she seemed to get were perverted men who, after seeing her pictures, offered to pay her for sex. I'd block those idiots and more would show up. It strikes me that maybe being the hot girl is overrated. Maybe it's better to be valued for who I am instead of what I look like.

Next, I wipe my hard drive clean of all of her pictures, then I log in to my email account and write a brief but what I hope is kind message to Dirk:

Hey there,

I know you're out of town and I feel really bad about doing this through email, especially because you've been so patient about meeting me, but I just don't think I'm ready for a relationship right now. You deserve someone who can be there IRL for you and I'm just not that girl. You're probably one of the sweetest guys I've ever known. Thank you for being my friend.

Maddie

I hesitate, thinking maybe I should tell him the entire truth about who I am, but then I think about how I felt earlier tonight when Hannah handed me that letter and I understood she had been lying to us since the day we met. I felt shocked, stupid, and used, and the truth is I don't want Dirk to feel that way, too. I thought pretending to be someone I wasn't was harmless, but I realize now that every little deception took away from my true self—a self that, since the transplant, I'm just starting to sort out. I finally click the send button and then add his email address to my blocked senders list so he can't contact me. I block his number on my cell phone, too. I feel a little sad as I do this, but also relieved. It's exhausting, putting so much energy into being an entirely different person than who you actually are. Now I can work at becoming the girl I want to be.

I'm hoping a big part of that girl will be someone who helps her mother get away from a dangerous marriage, so I open up a search engine on my laptop and type in the words "how to leave an abusive relationship." More than 3 million links are returned in under a second, and in some small way that comforts me, knowing I'm not the first person to sit in front of the computer and look up this particular subject.

The first thing I learn is that there is a National Domestic

Violence Hotline, so I quickly look up that number and pro-gram it into my phone, just in case my mom and I need to call. I review the list of things a person is supposed to do in order to prepare to leave a violent relationship and immediately be-come overwhelmed. We can't just walk out the door like I'd hoped we could barely an hour ago. We'll have to gather birth certificates, medical records, and money; we'll need to create an exit plan and maybe call the police to escort us to safety. And since I'm a minor, my mom can't just take me away and never come back. There are custody issues to deal with—if she and I just pack our bags and disappear, she could be charged with kidnapping.

A sinking feeling gathers in my chest as I realize how complicated starting over might be, and I begin to understand why my mom has stayed with Dad so long. The instructions talk about how important it is to have documentation of the abuse—pictures of injuries, records of emergency room visits, and police reports. I'm sure my mom has none of these, since up until tonight she kept what my father does to her a secret. Except from Hannah, who at this point, doesn't even count.

The back of my throat aches as I think about how she lied to us, how both my mom and I thought she was our friend. I think about how long I've felt bad for the parents of the girl who saved my life, and suddenly, knowing what kind of person she actually is, my guilt begins to fade. "Screw her," I mutter, but then a little voice chirps inside my head: *You lied about who you are, too. You lied to Dirk . . . to every single person you chatted with online.* Hannah said she was scared to be hon-est, just like I was scared to be honest with Dirk. Is it fair to be angry at her for doing to us for a couple of weeks what I've

safe with me 261

done for over a year, even if it was for an entirely different reason?

Not really wanting to think about the answer to that particular question, I quickly erase my browsing history as the instructions I just read suggested. As far as I know, my dad has never checked up on what I do on my laptop, but I figure it's better to be safe than sorry. Then, because I said I would, I call Noah.

"How was the mall?" he asks with a slight mocking edge to his tone. I sigh before launching into a description of what happened with Hailey and Jade. My head spins thinking that all of this happened just a few hours ago—it feels so much longer than that.

"Are you effing *kidding* me?" he says when I finish explaining my bogus arrest and how Hailey and Jade ditched me. "What a couple of bitches."

"My thoughts exactly," I say. "But whatever. Who needs them." I pause, panicking a little when I remember that my dad knows Noah's dad, worried that what happened will get back to him. It could ruin everything. I quickly try to cover my tracks. "My mom is being pretty cool, though. She paid the fines with her own money and she's not going to tell my dad."

"Why not?"

I blow out a quick breath between my lips. I have to tell the truth to someone. The instructions I just read said it's important that other people know what you're dealing with so if they can, they might be available to help. "Because he might hit her," I say, and the words catch in my throat like they have claws.

"*What?* No way. You're joking, right?"

"I wish," I say in a very small voice.

"Like he's done it before?"

"Yes." My heart races, wondering how Noah will react.

He's quiet for a moment, but when he speaks, it is with sincerity. "Whoa, Maddie, I'm sorry. That totally sucks." He hesitates before saying more. "My dad told me he's always thought your dad is kind of a prick. I guess he was right."

"I guess so," I say, unable to stop myself from feeling a little bit pleased he talked about me with his dad.

"Has she called the cops on him? Have you?"

"Not yet," I say, and then slowly, quietly just in case my dad comes to my bedroom door, I tell him the whole story, as much as I know. He listens for the longest time, not saying anything. And when I finally finish—when I tell him about meeting Hannah and finding out just a while ago who she actually is—he lets go of a heavy sigh.

"Dude, you've got *issues,*" he says, and I smile, loving that in a moment like this, he can make me laugh.

"You got that right." I pause, suddenly worried I've made a mistake in revealing this much to him. "You can't tell anyone *any* of this, though . . . okay? Especially not your dad. You understand that, right?"

"It's cool, Maddie. I get it. This is some heavy shit you're dealing with. I won't talk about it unless you say it's okay. Okay?"

"Okay," I say, exhaling in relief. There is a soft knock on my door, and my mother opens it, sticking her head into the room. I wave at her and hold up a single finger to let her know I'll just be a minute, so she steps all the way inside, closes the door behind her, and waits. "Noah? I have to go. My mom just walked in. I'll see you tomorrow." I pause. "And hey . . . thank you. You're a pretty cool guy."

"You're just pretty," he says, and I smile, grateful he's not there to see me blush.

We hang up, and Mom comes over and sits down on the edge of my bed, then leans in to hug me. She smells like sesame oil, garlic, and my dad's spicy cologne. "You look happy," she says. She pulls back and tilts her head toward a shoulder, a tired but amused smile on her face. "Is it serious? Should we be looking for a prom dress?"

"No," I say, blushing even more. "He's just really nice. That's all."

"That's wonderful," she says, and then she sighs. "What a day, huh?"

"Yeah," I say, searching her expression for some evidence of how things went with Dad downstairs. She looks exhausted—the lines around her mouth and eyes seem more pronounced than usual. "I'm sorry about Hannah, Mom. I know how much you liked her. I did, too." I have the random thought that now I'll have to find someone else to cut and color my hair. Not a big deal in the grand scheme of things, but still.

She bobs her head and sighs again. "Everything's kind of a mess, isn't it." A statement—not a question. Her bottom lip trembles as she speaks again. "I want you to know something, Maddie. I tried to leave your dad years ago. I was going to divorce him and start a new life with you. But then you got sick, and I knew if I filed for divorce, he'd try and take you away from me, honey. He'd try to prove I was unfit—"

"That's crazy," I interject, feeling guilty for being the reason she had to stay. "There's no *way* he could do that. You're the best mother I know." My voice cracks, and a single tear slips down my cheek. She reaches over and wipes it away with the edge of her thumb. She looks at me tenderly.

"Thank you for that, sweetheart. But you know your dad. He can do pretty much anything he sets his mind to." She frowns and then looks at me, reaching over to squeeze my hand.

We're both quiet for a moment before I speak. "What're *we* going to do?"

She sighs again. "To tell you the truth, I don't know. Your dad is acting like he believes what I said happened with Hannah showing up unannounced, but I'm not sure he means it. It was a pretty weak story. If he finds out who she really is and that I let her into our life . . ." She trails off, and I can almost hear the thoughts clicking together like gears in her head. The terror she feels at what he might do to her—to us—radiates from her body. "I was going to try and stick it out until you left for college so custody and visitation with him wouldn't be an issue." She gives me a halfhearted smile. "I thought I might get my degree in criminal justice so I could become a lawyer, like I always wanted. So I could get a good job and not depend on your dad for money. I even went to a class at Lakeview College last week."

I pull my chin into my chest. "That's awesome, Mom!" It strikes me that there is so much I don't know about my mother— the picture I've always had of her was just the woman who took care of me and put up with too much crap from my dad. Beneath the surface, it's like she's this whole different person.

"I don't know," she says. "With all that happened with Hannah and with you, I think it might be too risky if I go through with it. I can't do anything that might upset your dad."

"What about the police? Can't you call them and get a re-straining order or something?"

"It's not that easy," she says, nervously glancing at the door, then back to me. She reaches over to squeeze my hand. "There has to be an incident . . . more than one, really. Some sort of evidence. Pictures or witnesses. It'd be his word against mine, honey. And I've done a really good job of not telling anyone what he does to me." Her voice breaks and she clears her throat. "I don't have any proof."

"But you have *me*."

"You've never seen him hit me though, have you?" she asks gently. "You've never actually witnessed it."

"But I know he *does*! I've heard it. I've seen the bruises. I've seen you cry. And when we leave and he tries to tell a judge you're a bad mom, I'll say he's lying, okay? You don't have to worry about that." I grab my phone and quickly scroll down to the abuse hotline number, which I'd filed under the name "Si-erra" just in case my dad ever looked through my contact list, then tell her what it actually is. "Maybe we can call them and get some ideas about what to do. How to get ready to leave."

"Where did you find this number?" she asks, suddenly look-ing panicked again.

"Online. I was just looking around for things that could help us."

"Did you tell anyone? That boy, Noah?" Her voice is low, but insistent. She's regretting now that she told me the truth. I can tell by the look on her face.

I drop my eyes to my bed and gather a pillow to my chest. "He promised not to say anything."

"Oh, Maddie." The words are thick with a messy combination of disappointment and fear. "I have to think, okay? I have to figure some things out. Please don't tell anyone else."

"Okay. Sorry."

"It's all right." She drags her fingers through her hair, pulling it away from her face. Her eyes are droopy, her eyeliner is smudged. "But for now, I think we need to act like everything is the same as it's always been. Can you do that?"

Though I hate the idea of more secrets, I nod because I know she needs me to. She looks so fragile sitting next to me on my bed, as though she might shatter if I touch her. I suddenly feel more like her mother than her child, worried she's going to make a bad decision, but knowing there's nothing I can do to stop her. I can't *make* her leave my father.

The one thing I *do* know is that if the day ever comes that he raises a hand to me—if he hits me or punches me or even screams at me too loudly—there's no way I'll stay. With or without my mother, the first thing I'll do is gather up my things and walk right out the door.

Hannah

As much as she hates leaving Olivia and Maddie alone with James, Hannah knows she doesn't have a choice. Driving north on I-405 toward the 520 floating bridge, she wonders if telling them who she is in the middle of them trying to figure out how to leave James was the best decision she ever made, but in her gut she knows she couldn't keep the truth from them a minute longer.

Grateful she thought to put her headset on before leaving the Bells' driveway, she uses the voice commands on her phone to call Sophie, crossing her fingers that her friend answers.

"I'm so glad you called," Sophie says when she picks up, in lieu of an actual greeting. "I feel awful about this morning. I shouldn't have lectured you like that."

"No, you were right. And I did it. I told them who I am." Hannah sniffles and fights back her tears. "But there's more to the story, Soph. I need to talk."

"Oh, honey. Of course. Come on over. I'll send Robert

home." Hannah can hear the low rumble of a man's voice in the background.

"Can you meet me at the storage unit instead?" Hannah lets the words rush from her mouth before she can stop them. "I'm on my way there now, but I don't have the keys. Isaac gave you a set, right? I want . . . I just . . . I need to be with her." A rough sob escapes her and she bites her bottom lip to stop it. "I'm sorry to interrupt your night . . ."

"I'll be there in twenty minutes," Sophie says, ignoring her apology. "You just hold on. Everything will be okay."

Hannah thanks her and then hangs up the phone, quickly instructing it to call her brother. He doesn't answer, so she leaves him a voicemail. "I'm sorry I've been out of touch," she says. "I'm going through some stuff, but I'm okay. I'll be fine. Sophie and I are going to the storage unit tonight. It's time. I've put it off long enough." She sighs. "I love you, Isaac. Talk with you soon."

A few minutes later, Hannah turns in to the parking lot of the facility Isaac chose last year to hold her and Emily's possessions. She isn't sure why, exactly, she feels so driven to go through her daughter's things now, but she isn't in any shape to figure it out. She only knows that she needs to reconnect with a part of herself she shut down when Emily died. Maybe before that, even. Before Devin. If she's ever going to be happy, she needs to find a way to let go and try to move on. Not to forget her grief over losing Emily—she will never forget it—but to ease it somehow, to lessen its icy grip around her heart.

While she waits for Sophie to arrive, she can't help but think about Olivia and Maddie and worry about how James will react to the knowledge of who Hannah actually is. She's so certain that he will hurt them, she's tempted to call the police and report a domestic disturbance. But she's also certain that if he *isn't* hurting them—if Olivia decided it was safer not to tell James about Hannah's identity, just like she decided not to tell him about Maddie's arrest—then the police showing up at their front door would only put Olivia and Maddie in more danger. And that isn't something she wants to risk.

A few minutes later, a pair of headlights shine in her rear-view mirror and Hannah recognizes the grille of Sophie's black Camry. Her friend pulls up next to her, and they both quickly get out of their cars, Sophie rushing over to hug her. Hannah breathes in her friend's sweet perfume, grateful for her strength when Hannah feels so weak.

"Thank you for coming," she whispers. "You're such a good friend to me . . . I know I don't say it often enough—"

"Shush!" Sophie says, squeezing her once more before pulling back. "You don't have to thank me. I love you, *chérie*."

"I love you, too." Hannah takes a deep breath to try to relax the muscles in her chest. "Did you bring the keys?"

Sophie pulls out a single silver key from her pocket. "I almost forgot Isaac gave me this," she says. "I had to search for it and the address. I brought a flashlight, too."

Moments later, Hannah and Sophie enter the storage unit, careful to lock the door behind them. Sophie finds the light switch and flips it on, the space suddenly illuminated in the weak glow of a single bulb hanging from the center of the ceiling. Seeing the sheet-covered furniture and haphazard stacks of boxes—each labeled HANNAH or EMILY in her brother's scrawling script—Hannah's eyes sting with tears. She reaches out and runs her fingers over Emily's name. "God, I miss her," she whispers. "It feels like . . ." She trails off, and the muscles around her stomach convulse.

"Like what?" Sophie asks gently.

Hannah turns to look at her friend. "Like a piece of me has been amputated. Like I'm stumbling around without a prosthetic for the part of me I lost." She swallows, hard. "I know I didn't handle the situation with Olivia and Maddie the right way. I know that. But it was like I couldn't help myself. Meeting Maddie was almost like being able to see my daughter again . . ." She pauses to wipe away a few tears with the back of her hand. "I mean, I know she *wasn't* Emily. I'm not *totally* crazy."

Sophie gives her an understanding smile and reaches out to hold her hand. "No, not totally." Her friend sighs. "Maybe you just needed to see that you made the right decision. Not just the whole of-course-it's-the-right-thing-to-do-to-save-other-people's-lives thing, but on a deeper level, just for you and Emily." She cocks her head to one side. "Hell. Now *I* sound crazy."

"Oh, good." Hannah lets loose a sound that is half laughter, half cough. "I'm pretty tired of being the unstable one." She takes a deep breath and looks around the unit again. "I think I'm going to donate her clothes and toys to an organization that helps pay for families to stay near the transplant center," she tells Sophie. "Zoe—that coordinator I told you about?—mentioned it in passing once and said that the kids who have to stay there rarely have anything other than the bare necessities."

"I think that's a lovely idea," Sophie says. "You're donating all of it?"

Hannah shrugs, then opens the box next to her and reaches inside to pull out a blue sweater that Emily had particularly favored. A spasm of grief seizes her throat, and she pushes the sweater against her nose, trying to find a trace of her daughter's scent, but there's nothing there, only a stale, cottony smell of fabric packed away too long. *Emily is gone.* "Yes, all of it. I want her art projects and schoolwork, but except for some of what she wore as a baby, I don't need her clothes and toys. They should be put to better use."

She sighs again, trying to release the stress that buzzes through her body, a feeling that reminds her of the one she had in the hospital the day Emily died. She reaches into a box stuffed full with papers and begins reading the stacks of notes Emily wrote her through the years. There are the ones she drew in preschool—stick figures of Hannah and Emily standing together in front of their house, Emily attempting to write her own name in barely recognizable letters. There's the one she pushed under Hannah's door on a Saturday morning when she was seven that read: *I am watching cartunes. Can I have Luky Charms for brakefast today? Mark Yes or No.* Below this were two boxes for Hannah to indicate her answer.

"She was such a little sugar fiend," Sophie remarks fondly as Hannah hands her friend this particular note.

Hannah nods, unable to speak. Her throat clenches as she reads through her daughter's many *I love you, Mommy* notes, trying to remember the specific instances that prompted Emily's affectionate declarations. But it's harder than she thought it would be to recall the reasons why Emily decided to express her feelings. Perhaps it doesn't matter. Perhaps all that matters is that Emily loved her.

With this thought, Hannah dissolves into tears. Hiccuping sobs shake her body; her muscles quiver and quake. She cries for Emily and for herself. For her parents and for her brother, for Olivia and Maddie. She lets the pain take her to a place she's avoided for over a year—the deepest, darkest space inside her—and lets it breathe, lets loose the despair that has dragged her down, kept her from moving forward. Sophie puts her arm around Hannah, not speaking, just holding on through the waves of grief, letting her know she's not alone.

Finally, Hannah's tears begin to lessen, and Sophie gently pulls away. "You'll be okay," she says. "Everything will be okay."

Sniffling, Hannah nods, trying hard to believe her friend's words. As they go through the boxes, Hannah tells Sophie the entire truth about Olivia and her marriage to James, along with everything else that has happened that day. She lets Sophie read Maddie's letter, and ends by explaining how James walked through his front door.

"It's a sad story, yes. Horrible, even," Sophie says as she lifts up a box filled with all of Emily's old Halloween costumes. "These, too?" Hannah nods, and Sophie goes on. "But ultimately, don't you think that what Olivia does with her life is her own business?"

"What about Maddie?" Hannah says, feeling desperate. "Shouldn't I report James to CPS or something? That there's suspected abuse? Maybe they could help."

"You could," Sophie says, nodding. "But you just finished saying how there isn't any proof. And as far as you know, he's not hitting Maddie. So you'd basically be getting CPS involved for no good reason."

"It's not fair for him to get away with this," Hannah says, frustrated that there's really nothing she can do to help mend the situation.

"You're right. It's not. But it's not your call to decide how Olivia handles it. Especially now . . . no?"

Hannah doesn't respond for the simple reason that her friend is right. Olivia confided in her, and at this point, the very least Hannah can do is sit back, honor Olivia's wishes, and keep her mouth shut.

The next morning, Hannah wakes up and as usual, goes for a run. She and Sophie stayed at the storage unit well past midnight, sorting through boxes, deciding which tangible items of Emily's Hannah wants to keep. In the end, they carried only two boxes back with them to the cars, filled with Hannah's favorite pictures of her daughter, several of her art projects, all of her I-love-you-Mommy notes, and a purple scarf she liked to wear. She'll ask Isaac to help her get the remainder delivered to the transplant center's charity. Her furniture and other belongings in the unit will have to wait until Hannah decides if she's going to stay in her apartment above the salon. "Maybe I'll sell the old house and buy a new one for myself," she told Sophie last night. "Maybe it's time to really start over."

Now, as she sets out down the sidewalk at a slow, warm-up pace, Hannah thinks the truly important things for her to keep from Emily are the intangible ones—the way her daughter looked when she first stumbled out of bed in the morning, the stink of her breath and the warmth of her skin. Hannah will forever keep the memory of how it felt for her daughter to climb up in her lap, stick her face against Hannah's neck, and whisper, "I love you, Mama." She'll hold on to the bubbles of Emily's laughter, the way she sometimes sang "C Is for Cookie" in a Cookie Monster voice purely for Hannah's amusement. Thinking back, Hannah realizes that for the most part Emily was a joyful, happy child, and despite any mistakes she's made along the way, this is what she needs to hold on to—not mourning, not grief, not loss.

When she gets back to the salon, an hour later, dripping with sweat and breathing hard, she decides to pick up the phone before jumping in the shower. Her mother answers on the second ring. "Hi, honey," she says. "What a nice surprise."

"I hope it's not too early," Hannah says. "I just got done with my run and I figured you'd be up."

"You know me," her mother says, chuckling. "With the roosters." She pauses. "Is everything okay?"

"Yeah, everything's fine." Hannah pauses to run a finger over a small crack in the plaster. "I just wanted to let you know that I'll definitely be home for Thanksgiving. I'm scheduling myself the whole week off so we can have a good long visit." Unexpectedly, she tears up as she speaks. "I'm sorry I haven't been home more this year, Mom. It's been . . . well . . . it's been hard." She knows "hard" is too simple a word to describe what the months since Emily died have been like, but it's the only one that comes to her.

"Your dad and I understand, sweetheart. We worry about you . . . that's all."

"I guess that never goes away," Hannah says affectionately. "No matter how old I get?"

"No, it never does," her mom agrees. "You'll always be our baby."

"I'm glad," Hannah says, her throat thickening again. "I love you, Mom. I'll talk with you later, okay?"

They hang up, and it strikes her that for the first time in a year her mother didn't bring up the subject of her moving home; she wonders if her adamant refusal has finally made its point. Hannah vows to have a long talk with her parents over the holiday about finding someone else to help Dad manage the farm—someone he can trust and someday turn the operation over to so they don't have to sell any more land than they want to for their retirement. She is lucky, she knows, to still have her parents with her, and she plans to be more attentive to them.

Her next call is a harder one to make. Surprisingly, Olivia answers her cell on the third ring. "I'm so glad you picked up," Hannah says. "I wasn't sure that you would."

Olivia sighs. "I only did so I could tell you that I really can't talk with you anymore. It's just not a good idea."

"Did you tell James about me? About Emily?"

"No. But I can't risk that he'll find out another way. If he figures out Maddie wrote that letter . . ."

"I thought you were going to leave him," Hannah says.

"It's not that simple," Olivia whispers. "I have to go now. Please understand that it's safer for us if you just pretend we never met."

"Olivia . . ." Hannah begins, her voice breaking. She clears her throat so she can continue. "I just need to say that if I could go back to that day when you both walked into the salon . . . when Maddie sat down in my chair and talked about her transplant, I swear, I would change everything. I would have told you right away that it was possible Emily was her donor."

"I know." Olivia sounds as though she is about to cry, too. "But you didn't."

"I'm so sorry," Hannah says.

"Me, too," Olivia responds, sounding more hurt than angry. A moment later they hang up, and Hannah sits on her couch, staring at her phone, hoping that someday, there might still be a chance for them to be friends.

Olivia

The first couple of days after finding out about Hannah, Olivia tiptoes around her husband, terrified she might say or do something to set him off. Strangely enough, he doesn't pick at the edges of Olivia's story about what happened with Hannah. When he's at home, he seems unusually pensive and distracted—less vigilant about monitoring what Olivia does during her days.

"Is everything okay, honey?" she asks him as they are about to go to sleep on Saturday night. He barely spoke to her all day, and usually, his silence is a precursor to one of his rages. She wants to do whatever she can to placate him.

"Fine," he says tersely. He waits a moment and then speaks again. "My dad called the office yesterday."

Olivia tenses next to him in their bed, knowing how much of a hot button James's father is for him. "I thought your secretary knows not to let him through."

"The bastard gave her a fake name. Said he was a potential

investor." James laughs, a dry, empty bark. "As if he has any-thing to invest. He was looking for a handout. Can you believe that?"

Olivia brushes her fingers over his forearm. "I'm sorry."

James places his own hand on top of hers and grips it tightly. Her breath freezes in her lungs, worried about what might happen next. But then he lifts her hand to his mouth and kisses the inside of her palm. "I felt like I was ten years old again, talking to him. I wanted to be sick." Suddenly, he gathers her to him, holding her so tightly no air can enter or escape her body. He presses his mouth up against her ear so she can feel the wet heat of his breath. "Tell me I'm not like him," he says in a ragged voice. "Please."

Olivia swallows the bitterness that rises in her throat and tries to ignore the conflicting ache in her heart as she tells her husband what he needs to hear. "You're nothing like him," she whispers. The lie burns like acid on her tongue. "Nothing at all."

Thus reassured, James falls asleep with his head resting on her chest and one arm flung over her stomach. Olivia doesn't sleep, her mind twisting with worry and fear—but perhaps more disconcerting than that, love for her husband.

The next morning, James leaves for the office despite the fact that it's a Sunday. Olivia fights the urge to call Hannah, knowing she's anxious to reach out so she doesn't have to face changing her situation alone. Now that Maddie no longer just suspects James's abuse, Olivia can't pretend that everything will be okay. In the moments they have been without James, her daughter has been adamant about making a plan to leave—and like her father when he sets his mind on something, she will not be deterred. Still, despite Maddie's protests, on Monday morning Olivia calls the college and withdraws her enrollment. At this point, it's just too much of a risk.

"Reason for your withdrawal?" the nasally woman in the administration office inquires.

"Family emergency," Olivia says, thinking this is about as close to the truth as she can get.

"Hold for Professor Lang, please," the woman says, and before Olivia can protest, her call is transferred.

"Professor Lang," her teacher says, and Olivia almost hangs up on her, but something makes her stay on the line.

"Hi," she says awkwardly. "This is Olivia Bell? The office just transferred me to you?"

"Olivia," Professor Lang says. "I haven't seen you in class this week."

Olivia shifts in her chair, swallowing before she answers. "I, um, have a bit of a family emergency going on. I have to withdraw."

"That's why the office transferred you, then. I require that students tell me personally why they're dropping my class."

Olivia licks her lips nervously, worried the professor will try to get her to admit the situation she'd described was anything but hypothetical. "It's not personal. I think the class is great. I just . . . like I said. I have a family emergency to deal with." *Please drop it,* she thinks. *Please just let me go.*

"I'm sorry to hear that," Professor Lang says and then waits a beat. "Are you okay, Olivia? Do you need help?"

The muscles in Olivia's throat thicken; she's certain Professor Lang has sorted out the truth. "No," Olivia finally manages to say. "I'm okay. I mean, I will be." There's no way to know whether this is true, but Olivia has to believe it. To think otherwise is too frightening. "Thank you for asking, though," she tells her teacher. "I appreciate it."

"There's a lot of help out there," Professor Lang says quietly. "You just have to reach out."

"Okay," Olivia says hurriedly, wanting to get off the phone. She's already made the mistake of trusting Hannah with her story—she doesn't want to run the risk with her professor. "Thanks again."

After she hangs up, she logs on to her computer and runs a couple of Internet searches for women's shelters and counselors who specialize in domestic abuse, curious about the "other help" Professor Lang had mentioned. The pictures on the shelter websites are full of smiling, happy women of all ages, colors, and sizes—stock photos, the disclaimers at the bottom of the screen state, because of identity protection issues that go along with being a survivor of abuse. Olivia reads through several of the clients' personal accounts, weeping as she finds herself over and over again in these stories: the constant fear, shame, and self-loathing the women experienced; the terror that strangled their every breath. Will she need to take Maddie to a shelter while she and James sort out their divorce? Her stomach turns over as she imagines his response to her filing. If she doesn't have any evidence, will she still be able to list verbal and physical abuse as the reason for leaving her marriage? Would a judge believe her?

She clicks through to a few pro bono legal websites, shocked by the length of the waiting lists to see one of these professionals. She has the money to pay for a good lawyer, but she had set it aside to help support Maddie and herself when they are on their own. Hannah had said that James would have to pay her child support and for Maddie's insurance—they've been married over ten years, so she'd be due alimony, too, however distasteful it might feel to take it from him. But if he filed for custody and won, would he have to pay her anything at all? She sits back from her computer and closes her eyes, unsure if she has the courage to leave him, though she acts as though she's still certain she will when she picks Maddie up later that afternoon.

"I can get any kind of job," she says after she tells her daughter about dropping out of the class. "Waiting on tables or whatever it takes."

"But I thought you wanted to become a lawyer," Maddie says as they drive toward home.

"I used to," Olivia says with a small, wistful smile. "Now I think maybe I wanted to go back to school as an excuse, you know? A way to postpone having to leave." She reaches over and pats the top of Maddie's thigh. "I'll make some calls, okay? We'll figure it out."

Maddie nods, but Olivia can see that her daughter doesn't trust that she'll follow through. "You haven't told anyone about your dad other than Noah . . . right?" she asks, trying to keep the inquiry light.

"No, Mom. *I'm* not someone who goes back on my promises." Clearly, her words are meant to make a point, and they hit the mark. After everything Maddie's been through over the years, Olivia knows she owes her daughter a chance to live beyond her father's angry reach. But her insides churn at the very thought of packing a suitcase, let alone finding a lawyer, and then, possibly facing years of divorce disputes. And there's the chance that James would come after her—that he would attack them both for leaving. The fear of that moment paralyzes Olivia, making her feel that the only safe movement is no movement at all. She longs for someone other than Maddie to talk with, a friend who might help her find the strength she needs—but the only person she can think of is Hannah.

It's strange, really, how much Olivia misses her, considering how little she actually knows about the mother of Maddie's donor. Is everything Hannah purported about herself a lie, or was it just her link to the transplant that she kept secret? There is so much about Hannah that Olivia likes—her sense of humor, her insightfulness, her compassion. Olivia truly believed she had found an ally, someone who understood her like no one else did. She knows that grief can make people do crazy things—behavior they normally would never even consider. She knows that her own propensity to portray a pretty picture of her life with James—not only to the world but to her daughter—isn't something she ever consciously decided on. It happened gradually, the small lies became one big one. It became her life. At least Hannah was only dishonest with them for a couple of weeks—she admitted she was wrong, she apologized for hurting them. Olivia hopes that someday, perhaps after she finds the courage to break away from James, she can move past the hurt she feels; then she and Hannah can try again.

When they get home and Maddie is ensconced in her bedroom, supposedly doing her homework, but more likely chatting online with Noah, Olivia decides to call Waverly, whom she hasn't spoken with for months.

"Olivia!" Waverly exclaims. "Long time, no talk!"

"I know," Olivia says. "Life has been a little hectic around here."

"How *are* you, honey? How's Maddie?"

Olivia can hear the clink of silverware in the background. "We're okay," she says. "Did I get you at a bad time? Sounds like you're out for dinner."

"I'm at the Olympic Hotel bar, waiting for a drinks date. You should come join me! I'm sure my trainer has an adorable friend I could ask him to bring along."

Olivia shakes her head, realizing not much has changed about Waverly since she divorced her husband. "That's kind of you, but I can't. You know . . . still married to James."

"Oh, I know *that,*" Waverly says with a laugh. "But it doesn't hurt to feed your ego a little bit. You can look at the menu as long as you eat at home."

"I should just let you go," Olivia says, deciding it was a bad decision to call. There is no way she will tell Waverly the truth about her marriage. *I'm just feeling lonely,* she decides. *Sad about losing a friend.*

"No, no," Waverly says. "I'm sorry. I was just teasing you, Liv. Did you need something, or did you just call to catch up?"

"Well . . . honestly I was wondering if you were happy with the divorce lawyer you used. I have a friend who's looking for one." She knows the "friend" story is a childish one, but she figures this way, if Waverly tells her ex-husband, who works with James, about this call, Olivia can simply fabricate someone from the gym who asked her for the referral.

"A friend?"

"Yes," Olivia says, hoping she sounds convincing.

Waverly is silent a moment, and Olivia thinks she hears

the tinkling of ice cubes in a glass. "You can tell your 'friend' that I was extremely happy with my lawyer. Ronald Kress. He squeezed every cent he could out of that rat bastard I married."

Olivia can almost taste her friend's bitterness through the phone. "Okay, thanks. I'll tell her she should call him." She breathes a sigh of relief, feeling as though she's at least taken a small step in the right direction today. She's not sure if she'll actually call Mr. Kress, but at least she has his name.

"Anytime," Waverly says. "And Olivia?"

"Yes?"

"Tell your friend to document everything she can. Paperwork, pictures, account numbers, investments . . . whatever she might need to prove how much her husband is worth. If she hasn't been involved in managing their finances, he's likely hiding money."

"I'll pass that along."

"Also tell her that leaving was the hardest thing I've ever done," Waverly continues, and Olivia hears the bumpy hint of tears behind her words. "But it was also the best."

Olivia thanks her again, and after they hang up, she sits and stares out the window to the backyard, hoping with everything in her that she might someday be able to say the same thing.

Maddie

Sitting in the back of the computer lab with Noah about a month after Hannah revealed who she is, I look at him and sigh. "I honestly don't think she's going to leave him," I say.

Since the night Hannah left our house, the only things my mom has done are drop out of college and continue to pretend like Dad is a really great guy. They haven't had any major fights. He hasn't lost his temper or raised his voice; in fact, they seem sort of happy together—going on dates and cuddling on the couch. Dad even went *grocery shopping* with Mom last weekend, because—he said—he just wanted to spend more time with her. It's completely freaking me out.

"Has she *said* that?" Noah asks. "That she has decided to stay?" It's after school, and we are finished with our assignment, but not ready to go our separate ways for the night. We've sort of developed a routine—he walks me to all my classes and to the nurse's office when I have to take my meds, and we sit together at lunch, along with a group of other kids Noah introduced me to. One girl named Jen is particularly cool—with a shock of bright blue hair threaded through blond. She wears knee-high, laced-up Doc Martens with black leggings and a short military-style jacket almost every day, and like me, she wants to work with CGI. I'm supposed to go over to her house for a Halloween party next weekend—with Noah as my date, which I'm totally excited about. My mom knows we hang out together after school, and as long as we stay *at* the school, she seems fine with it. She picks me up around four, and a glance at the clock now tells me Noah and I only have about ten more minutes together.

"No," I admit, "but actions speak louder than words, right? She hasn't done anything like she said she would. When I bring it up, she shuts me down." I feel tears prick at the backs of my eyes, and Noah reaches over and takes my hand, lacing my short fingers through his long ones. I love how his skin feels—the slightly raised calluses on his palms. "From helping my dad work in the garden," he told me when I asked him about them. "It's kind of our thing." I try not to feel jealous that he's close to his father.

"That sucks," Noah says. I like that he just listens to me and doesn't try to tell me what I should do.

"I don't get how she can stay with him. She's totally wimping out."

He shrugs. "I dunno. Maybe it's harder than you think . . . leaving." I widen my eyes at him and start to pull away, but he doesn't let me go. "Hey. I don't mean you're wrong or anything. I just think she's probably not having the best time right now, either. Right?" He jiggles my arm and gives me a big, goofy grin.

I relax and smile back at him. "Yeah, I guess. Maybe I'm just being a bitch."

"A bitch about what?" Hailey asks, and I look up to see her standing in the doorway, one hand on her jutted-out hip. Neither Kyla nor Jade is with her, which is strange. It's unusual to find her without her minions.

"Nothing," I say, a little worried she may have heard all of my conversation with Noah. I let go of his hand, stand up, and grab my bag. "I gotta go," I tell Noah. "My mom'll be here any minute."

"Are you still in trouble for the mall thing?" Hailey asks. The morning after, at school, she grilled me on what had happened, and I gave her the barest details—that my mom had paid a fine and that I was banned from the mall for the next six months. If I don't commit any other offenses, my record will be wiped clean when I turn eighteen. Hailey didn't even thank me for not giving the police her and Jade's names, further confirming my assessment that she's a jerk.

"No," I say, pushing past her, but trying not to touch her. She stumbles a step or two backward and has to put her hand on the wall to keep from falling, which actually makes me sort of happy.

"No thanks to you," Noah mumbles, following right after me. He's taller than Hailey, so he looks down his nose at her.

"Noah," I say, not wanting to get into anything with her. I'd done my best to avoid any kind of interaction with her or her snotty friends.

"What was that, Brace-Face?" Hailey sneers.

"Oh, ha-ha," Noah says, dropping his backpack to the ground. "What are you, eight?"

"You're such a loser, Noah," Hailey says, making a nasty face at him, then directs her gaze over to me. "I guess you two make a perfect *freak* couple." She narrows her eyes. "What happened to your other boyfriend, Maddie? He get sick of you? Maybe he was repulsed by your disgusting *scar*."

My eyes fill with tears, and before I can stop him, Noah charges at Hailey so she is forced to push her back up against the wall. He doesn't touch her, but with his face less than two inches from hers, he speaks with contempt. "You shut your ugly mouth." He breathes hard, and bits of spittle fly. "Maddie is more beautiful than you could *ever* hope to be. Stay the *hell* away from us." He steps away, wiping at his chin with the back of his wrist.

Shocked, Hailey straightens her shirt and starts to walk away. But then she stops short, turning to glance back at Noah over her shoulder. "You'll be lucky if I don't tell the principal you just assaulted me," she says smugly.

"And *you'll* be lucky if I don't tell him you've been paying Riley to write your English papers since you were a freshman," Noah shoots back at her. "He kept the originals on his hard drive, along with the email where you asked him to do it, so don't even think you could lie your way out of it."

Hailey looks scared for a split second before she blinks rapidly, whips around, and struts down the hall on her own. Noah turns to look at me, and I slowly shake my head. "Holy crap. That was kind of awesome."

Noah waves the compliment away. "She's been a pain in the ass since kindergarten. Both her parents pretty much ignore her, so I try to feel sorry for her . . . but what she said . . . that went too far." He takes a step over to me. "You okay?"

"Yeah." The tears that threatened to fall when she insulted me have vanished. "You?"

He nods, then cocks his head. "What was she talking about . . . an old boyfriend?" He suddenly looks a little scared himself.

My face flames and I look down to the floor, then back up at him. "I sort of told her I was dating an older guy." He raises his eyebrows, and I quickly attempt to reassure him. "I wasn't . . . it was a lie. A stupid one. I'm really sorry you had to hear about it like this . . . I should have told you before." He's quiet, staring at me with a curious flicker in his blue eyes. "What?" I say. "Are you mad at me?"

Before I realize it's coming, he leans down and puts his lips on mine. They are just as warm as I thought they'd be—his touch is soft, tender, and sweet. I do feel his braces push against me a bit, but I'm too happy to care. My stomach is doing back-flips, and my heart feels like it might hammer its way right out of my chest. When he finally pulls back, he looks satisfied, like he's accomplished a goal.

"You're not mad?" I ask, a little breathlessly.

"Nope," he says. "Just wanted you to know that *I* want to be your boyfriend now." He pauses, suddenly hesitant. "Okay?"

I press my lips together and nod, thrilled as he takes my hand again and walks me out to my mother's car.

The next afternoon Noah has an orthodontist's appointment, but I tell my mom that we're studying after school as usual. When the final bell rings, I load up my bag, say good-bye to Jen at her locker, and then head to the public bus stop across the street. The number 21 will take me right past Ciseaux—I looked it up online last night.

I'm not exactly sure what I'm going to say to Hannah, I only know I want to tell someone else who knows what goes on with my dad that my mom doesn't seem to be planning to leave. It's possible Hannah won't even care—it might be too hard to see me—though if that were true, she wouldn't have hung around with us in the first place. Maybe it was true she felt blindsided the day we walked into the salon and then later, didn't want to get us in trouble with Dad. And the minute she got my letter, she *did* tell us who she was. I have to at least give her that.

The ride is short, and after I step off the bus, I check the clock on my cell phone, knowing I only have about an hour before I have to be back at school for my mom to pick me up. As I stand outside the cute little house where Hannah works, I think about how my mom might feel if she finds out I've come here, but at this point, there's no turning back.

I take a deep breath and open the front gate, taking in the sight of the garden that is slowly starting to wither away in the cool autumn air. Hannah has placed pretty pots full of spiky yellow, amber, and deep plum-hued blossoms on the stairs. I have no idea what they're called, but they look like pom-poms or exploding firecrackers. I put my hand on the doorknob, looking into the salon through the glass panel in the door. I see Hannah blow-drying a woman with long blond hair. She looks so pretty standing behind the chair of her station in her slim black pants, black ballet flats, and a fitted white blouse. Her hair is pulled into a casual knot at the back of her head, with a few wavy strands hanging around her face. She is concentrating so hard on what she's doing that she doesn't even look up when the bells on the door tinkle as I walk inside. No one is sitting at the front desk—the guy with cool red glasses is cutting a man's hair, and the other stylist is using a thick curling iron to style a client's long red locks.

I let the door swing shut behind me and I clear my throat, which apparently Hannah doesn't hear over the buzz of the hair dryer she's using because she still doesn't notice me. "Hannah?" I say loudly, and finally, her gaze snaps over to me.

"Maddie!" she says, her blue eyes wide open. She turns off the dryer and sets it on the vanity table in front of her client. "Um . . . can you wait a minute, honey? While I finish up here?" I nod, watching as she fluffs the woman's hair and goes over it with an aerosol spray. "There," she says, letting the woman eye herself in the mirror. "Good?" The woman nods and grabs her purse, and Hannah takes off the protective cape before ringing her up at the front desk.

When she finally turns to look at me, her eyes are a little shiny with tears. "I'm so happy you came," she says. "Let's go upstairs, okay? So we can talk?" I nod again, and she tells the other stylists where she'll be.

I follow her up a narrow stairway, holding on tightly to the strap of my book bag. "You don't have another appointment?"

"Not for half an hour," she says. "I try to schedule myself a little break here and there throughout the day to catch up on paperwork or whatever." She opens a door at the top of the stairs and motions for me to enter first.

I look around the room, a small space with little furniture. "Did you live here with your daughter?" I ask.

"No," she says quietly. "I moved here . . . after. I had a hard time being in our house." She pauses. "I'm thinking about selling the house, actually, and buying one for myself."

"Oh," I say, still holding on to my bag. I notice a few pictures on the fireplace mantel and step over to look at them. One is of a chubby but cute dark-haired baby girl with huge blue eyes, another of a slightly younger-looking Hannah holding that baby as a toddler, and finally, what has to be a recent head shot of a pretty girl with long black hair and blue eyes, who looks so much like Hannah it almost makes me gasp. She's smiling in that picture, one of those please-push-the-damn-button smiles. There is a light in her eyes—a kindness—but also a stitch of thoughtfulness above her brows, as though she often pulled them together as she sorted something out. I touch the glass and run my finger over her face. "Is this her?" I ask. "Emily?"

"Yes," Hannah says, and I can hear the tears in her throat.

"She's pretty. I mean . . . she was . . ." I trail off and turn my gaze to Hannah. "Sorry. I guess I don't really know how to talk about her."

She gives me a shallow smile. "It's hard for me, too. I'm trying to learn how to do it without completely falling apart." She pauses, then gestures to the couch. "Do you want to sit down?"

"I can't stay," I answer, straightening my spine. "My mom doesn't know I'm here."

"Oh, Maddie," she says, and her shoulders drop. "I don't want to keep anything else from her . . . you know?"

"I know. But it's not like she's going to call you . . . right?"

She stares at me a moment, holding in a breath. "I suppose not," she says with a sigh. "So, what's going on with you?"

I lift my chin in what I hope looks like a confident way. "I wanted you to know I'm not mad at you anymore. I don't think what you did was right, but I guess I understand why you did it."

"Thank you," she says, looking palpably relieved. "That means a lot to hear. I really am very sorry if I hurt you. That was absolutely not my intent."

"Okay," I say, looking around the room for more evidence about Emily's life. I assumed there'd be more of her here.

"Are you guys . . . okay?" she asks hesitantly. "Does your dad know what happened?"

"With you, or with me at the mall?"

"Both, I suppose."

"He doesn't know anything," I say, and for some reason, my eyes begin to sting. "She said she's going to leave, but she's not. Which means I'm not." She takes a step toward me, one of her hands outstretched, but I move backward, out of her reach. "We're fine," I say. "He hasn't yelled at her or hit her or anything. I think she thinks he's better."

She drops her arm back down, letting it hang loosely at her side. "Has he been that way before, though? Where everything seems like it's fine for a while and then it's . . . not?" I don't say anything, but I'm sure she can see from my face that she's right, because she sighs again. "I wish there was something I could do, Maddie. I wish I could change everything about the way we met."

"What was Emily like?" I ask, suddenly not wanting to talk with her about my mom and dad anymore. It feels too danger-ous.

"She was wonderful," Hannah says, glancing over at the pic-tures on the mantel. "Not perfect, of course—no child is—but perfect for me. She was smart, like you. Better with the computer than I am . . . I had to have her program my phone for me, too."

"I do that for my mom," I say.

"That doesn't surprise me," she says fondly. She moves her gaze from the pictures to the bay window behind me. "She talked back a little . . . she always thought she knew more or better than I did. Sometimes she was right about that, but as her mom, I had a hard time admitting it. She loved old movies—the black-and-white ones, with Fred Astaire and Ginger Rogers?" I nod, and she goes on. "She wanted to be an actress, I think. Or a veterinarian. She loved animals so much and was never happier than when we were visiting her grandparents' farm." She smiled and looked back to me. "She was funny, too. Oh my god, she could make me laugh until I cried." Her eyes fill then, and I feel bad for making her talk about all of this.

"Do you think . . ." I say, unsure if I really want to know the answer to the question floating around in my head, but going ahead and asking it anyway. "Do you think she would have liked me? Would she be glad that it's me she saved?" My bottom lip trembles and I bite the inside of my cheek to get it to stop.

"Yes," Hannah says without hesitation, staring right at me. "I know she would." She takes a deep breath. "*I'm* happy it was you that she saved, too. I think you're an amazing girl."

"Thank you," I say, and a tingle of relief rushes through me. I hadn't realized just how much hearing that would mean. I glance at the clock on the wall. "Oh crap. I'm sorry, but my mom's meeting me back at the school. I should go."

"I can drive you if you want," Hannah offers, but I shake my head.

"It's probably better if I take the bus. Just in case she might see you."

"She's still mad?" she asks, and I feel a little sorry for her, seeing the sadness in her eyes.

"I don't know," I say, trying to be gentle. "She isn't talking to me much."

"I'm sorry to hear that." She pushes her hair back from her face, then walks over to her purse, which is lying on the couch. "Just one second," she says as she roots around inside it, eventually coming up with a small picture removed from her wallet. She hands it to me, and I don't even have to look to know it's the same school picture as the one on the mantel.

"I can't take this," I say, holding it back out toward her, wanting nothing more than to take it home with me.

"Of course you can. I have plenty, and I want you to have it. Please?"

I hesitate a moment, and then nod, carefully slipping it inside my bag before letting her lead me back downstairs and out to the front porch. I feel the other stylists' curious eyes on us both and do my best to ignore them. I imagine she hasn't told them who I am or about the fact that she lied to my mom and me.

"Well," I say, "good luck with everything." I cough, even though I don't really have to. "With your move and everything."

"Thank you," she says, and it feels like her eyes see right through me. "I want you to know, Maddie . . . if you ever need anything. If something happens with your dad or your mom and you don't have anyone to talk with? I'm here, okay? I might not be your first thought, but I want you to know that you're not alone."

"Okay," I say, and then before she can say anything more, I turn my back to her and go.

Hannah

A few days after Maddie visited the salon, Hannah has a conversation with the couple who are renting her house. She calls them after work, when she's finished with her last client.

"I've been giving it a lot of thought," she tells the husband, an older man named Thomas. She remembers feeling comfortable with him and his wife as tenants because he reminded her a little of her father. "And it's time for me to put the house on the market." There is a twinge of regret in Hannah's chest as she thinks about letting go of where she lived with Emily, but she knows in her heart it's the right thing for her to do.

"Really?" Thomas says. "That's wonderful!"

Hannah feels a little confused, considering this news means he and his wife, Tara, will have to move out. She says as much, and he chuckles. "We won't have to move out if we buy it," he says, and a moment later, Tara has joined them in a conference call so Thomas can tell her Hannah is planning to sell.

"We've just fallen in *love* with the house and the neighborhood," Tara says. "Let us talk with our Realtor and we'll make you an offer, okay?"

Hannah nods, still feeling a little hesitant about her decision, but since visiting the storage unit and seeing Maddie again—feeling like she finally has taken a few steps toward closure—Hannah believes she's ready to make some changes.

A couple of days later, Hannah meets with John, the real estate agent Isaac referred her to, at his office. He reviews the offer Thomas and Tara's agent made her and confirms that it's a fair amount for the property. After they write up the paperwork to accept the offer and set a date to close escrow, they discuss where she might want to live.

"What areas are you interested in?" John asks as they sit at a large table in the office conference room. He is a short, brawny man, who with his bald head and small but matching gold hoop earrings, looks oddly like Mr. Clean clad in a navy blue suit.

"Not too far from Bellevue," Hannah says. "I'd like to be by the water, if I can." One of Emily's favorite things to do was go to the beach, and Hannah hopes that being near the water—or at least being able to see it from her home—will make her feel near to her daughter, too.

"Kirkland, maybe?" John says, typing rapidly on the keyboard of his laptop. "There are some beautiful cottages around the edge of Lake Washington. Waterfront might be a little out of your price range, but we could get you close. And it wouldn't be a terrible commute to the salon."

Hannah nods, and an hour later, Isaac meets them at one of the properties John pulled off the MLS as something Hannah might like. They visit five houses Hannah isn't thrilled with before pulling up to the last one on their list.

"It's tiny," Isaac says after he gets out of his car. He stands next to Hannah, his lanky arms hanging loose at his sides as he cocks his head and squints his brown eyes at the property.

"We prefer to say 'cozy,'" John says, but Hannah stays quiet, letting her eyes roam over the pale yellow house, immediately charmed by the white shutters and wraparound porch. There is a postage-stamp-size yard, filled to the brim with lush plant life—a single, delicate Japanese maple graces each side of the stairs, and the flower beds are thick with sea grasses and several tall rosebushes. Hannah glances over to the narrow driveway and wonders if her car could fit inside the small garage.

"When was it built?" she asks.

John glances at his smart phone, using his finger to scroll down the screen. "Nineteen fifty-two," he says, then removes the key from the lockbox on the front door. "But it has been fully renovated."

They enter directly into the living room, and Hannah immediately notes the shiny blond hardwood floor and the calming sage-green walls. Like John told her, the property isn't waterfront, but it is on a hill, and from the picture window Hannah can see the bright blue waters of Lake Washington. She wanders into the dining room, which really is only an alcove with enough space for a table for two, and then into the galley kitchen, which is updated with gleaming stainless-steel appliances and a mosaic backsplash made out of what look like random bits of turquoise sea glass. There are two bedrooms with bay windows and tiny closets; between those, a bathroom with white tiles and a claw-foot tub.

"I love it," Hannah says, taking in the built-in bookshelves in the hallway. She suddenly envisions placing Emily's pictures and art projects there and suspects a Christmas tree will look just perfect in the corner of the front room.

"You've barely looked around yet," says Isaac, ever the practical sibling. When they were kids, Hannah would be scaling a western white pine tree in the back woods of their parents' property while Isaac watched from the safety of the ground. While she leapt from heights far above the reservoir of the Boise River, Isaac cautioned against the possibility of sharp rocks below.

"It feels right," Hannah says, smiling up at her brother. "Can we make an offer, John?"

"Of course," John says, walking past her to set his briefcase down on the dining room table. "We can fill out the paperwork online and email it to the listing agent right now."

"Hold on, Hannah-banana," Isaac says. "Don't you think you should look at a few more options before you decide?"

"No, I don't," Hannah says, stepping over to give her brother a kiss on the cheek. "Life is short, Isaac. This is where I want to live it."

That night, Hannah goes over to Isaac's for dinner to celebrate finding the house. She sits at the island in his sleek black kitchen, sipping a glass of wine as she watches him sauté vegetables and check the temperature of the chicken breasts roasting in the oven. When they arrived at his house, he changed out of the slacks and blue button-down shirt he'd worn to look at properties into a pair of Levi's and a black T-shirt. Hannah notes that he moves with decided ease around the room, his long limbs reaching for a pan in the cupboard or into the fridge for fresh herbs.

"You'd make some woman a lovely wife," she says, teasing him. "Do you do windows, too?"

He smiles and halfheartedly flips her off. "No, but my housekeeper does. Cooking just happens to relax me, okay? When you travel as much as I do, the last thing you want is to eat out when you're at home." He starts to mash the boiled potatoes he just took off the stove with butter and milk. Hannah sees the sinewy muscles of his forearm work beneath his tan skin. "So what inspired the move, little sis?" he asks. "I've been out of the loop."

Hannah takes a deep breath and proceeds to tell him everything that has happened over the last six weeks, starting with Olivia and Maddie's first appearance at the salon and ending with Maddie's visit there just a few days before. "I screwed up," she confesses. "But all of it made me realize that I'd been existing in a sort of suspended state, you know? I was working, remodeling the salon, dealing with clients, running my ass off trying to pretend that everything was fine when inside I was crumbling."

Isaac stops mashing and looks right at his sister. "I think we all do that, to some extent. We put on a face that things are fine when they're not, or pretend to be something other than what we really are." He pauses to give the potatoes a quick stir. "What's dangerous is when we lose sight of who we are behind the mask, you know? It sounds like you showed Olivia and Maddie who you *really* are when you told them the truth. And Maddie coming to see you? That's pretty huge. Maybe Olivia will come around."

Hannah sighs. "I know, I'm just still so worried about them. I hate that there's nothing I can do to help."

"I know that feeling well," Isaac says, giving her a pointed look.

Hannah sets her wineglass down, then walks over to her brother and gives him a hug. He smells like lemon thyme and garlic. "I'm sorry."

He kisses the top of her head. "No need. I'm just happy to see you coming back to your old self a bit." She pulls away, and he feeds her a bite of potato, looking at her expectantly. "More salt?" She nods and leans her hips against the edge of the counter, crossing her arms over her chest.

"I'm going home for the week of Thanksgiving," she tells him. "We need to help Dad figure out what to do about managing the farm."

"I know," Isaac says. He looks at her with his big brown eyes. "I'm quitting my job, Hannah. I'm moving back there."

"What?" she exclaims. "All of a sudden you want to live on a farm?"

"It's not all of a sudden. I've been giving it some thought for a while now. More so since Emily died." His eyes shine with tears and he blinks rapidly to erase them. "Losing her really shook me up. Made me reexamine my priorities. My whole life has been my career, and all that just feels meaningless to me now. I've made more money than I know what to do with and I'm burned out on traveling. I just want to go home."

"Home?" she repeats, trying not to look as shocked as she feels. "But you live *here*."

He shrugs. "I know . . . but I miss the country. I miss the

quiet and the slower pace." He waits a beat. "I've also recon-
nected with Annie Mitchell."

"Annie?" Hannah says, picturing her brother's high school
girlfriend—a bouncy, curvy brunette with huge dimples and
personality to spare. "I thought she married Brett Richardson?"

Her brother blushes. "They divorced about five years ago.
We found each other on Facebook in June, and it got serious
again between us pretty quickly, like no time had passed at all.
I've been back to visit her, and she's come here, too, but not
with her kids."

"You said you went home this summer to see Mom and
Dad," Hannah says, trying to keep the accusation out of her
tone. She cannot believe she has been so deep in her own grief
that her brother didn't feel he could share all of this with her.

"I did go home to see them." He smiles. "And Annie, too.
I just didn't want to say anything to you in case it didn't work
out."

Hannah takes a couple of breaths and looks at her brother
with wide eyes. "She has *kids?*"

"Twin boys, Grayson and Liam."

"How old are they?"

"Ten. They're really great, Hannah, and actually seem to
be okay with me dating their mom, so I started thinking about
moving back . . . just to see where it all might lead."

"How could you not have *told* me about this?" Hannah demands, playfully smacking her brother's arm. "Especially at the
party for the salon opening when Mom was giving me such a
hard time about *me* moving back home!"

Isaac looks a little guilty. "You already had a lot going on. I
didn't want to make it worse. And honestly, I hadn't decided

for absolute sure I was moving back at that point. Now, I'm sure."

Something dawns on Hannah, thinking back to her last conversation with her mother, when she didn't mention Hannah moving home for the first time in a year. "So that's why Mom backed off pushing me to move home? You're doing it instead."

"She gets one of her kids returning to the nest, so I guess she's happy. I'm not going to live in their house, though. We're going to fix up the old cabin, the one near the edge of the property." Hannah nods, and then he waits a beat before speaking again. "Are you going to be okay if I leave? I mean, I know you're a grown-up and everything, but—"

"I'll be fine," Hannah says, gently cutting him off. "I'm happy for you, Isaac. Really."

They sit down to dinner, and he fills her in on all the details of reconnecting with Annie. His face lights up when he talks about her, and although Hannah really is happy for him, she can't help but be a little jealous that her brother has fallen in love. It somehow compounds her aloneness and makes her realize just how deeply she aches for someone to hold.

Inspired by Isaac's story about falling back in love with Annie, Hannah drives home from his house surprised to find herself thinking about Seth. He really does seem like a good guy. Granted, most people only show the best version of themselves to new acquaintances, but Hannah likes that at first glance, at least, he seems compassionate and self-aware. She also likes that he helps other people for a living.

Back in her apartment, after unsuccessfully trying to distract herself from thoughts of him by watching TV, she glances at the clock and wonders if nine thirty is too late to call. She decides it's not and heads downstairs to get his cell number off his client profile. She's not exactly sure what she's going to say, and she knows that she might not be ready to date him, but considering his profession, there's something she knows she can ask.

Sitting on her small couch, she holds her breath as the phone rings. "Hi," she says when he answers, exhaling the word. "It's Hannah . . . from the salon?"

"Hello, Hannah from the salon," Seth says warmly. "Calling to check up on how happy I am with my haircut?"

She laughs, nervously. "No, not exactly. Well, not at all, really. Not that I don't hope you're happy with it or anything." Realizing she's babbling, she clamps her mouth shut.

"You can rest assured I am," he says, an amused edge in his voice. "How are you?"

"I bought a new house today," she blurts out. "I'm selling the one I lived in with my daughter." *Why am I telling him this?*

"That's great," he says, sounding genuinely enthused. "Congratulations." They spend a few minutes talking about the new house, where it is and what it looks like. Finally, there is a moment of silence before Seth speaks again. "Is there something else you wanted to talk with me about?"

"There is, actually," Hannah says. Her mouth is dry and she swallows to try to moisten it. "Here's the thing. I have some things to work out. For myself, I mean. Trust issues, maybe? And my feelings around losing Emily." She feels the back of her throat tingle with impending tears, and she swallows again to fight them down. "So I was wondering—"

"Let me stop you there, Hannah," Seth says gently. "I don't

make it a practice to take on women I'm interested in dating as clients."

"Oh no," Hannah says, ridiculously pleased that he just said he wants to date her. "I don't want to see you professionally."

"Okay, good," he says, relieved. "You're calling to ask me out, then?" She's pretty sure he's joking, but still, it makes Hannah squirm.

"Um, no," she says, wishing she could start this entire conversation over. She is entirely too out of practice with this whole world; she probably just offended him. "I mean, I'd like to go out with you . . ." She trails off and tries to find the right way to tell him what she needs to say. She considers telling him everything about Olivia and Maddie, thinking maybe he'd have some better insight on how she could help them, but realizes she doesn't know him quite well enough to feel comfortable exposing that much about herself. Instead, she tries to focus on the real reason she decided to call. "Like I said, I've got some things to work through. Until I do, I'm not sure I'm exactly ready to take on any kind of serious relationship."

"You think we'd have a serious relationship?" he asks, and immediately, Hannah wants to take back everything she's said.

"Well, I don't know, exactly," she stutters, and he once again cuts her off, laughing a little bit as he speaks.

"Sorry, I shouldn't tease you. Go on with whatever it is you want to say. I promise to be quiet."

"It's nothing huge," she says, feeling her heartbeat flutter. "I know we don't know each other terribly well yet, but I'm wondering if you could recommend a colleague for me to see. A therapist, I mean. Someone who you think I might mesh with?"

"Of course," he says, suddenly sounding very professional. "Would you be more comfortable seeing a male or female?"

"Female, I think," Hannah says, considering what a hard time she has trusting men. "Thank you."

"No problem. Can I email you a list?"

"Great," she says. She gives him her email address but then hesitates before ending the call. "Seth?" she says, just after he tells her he should probably go. She likes the way his name feels in her mouth.

"Yes?"

"I hope . . . I mean, when I've sort of worked through a few things, I'd like to, well, take you out for coffee or something. If you want." In that moment, she feels more like a nervous schoolgirl than a grown woman. She just told him she wasn't ready to date yet, and here she is, asking him out? Men just adore women who send mixed messages.

"I'd love that," Seth says. "Maybe we can just be friends for now. Friends have coffee . . . right?"

"They do." Hannah smiles, feeling a little less like she's made a fool of herself.

"All right then, it's settled," he says. "We'll be friends, having coffee. Say, next Sunday morning? If we're feeling *especially* daring, we could have muffins. Totally nonserious, we're-just-friends baked goods."

Hannah laughs. They decide on a time and place to meet, and then hang up. She looks around her apartment with a small, hopeful smile, knowing it really is time to move on. No matter what happens with Maddie and Olivia, it's time to pick up the broken pieces of her heart and try again.

Olivia

"Are you sure you're going to be okay at the party?" Olivia asks as she sits on Maddie's bed, watching as her daughter applies a pair of silver-tipped false eyelashes. She is dressed up as a glamorous witch, with the standard black hat, draped black dress, and pointy-toed black shoes. Maddie has thrown a sparkly turquoise feather boa around her neck for a bit of pizzazz.

"I'll be fine, Mom," Maddie says, glancing at her in the mirror. "Jen's parents are home, remember? You talked with them. They have your number if anything goes wrong. Which it won't."

"You just haven't been to a party like this before," Olivia says, unable to stop herself from fussing around her child. "There might be kids sneaking alcohol into the punch or getting high in the bathroom . . ." She trails off, then looks at her daughter with wide eyes. She's afraid to mention what's going through her mind—she's never had to worry about anything like this for Maddie before—but she forces herself to say it. "You know about condoms, right? In case Noah and you decide—"

"Oh my *god,* Mom! I am *not* talking with you about this!" Maddie whips around and stares hard at her mother. "Please. Just trust me, okay? I'm not going to do anything stupid, and if other people are being stupid, I'll call you to come pick me up."

Olivia stands and walks over to Maddie, reaching out to straighten her long black wig. In full makeup, her daughter looks so much older than sixteen, and for some reason, this makes Olivia feel scared. What happened to her little girl? "Okay, honey. I'm sorry. I do trust you. This is all just very new to me . . . and you. I just want you to be safe."

Maddie's expression softens. "I want that for you, too." She pauses. "Have you called anyone yet? Do you think we might be able to leave soon?" She says this quietly, stealing a glance at the door, even though she knows her father is at the office.

So many things—her illness, a life ruled by her father's temper—have made Maddie a cautious girl. Olivia wants nothing more than to free her daughter from that fear, for her to get to live a life filled with openness and unbridled enthusiasm. But the truth is, a part of Olivia still feels stuck. A part of her hopes that if Maddie can just hold on until college, then Olivia won't have to leave.

"I've made a few calls," Olivia says, realizing that now she is not only placating James but doing it with Maddie, too. Understanding this makes her feel a little ill, like she's moving farther away from the version of herself she'd like to be instead of closer to it. "Nothing definite, though."

"What are you going to do tonight?" Maddie asks her.

"I'm making a nice dinner for your dad when he gets home," Olivia says, trying not to let her worries show on her face. "Are you hungry? Do you need to eat before you go?"

"No, Mom. There'll be food at the party."

"What if there's nothing gluten-free? You should eat something."

"I'll be fine!" Maddie sighs and grabs her cell phone from her dresser, sneaking it into the pocket of her dress. "Noah is going to be here any minute."

Downstairs, Olivia waits with her daughter for Noah to arrive, which he does, not a minute later than he said he would. He stands on the threshold, dressed in what looks to Olivia like a priest's floor-length black robe. His dark hair is slicked back, and opaque black glasses cover his eyes. "Hi, Mrs. Bell," he says. "Thanks for letting me drive Maddie to the party."

"Of course, Noah," she says with a smile. She likes this boy for Maddie—he seems polite and respectful of her. James hasn't met him yet, but Olivia is hopeful that because her husband likes Noah's father, he'll like Noah, too. "What are you supposed to be?" she asks him. *This is the kind of question a good mother would ask,* Olivia thinks. *At least, I hope it is.*

"Neo from the Matrix movies," he says.

"'There is a difference between knowing the path and walking the path,'" Maddie says in a deep, throaty voice, which makes Noah crack up laughing. Olivia must look confused, because her daughter says, "It's a line from the *movie,* Mom."

"Ah," Olivia says, suddenly feeling older than she'd like. "Got it."

Noah looks over Maddie's costume. "You look great," he says. "Very pretty. *And* wicked."

Her daughter ducks her head a bit and smiles. "Thanks."
She leans over and gives Olivia a quick kiss on the cheek. "I'll
be home by midnight," she says.

"Eleven," Olivia counters, and Maddie lets loose a heavy,
irritated groan.

"Eleven," Noah repeats. "We'll be here."

"Thank you, Noah," Olivia says. She waves as they climb
into his car and drive away, then she shuts the front door.

For a moment, Olivia stands in the quiet of the house, listening to her breath move in and out of her lungs. She knows
Maddie is disappointed with her, but she can't help but feel
that James really has turned some kind of corner. He hasn't
raised his voice or touched her in any way other than with
gentleness and affection for the past few weeks. Though he
still works seven days a week, he has made an effort to come
home earlier and to take Olivia out for dinner or just for a
stroll together around their neighborhood. She knows he's had
months like this before and then something always set him off,
but she's hopeful that this time, now that Maddie is doing well
and they're back to being a normal family, things have truly
changed.

When James arrives home around nine o'clock, which is
later than she thought he'd be, Olivia is in the kitchen putting
the final touches on his favorite dish—Hungarian paprikash
with homemade noodles. Olivia had worked hard to master
making it exactly the way he liked it, with plenty of smoked
paprika and cayenne pepper to up the spice.

"Hi, honey," she says as he makes his way from the front
door to the kitchen. "Did you get hung up at work?"

"Something like that." He takes off his suit jacket and loosens his tie, hanging them carefully on the back of one of the breakfast bar stools. He stares at her as though he's never seen her before.

"Dinner's ready," she says brightly, determined to snap him out of whatever foul mood he might be in. "Do you want me to pour us some wine?"

"Where's Maddie?" he asks. His voice is gruff, and a shadow falls over his eyes.

"At her friend's Halloween party . . . remember?" Every siren in Olivia's body begins to wail. "She'll be home around eleven."

James strides up behind her and puts his hands on her hips, kissing the back of her neck. "You sure she's not going to the mall?"

Olivia freezes. "What?" she says.

James moves his hands up and squeezes her waist. "Oh, right. She *can't* go there. Because, even though my wife didn't *tell* me, our daughter was arrested for shoplifting." He digs his fingers into her flesh until it starts to hurt. Suddenly sick with panic, she tries not to cry out. *How did he find out? Oh god, what else does he know?*

"I didn't want to bother you with it," she says, hearing the desperation in her voice. "I'm so sorry I didn't tell you. Maddie didn't actually steal anything, though. I promise you she didn't. The friends she was with stuck a pair of earrings in her pocket and then they left her behind to get caught." Her words come quickly, tripping over each other as they leave her mouth.

"You're a liar," James snaps. "And so is Maddie. A *thieving* liar." Olivia cringes and tries to turn around, but James digs his fingers into her even deeper. She can't move. "Imagine my surprise this afternoon," he says, as though reciting a story to a child, "when my good friend Jacob from the prosecutor's office meets me for lunch and tells me he ran across my daughter's name in the system. Imagine how stupid I felt when I didn't know what the *fuck* he was talking about." He kisses the side of Olivia's neck again, and a terrified shiver runs through her. The calmness in his tone frightens her—the eerily gentle precursor to disaster. She has to get out of this house. She has to leave, now. No suitcase, no plan, no lawyer in place. She just needs to run.

"And so," James continues, "he kindly explained to me that my wife had paid my daughter's fines in cash—from what account I don't know, because apparently she keeps those secret from me, too."

Oh god. I have to get out. What the hell was I thinking, that he had changed? A man like him isn't capable *of change.* Olivia glances at the back door, wondering if she can manage to wrench away from his grasp and make it out before he can stop her. She realizes she's still holding a paring knife—its metal handle has gone slippery in her sweaty grasp. If she has to, could she cut him? But before she can act on this thought, James lets go of her waist and slides his hand over the one of hers that holds the knife.

"Here, let me take that," he says. "I wouldn't want you to get hurt."

The muscles in her chest clench around her heart as she squeezes her eyes shut and lets him take the knife. "Please," she whispers. Blood rushes past her ears, and her entire body vibrates. "Please, I'm sorry."

James sets the knife out of her reach and slowly rotates her around to face him. She keeps her eyes closed, but a tear slips out as he cups her face in his hands. "No," he says simply, and with his next breath, he hauls back his hand and slaps her.

The impact jars her, but still, Olivia tries to get away. He wraps a long arm around her waist and jerks her back to him. "What else are you hiding from me?" he demands, delivering a swift kick to her shin. Olivia cries out with the impact.

"Nothing, James!" she sobs. "I swear, nothing else. Oh god, I'm sorry. I'm so, so sorry." Her breaths start to come in shuddering waves, their sharp edges tearing her insides apart. James hits her again, this time a punch to her stomach, and she bends over, gagging violently.

"How can I believe a word you say?" he bellows, grabbing her by the back of the hair and dragging her through the dining room and toward the living room. She trips on her own feet, trying to keep up with his pace. "How am I supposed to trust my own wife when she is clearly a lying bitch?" He yanks her hair with such force she's sure her scalp is bleeding, then throws her to the couch, where she curls up in a fetal position, arms around her face, trying to protect herself.

There's nothing she can do at this point, she knows. He's gone over the edge, lost it completely, and so she does what she can to float above what he's doing to her—the way he rips her arms from her face and punches her in the jaw with a closed fist. She tries not the feel the warm blood that runs down her cheek or the bright explosion of fireworks inside her eye when his fist lands there. She knows it's happening to her . . . she knows he is kicking her in the ribs, that he shoves her so hard against the entertainment center she feels the bone in her forearm snap, but the only way she can get through it is to let her spirit leave her body—to try to make herself believe this horror is happening to someone else.

At one point, after he has pummeled her too many times to count, she passes out. When she wakes up, she is unsure just how much time has gone by. Lying on her side on the floor, she is barely able to open one eye—the other is swollen shut. Her entire body is in agony. She sees James sitting on the couch, watching her struggle. His hair is disheveled, and there are small sprays of bright red blood across his white shirt. He sips at a glass of Scotch, the ice cubes clicking as he takes a final swallow.

"I've done everything for you," he says, still so calm it makes Olivia fear he might have truly lost his mind. "And I ask so little. Loyalty. Honesty. Affection. Is that too much to ask, Olivia? Tell me. Because if it is, I don't know what to do."

Olivia tries to open her mouth, but her jaw screams in pain when she attempts to move it. She closes her one eye against the nauseating wave that rolls through her. Her arm and ribs throb; her face feels as though her muscles are no longer attached to bone. She's certain he's going to kill her. She thinks about Maddie, her sweet daughter whom she was too weak to save, and all Olivia wants is another chance. She'd do the right thing this time—she'd walk out the door with Maddie wearing only the clothes on their backs. Nothing else matters, not money, not a divorce—nothing but keeping her daughter safe from this man.

"What?" James asks, sneering at her. "No answer for me? Nothing to say for yourself? Come on, Olivia. You've always known how to use your mouth."

She opens her eye then, staring at him with more hatred

than she's ever felt in her life. She doesn't know how her broken mouth is able to get these next two words out, but it doesn't matter because she's finally found the strength to say them. "Fuck. You."

"Fuck *me?*" James yells. He slams his glass to the marble floor, and it instantly shatters. He lifts himself from the couch and storms over to her. He shoves her, rolling her onto her back. The pain is like a thousand knives stabbing at her flesh, and she struggles to breathe as he straddles her at the waist.

This is the end, she thinks. The last thing she remembers is the look on his face as he wraps his fingers around her neck. And then the world falls black.

Maddie

When Noah pulls up to Jen's house, the party is already in full swing. There are at least ten cars parked in the circular driveway, and their entire yard is decorated like a cemetery, with rows of headstones scattered across the lawn and plastic skeleton arms looking like they're trying to claw their way out of the ground. As we pass by a huge oak tree, a screeching bat whips down next to my head. "Holy hell!" I exclaim, ducking and clutching Noah's long arm.

He laughs and puts his arm around me. "Did the big bad *fake* bat scare you?"

"Not funny," I say, breathing a little hard but also relieved to realize the animal isn't real. I am jumpy, considering this is the first real party I've attended in eight years. I didn't want to tell my mom I'm nervous about it going well, because she's already wound tightly enough. I don't want to give her anything more to worry about.

As Noah and I walk up the steps, he keeps his arm hung

loosely around my waist. I like the feel of him so close to me—it makes my heart beat fast and my whole body gets warm. I wonder if this is what it feels like to fall in love.

Jen answers the front door, fully decked out as a ghoulish zombie. Her blue-streaked hair is messy with fake blood, her skin is powdered a sickening shade of green, and she wears glowing white contacts that make her look like an actual member of the undead. "Hey, peeps!" she says, welcoming us inside. Her house is not as big as mine, but it's just as nice, filled with tasteful artwork and fancy furniture. "The party's downstairs in the rec room. Food, drink, video games. We're having an Xbox Zombie tournament—winner gets a hundred bucks!"

"Awesome," Noah says, and we follow her down a long hallway to a doorway leading downstairs to a huge room. There is a pool table, a Foosball table, a dartboard, and an enormous L-shaped couch sitting in front of what has to be a sixty-inch plasma television.

"Where are your parents?" I ask over the loud thump of music.

"Hiding in their bedroom upstairs," Jen says, laughing. "They'll check on us in a while, just to make sure we're not shooting up or having an orgy or something." I smile, and she gives me a quick, hard hug. "I'm so happy you came!"

I almost tear up when she says this, so unaccustomed to having a friend. Noah sees this and covers for me. "Where's the food, dude? I'm starved."

Jen motions over to the huge table by what is likely a second, smaller kitchen in the house. "My mom ordered some chicken pad Thai for you, Maddie. I told her about your gluten thing. Sodas are in the fridge."

We thank her, and then she runs back to join the group playing Zombie. Noah leads me over to fill our plates. "Sorry I'm such a wuss," I say under my breath.

"It's actually pretty cute," Noah says, piling four pieces of pizza onto his plate. He catches me staring at him, a little slack-jawed. "What?"

"Are you going to *eat* all that?"

"Yeah." He grabs a soda and balances his plate on top of it. "I'm a growing boy." He flashes me a grin, and we go join our friends playing the game.

Over the next couple of hours, I feel the most normal I think I ever have in my whole life. I laugh and eat and play a video game with friends; my boyfriend holds my hand when it's not our turn, and it suddenly hits me that if my mom divorces my dad, it's possible I won't get to keep any of this. I might have to move away and change my name, and the thought of that, the thought of losing all of these cool people, makes me think maybe my mom is right—we should stay where we are. It's only two years until graduation. And really, if he's not hurting her anymore, then why should we have to go?

Noah nudges me and snaps me out of my thoughts. "You okay? You're like, completely distracted."

I smile at him. "Yeah, fine. Just thinking about what a good time I'm having tonight."

"Me, too." He pauses, then tilts his head down the hall-way, toward the bathroom and Jen's bedroom. "Want to take a break?"

I swallow hard and nod, letting him lead me to Jen's room. No one seems to notice us leave—they're too caught up in the game. He locks the door behind him, and I turn on the small lamp next to Jen's bed. Her room is done up in crazy punk rock décor, mostly black and white with odd splashes of neon. "She really likes punk, huh?" I say, nervously pulling the feather boa I'm wearing off and dropping it to the floor.

"I guess," Noah says, taking a step toward me, looking a little nervous, too, which sort of makes me feel better. His Neo sunglasses are on top of his head, keeping his hair out of his face. He takes my hand and we sit down on the edge of her bed. We stare at each other a second before he leans in to kiss me, putting his arms around me and pulling me close. When he opens his mouth and slips just the tip of his tongue against my lips, I open my mouth, too, a little weirded out by the feel of his tongue on mine. He tastes like Hot Tamales, which he'd been munching on after his pizza.

He runs his hands over my back, then moves them, tentatively, around to my waist and then my chest. I suck in a quick, sharp breath when he touches my breasts. "Sorry," he says, snatching his hands back to his own lap. "I didn't mean to—"

Breathing a little hard, I smile. "No, it's okay. I just . . . well, it surprised me. But it felt good." I take his hands and put them back on the sides of my waist. Then, keeping my eyes linked with his, I begin to undo the top buttons on my witch's dress. He quickly glances down at what I'm doing, but then looks back up to me.

"Are you sure?" he whispers, blinking hard and fast.

"I want to show you," I say, trying to stop my hands and voice from trembling. When the buttons are undone to my waist, I carefully pull the top of the dress down off my shoulders, taking in a deep breath and holding it as my upper body is totally exposed to him. I close my eyes and wait, feeling his gaze move over my skin first, and then . . . his hands, his fingers running over the raised red ridges of my scar. Down the center of my torso and across my waist. His touch is so tender, so careful, it makes me want to cry.

"You're beautiful," he says, leaning in to kiss me again. And right then, just for that moment, I believe him.

On the drive home a little while later, I keep looking over at Noah, wondering if he's thinking about that moment in Jen's bedroom as much as I am. We only kissed a bit more after I showed him my scar, then I buttoned up my dress and we rejoined the party. I didn't really want to stop—I wanted to do more, to see and touch his skin, too—but I also don't want to lose my virginity at a random party in someone else's basement. It seems like it should be more special than that.

"You're okay, right?" I ask Noah after I tell him the gate code to put in and he drives up to my house. "That we stopped?" I am a little nervous that he won't like me anymore, since my general understanding of boys is that the only thing they want more of than pizza is sex.

"Yeah," he says, shooting me a sideways glance as he puts the car in park. "It wasn't easy though, 'cause you're smokin' hot." I smile and give him a playful punch on the arm. "Ow!" he says, pretending to be hurt. "Violent, too, apparently."

I look at the clock on the dashboard. "Ten fifty-eight. Way to make my mom happy."

"Moms love me," he says smugly.

"Because you're a brownnoser," I say, teasing him.

"Whatever it takes to spend more time with you," he says, and I roll my eyes.

"Oh my god," I groan. "*Total* brownnoser."

We both laugh, and he walks around to open my door for me, holding out a hand to help me out of the car. He doesn't let my hand go until we're standing in front of the door, face-to-face. "I had a really great time," I say, but before he can respond, we both hear what sounds like the shattering of glass.

"What the hell?" he says, but I am already digging through my pocket for my key, my heart working like a jackhammer in my chest.

"My dad" is the only thing I say, and hope he understands. I finally manage to find the key and fling the door open. "Mom?" I call out. "Dad? Is everything okay?" I wait a moment, hearing only a quiet grunting sound coming from the living room. I race in that direction, trying not to slip on the floor in my witch boot heels, Noah following right behind me. Glancing wildly around the room, I don't see anything except the back of my dad's head, level with the bottom edge of the bookcase. It looks like he's on his knees. *"Dad!"* I yell, but he doesn't respond.

I run over, and it's then that I see her—my mother lying beneath him, his hands around her neck. "Get *off* her!" I scream so loudly it burns the muscles in my throat. I see her bloody face, her arm twisted out from her body at a strange angle. Her eyes are swollen, bruised, and closed. I can't tell if she's alive or dead.

"Dad!" I scream again, grabbing him by the shoulders and trying to pull him back. My hands just slip right off him.

"Maddie, don't!" Noah says, trying to grab me, too.

"Call 911!" I shriek. *"Now!"* Noah fumbles to get his phone out of his back pocket just as I grab for my father's arm again, trying to make him let go of Mom. There is blood bubbling out of the corner of her mouth—*that means she's still breathing, right?*—and I have to fight back the vomit in my own. My dad continues to grunt, squeezing her neck, until I finally haul back and start pummeling his head and face with my fists, trying to beat him off her.

The punch comes out of nowhere, smacking me hard across the face. I fly backward, seeing stars, and land with a hard thump against the edge of the coffee table. "Maddie!" Noah screams. "Please, hurry. He's going to kill them!"

The police, I think, woozy from the impact to my cheek. *He's talking to the police.*

"You little liar," my father says, spitting out the words. Before I know what's happening he has rolled me over and hit me again, this time on the other side of my face. There is a wash of coppery blood inside my mouth. I can't run—I can't even move. My eyes flood with tears, and all I can think of is that this man—a man who is supposed to love and protect me, who is supposed to take care of his wife and daughter—might just beat us to death.

I look over to Noah, who has dropped his phone and grabbed one of the pokers from the fireplace on the other side of the room. He charges at my father and slams the poker down hard across the top of his back. Dad falls over sideways, howling.

"Get up and I'll bash in your skull, you fucking bastard," Noah says, breathing hard. Dad rolls over, and Noah raises the poker threateningly. "Try me," Noah says, and my father stops

moving. He holds up his hands in a defensive posture—palms
out, facing Noah.

"You're going to be sorry you did that," he growls, clearly
still in pain from the strike across his back.

Noah looks at me, and I can tell he's scared, too. His eyes
are wild and wide, and his entire body is shaking. But he's pro-
tecting me. He made my father stop. "Maddie?" he says. "Are
you okay?" I nod my head yes, but doing so causes the room to
spin. I vomit all over the floor.

"My mom," I say, creaking out the words.

"I know," Noah says. The whine of sirens approaches the
house. "Can you get up? We need to open the gate. They can
cut through it, but that will take too long."

"Don't you do it," my dad says, turning his head to look at
me with his angry green eyes. "I'll kill you if you let them in,
Maddie. I swear to god."

"Shut up!" I scream, the sound ricocheting inside my head
like a bullet. Wiping my mouth with the back of my hand, I
try and pull myself up using the coffee table. On wobbly feet,
I stagger to the front door and press the entry button for the
gate, and before I know it, officers are rushing inside my house
with their guns drawn. Red and blue lights flash in bright circles
in our yard, and the EMTs bring the gurney up the front stairs.
"She's in the living room," I say, pointing in the right direction.

"You're bleeding," one of them says.

"Just go help my mom," I saying, sobbing. "He was trying
to kill her. Please, please help her first." A second later Noah
rushes up next to me, putting his long arms around me. He's
still shaking. I am, too.

"They have him," he whispers in my ear. "It's okay, it's

okay. They put him in handcuffs. They're going to take him away."

I nod, my teeth chattering uncontrollably. "Mama," I whimper, and with the medic's assistance, Noah leads me back toward the living room, just as three police officers are leading my father out. His wrists are cuffed in front of his waist, and he stares at me with tears in his eyes, where only a moment before there had been hatred.

"I didn't mean it, Maddie," he pleads. "I'm so sorry. I didn't mean to do this. You're my angel . . . you're Daddy's sweet little girl."

I stop, staring right back at him, feeling the strength of Noah's arm around me. "No, I'm not," I say with a coldness I haven't felt toward him before. This man could be a stranger standing before me. This man is not my father. "You can go to hell."

"Maddie!" he yells as the policemen drag him out of the house. I can still hear his muffled cries from the back of the police car as the medic sits me down on the couch and examines me. Two other medics work on my mother, sliding her carefully onto a backboard, stabilizing her head between two bright yellow pieces of padding. She hasn't woken up.

"Is she okay?" I ask, tearfully. "Is she alive?"

One of the medics, a thickly built, dark-haired woman with kind blue eyes, nods. "She's critical, though, and we need to get her to the hospital. You'll follow in a different ambulance, okay? We'll make sure the nurses keep you posted. They'll need to run some more tests at the ER, but I think you probably just have a concussion." She pauses. "Is there anyone you can call? Another family member to come wait with you?"

"I need to call my parents," Noah says, as though just realizing this. "They'll be wondering where I am." He squeezes my hand and steps over to the other side of the room with his cell phone. He looks stunned, like he can't believe what he's just done. *I* can't believe how lucky I am he was with me tonight. If he hadn't been—if he hadn't thought to grab that poker—who knows what my father would have done?

"Maddie?" the medic prods me. "Someone to call? The police are going to want to take your statement. Since you're a minor, you'll need an adult with you."

Slowly, I bob my head and reach deep into my pocket for my cell phone, which amazingly didn't fall out during the struggle with my dad. I scroll through my contacts until I find the one I want.

Hannah answers on the third ring. When I hear her voice I start to sob—loud, body-racking movements that make it almost impossible for me to speak.

"Oh my god, Maddie!" Hannah says, panicked. "What's wrong? What's happened?"

I take a few hiccuping breaths as I attempt to calm down. "He tried to kill her," I finally say in a weak voice. "We have to go to the hospital. I have to talk with the police. We need you, Hannah. Can you . . . can you come?"

"Which hospital?" she inquires, and I look to the medic and ask the same thing.

"Swedish," the medic answers, and I relay this information to Hannah, who says she will meet me there. After we hang up, I can't help but feel that Emily made sure Hannah picked up the phone—that after all we've been through, her daughter wants me to be okay.

Hannah

As Hannah pulls up to the same ER where she was with Emily just over a year ago, she tries to not let the painful memories of that day overwhelm her. Entering through the familiar sliding doors, she takes a deep breath and then gives the nurse at the reception desk Olivia's and Maddie's names.

After a moment, another nurse guides her back to a curtained area where Maddie lies in a bed. Hannah can barely stand the anger she feels at the sight of Maddie's swollen and bruised face—both of her eyes are blackened and her bottom lip is split open. The nurse told Hannah that Maddie's injuries look worse than they are—she escaped her father's beating with no broken bones, just a mild concussion. *What about the injury to her heart?* Hannah thinks. *There's nothing mild about that.*

"Hannah," Maddie says when she sees her. Her voice is raspy and she sounds exhausted. Next to the bed stands a tall, slightly gangly boy in a black robe and a man who looks enough like the boy that Hannah assumes he is his father. The boy turns to look at Hannah, too.

"I'm Noah," he says, "and this is my dad. We didn't want to leave Maddie alone."

"Nice to meet you both," Hannah says, quickly shaking hands with Noah's father. "I wish it was under better circumstances."

Noah speaks again. "The police should be here any minute to talk with her about what happened. I gave them my statement back at the house."

"You were there?" Hannah asks. A brief, traumatized look flashes across Noah's face and he bobs his head, lips pressed together firmly. His father reaches over and squeezes his son's shoulder, then moves his gaze to Hannah. "I think I should get him home now," he says. "If you're planning to stay."

"I am," Hannah assures him.

"I want to stay, too," Noah says emphatically, glancing at his father. "Please, Dad?"

"Maddie needs to rest, Son," his father says kindly. "And so do you. We can come back in the morning . . . okay?"

Noah turns his attention to Maddie, who nods. He leans down and gives her a quick kiss on the cheek. "I'll text you, okay?" he says.

"Okay," Maddie says, tears filling her already red-rimmed eyes. He straightens and turns to leave, but Maddie's voice stops him. "Noah?"

"Yeah?"

"I know I already said this like twenty times, but . . . thank you."

"Eh. No biggie. Totally standard Saturday night." Noah

gives her a shaky grin, and then a moment later, he and his father are gone.

Hannah steps over next to the bed, reaching for Maddie's hand. "How's your mom?" Hannah asks. "Do you know?"

"She's in surgery," Maddie says, clearly trying not to cry. "The nurse told me she has broken ribs and internal bleeding. And a broken arm, so they're going to put screws in it so she hopefully can still use it."

"Oh, sweetie," Hannah says, not wanting to ask for specifics of the night's events yet, knowing the police will do that soon enough. "I'm so sorry. I'm sure the doctors will take good care of her." She waits a beat. "What about you? Are you okay?"

Maddie shrugs, then takes a shuddering breath. "I don't know what I would have done if Noah and I hadn't come home . . . my mom would be dead, Hannah. Dad was trying to kill her." Maddie dissolves into tears, and Hannah leans down to hold her, careful not to press against her bruised face.

"You're all right," she murmurs. "Everything will be all right." She keeps repeating this, smoothing Maddie's hair and letting her cry, until a few moments later, when a uniformed police officer pushes back the curtain and steps in to stand on the other side of Maddie's bed.

"Hi, Maddie," she says gently. She is a stocky woman with short blond hair and round, pink cheeks. "I'm Officer White, but you can call me Katie, okay?" Maddie pulls back from Hannah and nods, so Katie continues. "I need to ask you a few questions."

"Does she have to do this now?" Hannah asks.

"I'm sorry," Katie says. "I know this is a terrible time, but she'll remember the details better closer to the event. I'll go slow, I promise."

"It's okay," Maddie says with a sniffle. "I want to."

Hannah hands her a tissue from a table at the side of the bed, listening with growing horror as Maddie describes the scene she and Noah walked in on, and then what happened after that. Maddie couldn't say what led her father to attack Olivia—that would have to come later, from Olivia herself. Hannah can't believe the bravery Maddie and Noah showed, taking on James like that. No wonder Maddie thanked Noah; it sounds as though he might have saved her life.

"Has your dad ever hit your mother before?" Katie asks, keeping her voice low. Maddie nods, and the officer continues. "How long has it been happening?"

"As long as I can remember," Maddie says, and half an hour later, after Maddie has recounted everything she can think of about her father's abuse over the years, Katie says she has enough information for now, and it's time for her to go.

"I'll walk you out," Hannah says, wanting to talk with the officer alone. She looks at Maddie. "I'll be right back, okay?" Maddie nods, and Hannah walks with the officer to the waiting room.

"What happens now?" she asks Katie as they stand off to the side of the sliding doors. "To James Bell, I mean?"

"He's in custody," she responds. "And either an attempted murder charge or first-degree assault charges will be filed by the prosecutor's office. After that, there'll be a hearing, where his lawyer will probably ask for him to be released on his own recognizance. What happens after that all depends on which judge gets assigned the case."

"Do you think they'll release him?" Hannah asks, disgusted at the thought.

The officer shrugs. "That remains to be seen. It's more likely he'll have a high bail set, and Mrs. Bell will have to file a restraining order once he pays it and gets out. But considering the violence of his acts tonight, no judge is going to just let him walk. If he doesn't make a deal and it gets to trial, hopefully he'll do some serious time." She pauses. "Still, Mrs. Bell should find a good lawyer. She's going to need one to make sure she and her daughter are protected."

Hannah thanks her and returns to Maddie's side just as a doctor in a blue surgical scrub cap approaches the bed. "I'm Dr. Peyton," she says, pulling off her cap to reveal a headful of short, tightly woven black braids. She looks at Maddie with kind brown eyes. "I just finished working on your mom."

Maddie's chin trembles. "Is she okay?"

Hannah can't help it; she starts to cry, unable to think of anything other than the moment when the doctor first told her there was no hope for Emily . . . that her daughter would most assuredly die. She waits for the same words to tumble from this doctor's mouth about Olivia.

"She sustained some pretty serious injuries," Dr. Peyton says with a brief frown. "But luckily, we were able to stop the bleeding." She reaches over and runs a gentle palm down Maddie's forearm. "Don't you worry. After some time and healing, she'll be just fine."

Maddie lets loose a shuddering sigh. "Thank you," she manages to choke out. "When can I see her?"

"She's in recovery now," Dr. Peyton says. "The nurse will take you to her once she's settled into a room, most likely in an hour or so." She looks at Hannah. "And just so you're aware, Olivia will need to stay here at least a week, for observation. We're keeping Maddie overnight."

"Thank you," Hannah says, and then the doctor gives Maddie's leg a quick pat before walking away. Hannah pulls up a chair to sit next to Maddie's bed.

"Thanks for coming," Maddie says, rolling her head on the pillow so she can look at Hannah.

"Of course, honey," Hannah says. "I'm so glad you called me. It's hard to go through this kind of stuff alone."

"Noah's dad is freaking out that my dad did this to us," Maddie says. "They've worked together for like, a hundred years or something." She tears up again. "He thought my dad was kind of a jerk, but he never suspected . . . this. No one did."

Hannah puts her hand over the top of Maddie's. "A lot of the time, people see what they want to see. And no one wants to think someone they spend time with can do something like this." She waits a beat. "Your dad is a good actor, too, isn't he?"

Maddie nods, then releases a long sigh, her eyelids fluttering. "I'm so tired. I don't think I've ever been this tired, even when I was sick."

Hannah reaches for Maddie's blankets and tucks them up around her shoulders. "Why don't you try and sleep for a bit? I'll wake you when the nurse says you can see your mom."

"Promise?"

"Cross my heart."

"Okay," Maddie says with a weak smile, then closes her eyes. Only a moment later her breaths deepen, and Hannah watches her while she sleeps, remembering how many times she did this same thing with Emily. Especially in the months preceding the accident, when her daughter seemed to be pulling further and further away. Hannah would tiptoe into her room after she was certain Emily was asleep, staring at her daughter's relaxed, beautiful face, charmed by the odd way she pushed out bits of air between her lips like she was trying to blow up a balloon. Those stolen moments, when sleep robbed Emily of the ability to throw up walls between them and she was still just a little girl, are among the things Hannah misses most.

It strikes Hannah now that her brother was right when he said that at one point or another, everyone pretends to be something they're not. This tendency starts so young—just as it did with Emily, when she first began to push Hannah away. We try on personalities like second skins, learning to present only the best version of ourselves to the world, fearful of what might happen if we reveal just how imperfect and vulnerable we really are. But it's those imperfections, Hannah realizes, those struggles, that truly connect us. It's what linked her and Olivia so quickly when they first met. It's the reason she's sitting here next to Maddie's bed, worried for this child as much as she once worried for her own.

After a while, Hannah begins to nod off, too, only to be awakened by the same nurse who had brought Hannah back to Maddie's bed. "Olivia's in her room now," she says. "She's conscious, and asking for Maddie."

Together, Hannah and the nurse gently shake Maddie awake, then help Maddie ease herself into a wheelchair. Hannah pushes the chair, following the nurse down a long corridor lighted by cool blue, fluorescent bulbs. They take the elevator to the fourth floor, and the nurse leads them to a private room at the end of the hall. She opens the door, but Hannah hesitates before entering.

"Maybe you should go in alone, first," Hannah says, her hands suddenly sweaty as they grip the handles of the wheelchair. She isn't sure if Olivia will want to see her.

"I want you to come with me," Maddie insists, so Hannah steadies herself and does as Maddie asks. Olivia lies in a bed against the far wall, tubes stringing out from her body just as they had from Emily's last year. Hannah swallows hard, trying not to cry at the memory, trying to be strong for Maddie. And Olivia, too.

"Mama," Maddie says, and Olivia opens her eyes, turning her head toward her daughter's voice.

"Baby girl," she whispers. Her voice is raw, and it looks to Hannah as though it hurts her to speak; her throat must be raw from the intubation tube they used in surgery. And, Hannah realizes, from James's hands around her neck. "Come here," Olivia says, and Hannah pushes Maddie over to her mother.

Olivia's eyes are swollen, black and blue like her daughter's, but it's clear she sees Hannah standing behind the wheelchair. "You're here?" she says quietly. Not angry, not accusing. Just a question.

"I called her," Maddie says, her words made fragile by tears. "I asked her to come."

Hannah holds Olivia's gaze with hers for a long moment. She understands why Olivia asked her to stay away from them—to protect them all from James should he find out who Hannah is to their family. But Olivia was also hurt that Hannah kept the truth from her—dishonesty, even if it is for a justifiable reason, is far from an ideal foundation for a friendship. But Hannah hopes that after the events of this night, Olivia might be willing to start over.

But instead of saying anything to Hannah, Olivia looks at her daughter again. She visibly flinches as she takes in Maddie's bruises and swollen flesh. "Oh, honey, your *face,*" she whispers, trying to lift her arm to reach out to her daughter, but realizes the cast she's wearing prevents the movement. "Your father . . . ¿" Maddie nods, and Olivia clenches her eyes shut. "What happened¿" she asks, looking back at Maddie. "The last thing I remember is being in the living room . . . James hitting me . . ." Her voice breaks, and Maddie puts her hand through the railing on the bed to touch her mother's leg. Slowly, she explains to Olivia what she told Hannah and the police officer earlier—how she and Noah managed to fight James off and called the police to take him away.

"He's in jail, now, Mama," Maddie says. "He can't hurt us anymore."

Olivia swallows carefully, clearly still struggling to speak through the pain in her throat. "I should have left him before . . . you were right." She looks at Hannah. "Both of you were right."

"That doesn't matter now," Hannah says gently, not wanting Olivia to feel any worse than Hannah suspects she already does. "What matters is that you're both alive and that he pays for what he did."

"I'll tell the police everything," Olivia says. "Do you think it will be enough¿ My word¿ That he'll go to prison and I can divorce him¿"

"You can divorce him either way," Hannah says, wanting

to touch Olivia but not knowing where to put her hand that won't hurt her.

"Noah and I will testify, too, Mom," Maddie adds. "It won't be just your word anymore."

Olivia presses her split, swollen lips together and nods her head once. Hannah decides to place just the tips of her fingers on Olivia's white blankets before she speaks again. "I think the best plan for right now is to take things one step at a time. First, you need to focus on getting better." She pauses, unsure what Olivia will say to what she's going to offer next, but knowing it's what she wants to do. "And if you want . . . if you're okay with it, Maddie can stay with me until you're back on your feet. Anything else you need, anything at all, I'm here."

Maddie looks at Hannah and then back to her mother again. "It's okay with me, Mom," she says, reaching out to take Hannah's free hand.

Olivia is quiet a moment, still gazing at Hannah. There is a hesitance in her eyes and a slight stitch between her brows, making it clear that she's trying to sort out how she feels. "Thank you," she finally whispers, and Hannah knows she means this for so much more than just tonight.

And then Hannah smiles, realizing that no matter how quickly sorrow can demolish a life, a moment of kindness, a pure and simple act of forgiveness, can just as quickly save it.

Acknowledgments

The idea for this book came to me over a decade ago, and at the time, I tried to wrench the story onto the page with little success. Maybe it wasn't ready to be told. Maybe I wasn't ready to tell it. Whatever the case, I am so grateful to my wise and wonderful agent, Victoria Sanders, who trusted me enough to give it another chance when I suggested I wanted to try again, and who later called me twice on a Sunday as she finished reading to say how much she loved it. She is a remarkable and savvy advocate in this crazy business, and I'm so lucky to have both her and her formidable staff—Bernadette Baker-Baughman and Chris Kepner—on my side.

Thanks to my editor, Greer Hendricks, who possesses brilliant insight into the stories I want to tell and always finds the kindest, most effective ways to challenge me and help make my writing better. Her support is an unparalleled gift.

Thanks to so many others at Atria Books—Judith Curr, Ben Lee, Paul Olsewski, Sarah Cantin, Lisa Sciambra, Hillary Tisman, Carole Schwindeller, Isolde Sauer, and Carly Sommerstein. This list could go on and on—to every member of the sales team, the art department, and marketing, I extend my most sincere gratitude for taking such good care of me and my books. Special thanks to Cristina Suarez-Krumsick, my publicist at Atria, for her belief in my work.

Organ donation is a complex, variable experience for every individual or family member who goes through it, and while it would be impossible to adequately describe each of those experiences in a single story, my goal was to capture overall emotional truths. While conducting my research, I was fortunate enough to come in contact with Valerie Maury, family program manager at LifeCenter Northwest, a nonprofit organ procurement organization. Her patient and knowledgeable answers to my many, many questions about the psychological effects the process has on the recipients and the families involved were invaluable in the shaping of this book. (Any procedural inaccuracies are my own.)

I'm so grateful for the enthusiasm of my social media friends, who cheer me on through the tough writing days and say such kind things about my books. I cannot express how much it means to connect with you all. For this book in particular, I must especially thank Joanie Mack, who when I cried out for help on Facebook, gave me the perfect French-themed name for Hannah's salon.

I must also thank social media for bringing Laura Meehan into my life, not only as a valuable editorial professional but as a dear and hysterically funny friend.

And finally, I could not live this writing life without the love and support of my family—heartfelt thanks to Anna, Scarlett, and Miles for being so proud that I'm a writer, and thanks to Stephan, always—for everything.

safe with me

AMY HATVANY

A Readers Club Guide

Questions and Topics for Discussion

1. Consider the title of the novel, and the idea of safety—both of a physical and emotional nature—in the story. Who is keeping whom safe in this book?

2. If you had been in Hannah's position, do you think you could have donated your child's organs? Why or why not?

3. Did Olivia and James's relationship change how you viewed domestic abuse? Does Olivia match your vision of an abuse victim?

4. What is the book saying about the relationship between one's physical exterior and their emotional and psychological state? How does each character try to project an outward appearance that is different from their internal feelings?

5. Read the novel's epigraph as a group. What does the concept of destiny, or fate, mean to you?

6. Olivia has many reasons for not leaving James, not the least of which are financial. Consider the power dynamics at play in their marriage. How does James make Olivia feel helpless—and how does he also make her feel special?

7. Dishonesty is a theme throughout the novel. Do you think that there are degrees of dishonesty? For example, is there a difference between fabricating a story and obscuring the

truth? What qualifies as lying? And is dishonesty that has good intentions more excusable?

8. Turn to page 177, and as a group, read the scene where James brings Olivia breakfast in bed. Can you empathize with Olivia's thinking that, "even though she knows better, even though she's been through this with him a hundred times before, Olivia can't help but wonder if she really needs to leave him after all."

9. Maddie's experience at the mall with Hailey and her friends highlights the perils of being a teenage girl. Do you have any memories from this age that are similar? Do you think the challenges of being an adolescent girl have inherently changed?

10. On page 182, Olivia acknowledges that she worries sometimes, "that Maddie spends so much time interacting with what *other* people's imaginations have dreamed up that she'll never learn to imagine things on her own." For those of you who have children, do you worry about this as well?

11. Discuss the role that technology plays in this narrative. In what ways does it have an empowering, connective impact? In what ways does it have a distancing effect?

Enhance Your Readers Club

1. Do you know anyone who has received a donor organ? Learn more about organ donation at: http://www.organdonor .gov/index.html.

2. If you haven't read *Heart Like Mine* yet, consider reading it as a group. Discuss how Hatvany uses three alternating perspectives for different purposes in both *Heart Like Mine* and *Safe with Me*. What are some of the devices she uses to create unique voices for each of her narrators in these novels?

3. Many domestic abuse shelters accept items that we routinely replace and then have no further need for—like computers, cell phones, cameras, or even magazines. Consider bringing a few of these items to your next meeting and then find a local shelter to donate them to.